Every Fifteen Minutes

Also by Lisa Scottoline

Every Fifteen Minutes

Lisa Scottoline

ST. MARTIN'S PRESS ❧ NEW YORK

This is a work of fiction. All of the characters, organizations, and events portrayed in this novel are either products of the author's imagination or are used fictitiously.

EVERY FIFTEEN MINUTES. Copyright © 2015 by Smart Blonde, LLC. All rights reserved. Printed in the United States of America. For information, address St. Martin's Press, 175 Fifth Avenue, New York, N.Y. 10010.

www.stmartins.com

The Library of Congress Cataloging-in-Publication Data is available upon request.

ISBN 978-1-250-01011-7 (hardcover)
ISBN 978-1-4668-7461-9 (e-book)

St. Martin's Press books may be purchased for educational, business, or promotional use. For information on bulk purchases, please contact the Macmillan Corporate and Premium Sales Department at 1-800-221-7945, extension 5442, or write to specialmarkets@macmillan.com.

First Edition: April 2015

10 9 8 7 6 5 4 3 2 1

R0443335367

For Sandy, with love and thanks

Unexpressed emotions will never die.
They are buried alive and will come forth later in uglier ways.
 —Sigmund Freud

Every Fifteen Minutes

Chapter One

I'm a sociopath. I look normal, but I'm not. I'm smarter, better, and *freer,* because I'm not bound by rules, law, emotion, or regard for you.

I can read you almost immediately, get your number right away, and push your buttons to make you do whatever I want. I don't really like you, but I'm so good at acting as if I do that it's basically the same thing. To you.

I fool you.

I fool *everybody*.

I've read that one out of twenty-four people is a sociopath, and if you ask me, the other twenty-three of you should be worried. One out of twenty-four people is 4 percent of the population, and that's a lot of sociopaths. Anorexics are 3 percent, and everybody talks about them. Schizophrenics are only 1 percent, but they get all the press. No one's paying any attention to sociopaths, or they think we're all killers, which is a misconception.

It's not being paranoid to worry about us. You should be more paranoid than you are. Your typical suburban mom worries all the time, but she worries about the wrong things.

Because she doesn't worry about me.

People think evil exists in the form of terrorists, murderers, and ruthless dictators, but not in "normal" people like me. They don't realize that evil lives on their street. Works in the cubicle next to them. Chats with them in the checkout line at CVS. Reads a paperback on the train next to them. Runs on a treadmill at their gym.

Or marries their daughter.

We're here, and we prey on *you*.

We target you.

We groom you.

I took a sociopath test, not officially, of course. Only trained professionals can administer the real test, called the Hare test, but I found a version of it online. The first two questions went like this:

> **1. I am superior to others.**
> **Circle one: Doesn't apply to me. Partially applies to me.**
> **Fully applies to me.**

And:

> **2. I would not feel sorry if someone were blamed for**
> **something I did.**
> **Circle one: Doesn't apply to me. Partially applies to me.**
> **Fully applies to me.**

There were twenty questions, and forty was the top score. I scored a thirty-eight, which means I would be graduating with honors if I majored in being a sociopath.

I didn't need the test to tell me who I was, anyway.

I already knew.

I have always known.

I don't have any feelings, neither love nor hate, no like or dislike, not even a thumbs-up or thumbs-down like on Facebook.

I do have a Facebook account, however, and I have a respectable number of friends.

Ask me if I care.

Actually, I think it's funny they're my friends, because they have no idea who I am. My face is a mask. I hide my thoughts. My words are calculated to please, charm, or undermine. I can sound smarter or dumber, depending on what you expect to hear. My actions further my self-interest

I'm neither your friend nor your frenemy, unless you have what I want.

In that case, I'm not only your enemy, I'm your nightmare.

I get bored easily.

I hate to wait for anything.

Waiting makes me so restless, and I've been in this room for hours, even this video game is *boring*. God knows what idiots are playing online right now, forming their pimple-faced teams, exploring dungeons, going on quests, killing dragons, hookers, and Nazis, all of them playing a role.

I wonder if whoever invented World of Warcraft realizes it's practice for sociopaths.

The gamers I play online name themselves KillerCobra, SwordofDeath, and Slice&Dice, but I bet they're in middle school.

Or law school.

If one out of twenty-four people is a sociopath, I'm not the only gamer who tried to burn the house down.

My character name is WorthyAdversary.

I role-play every day in real life, so I'm very good at gaming.

I'm always a step ahead, maybe two.

I plan everything. I set everyone in motion, and when the moment comes, I strike.

I always win in the end.

They never see me coming.

Know why?

Because I'm already there.

Chapter Two

Dr. Eric Parrish was on his way out when he was paged to the emergency department. His gut tensed as he approached, though he'd been Chief of the Psychiatric Unit at Havemeyer General Hospital for five years. There was always the possibility of violence on an emergency consult, and last year in nearby Delaware County, a hospital psychiatrist on an ED consult was shot and his caseworker killed by a psychotic patient. The tragedy ended when the psychiatrist, who carried a concealed gun, returned fire, killing the patient.

Eric hustled down the hospital corridor, followed by two medical students on their psych rotation, a female and a male talking among themselves. He felt confident that he could protect them, and himself, without a gun. His employer, the PhilaHealth Partnership, had become hyperaware of security after the Delaware County shooting and had trained him in defensive strategies and escape procedures. Eric would never carry a gun in a hospital. He was a healer at heart and, he suspected, a bad shot.

Abruptly the loudspeaker system switched on, and a recorded lullaby wafted through the speakers. The hospital played the lullaby each time a baby was born in its labor and delivery service, but Eric cringed at the sound, knowing it would cause misery on his psych unit, upstairs. One of his patients was a young mother depressed after the stillbirth of her child, and the intermittent lullaby always sent her into an emotional tailspin. Eric had asked administration not to pipe the music into his unit, but they said it would cost too much to alter the speaker system. He told them to take it out of his budget, but they said no.

The chimes of the lullaby reverberated in his ears, and it bugged him that he couldn't get the hospital bureaucracy to listen to him. He knew it was part of the larger problem, that mental illness wasn't taken as seriously as physical illness, and Eric was on a one-man campaign to change that. He was living proof that there was hope, even happiness. Back in med school he'd developed an anxiety disorder, but he'd gotten his symptoms under complete control during his training. Since then, he'd ended talk therapy and weaned himself off his meds. He'd been symptom-free. Cured.

He pushed open the double doors leading to the ED, which bustled on a Friday night. Nurses in patterned scrubs hurried in and out of full examining rooms, a physician's assistant pushed a rolling computer desk, and a group of black-uniformed EMTs talked near an empty stretcher with orange head-immobilizing blocks, resting on a hospital gurney.

Eric approached the octagonal nurses' station, and a blonde nurse looked up from her computer monitor, smiled, and pointed to examining room D. Everybody recognized the hospital shrinks from the bright red W on their lanyard IDs. The W stood for Wright, the wing that contained the locked psych unit, but the staff teased that W stood for Wackos. He'd heard all the jokes— *How do you tell the psychiatrists from the patients in the hospital? The patients get better and leave.* Eric told the best psychiatrist jokes, though he never told the ones about psychiatrist's kids. He didn't think those were funny. He lived those.

The medical students quieted as he beelined toward the examining room, walked to the open curtain, and stood in the threshold, relieved to see that his patient was a sweet-faced older woman with cropped silvery white hair, resting comfortably in bed in a hospital gown. Next to her sat a young man, looking concerned as he held her hand. Standing behind him was Dr. Laurie Fortunato, a short, curvy figure in a crisp white lab coat, the black rubber stems of her stethoscope decorated with flower stickers for her pediatric patients. She and Eric had been friends since medical school and were running buddies, even though she was faster, which sucked.

"Hi, Laurie, good to see you." Eric entered the room followed by the medical students, whom he introduced briefly before they stood at the back wall, observing discreetly, per procedure.

"Eric, same, thanks for coming down." Laurie grinned. She had a bright and lively aspect, owing to her warm brown eyes, longish Roman nose, chubby cheeks, and a generous mouth that never stopped moving, whether she was yakking away, cracking wise, or making faces. She was appealing without makeup, which almost none of the female professionals bothered with in the hospital, but Laurie's earthy lack of vanity was her defining characteristic; she always twisted up her curly brown hair in a knot, held in place at the nape of her neck by whatever she could grab—pencil, pen, or tongue depressor.

"Happy to do it. How can I help?"

Laurie gestured to the patient. "This is Virginia Teichner and her grandson Max Jakubowski."

"I'm Eric Parrish. Good to meet you both." Eric took a step closer to the bed, and the elderly patient looked up at him with a sly smile, her hooded brown eyes making direct contact, a good sign. She had no evident injury, but she was on a saline IV drip and her vital signs were being monitored by a finger clip. Eric checked the glowing screen; her numbers were normal, if not great.

"Ooh, look at you, you're so handsome," Mrs. Teichner said, her voice raspy. She eyed him over in a mock-stagey way. "You can call me Virginia. Or honeybun."

"Now we're talking." Eric reached for the rolling stool, pulled it over, and sat down next to her bed. He enjoyed working with geriatric patients, and his first task was to establish a rapport with her. Humor usually worked. He smiled at her. "If you think I'm handsome, there's obviously nothing wrong with your vision."

"Not true, I got macular degeneration." Mrs. Teichner winked. "Or maybe I'm just a degenerate!"

Eric laughed.

Mrs. Teichner gestured at Laurie. "Dr. Parrish, how come you don't wear a white coat like her?"

"It makes me look fat." Eric didn't add that many hospital psychiatrists didn't wear white coats, to be more relatable to the patients, and he had on a blue oxford shirt and no tie, with khakis and loafers. The look he was going for was Friendly Suburban Dad, because that's what he was, but he suspected he'd achieved only Cialis Guy.

"Ha!" Mrs. Teichner laughed. "You're funny!"

Laurie rolled her eyes. "Mrs. Teichner, please don't encourage him. Dr. Parrish doesn't need any more female fans in this hospital."

Mrs. Teichner's hooded eyes twinkled. "You're just jealous."

"I agree." Eric smiled at Laurie. "Jealous."

"Hardly." Laurie snorted.

Mrs. Teichner cackled. "Now she's embarrassed."

"Bingo." Eric mentally ran through the elements of the MSE, the Mental Status Examination, whenever he met a patient, and he assessed their level of consciousness, appearance and behavior, speech and motor activity, mood and affect, thought and perception, attitude and insight, as well as his reaction to the patient and the patient's own cognitive abilities. Mrs. Teichner was already scoring well on most of the factors. Eric's gestalt reaction to her was that her mood was euthymic, or completely normal. "So, how can I help you, Virginia?"

"Eric," Laurie interjected, answering, and her expression changed, falling into professional lines. "Unfortunately, Mrs. Teichner has been dealing with congestive heart failure and advanced-stage lung cancer. Two months ago, she was admitted upstairs, spent three days in cardiology, and was just about to begin palliative care at home."

Eric listened, hiding his emotions. It was the worst possible prognosis, and he couldn't help but feel sympathy for Mrs. Teichner, as Laurie continued.

"She came in tonight because of a choking incident at dinner. I ordered new X-rays, and we found another mass growing in her throat, impacting her ability to swallow."

"I'm sorry to hear that," Eric said, meaning it, but he felt surprised by Mrs. Teichner's calm demeanor, given the dire state of her health. She didn't seem distraught or even depressed, nor did she present with the vagueness of aspect or speech that characterized any memory or other issue he'd expect in a geriatric patient, though he'd test her later to confirm.

"Thanks, Doc, but I know I have cancer, it's not new news." Mrs. Teichner's tone turned matter-of-fact. "My grandson, Max here, wanted us to call you. He's seventeen years old, so he knows everything. He keeps telling me I'm crazy and—"

Max interrupted, "Not crazy, Gum. Depressed. I think you're depressed, and the doctor can help with that. He can give you some antidepressants or something."

Eric shifted his gaze to Max, who was short and slight, maybe five two and 130 pounds, which made him look younger than his age. His face was round, and he had a small straight nose, eyes of a pale, washed-out blue, and a shy smile with a single dimple. His longish hair was light brown in a shaggy cut, and he had on baggy jeans and a black T-shirt that showed an undeveloped skinniness to his upper arms, as if he never lifted anything heavier than an iPhone.

Mrs. Teichner waved him off with a hand gnarled by arthritis. "He calls me Gum, Gummy, Gumbo, all kinds of names like that, because he couldn't say grandma when he was little. He likes to play with words. He's smart as a whip, he's a National Merit scholar, got perfect SAT scores, tops in his class, and that's why he's such a know-it-all—"

"Gummy, please," Max interrupted her again, gently. "We need to talk about *you,* not me, and about why you're not eating." Max turned to Eric, looking at him with a direct blue-eyed gaze that echoed his grandmother's. "Dr. Parrish, the cardiologist told us that if she eats, she can keep her strength up. He said he could give her a feeding tube if she doesn't eat, but she doesn't want the feeding tube and she doesn't want to eat either. I know that's the depression talking. I think she should get the feeding tube. She has to."

Eric realized why Laurie had called him. End-of-life care presented an array of emotional issues for patients and their families, and Eric knew he could do some good. "Max, thank you for that information, that's helpful. If you would step outside for a moment, I'd like to examine your grandmother."

"Sure, great." Max stood up, letting go of his grandmother's hand, and smiled at her. "You behave yourself, Gummy."

"Don't tell me what to do," Mrs. Teichner shot back, cackling, and Eric could see the love that flowed easily between them. Max shuffled out of the room, and Eric glanced at Laurie.

"Let's talk after I've evaluated Mrs. Teichner."

"Good. Come find me when you're finished." Laurie patted Mrs. Teichner on the shoulder. "My dear, you're in excellent hands."

"No kidding. Now get out so we can be alone." Mrs. Teichner cackled again, then gestured at the medical students, standing at the wall. "Can't they leave too, Doc? I need a peanut gallery like I need a hole in the head."

"They have to stay," Eric answered, amused. "Try to ignore them."

"How'm I gonna do that? They're *looking* at me."

"I do it all day, it's easy. Now, seriously, tell me how you are. Are you feeling depressed? Blue? No energy?"

"No, I'm right as rain." Mrs. Teichner shook her head of short white hair, which swiveled on her neck like a baby snow owl.

"You sure about that? It would be natural, given your illness."

"I tell you, I'm fine." Mrs. Teichner snorted. "I don't need my head examined, but where were you when I married my second husband? Sheesh!"

Eric smiled. "Okay, let me ask you a few questions. What is today's date?"

"What difference does it make?"

"I'm doing an assessment and I need you to answer a few questions. Who's the president of the United States?"

"Who cares? All politicians are crooks."

Eric smiled again, persisting only because he had to for legal reasons. "Listen carefully, I'm going to say three words."

"I love you?"

Eric chuckled. "The three words are banana, strawberry, milkshake. Can you repeat those words?"

"Of course! Banana, strawberry, milkshake! Dr. Parrish, there's nothing wrong with my brain." Mrs. Teichner's smile vanished into her deep laugh lines, evidence of a life well-lived. "I'm not depressed, I'm worried."

"What about?"

"My grandson Max. He lives with me, I raised him. He's the one who's depressed, and I don't know what's going to happen to him after I die." Mrs. Teichner's forehead buckled. "He's different, Max is. He's got no friends, he's always alone."

"I understand, but you're my patient tonight." Eric didn't want to neglect her, even if she was inclined to neglect herself. "You're here seeking treatment, and I'd like to evaluate and, if necessary, treat you."

"I'm not asking you for treatment. Max wanted us to call you, not me. I let him do it because I think *he* needs the help. I can't get him to a psychiatrist any other way, he won't go."

"You mean he's the real reason I was called down?" Eric was coming up to speed. It was one of those situations where the identified patient wasn't the real patient.

"Yes. He knows I'm dying, but he can't really accept it and he'll be all alone when I'm gone. Can't you help him?" Mrs. Teichner grasped the sleeve of Eric's shirt, newly urgent. "Please, help him."

"Explain to me what makes you say he needs help."

"He tells me that if I just eat, I'm going to get better or live longer or whatever, but I'm not. I'm going to die, and he can't deal with it." Mrs. Teichner didn't blink, her gaze steady and knowing. "I don't want a feeding tube. I'm ninety, I've lived a long time, and when my pain pills wear off, I hurt all over. I want nature to take its course, at home."

"I understand." Eric hoped that he would face his own demise with as much bravery. He decided it wasn't necessary to conduct a mini-evaluation. Mrs. Teichner was remarkably sane, and since she was refusing treatment, he was on safe legal terrain if he addressed what was bothering her about her grandson. "Where are Max's parents? What do they say?"

"My daughter is his mother, but I'm embarrassed to say, she's worthless. She lives with me, but she's never home. She drinks too much and she can't keep a job. She used to work for the phone company but they fired her for absenteeism."

"How about his father?"

"His father ran away when Max was only two. He drank, too."

"That's too bad." Eric felt a bitter pang of resentment, one that would never go away. His father had been an alcoholic, a truck mechanic who'd been driving drunk when he swerved into a tree, killing himself and Eric's mother. Eric had just left for freshman year at Amherst. But he pressed the memory away, to stay present. "Does Max have any brothers or sisters?"

"No, he's an only child. He doesn't even have any friends. At home, he never leaves his room except to take care of me or eat dinner and he plays those computer games all night. I'm all he has." Mrs. Teichner blinked away tears. "What's going to happen to him? He could hurt himself, after I'm gone."

"Please, take this." Eric pulled a Kleenex from a box on the bedside table and handed it to her. As a psychiatrist, he spent a lot of time handing people tissues, but it still tore his heart out when women cried, especially older ones. They reminded him of his mother, whom he still thought about, every day.

"I don't know what to do, I'm worried sick about him."

"Do you really think he'd harm himself?"

"Yes, I really do." Mrs. Teichner dabbed her nose, which came to a curved point. Pinkish mottling on its sides told him her oxygenation was poor, which was to be expected. "He's an odd duck but he's a good kid, with a good heart."

"Has he ever tried to hurt himself? Or said words to that effect?"

"No, he doesn't talk about himself or his feelings. His father was the same way, that good-for-nothing."

Eric let it go. "Has Max gone to a therapist or gotten counseling at school?"

"No, he's embarrassed. He says he'll get teased if people find out." Mrs. Teichner sniffled, wiping her nose. "I'm beside myself. I pray on it all the time. It's just so hard. I've asked around but nobody comes through. Please, help him."

"Well, I do have a private practice," Eric found himself saying, though he hardly needed a new client. "I could make time to see him if he wanted."

"Really?" Mrs. Teichner's hooded eyes rounded with hope. "Would you?"

"I would, if he wants to come."

"Thank you so much!"

"You're welcome." Eric's heart eased to see her relieved. "But you have to understand that psychotherapy is a serious undertaking, and you've probably heard that it helps only if the person really wants to do it. I'll make the offer to Max, but it's up to him."

"He'll go, I know. You've lifted such a load off." Mrs. Teichner clapped her arthritic hands together, holding her Kleenex. "Really, there's nothing on earth that matters to me as much as that boy. I can be at peace if I know he's okay. You understand, if you have kids."

"I do." Eric thought of Hannah, but kept that to himself. His daughter was only seven years old, and he worried about what would happen to her if he wasn't around. Since his separation from his wife, that worry had become more than academic.

"And, Doc, I can pay you, don't worry about it. What does it cost to see you, fifty or sixty dollars an hour?"

"About that, yes," Eric answered. His fee was $300 an hour, and for clients who couldn't afford that, he had a sliding scale that was never less than $250—except for crying old ladies facing terminal diagnoses. Psychiatry was among the lowest-paying medical specialties because it required virtually no procedures, with the highest fees generated by procedure-heavy practices like orthopedics, with its hip replacements and Tommy John surgeries, or plastic surgery, with its face-lifts, nose jobs, and boob jobs. Every psychiatrist hated the irony that the best-paying specialty was cosmetic surgery, as if you could fix your psyche by changing your face.

"Then it's a deal. Thank you so much!"

"Happy to help." Eric rose, brushing down his khakis. "Before I leave, are you sure you don't want to talk to me about yourself? I've treated patients coping with a diagnosis like yours, and it's understandable if you want some help."

"Nah. I'm a tough cookie. Except for the cancer, I'm fine." Mrs. Teichner waved him off with an ironic smile.

"Virginia, it was a pleasure meeting you." Eric slid his wallet from his pocket, extracted a card, and set it down on the bedside table. "If you change your mind, feel free to call me. Don't hesitate. You *are* one tough cookie."

"You bet your ass," Mrs. Teichner shot back.

Eric smiled, trying not to wonder if he would see her alive again. He gave her a final wave and motioned to the medical students to leave. "Mrs. Teichner, 'bye now. I'll send Dr. Fortunato in. Best of luck."

Eric followed the medical students out of the room, then spotted Laurie at the nurses' station and Max heading for the vending machines. Eric was about to go see him when he felt a touch on his elbow and turned to see it was the female medical student, Kristine Malin. "Yes, Kristine?"

"That was such a sweet thing to do, Dr. Parrish," Kristine said, her hand on his arm. She had a gorgeous face, big blue eyes, long dark hair, and a dazzling smile, like a toothpaste model.

"Thanks," Eric answered, surprised. He didn't know why she was standing so close, much less touching him, but he didn't have time to worry about it. He was thinking about Max, who was standing in the small glass-walled room that held the vending machines, off the waiting area. "Excuse me, I have to go."

Chapter Three

"Max, hi." Eric walked to Max, who stood in front of a vending machine, staring at it blankly, his numb expression ghosted in the glass. The room was otherwise empty, and beyond it was the children's waiting area, its primary-colored walls and boxes of toys an incongruously cheery backdrop.

Max turned. "What do you think? Can you help her? Give her something to lift her mood?"

"I understand that you believe your grandmother is experiencing depression, but I don't agree."

"Why not?"

"I evaluated her, and in my opinion, she's fine, given the circumstances. She's a special person—"

"What about the feeding tube?" Max's blue eyes weren't challenging, but pleading. "Why would she refuse a feeding tube if she wasn't depressed? That's, like, suicide. Like saying you don't care if you die."

"It's not an irrational choice, Max. Many patients in her circumstances refuse feeding tubes." Eric kept his tone gentle. "You know there are two kinds, one tube that goes through the nose or one that goes through the stomach. Either is a very intrusive thing and—"

"But she'll *die* if she doesn't eat. She'll *starve*." Max's eyes flared, pained, and Eric's heart went out to the boy, who was too young to deal with this on his own.

"I understand that, and so does she. Still, I gave her my card and told her to call me if she feels the need for treatment. She's facing her diagnosis with an acceptance—"

"I can't let her starve. She has to get a feeding tube. Can't I *make* her?"

"Max, I know this is hard to hear, but that's not your decision. It's hers. She'll make it with her doctors and the hospice workers."

"But she's choosing wrong."

"You have to let her decide. It's her life." Eric could see that the boy was trying to hold it together, his face flushed with emotion.

"What if she changes her mind? Can she get a feeding tube in hospice, even at home?"

"Yes, she can, but that's not my bailiwick." Eric paused. "I know how much you care about her, I can see that. Once she enters hospice, she will get a first-rate social worker to help her. They'll call me if she develops depression or any other emotional problems."

"For real?" Max's eyebrows slanted downward under his raggedy bangs.

"Yes, and they have ample experience." Eric placed a hand on the boy's shoulder. Oddly, he wondered what it would be like to have a son. He hadn't thought that in ages, not since Hannah was born, but something about the physical connection sparked the thought. "Max, this is going to be a difficult time for you both. Your grandmother believes that you'll benefit from therapy, and I'm offering to see you in my private practice, nights or weekends." Eric slid his wallet from his back pocket, extracted a business card, and handed it to the boy. "Please, take this. Don't hesitate to call me if you want to schedule an appointment."

Max accepted the card and glanced at it, blinking. "Okay, thanks. I appreciate it."

"I'm not going to try to convince you because it has to be up to you. But if you don't call me, then please do avail yourself of the support groups that hospice will offer. One of the best things you can do for your grandmother is to take care of yourself."

"Yes, that's what she says."

"I hope you listen to her." Eric took his hand from the boy's shoulder. "I wish you the best of luck."

Max managed a shaky smile. "Thanks."

"Take care." Eric turned away, with difficulty. He couldn't help feeling that he was turning his back on the kid, but that was the hardest part of his profession, knowing that he could help only those who came to him. He walked back to Laurie, who was waiting.

Laurie smiled sadly. "I knew you'd come through for him, the poor kid. I owe you one."

"So you were in on this, too?"

"Yes. I could see that her problem was him, really. Thanks for the consult."

"No worries." Eric looked around for the medical students. "Where—"

"They went back upstairs. The girl got paged. What's her name, Kristine? Dude, she has a lady boner for you."

"No, she doesn't." Eric had missed how blunt Laurie could be. They hadn't gone running for a few months, since he'd been going through the worst of his separation.

"When you were talking to Max, she was gushing about how nice you were. Besides, she bugs me. There's always one of them."

"One of what?"

"She's the Girl Who Dresses Too Hot For Work. Every rotation has one, probably every job."

Eric hadn't even noticed what Kristine was wearing, but she was pretty. He wasn't blind.

"Also did you see Sandy at the nurses' station? She was so excited I called you down. They're champing at the bit, now that you're divorced."

"I'm not divorced yet."

"Oh please. You filed, right?"

"Yes, but nothing's final."

"So there's a waiting period. Whatever."

Eric didn't understand why he was making such a pointless distinction. "Permit me my denial. I'm a professional."

"Well, in the good-news department, there's no waiting period for single doctors."

Eric checked his watch. "Can I go now? I'm late."

"Where're you going?"

"Home," Eric answered reflexively.

Laurie scoffed. "You mean your soon-to-be ex-wife's house? Why?"

"I have to drop off a check."

"Ever hear of the mail?" Laurie lifted an eyebrow. "You put your check in something called an envelope, and they bring it to her door."

"I told her I'd do some yard work. Mow the lawn."

"At night?"

"It doesn't get dark until nine." Eric could feel a lecture coming on. He'd observed that doctors in hospitals tended to become their specialty. He'd become more cerebral as a psychiatrist, but Laurie had morphed into an emergency doctor to the max. She went right for the wound, exposed it, and flushed it out, no matter how much it hurt.

"Can't she mow her own damn lawn? Or pay somebody?"

"I like to mow the lawn, and if I go over, I get to see Hannah when it's not my night." Eric didn't want to hear it, not right now.

"Why do you care?"

"I don't like seeing you get used. It's not right."

"She's not using me."

"Whatever, I never liked her, she's a bitch."

"Okay, let's let it go." Eric didn't like to hear bad things about Caitlin. He still was sorting out why she'd wanted a divorce, though he suspected its roots went back years. They had met at Amherst, and she'd married him after graduation, but when he developed an anxiety disorder, he could feel his cool factor vanish and her disillusionment begin. She'd wanted him to be the take-charge, confident, alpha male he seemed to be, killing it in college, summa cum laude, headed for Penn Med. She had fallen in love with a cardboard cutout of a man, a résumé rather than a human being, and when he'd showed a chink in the armor, it sealed his fate with her.

Even after he'd gotten over the anxiety and they'd had a child together, she never looked at him the same way again. And the child
only made things worse.

"All right, I'll lay off, I'm sorry." Laurie sighed. "It must be hard
on you not to see Hannah. You're a great dad, and she was always
closer to you than to Caitlin."

"Thanks." Eric never allowed himself to think such things, much
less say them, but it was true. He was closer to Hannah than Caitlin had been. He and his daughter had so much in common. Too
much, according to his wife. Er, ex-wife. Eric wanted to change the
subject. "So what's new with you?"

"Nothing." Laurie shrugged her broad shoulders. "I'm here all
the time. We lost two part-time docs and I'm taking extra shifts."

"That's tough." Eric admired Laurie's work ethic. She was an absolutely dedicated emergency physician. "And how about that guy
you were seeing, the new one?"

"Which one?"

"The fix-up."

"The fix-up who texted too much or the fix-up who texted too
little?"

Eric smiled. Laurie's dating tales were the stuff of ED legend.
"I'm behind on your love life. I meant the ethics professor."

"Need you ask? *Ethics professor?* That says it all."

"What? I think that sounds good."

"You would." Laurie rolled her eyes.

"Another one bites the dust, eh?" Eric felt a twinge of sympathy
for her. She was too attractive to be single: smart, funny, and fun
to be with. "Well, you'll meet someone. You're awesome."

"I'm *so* awesome." Laurie grinned. "Men are threatened by me,
what can I tell you?"

"They don't last long enough to be threatened by you."

"I'm threatening right off the bat. I don't want to be less than,
so some guy can feel more than. *Capisce?*"

Eric smiled. "How's that working for you?"

"Don't ask." Laurie laughed. "Anyway, enough. I think we should
start running again."

Eric groaned. "I haven't run since I moved out."

"We'll start slow. How about next week, after work? I can't Monday, but can you Tuesday?" Laurie glanced over at the examining room, and Eric turned, too, to see Max talking with his grandmother.

"Poor kid." Eric watched Max take his grandmother's hand. "How much time does she have?"

"Can't say for sure. It's been three days since she's eaten. Older people don't need the calories, but she's dehydrated. We're giving her two bags of saline, but she'll lose that in a day or two."

Eric recognized the answer-that-wasn't-an-answer. He did it, too, hedging his bets when he answered questions from anxious families, *will she get better, will he try to kill himself again, will she keep cutting herself, will the Klonopin work, does he really have to be admitted?* Eric repeated, "How long does she have?"

"Two weeks, tops."

Eric eyed Max and his grandmother, with sympathy.

Chapter Four

Eric turned the corner onto his old street, leaving behind the rush-hour traffic, the hospital, his patients on the unit, even Max and his grandmother. He decreased his speed and heard the reassuring rumble of gravel beneath his BMW tires. He looked forward to seeing Hannah, and Caitlin had even invited him to have dinner at home, which he took as a good sign—of what, he didn't know.

He cruised along the winding road, lined with tall pin oak and horse-chestnut trees. He cruised past the trees, noting which were gaining buds or shedding bark. He was his mother's son, she'd been an avid gardener who loved nature, and he'd come to know the trees, as well as all the other flora-and-fauna along the street; the Daleys' forsythia that was sadly short-lived, the fragrant lilac bushes clustered around the Menghetti driveway, and the privet hedges that the Palumbos let grow tall, so they thinned out like older people. It reminded him of Mrs. Teichner, and he felt it like a brick in his stomach.

Two weeks, tops.

Eric never got used to death at the hospital. It was one of the advantages to psychiatry: they didn't lose patients unless to suicide, which was every psychiatrist's nightmare. It had happened to him only once, when he was in training; he had lost a heroin addict to suicide, and he still thought about that patient late at night, when he was trying to sleep. A professor he never liked used to say, "You never forget your first," but Eric wasn't laughing.

It was one of the reasons he valued his private practice, in which he curated his patients carefully, choosing them to be different from the psychotic or even violent patients at the hospital. The DSM listed personality disorders in clusters, with Cluster A being eccentrics, Cluster B being dramatics, and Cluster C, the anxious. As a former Cluster C himself, Eric retained his team loyalties and maintained a Cluster C client base in his private practice, which contributed to the mental relaxation he felt approaching home. He was still getting used to seeing patients in his new house; he didn't like the change any more than his patients did. Cluster C liked everything to stay the same, forever.

Eric drove on, spotted his neighbor Bob Jeffries getting out of his white Acura, and gave him a wave. Bob waved back, flashing a surprised smile. Eric didn't know whether Bob knew that he and Caitlin had broken up. Caitlin wasn't home enough to know the neighbors, but Eric was, and he had helped Bob's black-sheep brother get into a ritzy drug rehab center, writing a recommendation as flowery as if it were an Ivy League school.

He steered the car around the curve that led to his house, knowing that the first thing he'd see when he rounded the bend was the row of abelia bushes that he'd planted when Hannah was born, their delicate pink flowers in honor of their newborn girl. Eric had thought of that moment tonight in the hospital when he'd put his hand on Max's shoulder, but dismissed it. He was truly glad he had a daughter, and Hannah was a daddy's girl who couldn't be improved upon in his eyes.

Eric pressed the gas and spotted the abelias, but behind them was something he'd never seen on his front lawn. **FOR SALE,** read the Remax sign in bright red letters, and underneath it said, UNDER CONTRACT. Eric didn't understand what he was seeing. The house wasn't up for sale, much less under contract. He flipped up the visor and cruised to a stop in disbelief. It had to be a mistake.

Eric pulled over, cut the ignition, and climbed out of the car. Suddenly the front door of the house opened and Caitlin hurried out, dressed in jean shorts and a white T-shirt, carrying a few Wegman's bags to her silver Lexus in the driveway. She didn't notice him, hustling to her car, chirping open the hatchback, and tossing in the plastic bags. She was so cute, her figure gym-toned and sexy, and in any other circumstances, Eric would have felt a stab of suburban lust.

"Caitlin!" Eric hustled past the abelias while she stopped in front of the door and turned to see him, her ponytail whipping around and her eyebrows lifting in surprise.

"Eric. Oh, no, I forgot you were coming over. Sorry, we have to go out."

"What's going on?" Eric realized she hadn't meant for him to see the sign. "You're *selling* the house?"

"Yes." Caitlin pursed her lips, unhappily but firmly. She was a strong, smart lawyer, an assistant prosecutor with the Chester County D.A.'s Office.

"You can't do that."

"Yes I can."

"No you can't." Eric wanted to raise his voice but didn't, because Hannah was home and the screen door was open.

"I own it, remember?" Caitlin's eyes narrowed to sharp blue slits. "I bought you out. You sold it to me."

"I let you buy me out because we agreed Hannah would stay here." Eric couldn't believe he was explaining this to the person whose idea it was in the first place. "We said it was in Hannah's best interest to live in the house she grew up in. You said it was closer to work for you, so it made sense for me to move, even though I saw patients here. We did it for Hannah."

"None of that is in the settlement agreement."

"Does it have to be?" Eric couldn't believe his ears. "We understood what we were doing and why. We sat down with the lawyers. We agreed what the reason was. We're not even divorced yet."

"So what?"

"You can't turn around and sell the house, just like that." Eric couldn't bring himself to say that selling the house made it real. That they weren't getting back together. That their marriage really was over. He was in professional denial.

"I own it, and I'm selling it. I sold it." Caitlin put her hands on her hips. "Now lower your voice. The neighbors will hear us."

"Caitlin, why sell it?" Eric didn't understand. "It's a great house and Hannah loves it. It's her *home*. What did she say about this?"

"She doesn't know."

"She saw the sign, didn't she? She can read."

"She didn't see it. She fell asleep in the car on the way back from the mall."

"The mall?"

"We went to the mall. I took the day off. She didn't see the sign. It sold before it was on the market and they only put the sign up to promote themselves."

"So when were you going to tell her? Or me?" Eric couldn't remember the last time Caitlin had taken a day off from work, but he let it go.

"Look, it just happened today. Like I said, it didn't even get listed yet, but the broker had a buyer for me. I didn't turn it down, not in this market."

"But you knew you had it with a broker. Why didn't you say anything?"

"I didn't know when it would sell, or even if." Caitlin scoffed "What am I supposed to tell her, someday Mommy might sell the house?"

"Why not tell *me*?"

"I knew you wouldn't agree and I didn't need your permission. I decided I didn't want to live here, with the memories. It's not good for Hannah."

"I'm not dead, Caitlin. I'm her *father*." Eric thought Caitlin had lost her mind. "Are you taking her out of the school district? You can't do that. She's only in second grade. She just started—"

"No, I'm not."

Eric's heart eased. At least, that. "Where are you going to go? When's settlement?"

"I don't have to tell you."

"What? Why wouldn't you?"

"When it's final, I'll tell you. This is about you, not her."

"But I'm concerned about her. Can't you think how this will affect her? It's too much for her to deal with, all at once. She's still working out that we broke up."

"She'll be fine."

"Not necessarily. She's a sensitive kid." Eric knew Hannah's emotional health had been a major problem during their marriage. He feared that Hannah had inherited his anxiety disorder, which was genetic, but Caitlin always argued that he reinforced Hannah's anxieties, so that she played them up for him. Caitlin would never believe that Hannah wasn't perfect, like her.

"We'll start over. Fresh."

Eric switched tacks. "Can I buy the house from you? I'll buy it back. My *own* house."

"No. It's a done deal, cash, for full ask."

Eric didn't know when Caitlin started talking like a Realtor. "What did they pay? I'll pay more. I'll top it."

"No, it's done." Caitlin threw up her hands. "Let it *go.* You never let anything *go.*"

Eric felt his temper flare, but stayed in control. "Where's Hannah? We were supposed to have dinner tonight."

"We can't. We have softball practice."

"Since when does she play softball?" Eric felt as if he'd stepped into bizarro world. Hannah didn't like sports. The child had absolutely no athletic prowess. She liked to write, draw, and read. She was a bookworm, like him.

"It's the first night, a practice, in the summer league on the playground."

"You can't sign her up for softball without talking to me about it. We're supposed to agree."

"We're giving it a try for one practice. I don't need your agreement to try." Caitlin waved him off with a manicured hand.

"Yes, you do. We have joint legal custody." Eric felt everything slipping away. His life, his home. His wife, his daughter. Control. He was big enough to admit that, too.

"What possible objection could you have?"

"You know my objection. You push her into sports. You want her to be an athlete because you were. You don't care whether she wants to play."

"What's the big deal? Let her be a normal kid, for God's sake." Caitlin waved him off like a fly. "Normal kids like sports. Don't you want her to be normal?"

"I want her to be who she is—"

"No," Caitlin snapped. "You want her to be *you.*"

"And you want her to be *you,*" Eric shot back, wondering when exactly they'd gone from I-hope-our-little-girl-is-exactly-like-you to I-hope-our-little-girl-is-the-exact-opposite-of-you.

"Leave, Eric. You have no right to be here."

"Where is she? I want to see her."

"No, you can't. She has to get dressed. We're running late."

"I can't see her? Really?" Eric stepped toward the door, but Caitlin blocked it with her body, folding her arms. He was a big guy, but he wasn't about to intimidate her and she knew it. It was the last thing he would do, ever.

"We got cleats and a uniform. She's excited. Don't mess it up for her."

"I'm not going to mess it up for her, I'm going to say hello. She expected to see me—"

"You can't see her." Caitlin's blue eyes flashed coldly. "It's not your night."

"She's my *child.*" Eric hated this my-night/your-night business. He missed seeing his daughter every day, and he got to see her only every other weekend and one dinner a week. It was a custody plan the lawyers said was conventional, but Eric had been doing it for three months and it wasn't getting any easier.

"I'm calling Daniel." Caitlin slid her iPhone from her shorts pocket and hit a button. "You better call Susan."

"Battle of the lawyers? No thanks. Please stand aside."

"Knock yourself out." Caitlin stepped aside, phone to her ear, then said into the phone, "Daniel, I have a problem—"

Eric passed her, entered the house, hustled through the entrance hall, then took the hardwood stairs two-by-two. He reached the landing and put on his game face.

"Daddy, is that you?" Hannah called from her bedroom, excitedly.

Chapter Five

"Daddy!" Hannah ran down the carpeted hall to him, and Eric caught her up in his arms, hoisted her into the air, and hugged her close, breathing in the fruity perfume of her Disney Princess shampoo mixed with the oddly synthetic odor of the yellow polyester jersey, which read David's Dental For Kids.

"How did you know I was here?" Eric stopped himself before he said *home*. He had no idea where his home was, now. For Sale. Sold. Gone.

"I heard you on the stairs. You have big feet." Hannah wrapped her bare arms tight around his neck, clinging like a kitten. Her straight, chin-length light brown hair framed a face as round as a button, and she was skinny, with coltish knees. She had on matching jersey shorts and her feet were bare.

"I love you, honey." Eric kissed her on the cheek.

"I love you, too."

"How did Mrs. Williams like your diorama?" Eric set her down on the carpet. She looked so cute with her softball gear and pink plastic glasses. She was farsighted, so her prescription lenses magnified her sky-blue eyes, and there was something about a little girl in glasses that stole his heart.

"She loved it!" Hannah beamed, showing mostly even teeth,

except for one missing on the upper left. "She said it was one of the best in the class."

"That's great, I knew she would."

"Three other kids made their diorama about *James and the Giant Peach,* but I was the only one that showed the magic crystals."

"Way to go." Eric knelt down and touched her jersey. "Hey, I like this cool uniform. I hear you're going to play softball tonight. That sounds like fun."

Hannah fell suddenly silent, frowning, but Eric didn't want to project his feelings onto her, so he tried again.

"I hear you get to wear cleats, too. Cleats are very cool."

"No, I hate them. They're weird. You can't walk in them unless you're on the grass. We went to the mall and got them." Hannah wrinkled her upturned nose, a miniature version of Caitlin's. "Mommy used to wear them when she played feel hockey."

Eric hid his smile. Caitlin had played varsity field hockey, but she wasn't as good at feel hockey.

"We got ice cream, and Mommy got me my own glove, too. You have to put it on your hand and it helps you catch the ball." Hannah brushed her bangs from her forehead. "And we got Croakies for my glasses, to keep them on. In yellow, to match my uniform."

"Wow, that sounds great." Eric realized that Caitlin had staged a charm offensive, mall trips and ice cream. "Looks like you're ready for softball. That sounds like fun, doesn't it?"

"No." Hannah looked up from under her bangs, pained. She reminded Eric so much of himself, not her looks, because her fair coloring and clear blue eyes resembled Caitlin more than him. But the way Hannah acted, her mannerisms, her *gestalt*—he couldn't help using the psychiatric term of art—it was all him.

"Why not? It sounds like fun to me."

"I'm not good at it. It's so hard."

"What's hard about it?" Eric kept his tone light, but his heart ached for her.

"It's just hard." Hannah shrugged, averting her eyes.

"But, how?" Eric knew that helping her express herself was better than bottling it inside. He'd always used his expertise to benefit Hannah, like her resident Shrink Daddy.

"You only get three chances to hit the ball. If you don't get it in three times, you have to sit down."

"Just have a good time, honey. It's only practice, to see if you like it. Give it a chance."

"They'll get mad at me. They already don't like me, from school." Hannah's eyes met his directly, her eyebrows sloping down unhappily. "I'm not good enough to be on the team. I never hit the ball, I don't know how to catch it. I only caught the ball one time in recess, but Sarah T. ran into me and I dropped it. What if I drop the ball and they laugh? What if they make fun of me?"

Eric heard her anxiety, the litany of what-ifs that ended in disaster. Hannah's signs of an anxiety disorder had been evident from toddlerhood, when she had been shy around the other kids in preschool and generally phobic: afraid of bees, flies, the dark, the windows at night, even butterflies. As she had gotten older, she had become only more cautious, careful, and worrisome, articulating fears that went beyond reasonable. Eric gave her shoulder a gentle squeeze. "The best thing is to try and have fun."

"How?"

"Just say to yourself, it's fun to be outside in nature. Like James with Miss Spider and the caterpillar."

Hannah blinked, dubious. "Mommy says I have to try it for the summer, then I can quit."

"I see." Eric kept his thoughts to himself. So much for Hannah's trying it only one night. "Your mom wants you to have fun outside, that's all."

"What if I don't know the rules?"

"You'll learn them."

"Ms. Pinto has to tell me in school." Hannah began to finger her hair, taking a few strands between her thumb and index finger, a nervous habit. Eric prayed it wasn't a precursor of trichotillomania, in which kids pulled hair from their heads. It wasn't uncommon among his patients at the hospital; most recently, he'd treated a high-school girl who tore out her eyebrows and eyelashes.

"Hannah, listen to me. They'll help you understand the rules. It's not like they expect you to know them. That's what practice is for. To learn."

"Everybody else knows them already." Hannah twisted her hair. "I'm the only one who doesn't. Emily is the captain and she says I'm a loser."

"Aw, no, you're not a loser, honey." Eric gathered her up in his arms and gave her a kiss. "Emily is a bully, and what do we know about bullies?"

"They have low self-steam."

"Exactly right." Eric smiled. "They have low self-steam. You know what they are? Knuckleheads."

Hannah giggled, and they both turned at the sound of Caitlin's coming up the stairs.

"Hannah, you ready to go?" Caitlin called out, her tone falsely casual. "We don't want to be late."

"Mommy, guess what?" Hannah called back, grinning. "Daddy said Emily is a knucklehead."

Caitlin walked toward them with pursed lips. "Don't call names, Hannah. Emily's a nice girl."

Eric stood up, resting his hand on Hannah's head, tousling her hair. Her head felt warm under his palm, a wonderful sensation. "Emily sounds mean to me. She called Hannah a name."

"Two wrongs don't make a right," Caitlin said coolly, then handed Eric her iPhone. "Here, Eric, take this. I have Daniel on the line and I think you should speak with him."

"Great, thanks." Eric took the phone, pressed End Call with his thumb, then handed it back. "Here you go. Tell Daniel I said hi, would you?"

"Fine." Caitlin shot him a warning look, muted because they were in front of Hannah.

Hannah looked up at Eric, her giggle gone. "Daddy, can you come to my softball practice?"

"Sure," Eric answered. "I'd love—"

"No, he can't," Caitlin interjected, maintaining her ersatz politeness. "Tonight isn't a real game, it's just a practice, and Daddy has to mow the lawn and fix the fence. I'll make sure he has a schedule of your games, so he can go and watch you play." Caitlin motioned to Hannah's bare feet. "Why aren't your socks and cleats on, honey? We have to get going."

Hannah pushed up her glasses. "They're in my bedroom. The shoelaces are too long and they didn't put them in the holes and I tried but I don't know how to do it."

Caitlin waved her down the hall. "Go get them and we'll put them on in the car. Hurry up, now."

"Okay." Hannah ran off down the hall to her room.

Eric waited until Hannah was out of earshot, then turned to Caitlin. "As I suspected, she's not excited about playing softball, but I have no problem with you giving it a try. I would've liked to go and see her practice, and I have every right to do so."

"If you had taken Daniel's call, you would know that you don't have every right to do so."

"As you say, 'What possible objection can you have to my being there?' " Eric wasn't above throwing her own words back at her. "If softball is so great, why can't I watch my daughter enjoy it?"

"She won't enjoy it if you watch. She'll act like she doesn't like it so you'll feel sorry for her."

"No, she won't." Eric felt stung for Hannah. "She's just a little kid trying to deal with big emotions. We're supposed to help her do that, even if we don't want her to have those emotions. Even if those emotions are inconvenient for us."

"Give it a rest, Freud. Why do you have to burden everything? Why is everything so *freighted*?"

"Actions have consequences, Caitlin. People are allowed to have emotional reactions to decisions, especially children."

"Gimme a break." Caitlin clenched her perfect teeth. "Kids play softball. Bad things happen and good things happen. People get divorced, and everybody has to learn to move on. Me, you, and Hannah." Caitlin lowered her voice because Hannah was walking toward them, holding her socks and her cleats, trailing overlong shoelaces.

"Mommy, I got my shoes!"

"Can you walk faster?" Caitlin hurried toward Hannah and hustled her down the hallway to the stairwell, just as Eric's phone started ringing in his pocket. He slid it out quickly, a psychiatrist's reflex. He glanced at the screen, which read Susan Grimes, his lawyer, so he slid the phone back into his pocket and hurried after Caitlin and Hannah. He followed them downstairs, where Caitlin gave him the job of carrying shopping bags of healthy snacks to the car, while she laced Hannah's cleats. When it was time to go, Caitlin locked the front door, then she and Hannah piled into the car.

Eric waved good-bye as they reversed out of the driveway, turned right, and disappeared around the bend, out of sight. He realized that the FOR SALE sign was gone and assumed that Caitlin had removed it while he was upstairs. He turned away and headed to the garage, where he spotted the sign behind the beach chairs. He moved the chairs, retrieved the sign, and threw it in the trash can out back. He didn't bother thinking about it, he just did it, and it felt good and childish, both at once.

He went back to the garage, changed into the sweatshirt and jeans that he stowed in his workshop, then got his tools, carried them out to the back fence, and fixed the rail as it grew dark. He tried to ignore the tension tightening his chest. He reminded himself that it was just an overactive amygdala, the brain's emotional control center, which was hyperactive in those with anxiety. He pictured his neuroscience textbook, which showed thermal images of the brain, the amygdala hot with electrical activity, in vivid reds and orange flares, like sunspots.

Eric put the tools back, started the tractor, and mowed the lawn, finally calming down as he drove back and forth in strips as straight as wound tape, getting as close as possible to the trunks of the trees so he didn't have as much to weed-whack, tending a yard that his daughter would no longer play in, on a property he no longer owned, with a house that was no longer his home.

By the time the sun abandoned the sky, Eric barely noticed. Because he was already in darkness.

He didn't see the text until he got home.

Chapter Six

Eric opened his door into his entrance hall, set his keys and mail on the side table, then slid his iPhone from his pocket. The screen showed a text he must have missed. He hadn't felt the phone vibrate while he was mowing the lawn, and he'd started making calls almost as soon as he hit the car; first to his lawyer, whom he didn't reach, second to the Remax Realtor, whom he didn't reach either, and finally he returned calls to his private clients. Luckily, nothing had been pressing, just hands held, dosages tweaked, and pharmacies called, and then he was here, his new home.

He felt tired, sweaty, and hungry, covered with a fine yellow-green dusting of pollen. His T-shirt hung on his body, his jeans and sneakers were covered with grass clippings. He touched the text icon, and the text popped onto the screen. He didn't recognize the phone number but the text read:

> U wanted 2 talk about Jacobs but I didn't C U before U left.
> I'm free 2 meet 2 nite. Kristine

Eric blinked, surprised. It was from his medical student, Kristine Malin. He'd never gotten a text from her, or any other med student, before. He didn't know how she got his cell number, then he realized she would have password access to the online hospital directory. True, he had told her that he wanted to talk to her about Armand Jacobs, a seventy-something patient whose borderline personality disorder wasn't helped by a relapse into alcoholism, but that could wait until tomorrow. The matter had slipped Eric's mind and he'd left work from the ED, after talking with Laurie.

She has a lady boner for you.

Eric wondered if Kristine was asking him out and using the case for an excuse. He would never date anyone under his supervision, much less a medical student, but he was tempted. After all, his new place was empty, the silence practically echoing. He still hadn't furnished it completely because he'd been holding out hope that he and Caitlin would get back together, but that wasn't happening. The last time he had sex was eight months and about three weeks ago. Still, he didn't need a date, he needed a lawyer.

Eric thumbed to the phone function, scrolled through his contacts, and pressed Call, then wandered into the kitchen while the phone rang. "Susan?" he said, when the call was picked up. "Hi, did you get my message?"

"Yes, hello." Susan's voice was hard to hear over some background noise. "I'm at my son's basketball game. Sorry I didn't get a chance to call you back."

Eric thought of what Caitlin had said, *normal kids like sports,* but he pressed that thought away. "Do you have time to talk? It's important and I'm one of those clients now, who call at all hours."

Susan laughed. "Go ahead. I understand from Daniel you had an issue at the house today. What happened?"

Eric filled her in as succinctly as possible. "But can she sell the house without asking me?"

"Unfortunately, yes. We agreed that you were giving her the house because it was the best thing for Hannah, but we didn't provide for that in the agreement. In my defense, the only thing I can say is that sort of thing is never in an agreement."

"Damn it." Eric went to the refrigerator and opened the door.

"The most I could have done is to try and get you the right of first refusal. My sense is that she knew she wanted to sell the house when she signed the agreement. I said as much to Daniel. He didn't deny it but he didn't confirm it either."

"Can we change the agreement to put in the right of first refusal?" Eric scanned the refrigerator, which contained expired milk, a six of Bud Light, and leftovers from Chipotle, Saladworks, and Outback Steakhouse. He ate so much takeout that he saw tinfoil lids in his sleep.

"No. We can't amend it because they won't agree. They never would have."

"I see." Eric wasn't giving up. "But isn't there anything we can do to stop her?"

"Sorry, but no."

"Can I buy the house back? I called the Realtor, but he hasn't returned it yet."

"I have to advise against you doing that, Eric."

"Why? If I'm crazy enough to buy my own house, why should anybody stop me?"

"If the house is under contract and you start making phone calls that disrupt that transaction, she could sue you."

Eric scoffed, incredulous. "For what? Trying to buy a house I used to own?"

"It's called tortious interference with contract."

"But what if it's for a higher number? She said she got the full asking price, but whatever it is, I can top it. How is that interfering with the contract?"

"Not so fast, I doubt you can top it. After I spoke with Daniel today, I called my cousin who's a Realtor at Berkshire Hathaway, and he did some digging for me. Caitlin got $510,000 for the house."

"*What?*" Eric grabbed a Bud Light and closed the refrigerator door. "That's not possible. The estimator valued it at $450,000. How did she get that much?"

"My cousin thinks it's a foreign buyer."

"What foreign buyer? This is the Philadelphia suburbs, not London."

"He says that the houses in your neighborhood are getting snapped up for the executives, ever since Centennial Tech merged with that Japanese company. They paid way too much. Three bed rooms, two baths, for 510? On *that* parcel?"

Eric felt his heart wrench. He loved that parcel. "Well. That shuts me down. We both know I don't have $510,000 in cash lying around."

"Especially since you let her buy you out for a hundred grand. She makes great money, and by all rights, she should've paid fully half." Susan clucked. "I tried to warn you. No good deed, Eric."

"It was my kid's house." Eric tucked the phone under his ear, went to the silverware drawer, pulled out the church key, and pried the lid off his beer.

"Yes, it was, and Caitlin made herself a bundle."

Eric couldn't say anything, trying to process the information. He didn't know how Caitlin could bring herself to sell the house, even for that much money. He didn't know how she could let him go. He loved her still, but she was gone and somehow she'd ended up with everything—Hannah, a windfall, and a perfectly mown lawn that didn't even need weed-whacking. He took a slug of beer, which tasted bitter.

"Eric, are you there?"

"Yes, but I'm suicidal. Luckily, I know a good shrink."

Susan chuckled.

"Okay, let's switch gears. Talk to me about softball. Caitlin said I wasn't permitted to go to Hannah's practice. Was that right?"

"No, she was just trying to back you down, and so was Daniel. I'm glad you didn't take his call. He never should have talked to you. He knows you're represented. Anyway, softball practice is a public event. You're permitted to go."

"Doesn't she have to ask me before she signs Hannah up for summer activities? Isn't that what legal custody means, that we decide major decisions together?"

"The term 'shared legal decisions' are major things, like choice of religion or enrolling the child in a different school."

"So what do we do about softball?"

"Nothing. If we went to a judge and asked him to restrain Caitlin from enrolling Hannah in a softball league, we would lose. It would look like you were overreaching. Micromanaging."

"You make it sound like nothing, and it's not for a kid like Hannah. I told you, she's anxious and she doesn't want to play softball. She's not as good, and the other girls bully her. Couldn't we say that to the court?"

"No. A court doesn't want to be in the business of telling parents whether or not their kids should play softball. I know you think she has an anxiety disorder, but she hasn't been diagnosed with one."

"I diagnose her as having one."

"But the court would say that you weren't independent, and you're not. If you want me to get an evaluation of her psychological status, we can do that."

"I don't want to stress her more, to prove a point to some judge." Eric hated this whole legal process, asking a judge what was best for a child he knew better and loved more than life itself. "She's already under the stress of the separation, and now, a move."

"Kids are resilient, Eric."

"Not that resilient." Eric disliked the skepticism in Susan's tone. Kids with anxiety issues were in psychic pain, and nobody knew that better than he did. Anybody could be pushed over the edge, given the right circumstances. He wondered how many school shootings it would take before people woke up.

"Eric, here's what I suggest. See how the practice goes. Let her try it one or two times. That will make you look reasonable to the court if we have to go."

Eric was getting a new idea, a bold one. "Listen, I really got blindsided by this house business, and it raises the question of whether I should have given Caitlin primary custody. If Caitlin is going to change so many things, then Hannah isn't going to get the benefit of the continuity that I bargained for."

"Where are you going with this?"

"Can we apply to the court for me to be primary custodian?"

"Are you serious?" Susan asked, surprised.

"Yes, why not?"

"But you and Caitlin agreed the other way. We just filed a custody agreement that gives her primary physical custody."

"That was before I knew she was selling the house." Eric took another swig of beer. Either the Bud Light was improving his reasoning powers or he was getting blitzed. "Think outside the box. Why shouldn't I be primary custodian? I can work fewer hours than Caitlin and I have more flexibility. Hell, if I wanted to, I could quit my job at the hospital and see patients only at home."

"Slow down, Eric. You're talking about changing your life."

"Maybe I need to change my life." Eric felt his heart lift. Months of watching his fatherhood whittled to nothing had been getting to him more than he realized. "It's time to get aggressive, isn't it? Caitlin is."

"It's not a contest between you and Caitlin. It's about the best interests of Hannah."

"I know that, and I think it's in Hannah's best interest to be with me, now."

"Why? Just because your ex is selling the house?"

"No, not *per se,* but it got me thinking. I went with the least disruptive thing for Hannah, but that purpose just got defeated. If she has to move, let her move in with me." Eric took anther swig of beer. "I thought it would benefit Hannah if we didn't fight over her, but I shouldn't have tried to avoid the conflict. I should fight for what I think is right."

"Why is it right for you to be the primary custodian? It's unusual for a female child."

"I'm very close to Hannah, closer than Caitlin. I *get* her in ways that Caitlin doesn't." Eric knew it in his heart, even if Caitlin would never admit it. "I think if you asked Hannah, she would choose to live with me over Caitlin, but I'd hate for Hannah to have to testify. Would she have to?"

"No. The judge could ask her in chambers whom she wants to live with, but she's too young for it to be dispositive. If you want primary custody, then I would withdraw our papers, right away."

"Then what?"

"We would open the custody discussion and negotiate. If we couldn't agree, then we battle it out in court. It's not pretty, but if it's what you want, we can do that." Susan hesitated. "You know, before we go there, there is a middle ground."

"What?"

"We could ask for fifty-fifty physical custody. Hannah would be one week at your house, and one week at Caitlin's."

"I don't like that idea, for Hannah. She'd have to get used to two new houses, and kids with anxiety don't do well with change, shifting back and forth. It's hard for them to adapt and it creates even more adjustment problems."

"Okay. Sleep on it over the weekend. Call me Monday morning and let me know what you decide."

"If we go to trial, will we win?"

"It's a borderline case, and I don't know. All I can say is, if you decide this is the way to go, I will do my very best."

"Thanks." Eric felt a warm rush of gratitude.

"In the meantime, toe the line. Don't call Caitlin and fuss about softball. Don't call Hannah and ask her how it went, either. Bow out. Let it be between the two of them."

"I'm allowed to talk to Hannah, aren't I? I call her every night. We gave her a cell phone so she could talk to me."

"Yes, but don't pump her for information. Courts frown on that."

"I don't do that."

"So far. But everything is about to become adversarial, which it hasn't been before. Caitlin isn't going to take this lying down. You don't need me to spell that out, do you?"

Eric didn't.

"Everything you do now goes on the record. The court will see all of it." Susan sounded like she was wrapping up. "Do you follow me?"

"Yes, thanks."

"You're welcome. Let's talk Monday. I have to go. My son's game is over."

"Did they win?"

"If they won, I'd be cheering. Have a good night "

"Great, take care. Bye." Eric pressed End Call and took another swig of beer, draining the bottle. He set it and his phone down on the counter, and on the screen glowed the red alert on the text icon, from young Kristine.

He headed for the shower, to consider his decision.

Chapter Seven

Eric lathered up, letting the hot water relax his neck and shoulders. His thoughts ran free, fluid, and easy, if somewhat disorganized, which was unusual for him. His initial enthusiasm about trying to get primary custody of Hannah worried him, and he challenged it in his mind. He loathed to put her through a custody battle, which pitted her against her own mother. If the judge asked her whom she wanted to live with and Hannah chose him, then that would burden her in a new way.

Eric turned around, and water sluiced down his back. His mind stayed on track. As long as both parents were fit, a custody battle seemed the classic no-win position for her; Hannah would lose either her mother or her father as a hands-on parent. Eric didn't like being the odd man out, but he knew that he was better behaved than Caitlin. If Caitlin were the loser in the battle of Hannah, she would never forgive him. He would lose her, even as a friend, until the end of their days. So he had a no-win decision of his own.

Eric shut off the water, thinking. Like any married couple, he and Caitlin knew each other's secrets, and many of hers concerned being a mother. Caitlin's own mother, Teresa, whom she used to ironically call Mother Teresa, had been a cool and distant mom, and Caitlin had always worried that she wasn't maternal. She'd felt guilty that she enjoyed being a prosecutor, and she'd always doubted that her postpartum depression was truly hormonal. She hadn't wanted to stay home when Hannah was born, not even for a month, and she quit nursing after two weeks.

Eric opened the glass door of the shower, stepped out, and reached for a towel, drying himself off. He began to think he could be the natural primary custodian for Hannah. The fact that he was a father, not a mother, was simply beside the point, wasn't it? What defined a man? A father? Did he have the balls to quit the hospital and work only at home? How much of his own self-worth was tied up in being chief at Havemeyer General? Would it affect his career? His status in the profession? His private clients?

Eric tucked the towel around his waist, catching sight of himself in the mirror. His eyes were an intense blue, close together and sunk into his eye sockets; Caitlin always called them mournful, but he preferred to think of them as intense because it didn't sound so symptomatic. His short blondish hair stuck up like a brush, even dripping wet, but she used to think that was cute. He had a strong nose, narrow with just a slight bump, and thin lips; she had liked his smile. He was tall and strong, with broad shoulders, pronounced shoulder caps, and fairly cut abs from running.

You have the best body of all the husbands, Caitlin used to say.

Eric realized that he couldn't look at any of his features without reference to her. He didn't know if that happened to every married guy, but he'd come to see himself only through her eyes. Caitlin had gone from being his girlfriend, to his best friend, to his wife, to the mother of his child. She was his only family and now he had to decide whether to take their only daughter from her; make *her* the every-other-weekend parent, the afterthought, the footnote, all the bad things he'd felt lately. He didn't know if he could do it to her.

He left the bathroom, securing the towel around his waist because he hadn't had a chance to put up curtains. He'd discovered this was a problem in his second week in the new house, surprised to catch the older woman across the street watching him through binoculars. Caitlin used to tell him that old ladies always had a thing for him, but he shooed that thought away. Then he flashed on poor

Mrs. Teichner and her grandson, but he put that thought out of his mind, too.

He walked barefoot down the narrow hallway, with its hardwood floors and eggshell-colored walls, trying to imagine how the house would work with Hannah here, full-time. It was a charming carriage house in Devon, with weathered brown shingles and forest-green shutters, only ten minutes away from his old house, in the same school district. It had two bedrooms roughly the same size; one facing north for him and the other facing south for Hannah. She loved it and never got homesick, even overnight, which they did only on weekends, so she wouldn't be shuffled hither and yon during the school week. Here, she played in the same playground, went for ice cream at the same Baskin-Robbins, and picked out books at the same local library, Wayne Memorial, and bookstore, either the Barnes & Noble in Valley Forge or their favorite indie, Children's Book World.

He stopped in the threshold of Hannah's bedroom, assessing it with new eyes. It was a good size and held a double bed, a white dresser and bookshelf, and a matching white desk, situated next to a large window that overlooked the backyard. It was sunny and inviting in daytime, but right now it looked unfinished and unwelcoming; there was no headboard on the bed, nor any curtains on the windows. He had bought her a plain beige blanket, unlike the flowery quilt she had at home; the walls were the same white as throughout the apartment, although Hannah's room at home was a girly pink, her favorite color. If Hannah was going to be here full-time, he would have to warm the room up.

Eric felt a surge of new energy. He had painted to earn money in high school, and he could turn this bedroom into a pink palace. He checked his watch, and it was ten o'clock, so Home Depot was still open. Then he could run over to one of the big box stores and buy a lot of pink things—a comforter, some pillows, stuffed animals and games, more books, some pink flowery curtains.

His thoughts clicked away, and a vision came together in his mind. Hannah had also been talking about missing Peachy, their gray tabby cat who had died last year. Maybe it was time to go to the shelter and rescue a new kitten. Unlike Caitlin, Eric loved animals and wasn't embarrassed to say he was a cat man.

His phone started to ring in the bathroom, and he hurried back down the hallway, dashed to the bathroom, and picked up his phone, its screen glowing in the dark. The number on the screen wasn't one he recognized, but it wasn't Kristine's either. He picked up.

"Dr. Parrish, it's Max Jakubowski." Max's tone sounded urgent. "I met you at the hospital, with my grandmother."

"Sure, hello, Max." Eric's heart leapt to his throat, thinking the worst. "How is she? Is she okay?"

"She's fine, she's asleep, but we talked, like, about me. I decided, I would like to come and see you."

"Good." Eric felt relieved. The boy was in crisis, and it was a good sign that he was asking for the help he needed. "When would you like to come in?"

"Can it be as soon as possible? Did you say you see clients on weekends?"

"Yes.

"What about this weekend? Can I come tomorrow?"

"I think so, let me check." Eric thumbed to the calendar function on his phone. He was booked from nine o'clock until three, but he could start earlier. "You can be the first appointment, at eight o'clock. Does that work for you?"

"Yes, totally, thank you so much."

"Good. You have the address on my card, right?"

"Right."

"Make sure you use the driveway on the left, which is the office entrance." Eric's new office was a sunroom on the back of the carriage house he rented and, because it used to belong to an orthodontist, had its own separate entrance and driveway.

"Yes, thank you so much. I'll see you tomorrow at eight."

"Great. Good night. Give my best to your grandmother."

"I will, thanks." Max sounded calmer. "Good night."

Eric hung up, then scrolled to the text function, where Kristine's text was staring him in the face, unanswered. He deleted it and got dressed to go out. He couldn't believe he was choosing Home Depot over Hot Medical Student.

At this rate, he would never have sex again.

Chapter Eight

3. I lie easily and well.
Circle one: Doesn't apply to me. Partially applies to me.
Fully applies to me.

I can't sleep. I'm too hyper. I've cleared the first, maybe the biggest, obstacle. It took time, but it's working.

The enemy has been engaged.

I can't settle down. I feel a thrill, a tingling, not excitement but more nervous, like anticipation, if darker.

The clock by my bed reads 3:02 A.M., but I keep tossing and turning, shifting onto my right side, then my left. I get up to fiddle with the air-conditioning, twisting the knob to HI, then to LO. Why can't they spell English?

Idiots.

I go online and play a video game, but I can't focus, so I go back to bed. I'm bored with these losers and I don't want to be Worthy-Adversary tonight. I found myself a real-life game, and my character is about to destroy someone who needs to be taken down because he's unworthy and weak, a lesser angel.

I haven't felt this good and bad in a long time, and lying here in the darkness, naked under the sheets, it feels like the cotton is burning into my skin, setting it tingling.

Everything is inferior to this feeling, the beginning of a plan. It's like the Friday night to the weekend that I've been waiting for.

I turn over and stuff the pillow under my neck, but still can't calm down. Even though the room is dark and I am still, the night feels somehow alive, my body suspended, floating, flying, my nerves electrified, my heart pumping, my blood racing, adrenaline racing through my system, setting all of my neurons firing.

Sizzle! Bam! Pop!

I'm a video game.

This is as excited as I get. Sociopaths have underactive amygdalas, the emotional center of the brain. You can go online and see for yourself, thermal MRIs of a sociopath's brain show where the amygdala is supposed to be hot red and orange, a sociopath's amygdala is dark, black, and cold, like permanent midnight.

Works for me.

Right now, my thoughts are running free, corkscrewing back in time, to the very beginning, to the very first time I felt this feeling.

I remember it.

I was seven years old, and my mother had a boyfriend over, and this one had a kid of his own, a fat-faced son named Jimmy. She put me in the backyard to play with him while they went inside the house and we knew what they were doing, even then I knew what she was doing, I heard the noises.

By the way, it's not my mother's fault I'm a sociopath.

And she can't take the credit either.

The fact is, I was born this way.

I've always known I was different, right from the beginning, and so did my mother, that's why she kept her distance. She was scared of me, I could see it in her eyes, and she could see it in mine, who I was, the truth.

I never felt like anybody else, I always knew I was better. Smarter. Special. But I knew how to imitate them, how to make them think I was like them, and I was pretty good even way back when, like that day when Porky Pig Jimmy came to visit and I gave myself my first test.

I left Porky to play in the backyard, went inside the house, and took his father's blue plastic Bic lighter from the end table. The noises came from the bedroom so I knew my mother was still busy, and I took the plastic lighter, set fire to a newspaper on the couch, and slipped the lighter in Porky Pig's Ninja Turtles backpack. Then I went out to the backyard, where Porky was writing his name in the dirt with a stick.

It only took five minutes for mom and her boyfriend to come running out, half-dressed, puffing and panting, scared that the house almost burned down. At first my mother thought she left a cigarette burning, but the boyfriend figured out that it was a set fire and accused us.

Of course I denied it, and so did Porky.

But then the boyfriend realized his lighter was missing and went looking, and lo and behold, where did it turn up but behind old Leonardo, Michelangelo, Donatello, and whoever the other one was, I forget.

What I remember is how fast the boyfriend grabbed Porky by the scruff of the neck and cracked him across the face, sending the kid flying backwards.

I covered my face.

So nobody could see me smile.

That's what I feel like right now.

Awesome.

Chapter Nine

The next morning, Eric opened the door to his waiting room to find Max Jakubowski sitting in one of the wooden chairs, hunched over his phone, scrolling the screen with his thumb. "Max? Good morning."

"Oh, hi." Max looked up, slipped his phone quickly into his back pocket, and jumped to his sneakers, as if he were coming to attention.

"Have trouble finding the office?"

"No, used GPS."

"Good. Come on in." Eric gestured Max through the open door to his office, and as the boy shuffled past, Eric thought he seemed more troubled than he'd been in the hospital. Max hung his head and had darkish circles under his eyes, as if he hadn't slept much. His forehead was knit under his bangs, and his mood seemed generally depressed.

"Thanks for seeing me, Dr. Parrish." Max stopped in the center of the office, his eyes grateful, if guarded. Up close, Eric could see that his pale, smooth skin had no trace of beginning stubble.

"No problem. Please sit down." Eric gestured him to the over-sized forest-green chair across from his own.

"Thanks." Max eased onto the chair, bending from the knees sharply, as stiff as a stick figure. He had on loose jeans, another black T-shirt, and worn Converse sneakers. "I didn't realize you were such a big deal at the hospital. I looked you up online."

"That's me, a very big deal." Eric smiled, trying to put him at ease.

"So this is what a psychiatrist's office looks like." Max looked around, wheeling his scruffy head.

"Don't draw too many conclusions. It used to belong to an orthodontist."

Max smiled uncomfortably, still looking around, and Eric took a moment to scan the pale green walls, which had four panels of double-hung windows on three sides. On the right was his modern desk of tiger maple, which he kept uncluttered, a green-gray Aeron ergonomic chair, and a low walnut bookcase stuffed with his textbooks, professional journals, and the DSM. Atop the bookcase was a Keurig coffeemaker, next to a few clean mugs and stethoscope and blood-pressure cuff he used to check vitals. Three oversized chairs of a matching green-patterned fabric faced each other in the center of the room. He hadn't had a chance to hang anything on the walls, but there wasn't much wall space anyway. He kept his diplomas in his office at the hospital.

"There's no couch."

"That's for something called psychoanalysis." Eric smiled again. It was a common misconception. "We can sit here and talk."

"Oh." Max gestured outside the window, where butterfly bushes shaded the room from direct sunlight, making shifting shadows. It was quiet outside, except for the chirping of some noisy blue jays and a rumble of a distant leaf blower. "I like the trees and all."

"I like that, too."

"Is that your family?" Max's gaze fell on the bookcase, with its photographs of Caitlin and Hannah.

"Yes." Eric nodded, but didn't elaborate. He used self-disclosure judiciously, mostly because he didn't want to waste time. Not all psychiatrists kept personal photos in their offices, but since his private clients were never dangerous, he didn't worry about his family's safety.

"So, what do I call you? Dr. Parrish, like at the hospital?"

"Yes, Dr. Parrish is fine." Eric lifted his computer tablet from the end table, then rested it in his lap. He always picked it up at the beginning of the session, so his clients wouldn't attribute any significance to when he reached for it, later.

"I have a note from my grandmother, to say I can come."

"That's not necessary, you can consent to therapy on your own."

"She thought it was like school, and it has the check." Max reached into his pocket and pulled out a piece of stationery, which he handed to Eric, who skimmed it—*Dr. Parrish, God bless you for taking care of my Max*—written in a shaky hand that summoned a lump to Eric's throat. A check was inside, and he set them both on the end table.

"Perfect, thanks. I'm glad you decided to come." Eric typed *Max Jakubowski* and the date on the notepad. Later he'd print the notes and put them in a patient file, which he kept locked in his home office. He never recorded his sessions.

"My grandmother really wanted me to come. She likes you a lot." Max clasped his hands together in his lap, his nervousness making him rigid.

"I like her too. How is she today?"

"Not great, to be honest. She was tired this morning. She usually tries to have some coffee around seven o'clock—she likes instant coffee, crystals or whatever—but not today. She got up but she went back to sleep without her coffee." Max bit his lip. "It kinda worried me, like, I was thinking, it's so weird to know that, well, one day I'll go to wake her up and she won't wake up, and like, that can happen anytime."

"That's very difficult."

"Yeah, like, I don't know if it's better to know or not know. I can't really believe it's happening."

Eric thought of Laurie's telling him that Mrs. Teichner had two weeks to live, but he didn't share that. "I'm sure. It's a very difficult thing to cope with."

"I know, and I had to come see you, but not because she says so. She doesn't really know what's going on, with me. I keep it from her." Max paused, blinking. "I guess I have to tell you, I want to, it's why I'm here, why I knew I would come, like, sooner or later. My symptoms are getting worse."

"What symptoms?"

"I have OCD."

"Tell me about your OCD." Eric used Max's term, but wasn't taking it at face value. He would have to know Max better before he made a diagnosis, and he'd have to learn the boy's family history, to determine his biological vulnerabilities. Late adolescence and early adulthood was a dangerous time, especially for boys; it was around Max's age that "first breaks" usually occurred, in that bipolarity and schizophrenia reared their ugly heads.

"Dr. Parrish, I really need you to give me some meds. I've done the research, I know meds can help OCD. Isn't that right?"

"Yes, it is." Eric encountered this all the time in practice; if a pill existed, patients wanted it. He wasn't anti-meds, but he wasn't about to order anything unless it was called for, especially with an adolescent.

"Luvox and Paxil are good for OCD, I read. Is that what I'll get?"

"Before we talk about meds, let's talk about your symptoms." Eric usually prescribed an SSRI for OCD, like fluoxetine, which was FDA approved, or Celexa, Zoloft, and Luvox, but all of them came with black box warnings for adolescents, which meant they could result in suicidality.

"What about my symptoms?"

"Your OCD, as you say. How does it manifest itself?" Eric wanted to get Max talking, the goal in a first session. "Many people use the term OCD as slang. I need to know your symptoms."

"I have a thing I have to do, like, every fifteen minutes. I have to tap my head and say something and right on time." Max frowned. "I researched myself online. It's called rituals."

"Right. Ritualistic behaviors."

"Yes." Max nodded, jittery. "Once at work, I slipped and said the ritual words out loud and my boss heard, which was terrible."

Eric didn't interrupt, but typed a note, *work?*

"Nobody knows, not even Gummy—I mean, my grandmother." Max knit his hands, his expression showing the strain. "It's horrible, like, a secret I keep. I feel kind of crazy, and nobody knows, like, I have a double life."

"I understand. Tell me when the rituals started." Eric knew exactly how Max felt, though he wouldn't tell him that he'd had an anxiety disorder, yet. Eric used to question how he had the right to treat anybody when he'd had a mental disorder of his own, but every one of his colleagues had something, and people became psychiatrists for a reason. In truth, he believed his old anxiety disorder gave him insight he wouldn't otherwise have.

"A few years ago, maybe two years ago, it got worse. Really bad. I have to touch my head, my right temple, one time, right on time. Every fifteen minutes."

"Around the clock, you mean?"

"Yes, if I'm awake, every fifteen minutes, I have to do this." Max demonstrated, tapping his temple with a slim index finger. "I can't do it too late. I hide it at school or at work by pretending I'm moving my hair or touching a zit or something."

"So you have to watch the clock."

"Yes, constantly. I count down the minutes sometimes, to get to fifteen. It's always on my mind. It's all about the clock, twenty-four/seven."

Eric could imagine how hellish it would be. "Do you count anything else?"

"Like what?"

"Ceiling tiles, sidewalk blocks, the number of times you chew, for example?"

"No."

"Do you do things in numbers, like everything you have to do, you do three times?"

"No." Max shook his head.

"Do you have to even up things, like make something symmetrical?"

"No."

Eric took notes. "What certain words do you have to say when you tap?"

"I have to say red-orange-yellow-green-blue-purple-brown-black, all at once, fast." Max recited the colors together, in a rush. "I have to keep an eye on the clock and make sure I do it right on time. It drives me crazy."

"I'm sure. Is there any significance to the colors?"

"I don't know." Max paused. "But the picture in my head is watercolor paints I used to have when I was a kid, you know the kind everybody has, the lid flops open and there's wells for the paint, with a crappy brush that all the hair falls out of, like eyelashes."

"I remember." Eric did. Hannah had one, too.

"That just comes into my head and I have to say it."

"Why every fifteen minutes, do you know?"

"No, just that fifteen is a good number. I love numbers. I like fifteen, as a number." Max shrugged unhappily, his narrow shoulders going up and down in the T-shirt. "I hated turning sixteen because I had to leave fifteen."

Eric made a note. "Did something good happen to you when you were fifteen?"

"No, not at all."

"Did anything happen that could have precipitated these rituals?"

"No." Max shook his head, nonplussed.

"Your grandmother's diagnosis was about two years ago, wasn't it? You told me so last night."

Max blinked. "Yes, that's true."

"So that was when you were fifteen."

"Right. Does that make a difference?"

"Possibly." Eric thought it seemed too easy. "Sometimes events like that can trigger or exacerbate OCD symptoms."

"Oh." Max's forehead eased. "So that's why?"

"No, not there yet." Eric held up his hand. "Do *you* have any idea why you do these rituals?"

"No."

"Does it happen more in the morning or at night?"

"All the time, no matter what, it's hard to hide. I drop things, like, to hide it. Disguise it. I don't go out because it's too hard to hide. Anytime I'm out, it's harder." Max's eyebrows sloped down miserably, his smile vanishing. "I don't want to do this crap anymore. I can't keep this up. It's always on my mind. I watch the clock, I check my phone and my watch, all the time. I want to be normal, like everybody else."

Eric felt it strike a chord. It reminded him of Hannah, and how Caitlin wanted her to be normal. And himself, back when he was in the throes of his anxiety disorder, how much he wanted to be normal. Normal was the simple wish of everyone with a mental illness. Normal was what everyone else, the worried well, took for granted. Eric had been on both sides of that line, so he knew it was an illusion. "Do you think something will happen to you or someone else if you don't tap and say the colors?"

"Yes."

"What would happen if you didn't?"

"I don't know, I couldn't deal, I don't want to try. I just know I have to."

Eric made a note. "Does anyone in your family exhibit any tendencies that way?"

Max rolled his eyes. "No, my mom is a slob, she never checks anything."

"Point of information, it's a myth that everyone with OCD is neat. For example, hoarders have a form of OCD." Eric assumed there were issues with Max's mother, given what he had heard at the hospital, but he didn't want to change topics.

"Oh, okay, but still, there's no history of it in my family, that I know. My grandmother, she's great." Max smiled briefly. "She's a total character."

"She sure is." Eric smiled back. "Tell me about your relationship to her. It looked like you two were very close."

"It's great, she's great, you saw. I take care of her. Her eyes are bad, so I get her meals, I make them before I go to work in the morning." Max's smile vanished again. "I used to when she ate. Now I get her coffee, but she didn't have that today, like I said."

Eric made another note. "You said you work. What's your job?"

"I'm an SAT tutor at PerfectScore. I tutor for the math section of the PSAT, SAT, and Achievement tests." Max smiled, again briefly. "I got perfect SATs."

"Really?" Eric allowed a note of admiration to creep into his voice, though he remembered that Max's grandmother had already told him that. "Where do you go to school?"

"Pioneer High, I'm a rising senior. I'll probably be salutatorian, and thank God I'm not valedictorian because I could never make a speech, like, in front of everybody."

"Congratulations." Eric wasn't surprised that Max had above-average intelligence, which squared with the OCD profile, but he needed to know more about Max's family history. "What about during the school year, do you take care of your grandmother, then, too?"

"Same thing, before I leave, every morning. She couldn't eat normal food for the past few months because of the cancer, so I had to puree it in the blender." Max made a hand motion, like a blender whirring. "She can't swallow anything if it doesn't have thickener in it, not even water. It comes in a packet."

Eric knew that had to be a burden, remembering how hectic mornings could be at home during the school year. Still, he missed those mornings. "And at night, for dinner?"

"I do it then too."

"What about your mom? Does she help?"

"Are you kidding?" Resentment flickered through Max's eyes. "She drinks. She works off and on, but she's always with her boyfriend. He lives in the city."

"How about your dad? Is he around?" Eric knew the answer from Max's grandmother, but he wanted to hear it from Max.

"No." Max raked his thin hair back with his fingers, his fingernails bitten to the quick. "He left when I was little. He was a drunk, too. I hardly remember him."

Eric could see it was topsy-turvy, with Max parentified and the parents abdicating their roles. "And no brothers or sisters?"

"No, just me." Max smiled crookedly. "Red flags, right? Abandonment issues, mother issues, father issues?"

Eric wanted to deflect Max's tendency to diagnose himself. "Do you drink or use other substances?"

"No."

Eric met his eye. "You can tell me."

"Okay, sometimes. I drink a little and I tried weed in a brownie, but I threw up."

Eric made notes. "You absolutely should not do any drugs or smoke weed, as an OCD sufferer. Do you understand?"

"Okay, chill." Max's eyes flared. "I didn't know that. I mean, it's practically legal now."

"It's not about the law. This is medicine, and the law is behind the science, as usual. Now, tell me about your friends."

"My what? I don't have any." Max chuckled, a *huh-huh* sound without mirth.

"Acquaintances?" Eric felt a pang for him, but kept his face in a professional mask.

"Not really. I mean, I hardly ever talk to people, IRL."

"IRL?"

"In real life. I have online friends, I'm a gamer. Hardcore."

"What do you mean by hardcore? How many hours a day?" Eric remembered Max's grandmother had mentioned it at the hospital.

"I play a lot." Max checked his watch.

"How much is a lot? This is a judgment-free zone."

Max smiled, tightly. "Six hours at night, like, until late."

Eric made a note, *gamer.* "Are you in any activities or sports, at school?"

"Do I *look* like I play any sports?" Max chuckled again, nervously.

"What about activities or clubs?"

"I'm a mathlete. Too bad they don't have mathletic scholarships, huh?" Max smiled ruefully, and Eric smiled back, trying to hold his eye contact until the boy looked away.

"What is school like for you during the day?"

"What do you mean?"

"What's it like, a typical day? Are you lonely?"

"I'm on my own, but that's fine. I like being alone because no-body's around to see me tapping."

Eric's heart went out to him. He knew firsthand how having a mental disorder could be so isolating, and sufferers tended to hide. "Are you bullied?"

"Not really." Max checked his watch again. "I'm ignored."

"How so?"

"Like, for example, my Spanish class had a Halloween party and I went as The Invisible Man, like that old movie. Gummy turned me onto it, she loves that movie. Anyway, I put on sunglasses and a trench coat. I wrapped my face in an Ace bandage." Max gestured around his head. "But nobody noticed. How ironic is that?"

Eric made a mental note, listening. It wasn't hard to hear the loneliness behind the story. "What about teachers? Do you have a favorite teacher? Or one that you're close to?"

"No. They're all okay except my Language Arts teacher, who's a bitch." Max's small hand flew to cover his mouth. "Sorry, can I say that, here?"

"Of course."

"Anyway, whatever, socially, I'm on my own. There's nothing more to say about it."

"If there were nothing more to say about it, I'd be out of business." Eric was trying to relax him, make him laugh, but Max didn't. "Let's go back to how you feel about the way things are, socially."

"Obviously, I don't feel great about it, but there's nothing I can do about it, it's too late." Max's face darkened, and he glanced at his watch. "I think it happened because my house sucked so bad, like when my mom would drink, I didn't have friends over. And when people have you over, you're supposed to have them over, and I knew I could never do that, so I avoided everybody. Then in high school everybody got in their group—the jocks, the stoners, the hipsters, the rich kids, the geeks, the black kids, the hot girls, and the slutty girls who think they're hot. I don't fit in anywhere, I end up on the outs."

Eric noted that Max dismissed his own feelings about being

isolated, glossing over them in favor of explaining why he got that way. "Is there a gamers' group?"

"At school? No, that's online."

"What about dating? Do you date?"

"No." Max flushed under his pale skin. "I know a few girls, but I get friend-zoned."

"Any girl you're interested in, like a crush or anything?"

"No, not really. I don't get my hopes up."

Eric felt another stab of sympathy, then tried a different tack. "Have you ever had thoughts that you would consider gay or bisexual?"

"No, dude!" Max's eye flared in surprise. "I'm straight!"

Eric remained silent for a moment, waiting. Silence had a lot of uses in psychotherapy, and he sensed that a client like Max would rush to fill it.

"Dr. Parrish, I'm totally *not* gay." Max pursed his lips. "You don't look like you believe me."

"I do." Eric saw an opportunity. "Let me be clear. If you tell me something is true, then I'll believe it. In return, I will never lie to you, ever. And anything you tell me is confidential. This is a safe place for us to talk to each other, to be completely honest, and everything we say stays here. Do you understand?"

"Yes." Max paused. "Even if my grandmother pays?"

"Correct, and by the way, when you go home, don't feel as if you have to talk with your grandmother about what we discuss."

"Okay." Max swallowed, his Adam's apple going up and down his skinny throat, like an elevator. "Um, then, there is someone. A girl."

Eric made a mental note, it was a small triumph. "What's her name?"

"Renée. Bevilacqua. I see her at work. She goes to a different school, Sacred Heart, but she comes in for tutoring."

"How long ago did you meet her?"

"A month ago, when she came to tutoring."

Eric wrote, *Renée Bevilacqua.* "What do you like about her?"

"Everything." Max burst into unaccustomed laughter, flushing.

"She's *beautiful,* she has curly red hair and tons of freckles. I like them even though she feels weird about them. I know because she puts makeup on her face to hide them." Max's face lit up, for the first time in the session. "Her eyes are a bright blue, like *really* bright, and she sucks the tip of her tongue while she thinks. She's not good at trig but she's smart, she just has a mental barrier."

Eric let him talk, just to see him look happy, however briefly, like any other young man in love. "Would you like to ask her out?"

"No!" Max widened his eyes, as if the question were plainly ridiculous. "She has a boyfriend, but I don't like how he treats her. Like one day she came in and I could tell she had been crying, and I asked her if she was okay, and she said he said something mean to her but she wouldn't say more." Max sighed. "How is telling you this going to help me stop tapping? Are you going to give me a prescription or not?"

"First I need to understand more and get to know you better." Eric thought it did sound like OCD, not an uncommon form. Luckily, it was highly treatable because OCD sufferers had a high degree of insight, in that they knew the disorder they had, and were ego-dystonic, which meant they wanted to be free of the symptoms.

"Like what?"

"Now, the thing about OCD is that the compulsion, in your case, the ritual of counting and tapping, arises as a way to cope with an obsession. Put differently, the ritual provides a relief from the anxiety created by the obsession. So the question is, what's your obsession?"

Max frowned. "Are you saying Renée's the obsession?"

"You tell me. Do you think about her a lot? Is she on your mind?"

"Yes, but . . ." Max looked stricken. "But the thoughts about her, they aren't good. They're weird and strange. They, like, *disturb* me."

"Obsessive thoughts are rarely pleasurable. In fact, that's the definition of obsession. It's an unwanted, intrusive thought."

"I didn't know that."

Eric wrote, *obsession with Renée.* "What are your thoughts about?"

"It's like I get this weird thought that I'm going to hurt her, not that I would mean to hurt her, that somehow I would hurt her accidentally. I would *never* hurt her, not on purpose, ever." Max hesitated, then raked his hair again. "I mean, she's amazing, she's great. She's so nice and sweet. I would never want anything bad to happen to her."

Eric took notes. "That's common with OCD, the fear that you might harm someone else without meaning to."

"Really?" Max's eyes rounded slightly. "I can't believe that."

"It is very common."

"I thought it was only me. It makes me feel like a terrible person."

"Consider this for a moment, Max. You don't have control over your thoughts, not really. They come to you. You don't have any agency in them, do you understand what I mean? You don't cause them. You can't will them to come or wish them away. They're just there, like clouds."

"Okay."

"Actions are completely different. Actions are separate from thoughts. You can have all the thoughts you want all day long, whether they're scary, or evil, or sexual, or whatever. You don't have to act on your thoughts. Most people never act on their thoughts, one way or the other, but don't blame yourself for having your thoughts. You're no more to blame for having your thoughts than you are to blame for breathing. You're a human being, so you're going to think. You with me so far?"

"Yes." Max smiled slightly, and Eric took that as a plus, trying to create a safe atmosphere in which the boy would open up.

"And, if you blame yourself for the thoughts, you're sending yourself the wrong message about yourself. You're alienating yourself from yourself, and that's not healthy. Just let whatever thoughts you have come, and in time, as we work together, you'll get to the point where you can say, 'that's just a thought I'm having.' 'It doesn't mean I'm a bad person.' 'And it doesn't mean I have to act on that thought.'"

"All right." Max checked his watch, and Eric knew he was counting down until he tapped his forehead again.

"Therapy is a process that takes time, and it's a process that helps you pay attention to the thoughts you have, even examine them. It helps you open yourself to yourself, and you explore who you are deep inside, your deepest intentions, motivations, scripts, responses. It's like we're in a cave together and you're exploring it, using a flashlight. I'm there with you and I hold your hand. That, in a nutshell, is talk therapy."

Max smiled. "The cave is me?"

"Yes."

"What's the flashlight?"

"A phallic symbol."

Max burst into laughter, which made Eric smile.

"Sometimes a flashlight is just a flashlight. I think Freud said that." Eric could feel Max responding, beginning to connect, which was a good thing. "Now, let's return to your thoughts, but try and remember, don't judge yourself for having them. Tell me about them. And never forget, they're only thoughts."

"Okay, well, they're horrible." Max's brow knit, his smile vanished in an instant. "They always start the same, with me worrying about Renée, worrying that something will happen to her."

"Like what?"

"Okay, she's not that great a driver, every time she comes to her tutoring session, she drives herself and she's always on the phone. I see her when she comes, I can look out the window. She turns really fast into the driveway. I worry that if she drives like that and I don't see, she could really hurt herself."

"Then how do you get into the picture, in your mind?"

"Then I start thinking about her driving, but I see her from the outside of the car, like her hair is all cute and curly, and then I start to look at her face, then her neck. She has this little necklace she always wears, like a gold square, and it says 'fearless.' I think it's so, cute, but then, I start thinking and it gets weird." Max squeezed his hands together. "I don't even know how it starts, but I start to imagine like my hands are on her face, and move her hair back from her face, and then I touch the necklace and then, I know it sounds horrible, but my hands are on her neck, and I, like, *strangle* her."

Eric didn't fill the silence, but waited, remaining calm so Max would be encouraged to talk without judgment.

"It's like, my hands are around her throat, and I'm squeezing and squeezing, but I can't stop myself from squeezing, and then all of a sudden"—Max's upper lip curled with revulsion—"it's *horrible,* she's just lying there *dead.*"

"Tell me more about that." Eric didn't make notes, to maintain eye contact.

"What more is there to tell?" Max threw up his hands, his boyish features etched with deep guilt. "She's dead, I strangled her, and I get horrible, awful pictures in my head, like you see on *CSI* or *SUV,* or whatever. They always show the dead girl, staring. I would *never* do it, I never want to, it's just a thought that comes in my head and I can't get it out. I want to get it out, but I can't get it out. It's too awful!"

"Try to relax, Max. Breathe in and out."

"I *know* how to breathe!"

"I can see you're upset, I understand why. Thoughts like that would upset anyone—"

"They're horrible, the worst thing ever! I don't understand why I have them because I like her, I'd never hurt her, she's so cute!" Max checked his watch. "Wait. Stop. I have to stop now, I know it's time. I can tell without even looking it's been fifteen minutes, almost." Max's attention stayed glued to his watch, completely absorbed. "I have to wait ten more seconds. That's why I have to use my watch and not my phone. It has a second hand. It has to be exact. Now it's time to tap. Fifteen minutes exactly." Max tapped his temple with his right index finger as his lips moved silently, then he stopped. "Now I'm saying the colors in my head. There."

Eric watched the ritual end, with compassion. It had to be maddening to endure, a routine that chopped up a life that should be carefree, stalling a future by counting around the clock, a twenty-four/seven source of deep shame. "How are you feeling, now?"

"Fine, better, but not much." Max sighed. "It's, like, a little relief. There's less pressure, it leaks out, until it builds up again. You have to help me. You have to give me meds."

"Max, do you ever masturbate to her?"

"Dr. Parrish, that's so random!"

"It's okay, Max. People masturbate."

"Okay, then . . . yes. I feel *so weird* telling you this."

"Do you use pictures of her or anyone else, or just your imagination?"

"Uh, well, both."

"Where do you get the pictures?"

"Her Instagram and Facebook page." Max knit his hands together. "And once, well, uh, I took her phone."

Eric felt a red flag go up. "What do you mean?" he asked, modulating his tone.

"Uh, I didn't really take it, like *steal* it from her. She left it at work, on the chair, and I, uh, I kept it. Her mom called and asked if she left it there, but I said no."

"So do you have the phone?" Eric didn't like what he was hearing. It crossed a line, and he didn't like any obsessive type having a tangible item that belonged to his object. He made a note.

"Yes." Max looked down again, his brow furrowing deeply.

"Where is it now?"

"Hidden, in my room."

"Do you take it out and look at it?"

"I did." Max sank into the chair, and the cushions bent up as if they were swallowing him alive.

"What do you look at?"

"Her contacts, her emails, but then I stopped. I'm afraid to turn it back on, in case she has an app for that. I don't even know . . . why I took it. But I have it."

Eric made a note, *has her phone*. "Are your symptoms worse around her, or better?"

"No, the same, I mean, I'm nervous around her, but I keep it together."

"You tutor her."

"The math sections. I do think about her, a lot. I guess I am a little obsessed with her. Can you help me?"

"Yes, I would be happy to work with you. I think we can fix your problem together. It will take time and lots of talk. We also use CBT, cognitive behavior therapy."

"What's that?"

"A behavioral treatment for OCD, called exposure and response prevention therapy. I'll help you face your fears and recondition your responses to them."

"Do you think it will work?"

"Yes," Eric answered. He had tried a form of exposure therapy himself, called flooding, for his anxiety, but it hadn't worked. It involved exposing him to the things that made him anxious, but it only made him more anxious. Happily, the prognosis was much better for OCD patients.

"What about meds?"

Eric was worried about the boy, with his grandmother's death imminent. It would exacerbate the OCD symptoms. "Medication is not always the answer, because of side effects. I want to see you tomorrow, and we'll talk about it again."

"Tomorrow? Sunday?"

"Yes, same time, first thing in the morning, then we'll work out a twice-a-week schedule. Can you do that?"

"Okay."

"Good," Eric said, but in the back of his mind was that phone.

Chapter Ten

That afternoon, Eric stood on the plastic tarp, surveying the walls of Hannah's bedroom to see if the first coat of paint had dried. The walls were as pink as a newborn, and the air smelled of latex, a clean scent he associated with fresh starts. The late-day sun filled the room, and a box fan on the floor kept the air moving, helping the paint dry. The sounds of the TV next door, playing a golf tournament, wafted through the open screens.

He'd had a long day of seeing patients, but the one that stuck in his mind was Max. The boy presented a fairly straightforward case of OCD, and Eric knew he could help him, but the worst was to come, with the grandmother's death imminent. Her death could aggravate Max's OCD symptoms, and Eric had wanted the boy stabilized, which was why he wanted to see him Sunday, too. Eric worried mildly about Renée Bevilacqua too, but he didn't have a solid reason to be concerned for her safety, it was just his nerves jangling.

Eric eyed the wall without really focusing on it. He wasn't sure what to do about custody of Hannah, but he felt pleased that he'd gotten around to fixing up her room. Home Depot had had enough selection of pink paint to satisfy every little girl in the tri-state area, and he'd gone with the Powdered Blush instead of Ballerina Pink or Primrose. In his opinion, there was a fine line between Primrose and Pepto-Bismol.

Eric went to the wall and swiped it with an index finger to see if it was dry enough. It wasn't completely, and he'd be pushing it if he put on a final coat now. He shifted plans and decided to go to Bed Bath & Beyond for the comforter and other things. He left the room, headed down the hallway, and went downstairs. Suddenly his cell phone rang, and he reached into the pocket of his khakis, slid out the phone, and checked the screen. Martin Baumgartner, it read, a colleague of his, so he picked up. "Martin, to what do I owe the pleasure?"

"Hey, buddy, how have you been? It's been too long, but you know tennis elbow. Recovery takes forever."

"How much longer do you have to rest it?" Eric hit the ground floor and grabbed his keys from the console table. He realized that if he had full-time custody of Hannah, there wouldn't be a lot of tennis in his future, but he was fine with that.

"Two more weeks, but I already bought court time. I can't wait to kick your ass."

"Spoken like a true friend." Eric went out the front door and locked it behind him. The sun was out, the air muggy and humid, and the sounds of the golf tournament sounded louder.

"Anyway, how's Hannah?"

"Fine, why?" Eric answered, puzzled. He realized that Martin didn't know that he and Caitlin had separated, since they hadn't spoken in a while.

"I saw her and Caitlin in the emergency room earlier this morning."

"What?" Eric crossed the front lawn toward his car in the driveway. "What are you talking about?"

"Wait, didn't you know? Are you out of town?"

"Where did you see them?" Eric chirped the car unlocked, worried.

"At Whitemarsh Memorial, my hospital. We have a pediatric emergency department, and I saw Caitlin and Hannah going into one of the examining rooms, but I didn't find out what happened. I told Jenny, and she gave me hell because I didn't call you to see what happened."

"Thanks, but I have to go."

"Okay, buddy, talk soon."

"Right, thanks, good-bye." Eric hung up as he jumped in the car and started the engine. He was surprised that Caitlin hadn't called him if there was a medical problem with Hannah. He'd always handled their family's medical problems. He was a physician, after all.

He scrolled to Caitlin's number and pressed Call while he reversed out of the driveway, the phone to his ear. It was ringing, but Caitlin wasn't picking up, then the call went to voicemail. He hung up immediately and called again. Caitlin was supposed to call him if there was a medical emergency on her weekend with Hannah, and his hospital was a lot closer to the house than Whitemarsh.

He straightened the car and drove down the street while he listened to the phone ring. The voicemail came on, and he left a message: "Is everything okay with Hannah, I heard she was in the emergency room. Give me a call." Eric scrolled to Hannah's number and pressed Call, telling himself to remain calm. It could be anything, it could be nothing. Still, Caitlin should've called him.

He reached Lancaster Avenue and stopped at the red light, joining the long line of people running their Saturday errands. The lush lawns lining the street were dappled with sunlight and the branches of the trees swayed in unseen breezes, but he didn't stop to take in the idyllic scene.

He hit the gas when the light turned green. Hannah wasn't picking up either, but that didn't mean much. She wasn't that good with the phone, which made him proud. She had the rest of her life for the phone, computer, Facebook, Twitter, or whatever electronic horror they came up with next. He'd seen too much depression in kids spending more time with machines than people, and he'd read the papers in his neuroscience journals, their data suggesting that computer and video game use altered brain circuitry. He wondered fleetingly if that was contributing to Max's problems, too.

Hannah's voicemail clicked on, with her cute little voice: "Hi, please leave me a message, thank you!"—she didn't identify herself by name, per his insistence. Eric had treated a pedophiliac during training and he still shuddered to think of the trivial things that triggered the man's fantasies, even the knowledge of a child's nickname. Caitlin had thought he was being ridiculous, but he wasn't taking any chances.

Eric stopped at a red light and left Hannah a message: "Hey, honey, it's Dad and I wanted to say hello and see how you are. Love you, and give me a call when you can. Bye-bye." He hung up, and when the light turned green, he cruised ahead, heading home.

Not your home, he reminded himself. *Not anymore.*

Fifteen minutes later, Eric rounded the bend on his street, driving past the abelias, and the sight eased his worry. Hannah was in front of the house and she didn't seem to be sick or hurt. She was sitting cross-legged on the sidewalk with another girl, drawing on the concrete with oversized chalk. The other girl was watching, and Eric didn't recognize her; she was taller than Hannah, with a long blonde ponytail, a red T-shirt, and bicycle shorts. Hannah's concentration was typically complete, her glasses sliding down her nose and her hair falling forward.

Eric pulled up and cut the engine. "Hey, honey!" he called to her, getting out of the car.

"Daddy!" Hannah called back, breaking into a smile so big it showed her missing tooth. She started to get up, and Eric noticed that her right ankle was covered to the calf with an Ace bandage.

"What happened to your ankle, honey?" Eric met Hannah on the grass that bordered the sidewalk, knelt down, and gave her a hug. "Did you hurt yourself?"

"I fell down, I slipped." Hannah kissed him on the cheek, then released him with a sweet smile.

"Let me see how it looks." Eric examined her ankle, palpating it. Everything felt in order, though there was swelling above the bandage. "You sprained it, huh?"

"I think so."

"Does it hurt to walk?"

"Only a little."

"How did you fall? Where were you, the hallway?" Eric had been intending to tack down the carpet in the hallway, a tripping hazard.

"No, in the grass. It was wet. I was trying to catch the ball but it was too high for me to jump up."

"Oh, this happened last night, at the softball practice?" Eric was putting two and two together. He should have realized it on the drive over, but he'd been too focused on the injury. "And you went to the hospital this morning?"

"Yes, I couldn't sleep because it hurt and got swollen."

"Did Mommy ice it last night?"

"Ice it?" Hannah blinked.

"Put ice on it, so it wouldn't swell." Eric was surprised that Caitlin hadn't iced it, she usually knew better.

"No, so we went to the hospital today and they taked X-rays but they said it's not broken. They said it would really hurt if it were broken."

"Right, it's not broken. It's not a big deal, at all. It'll hurt you for a while, then go away." Eric realized that Caitlin hadn't called him because she was hiding it from him, probably because it had happened at softball practice. It occurred to him that if he had primary custody, he wouldn't be on the outside, playing games with Hannah's health. Also, he doubted that Caitlin had told Hannah they were moving, because Hannah seemed fine and hadn't said anything to him.

"HEY, LOOK AT THIS!" the other little girl called out, and Eric turned to see her doing perfect cartwheels across the grass, her ponytail whipping around and her limbs forming a human pinwheel.

"Wow!" Eric called to the girl. He patted Hannah's side. "What's your friend's name, honey?"

"Michelle." Hannah blinked. Her smile faded as she pushed up her glasses. "She does gymnastics. She's on a team, and they go to competitions. She's one of the best ones."

"Good for her." Eric had never heard the name Michelle, and Michelle seemed nothing like Hannah's usual friends Maddie and Jessica, who were verbal and bookish, like her. "Is she in your grade? She looks so tall."

"No, she's going into fourth. She's older."

"LOOK, LOOK!" Michelle called out again, and Eric and Hannah turned to see the girl cartwheel across the grass in the opposite direction.

"Way to go, Michelle!" Eric called back, but Hannah turned away.

"She really likes gymnastics. She does it all the time. She did it last night and the softball coach told her to stop and watch out for the ball."

"Is that how you know Michelle?" Eric asked, coming up to speed. "Is she on the softball team?"

"YOU MISSED IT! I DID IT PERFECT THAT TIME! WATCH OR YOU'RE GONNA MISS IT!"

"Yes," Hannah answered, ignoring Michelle. "The coach told her to pay attention to the game. She got yelled at two times."

"WAIT, WAIT! NOW WATCH ME!"

"Great, Michelle!" Eric glanced over, then turned back to Hannah and tugged a strand of hair from the hinge of her glasses, where it always got caught. "So, did you like softball?"

"It was okay, but now I can't go anymore because of my ankle." Hannah didn't sound too broken up, and Eric let it go. Hannah brightened suddenly. "Daddy, do you want to see my drawing?"

"Yes, sure."

"YOU'RE NOT WATCHING! MY KNEES WERE SOOOO STRAIGHT THAT TIME!"

"It's this one." Hannah took his hand and led him, with a slight hitch in her step, to the sidewalk block that contained her drawing, which showed farm animals in bright pastels, their outlines indistinct, owing to the thickness of the chalk.

"Wow, that's great! It looks like a farm."

"It is." Hannah looked down with pride, tucking her hair behind her earpiece. "It has chickens in it and pigs and also Charlotte the pig. Do you remember Charlotte the pig?"

"Of course." Suddenly they both looked up as the front door to the house opened and Caitlin came out, striding toward him. She was wearing a white tank top, jeans shorts, and a forced smile.

"Hey, Caitlin, hi," Eric called to her, waving. He wasn't about to make a fuss, especially since Hannah hadn't been injured seriously.

"LOOK, CAITLIN! LOOK AT THIS!"

"Excellent, Michelle!" Caitlin nodded at Michelle as she passed her, then kept going, crossing the lawn toward Eric and Hannah. "Eric, what a surprise," she said when she reached them. "I didn't expect to see you today."

"I just thought I'd stop by." Eric kept his tone casual. "I heard through the grapevine that Hannah was in the emergency department at Whitemarsh Memorial, so I thought I'd see if she was okay. Next time you guys have a medical problem, feel free to give me a call, okay?"

"CAITLIN, WATCH! I CAN DO IT AGAIN! WATCH MY KNEES!"

"Great!" Caitlin called over her shoulder to Michelle, then returned her attention to Eric, her eyes narrowed against the sunlight. "I didn't want to bother you with it. It's only a sprain, and she could've done it anywhere."

But she didn't, Eric thought, but didn't say. He became aware that Hannah was looking up at him and then at Caitlin, her head swiveling. He hated to stress her, so he lightened his tone. "I know that, and I'm glad to see it's nothing serious."

"Of course it isn't, but thanks for stopping by." Caitlin gestured at his car, a less-than-discrtee invitation for him to leave, so he took his cue.

"Anytime, no problem." Eric bent over, kissed Hannah on the head, and then on the cheek. "Bye, honey. I have to go run some errands. You and Michelle have a good time today, and I'll see you soon."

"Okay, Daddy. Bye-bye!" Hannah smiled and waved to him, and Eric headed toward the car.

"CAITLIN, LOOK AT THIS ONE! YOU'RE GONNA MISS IT!"

Caitlin put her arm around Hannah, as if she were taking physical possession. "By the way, Eric, I saw the sign."

"Sign?" Eric stopped beside his car, his hand on the door handle.

"The one you left for me, in the trash. Got the message."

"Oh." Eric realized she meant the For Sale sign.

"DADDY! DADDY, LOOK!"

Eric looked over reflexively at the sound of "Daddy," to find that Michelle wasn't calling to him, but toward the house. He didn't understand what was going on. He looked in confusion at Caitlin.

Caitlin snapped her head quickly away, to face Michelle. "Great job, Michelle! I saw it! That was great!"

"DADDY, YOU'RE MISSING IT!" Michelle started running toward the house. "DADDY, I DID IT PERFECT!"

Eric watched as Michelle ran inside the house, calling for her father, and all of a sudden, he realized what was going on. Caitlin was seeing someone else, and the man was in the house, *his* house, right *now*. It couldn't have been an innocent relationship, because the man would've come out and introduced himself. Instead, he had stayed in the house, and Caitlin had come out, that's why she'd been giving Eric the bum's rush. She hadn't wanted him to know the man was there, the same way she hadn't wanted him to know she was selling the house.

"Hannah, let's go," Caitlin said tersely, walking her toward the house.

Eric watched them go, their backs to him. Caitlin had moved on, and her new boyfriend had a kid who played on the softball team—a completely annoying kid who played softball, gymnastics, and God knows how many other sports—just like Caitlin herself had done when she was little. And so now, Hannah—his bookish, adorable, klutzy daughter who hated sports—had to play softball. No wonder Hannah and Michelle hadn't made sense to him, as friends.

Eric stood at his car, and it dawned on him fully. He didn't know how he could've been so blind, so stupid, in so much denial. He'd actually believed he'd get back with Caitlin, they'd reconcile, and she'd love him again. He'd thought he could weed-whack his way into her heart.

His mouth went dry. He felt stunned, angry, heartbroken. It

killed him to lose Caitlin, but worse, it killed him to see Hannah put second, her interests subordinate to Caitlin's new boyfriend and her health sacrificed for God-knows-what-reason. No reason was good enough, not to him.

He stood still, after Caitlin and Hannah had vanished inside the house and closed the front door behind them.

Leaving him on the outside.

Chapter Eleven

Eric painted with a vengeance, his brain on fire. He had no idea how late it was, he wasn't tired. He wasn't going to bed. He knew he wouldn't sleep anyway. It was dark outside, and the windows were open, with no sound but the crickets. Gnats flitted through the screens, and the box fan whirred on the floor.

Eric rolled the brush like a madman, picturing Caitlin with her new boyfriend, imagining them making out in the kitchen of his own house. Having sex in *his* bed. In *his* bedroom. A wave of intense sexual jealousy flooded his brain.

Eric tried to think when they had started seeing each other, but he didn't know. He tried to remember the littlest things, sifting for clues about when she met him and who he was, driving himself nuts. He rolled the brush into the ribbed bottom of the pan, then held the roller up, but dripped on his jeans. He brushed them off and when he looked down, the front of his blue work shirt was also spattered with a fine pink spray. Obviously, he wasn't paying attention, but he couldn't.

Eric rolled paint on the wall, listening for the telltale tacky sounds. His thoughts turned to Hannah, with her hurt ankle, and though it was true that it could've happened anywhere, it made his blood boil that it happened at softball, which she wouldn't have been playing but for the fact that her mother was sleeping with another man, whose kid was on the team. It made him sick to his stomach that Hannah was being used, or pushed to do something she didn't want to do, and he considered again the decision about going for custody.

Eric kept painting, his thoughts elsewhere. He found himself wishing that he had someone to talk it over with, but Caitlin had been his best friend. His other friends were tennis players, but this was too heavy a thing to lay on them, though he'd told them that he and Caitlin had separated. Two were divorced dads, but neither would want primary custody, and he wasn't sure they could relate. Otherwise, he had become friendly with his three attending psychiatrists at the hospital, but they reported to him as chief and he had to maintain a professional distance. He knew in his heart whom he truly wanted to talk to, anyway.

He left the roller in the pan, reached into his back pocket for his phone, and scrolled through contacts until he found the number for Arthur Markusson, then pressed Call. Arthur was Eric's former psychiatrist, who had treated him so successfully. Arthur had a law as well as a psychiatry degree and had become a mentor, colleague, and surrogate father. Eric felt himself smile as the call was picked up. "Arthur?"

"Eric, my boy!" Arthur's voice sounded instantly friendly, if thin with age. His Norwegian accent hadn't completely disappeared, though he'd lived in the United States all of his professional life. "What a surprise!"

"How are you doing?"

"Delightful! Retirement agrees with me, I must say. I have all the time I wish to read. Reading without guilt, can you imagine?"

"Good for you." Eric sat down on the tarp, plucked his leftover turkey hoagie from the oily brown wrap, and took a bite.

"The weather down here takes getting accustomed to, but I fish now. Me, a sportsman."

"You? You used to be so indoorsy."

"Ha!" Arthur laughed with him.

"How's Ina?"

"Fine, thanks. Does water aerobics with a clutch of other octogenarian hens. Between the two of us, we're on the water more than the land. Perhaps we'll devolve into a lesser life form. Become geckos or the like."

"Don't do that, I need you the way you are."

"What's going on with you? How's Caitlin and Hannah? I haven't heard from you in a while. I always worry when that happens."

Eric set the elbow end of the hoagie roll back into the paper, not relishing telling Arthur the bad news. "Caitlin and I separated, and I have a decision to make about custody of Hannah."

Arthur moaned. "Oh, that's unfortunate. May I ask what happened?"

"I don't know where to begin," Eric said, meaning it. "Caitlin has been pulling away for a long time."

"I'm sorry." Arthur's voice turned sympathetic. "I know it must be painful, the ending of a long-term marriage, and I realize how much she meant to you."

"I know." Eric couldn't help adding, "I just found out that she's seeing someone else, which ticks me off no end."

"Of course it does. But you will move past that." Arthur hesitated. "Now that you're healthy, that's a good thing for you, which is my only concern. It's a good thing for Hannah, too. You've always been very close to her, and it doesn't surprise me you're thinking about filing for custody. I assume Caitlin will oppose you."

"Yes, I'm sure she will."

"How are you feeling about it? What have you decided?"

"I haven't yet. That's why I called, to see what you thought."

"I hardly have the answers. However, I do think that your relationship to Hannah has been extraordinarily close. You've been a better father than anyone I know."

"Thank you," Eric said, feeling a warm rush of gratitude.

"I remember when she was born, how involved you were even in the early infancy stages. I think the simplicity of your relationship to her cut through any residual anxiety you felt. It was a joy to see, when I was treating you."

Eric thought back to those early days, and the memories came flooding back. "I remember that I didn't know what to do with her, or how to be, but it wasn't as if I had to perform or achieve. It just felt natural."

"Exactly. You followed that feeling, and Hannah responded."

Eric had a nagging worry. "Do you think it was because we both have a propensity for anxiety?"

"No, I think that once Hannah was born, you allowed yourself to get out of your own way. You stopped focusing on yourself and started putting her first, as any good father would." Arthur paused. "Hannah gave you a meaning in your life and a dimension that you hadn't previously had, and I think she helped you to be healthy. Likewise, you helped her to be healthy. It isn't anxiety that binds you to Hannah, it's love."

Eric couldn't speak for a moment, touched.

"That said, I know you would be willing to make the sacrifices necessary for her and I think you could arrange your practice accordingly."

"True."

"You've written so many excellent papers. Your CV is the best. You can write and publish anywhere. You'd probably have more time for that if you cut back on the hospital, and you still have your private practice, don't you?"

"Yes." Eric was really coming around to the idea, and the more Arthur spoke, the more it resonated in his chest.

"Whatever decision you make, it will be the right one. I have absolute confidence in you and your judgment."

"Thank you," Eric said, feeling a sense of resolve.

"What's new with your cases? Keep me in the loop, it prevents an old man from rusting."

Eric thought instantly of Max. "I have a new patient with OCD, a seventeen-year-old."

"A washer? A checker?"

"Neither, he does some ritualistic thinking. He has obsessive thinking about a girl and he worries that he's going to harm her."

"So, that's typical for OCD."

"I know." Eric felt reassured to hear Arthur say it so lightly. "But there's other things he's done. He kept a cell phone that she left behind."

"Hmm. It happens."

"Something about it bothers me. Do you think she's in danger?"

"Not at all." Arthur scoffed. "They fear they'll harm inadvertently, or even intentionally, but an OCD patient rarely turns aggressive on the object of his obsession. They never act, that's the point, you know that."

"Right, I do."

"Nevertheless, you sound worried."

"Yes, it's on the back of my mind. During session I thought to myself, do I have a *Tarasoff* issue here?" Eric was referring to the seminal *Tarasoff* case, in which a patient had told his psychiatrist that he wanted to do harm to a young girl, and the psychiatrist didn't warn her or the police because of his duty of confidentiality. Subsequently, the patient killed the girl, and her parents sued the psychiatrist. The court held the psychiatrist liable and established the hornbook law that a psychiatrist had a duty to warn the police or the intended victim's of threats to her physical safety, made in the therapeutic context.

"I'm not hearing a *Tarasoff* issue on these facts. I only had one in forty-odd years of practice."

"You're probably right." Eric had never had a *Tarasoff* issue, and they were rare, though every mental health professional dreaded the dilemma. To warn the police or victim would risk losing the client's trust forever, increasing their risk of danger to themselves or others.

"How long have you been treating him?"

"Just the one session."

Arthur chuckled, softly. "You're jumping the gun, don't you think?"

"Probably," Eric said, relieved.

"The old Eric would've been anxious about it, but the new Eric is a member of the worried well. Press on, regardless."

"I hear you." Eric brightened.

"I'm glad you called, but it's almost bedtime, and this old man has to sleep. My bride calls."

"Thanks, and give her a hug for me, will you?"

"Sure thing, and call anytime. You know I love to hear from you."

"Good night." Eric hung up, then wolfed down the hoagie and got back to work.

Chapter Twelve

Sunday morning, Eric opened the door, but Max had been pacing in the empty waiting room. "Good morning, Max. Come on in."

"Hi. Thanks." Max barely looked up when he entered his office, his head down. He wore the same clothes as yesterday, and it smelled as if he needed a shower, so Eric was concerned. He tried to catch Max's eye, closing the office door behind them.

"How are you?"

"Terrible, I can't sleep at all, I'm still tapping, and Gummy's worse. She's not eating anything, she only had coffee and crackers all day yesterday." Max stayed standing. When he finally looked at Eric, his eyes were pained and defiant. "I'm a mess, I really think I should start on the medication. Can't you start me now, Dr. Parrish?"

"Please, sit down, and let's table that discussion—"

"Why won't you give me meds, Dr. Parrish?" Max threw up his hands. "I mean, that's why I'm coming to you. The tapping, the thoughts, everything, I need help!"

"Max, I don't expect things to get better after only one session, and we have to be realistic."

"I know it takes more than one session to get better and I want to get better, that's why I need the medication!"

"Sit down, please." Eric gestured at the chair. "I think I told you, many medications have adverse effects on adolescents—"

"Like what? I'm not going to kill myself, I promise." Max flopped into the chair.

"That's only one of the adverse effects, but it's the most concerning, obviously." Eric met Max's eye and sat down opposite him, taking his tablet onto his lap.

"I'm not going to, I swear." Max lowered his voice, sulking. "Gummy needs me, I'm fine, I just need some help."

"I understand that, but we need to talk more to determine how best to treat you."

"We've talked enough."

"I'm just starting to get to know you." Eric worried that Max was entering a crisis, but he couldn't admit him to the hospital unless he were a danger to himself or others, basically, unless he were suicidal, psychotic, or homicidal. "Let's switch topics. Tell me more about your grandmother."

"She's pretty bad, I mean, bad. The hospice people came yesterday, a nurse in the morning, then a social worker." Max's face fell and he raked his hair back with spread fingers.

"How was that?" Eric noticed the boy's hair looked greasy and made a note.

"They were nice. They gave me, like, a log for their visits and some pamphlet called *When the Time Comes* or something like that." Max snorted. "It's like they don't know there's an Internet that you can look all this up, which of course, I did. At least they helped me move Gummy into the living room, and they sent us a bed, like a hospital bed, and an oxygen tank. They even gave me this kit with morphine and a tranquilizer."

"Usually, it's Ativan." Eric didn't like the sound of the boy's having unfettered access to the drugs, especially benzos like Ativan, Valium, Klonopin, or Xanax. They caused dependency and were disinhibitors, like giving Max a few drinks. "I'm disappointed to hear they left that with you, a minor."

"They didn't. My mom was there to meet the nurse, and they gave it to her, then she left. She's good at keeping up appearances. She told the nurse she was home every night."

"You won't be touching those drugs, are we clear?"

"Of course not, and it's sealed, and the nurse said we have to call her if my grandmother's pain starts to get bad or if she gets agitated. Rather, *I* have to call her because my mom left right after." Max's eyes flickered with pain and he pursed his lips. "It's called terminal agitation, they said. It happens, I read it online."

"Was your mom there when you met with the caseworker alone?"

"No, not the caseworker." Max snorted. "I can deal, I do it, I'm not complaining. If I do it, at least I know it'll get done right."

Eric tried to imagine the weight of responsibility on the boy. "So is no one helping you? Who's home with your grandmother now?"

"Hospice sent a day nurse, and she's there today. Her name is Monique and she's Jamaican. She has such a thick accent, neither of us understand what she's saying, but we like her." Max brightened. "Gummy likes to sing, and Monique sings with her, old songs like from Judy Garland and people like that. They were singing 'You Made Me Love You' when I left today, and Monique is going to bring some Red Stripe tomorrow."

Eric smiled. "Good for her. Whatever she wants."

"That's what I say." Max chuckled, but it stopped abruptly. "I wish I could be there, but she wanted me to come see you, then go to work, to try to keep everything normal."

"I understand that, don't you?"

"Yeah, but I told my boss I'd only be in in the mornings because that's when she's asleep anyway. In the afternoon, her TV shows are on, and we watch them together." Max smiled, in a bittersweet way. "She's a *Golden Girls* junkie."

Eric smiled, touched by the boy's kindness, though he couldn't help but wonder if Renée Bevilacqua came to her SAT tutoring in the morning. "You work on Sunday?"

"Yeah, a lot of our students have summer jobs, so they're only free on the weekend."

Eric made a note, *Renée in morning*? "This is a very difficult thing for you to go through, and still work."

"I know, I guess." Max paused, seeming to lose his train of thought. "It's weird, like, thinking that this is the . . . end of her life. I keep thinking, how much time does she have left? Like, how long can you live, if you can't eat or drink anything? I keep asking Monique, but she says it depends on the person. What do you think?"

"I think the hospice nurse has more experience than I do."

"I just want to know, since you are a doctor, what you thought? How long does she have? Online it says if you can't eat or drink, you live three to five days."

"I can help you to deal with it, whenever it comes, and I'd like you to talk about it. Take your time, think about your feelings. Our treatment goal is to help you express your emotions, so we can examine them, and you'll inevitably feel better and happier."

"If I had medication, I just wouldn't feel the feelings, so I'd automatically feel better and happier."

"But this is talk therapy—"

"Dr. Parrish, I bet I could buy whatever I needed from kids at school. I know of a kid who sells his mom's Valium, and you can get Ritalin or Adderall, easy."

"Don't do anything like that. Take nothing from anyone else, and nobody else should either." Eric let it go, not to engage him in a downward spiral of argument, which would do nothing to open him up. "Give me some background. Where is your mother? You said she works. Where does she work?"

"In Center City at an insurance company, RMA. She's in the billing department."

Eric made a note. "What time does she come home?"

"She doesn't, not every day anyway. She stays in town with her boyfriend. Sometimes she calls." Max checked his watch and Eric knew he was counting the moments until eight fifteen.

"Does she understand what hospice care is?"

"Of course."

"And yet she still doesn't come home?"

"Nope." Max's lips contorted in disgust.

"When she calls, does she ask about her mother?"

"No, but I tell her."

"Does she ask about you?"

"No, but I tell her that anyway, too."

"Why does she call then?"

"Why do you think?" Max burst into derisive laughter. "She calls for money! Like, she needed two new tires, and she didn't have the money, so she has to make sure money got put in her account for that."

"How do you do that?"

"I do it online. My grandmother gave me her password and I pay all her bills online. Gummy puts money into my mom's account every week. I mean, I do, for her." Max snorted again. "My mom wants me to put it on automatic pay, but if I do, I'll never hear from her."

Eric suppressed a sympathetic pang. "This must be hard to deal with on your own."

"Not really, I'm used to it. I do it all the time. I like taking care of Gummy. She needs me."

Eric heard warmth in his tone, for the first time. "It's a good feeling to be needed, isn't it?"

Max nodded. "It is, yes."

"Does it ever feel like a burden? That it's too much for you to handle, on your own?"

"No, not really." Max shrugged his shoulders.

"Explain that to me, because I think a lot of people your age would find this a very difficult burden."

"She can't help that she got sick, and you saw her, she's fun. I think I just like her so much, really, that it doesn't feel like a bad thing. It feels like a really good thing."

Eric felt his throat constrict, and it was almost as if he could see the bond between grandson and grandmother become visible. "I think that's called love, Max."

Max's eyes filmed suddenly, but he wiped them roughly. "Are you trying to make me cry?"

"Absolutely." Eric smiled, because he knew Max needed one. "That's my job."

"Ha!" Max wiped his eyes again, then his gaze fell on the Kleenex, but he didn't get one out of the box.

Eric made a note, *no Kleenex.* It was his tell. He had noticed that many patients stopped themselves from taking Kleenex, as if it were a sign of weakness, and in his experience, he had noticed the outcomes were the best for those patients who took the Kleenex. So he worried about Max.

"I feel so dumb, it's embarrassing." Max shook his head, exhaling loudly. "Like, if anybody in school found out I was sitting here crying over my grandmother, they'd think I was the biggest idiot on the planet, which they already think anyway."

"The emotions you're feeling are very natural and they show that you make connections to other people. That's actually a sign of good mental health."

"What?" Max's weary eyes widened in disbelief. "How can you say that somebody with OCD is mentally healthy?"

"Think of it as a mental ailment, like any physical ailment. Just because you have diabetes doesn't make you a sick person. It makes you a healthy person, with diabetes. If we can fix the diabetes, you're good to go." Eric thought about it, though he hadn't before. He still learned new things every day, from his patients and from the process of talk therapy itself. "Max, we'll get you through this. You'll become healthier and happier quicker because you are mentally healthy. Now, tell me, are you having intrusive thoughts about Renée?"

Max checked his watch. "I think about her all the time, I have to tap and go through all the other rituals."

"Did you see her yesterday?"

"Yes . . . uh, I did," Max answered, hesitating.

"Why are you hesitating?"

"Well, I didn't only see her at tutoring."

Eric felt Max was being evasive. "Where else did you see her then?"

"I sort of saw her in town, like, where she works."

"Where does she work?"

"The frozen yogurt shop, Swirled Peace, in that strip mall?"

"How did that come about, that you saw her?"

"I just was around town, and I saw her, like, driving to work. She was on the phone again." Max's expression tightened, his lips forming a firm line, and his hands found each other, clinging together. "Like I told you, it's dangerous and she doesn't even use a wire or hands-free, and she texts a lot too."

Eric made a note. "So did you see her driving or in the yogurt shop?"

"Um, kind of, I saw her at both, if you really want to know"— Max began to knit his fingers, and anxiety crept into his voice—"I mean, I was home gaming on my laptop, and my grandmother was asleep and I know Renée works on Saturdays, so I went over to get some fro-yo but then I didn't go in."

"Why not?" Eric made another note.

"I don't know, I thought I would have a hard time explaining it and she would know I was crushing on her, so I didn't go in."

"What did you do?"

"I waited in the car, and when it was the end of her shift, I left then too, to make sure that she didn't get into any trouble or have an accident on the way home, you know. I mean, like, I just wanted to make sure she was okay and she got home okay."

"So you followed her home?" Eric kept the judgment from his tone, and the concern, not only for Max, but for Renée. He wrote, *waited for her after work, stalking? Tarasoff?*

"No, not really, well, I guess you could say that." Max shifted forward on the chair, leaning over urgently. "But it wasn't in a creepy way, I swear to you, it's not like I'm stalking her or anything."

Eric met his eye. "How is it different from stalking her?"

"Stalkers follow you to hurt you or upset you, but I would never hurt her. I'm watching over her. It's, like, I know she does all these things that cute girls do, like how they're on the phone all the time and always texting each other, I see it in school, in the cafeteria, and in the library, everywhere she is, she's always on the phone."

"Renée, in particular, is always on the phone?"

"Renée has a lot of friends, she's cute and popular. That's how girls are, the cute ones anyway, they're always on the phone and if she keeps talking on the phone when she's driving, she'll hurt herself." Max knit his hands. "I'm not trying to hurt her, I'm trying to *protect* her."

"So paint me a picture. You're driving behind her, a car length or two?"

"Yes, that's all, I just keep an eye on her to make sure she's okay."

"How does that protect her?"

"What do you mean?"

"I mean, what would you do, if she gets on the phone and you're behind her?"

"I'd just watch her. I watch her to make sure she's okay."

"Have you done this before?"

"Yes." Max grew suddenly still.

"How many times?"

"Twice, I followed her twice."

"Do you drive by her house?" Eric made some notes.

"Yes."

"How many times?"

"A lot." Max checked his watch.

"Would you harm her?"

"No. Never." Max's eyes rounded again, horrified. "It's weird, I go to make sure I didn't harm her, and nobody else did."

"Max, in your past, did you ever hit anybody, or get physical with anybody?" Eric wasn't taking any chances with the girl's safety.

"No."

"Ever get into fights at school?"

"Are you kidding?" Max asked, incredulous. "No way. I'd get my ass kicked!"

"Did you ever throw something in anger?"

"No."

"Have you ever been violent at all?"

"No, no!"

"What about toward animals? Cats or any pets like that?"

"Is this for real? You're kinda freaking me out right now." Max recoiled, bewildered, and Eric scrutinized him. He thought Max's taking the girl's phone and following her home were beyond the pale, but it didn't involve any physical threat to her. Eric understood Max's logic, acting as a protector, not a threat. Also Max's tone sounded genuine, which didn't mean the behavior wasn't concerning, but it fell short of the level of dangerousness required for being admitted to the hospital or triggering the *Tarasoff* duty to warn.

"I was asking out of concern for Renée."

"I'm not following her for a bad reason, I want to make sure she's okay. I'm not, like, a creeper or anything. It's just the opposite. I'm, like, her guardian angel. I'm looking out for her, and she needs me to look out for her."

"So you believe she needs you." Eric caught Max's eye and held his gaze for a moment.

"She *does* need me."

"And does that ring a bell, in terms of what we were just talking about?"

"No, what do you mean?" Max checked his watch.

"With your grandmother."

Max recoiled, rolling his eyes. "Dr. Parrish, I know the difference between Renée and my grandmother. That's gross."

"I understand that, but is your feeling about them the same, and is it related? Consider what I'm saying. Is your worrying about your grandmother tied to your worrying about Renée? So that now you're worrying more about your grandmother, you're worrying more about Renée?"

Max blinked. "Do you think?"

"You tell me."

"Maybe, kind of, I guess that could be true."

"Do you think you tap to prevent harm from coming to others, like Renée or your grandmother?"

"I have to think about it, but whatever the reason is, it's not helping to know it, like, it doesn't change anything, I still want to tap, I have to tap. I need to right now, I know it's almost time." Max checked his watch, his hair falling into his face. "Fifteen minutes exactly. Time to tap and say the colors." Max tapped his temple with his right index finger, then his lips moved silently. "There."

"Did that help?"

"Not really, it's not like doing it makes me feel better. It's not working the way it used to. That's why I say it's getting worse, why I came to you. Now I have to do it not to freak out."

"How about other intrusive thoughts of Renée, the ones you mentioned to me last time, in which you were afraid you would harm her?"

"I had them last night, I just worry about, like, that I'll hurt her."

"How specifically?"

"Like all kinds of ways, like I told you last time, and just this morning, it makes me nervous, and I worry that, like, I would go over there and somehow hurt her"—Max's words ran into each other as his anxiety gathered momentum—"or I would see her face and neck, and the necklace with the little gold plaque, and then my hands are on her neck, squeezing. It's upsetting me so much, that these ideas keep coming into my head and I just can't stop them, it's like if you have a nightmare only you're awake and you have it ten times a day, or twenty, and there's nothing you can do to stop it, nothing at all, no tapping or colors or anything relieves the pressure in your head." Max took a breath, ragged with emotion. "I can't take it anymore, Dr. Parrish, I really can't. I just want it to stop. It has to stop."

"I understand." Eric reached for the Kleenex, tugged one from the box, and handed it to Max. "Here, use this, please."

"Thanks." Max wiped his eyes, leaving pinkish streaks on his fair cheeks. "Sorry, I mean, this is ridiculous to sit here and cry like a baby."

"It's not ridiculous, it's human. You're doing excellent work here, and I know it isn't easy."

"It isn't, it sucks, it just . . . *sucks.*"

Eric felt confident in his differential of OCD and knew how to treat it, going forward. "Max, I am going to give you a script for some medication. It won't work right away, but be patient. You'll have to get some bloodwork done, too. I want to see you Wednesday night, at eight, here. It's my next available opening."

"Great." Max looked relieved, his forehead relaxing. "What meds are you putting me on?"

"Fluoxetine, or Prozac." Eric had good results with it, but he had to watch for short-term side effects. "Call me right away if you feel unusual restlessness. Understood?"

"Yes, thanks," Max said, wiping his eyes.

Chapter Thirteen

Monday morning, Eric got off the elevator in Wright and walked down the glistening hallway, taking his keys from his pocket, preoccupied. He'd spent most of the night worried about Max, his grandmother, and Renée, then about whether to file for primary custody of Hannah. He'd finally come to a decision and he'd call his lawyer after the morning staff meeting. He reached the door to the psychiatric unit, swiped the ID card on the lanyard around his neck, and inserted his key in the lock, then unlocked the door, closing it behind him, per safety procedure. Inside was a small anteroom and another locked door that served as a security airlock. His unit hadn't had an elopement, or a patient leaving unauthorized, since Eric had started here and he intended to keep it that way.

He opened the door and entered the unit, which was laid out like a rectangle, so that after the locked entrance was a small nurses' station in front of a large TV lounge containing an overstuffed sofa, matching chairs, and a wall of donated books and old computers with restricted Internet. To the left was the north hall of patients' rooms and to the right was the south hall of conference rooms, offices, a kitchen, and a few patients' rooms, reserved for patients whose dangerousness required they be segregated; all twenty patient rooms were singles for security reasons. Patients ranged in age from eighteen to ninety, suffering from depression, bipolar disease, schizophrenia, and other major mental disorders. One of the patients was currently on suicide watch, and two were on alert for self-harming behaviors like cutting. These numbers were low because of the summer months, but would double during the winter holidays.

Between the north and south halls at the center of the unit was the dining room, and behind the dining room was the main nurses' station, enclosed in thick Plexiglas for security reasons. The nurses had a good view of the outdoor patio beyond them, which was mandated by law for all mental health units in the state. Evidently, the Pennsylvania legislature believed that fresh air was beneficial for mental patients, so Eric wouldn't tell them that his patients used the patio to smoke. The hospital was smoke-free, but he didn't have the heart to deny a psychotic his cigarettes.

Eric took a left down the south hallway toward his office, dropped his messenger bag inside, hustled to the small conference room, and opened the door. His staff milled around, sipping their first coffee of the day and finishing their how-was-your-weekend chatter. Eric greeted everybody and made small talk, and the staff eventually made its way around an oblong conference table, too big for the room, of the same modern black fake-wood with black knock-off Aerons used throughout the hospital.

Eric pulled out a chair at the head of the table while the staff settled into their customary seats. He supervised three attending psychiatrists who sat in a row to his right: the most senior was Sam Ward, their resident intellectual with wire-rimmed glasses, pale blue eyes, and a vague scruffly brown haircut. Sam had published a number of significant papers on newer therapies of ADHD, even though he was only in his mid-thirties. Sam, a married man with a young son, had been at HGH for eight years and was Eric's personal choice to succeed him as Chief.

Sitting next to Sam was Jack D'Vergney, though the two psychiatrists barely liked each other, owing to their differing temperaments. As committed as Sam was to the scholarship of psychiatry, Jack made it known that he'd chosen the field because his father was a well-known neuroscientist in France; at one staff Halloween party, Jack had come as his famous father in a tailored suit and a button that read Ask Me About My Father Issues! Jack was handsome, flirtatious, and popular among the nurses for his dark good looks and vaguely European vibe; he'd been a champion NCAA fencer at Yale and kept his well-built frame insanely fit with something Eric avoided knowing about, called kettlebells.

The third attending psychiatrist was skinny, slight David Chu; he was also single, a decent-looking young man who had the misfortune to be compared most frequently with his pal Jack and found wanting. David had been on the unit for only two years, and like the baby in any family, got away with murder, playing dumb practical jokes and posting silly signs. David's most recent stunt was to put a sign on every stool that read STOOL SAMPLE. Actually, Eric had thought it was funny. Next to David sat a lineup of four nurses, Pam Susepeth, who was heavyset and sweet-faced, like her best friend, Beverly Gladfelter. The next pair of nurses were both new, hired since the freeze had been lifted last month: Allison Sterling and Sue Barrington, both of whom had short brown hair. The remaining chairs were occupied by staff who rarely had input at staff meetings: two psych techs, two nurse's aides, a nursing student, an art therapist, two caseworkers, and the two medical students from Jefferson, one of whom was Kristine Malin, whose eye Eric had been avoiding from the moment he'd entered the room.

"Okay, let's get this party started, Amaka," Eric said to his charge nurse Amaka Ademola-Gibbs, sitting to his left behind a tall stack of patient files. Amaka was in her fifties, a West African woman raised in the UK and married to a Brit, with an accent that reminded him of Downton Abbey. She was smart, skilled, and confident, and she had the most demanding job on the unit, which was to monitor the clinical care of the unit's patients. She was always the first one into work every morning, so she could meet with the nurses getting off the night shift at seven o'clock, get their reports, check their charting, and distill the data in order to update Eric and the rest of the team, now.

"Fine, Chief." Amaka sipped her tea. "I'll begin with Julius

Echeverria, who you will remember was admitted ten days ago with depression, arising out of the death of his teenage son in a car accident." Amaka opened the top folder on the stack in front of her, crossing her slim legs in her maroon scrubs. "Mr. Echeverria had a good night. He slept fully seven hours and was compliant with his meds."

Eric nodded. "That's good. So he's not trying to cheek them anymore."

"No, he's not." Amaka shook her head, and her little silver earrings wiggled back and forth. She had a thing for silver jewelry, which looked great with her dark skin and the graying tendrils woven through her hair, which she wore in a short natural cut. "His vitals were fine, and his wife Rosa visited him last night. She thinks he's improving, too. They had a nice chat."

"Good, good, good." Eric felt heartened. His psychiatry service integrated family members into the treatment plans for its patients, encouraging spouses, significant others, and even friends to join therapy sessions whenever appropriate, as an essential element of the patient's recovery. It was just another way in which psychiatry was different from every other service in the hospital; the outcome for a patient with a physical disease didn't depend on anyone else, in that a patient with colon cancer didn't improve because his family visited every day. He felt sure that Mr. Echeverria's depression would be helped by the support of his wife, who mourned the same tragic loss.

"By the way, Mr. Echeverria is almost out of days on his insurance. He has only three left."

"Duly noted." Eric filed it away. He knew that about 90 percent of the patients on the unit had some form of insurance, and he and Amaka kept a running tab of how many days each patient had left, trying daily to make progress within the strict parameters of managed-care, fighting the insurance companies for the mental health of his patients. "Whose patient is Mr. Echeverria? He's yours, right, Jack?"

"Yes." Jack nodded, shifting up in his seat and linking his long fingers in front of him. He had on a dark blue cashmere vest over a fitted white shirt, with slim-cut wool slacks and Gucci loafers. Eric remembered that Caitlin always said he could've been a male model.

"How close to discharge is he?"

"I'd say he's almost good to go."

"So when do you recommend we discharge him?"

"Tomorrow or the next day?" Jack shrugged cavalierly.

"Which is it?"

"Day after tomorrow."

"Okay." Eric let it go. He didn't say so, but he always felt that Jack was a little too glib for his own good, as if the attending lacked the true compassion required to be a successful psychiatrist, much less a scientist as prominent as his father.

Amaka retook the floor. "Our next patient is Leah Barry, who is on her third hospitalization after the stillbirth of her child. One of the night nurses noted that at dinner, she tried to slip a plastic knife from the dining room into her pocket, and the nurse worried that she was going to use it to self-harm."

"Oh no." Eric felt it tug at his chest, and the faces around the table went grave. Nobody ended up on a psych unit without a heartbreaking story, and Leah Barry's touched all of them. There was always one patient they called The Ghost, because she haunted you. This time, The Ghost was Leah Barry.

Amaka continued, "In addition, Mrs. Barry became very upset when the nurse took the knife away, and she barely slept. She expressed to the nurse that she wants to go home, though she knows she isn't well yet, and she continues to isolate. In particular she complains about being checked on."

"What's that about?" Eric asked, turning to David. "She's yours. What is she talking about?"

"You know how we have the bed checks every fifteen minutes. She finds it annoying. She wishes we could stop, at least at night, but I told her that we couldn't."

"Hmmm, we can't. But we'll have to do something else for her." Eric had instituted the fifteen-minute checking practice after one of the patients at another hospital in their system hanged himself.

The patient hadn't been checked in for an hour, and Eric vowed that would never happen in his unit. At the same time, he knew it could be annoying for the patient to be interrupted by a falsely cheery nurse's aide, saying "how are you doing" every fifteen minutes. It struck him that it was like Max Jakubowski, performing his ritual every fifteen minutes.

Eric eyed David. "So what can we do for Leah Barry?"

"I asked the nurse's aide who checks at night to make sure she doesn't shine a flashlight in her eyes. You don't have a problem with that, do you, Chief?"

"No, of course not. Can we do better than that? Think about it. Take some of the checks during your rounds, so it cuts down on total interruptions."

"Will do."

"Good. So, David, do you want to change your treatment plan for her? What would your recommendation be?"

"I have her on an SSRI, and we can increase the dosage just a bit. I'll also make a point of spending more time with her off-rounds."

"Good," Eric said, with a smile. David had to be a little less timid in his approach, but Eric knew that would come with time and experience. David Chu was a supersmart kid, but he tended to get in his own way. He turned to Amaka. "Okay, sorry to interrupt you, boss lady. Go ahead."

"Unfortunately, Mr. Perino doesn't present as sanguine a picture." Amaka went to the next folder on her stack, shifting the first to the bottom. She always presented in order of room numbers because she regarded it as more organized. Eric would have preferred the updates of critical patients first, but he believed in letting his people do their jobs their own way. Amaka opened the second folder. "Mr. Perino was disruptive at dinner last night. He pushed another patient in the dessert line."

David snorted. "Watch out. Don't get between dessert and Chubby Hubby."

Jack chuckled. "Like he needs another chocolate pudding."

There was chuckling around the room, but it fizzled when Eric didn't join in. He liked to laugh, but never at a patient's expense.

"So we'll have to file an event report," he said. Any type of inter-patient violence, however insignificant, had to be reported to the Commonwealth. "Amaka, will you?"

"Yes, I'll take care of it." Amaka checked her notes. "After the incident, Mr. Perino isolated in his room and at bedtime, he coughed up his meds. When they tried to readminister, he declined."

"How exactly did he decline?" Eric enjoyed Amaka's polite Brit-ishisms, but he needed facts. "I'm guessing it wasn't just a 'no, thanks.' "

Suddenly, there came the sound of shouting from the hallway and the loudspeaker crackled, "Dr. Parrish and Dr. Ward to Room 505, Code Gray. Dr. Parrish and Dr. Ward to Room 505, Code Gray."

"Let's go." Eric leapt to his feet just as the door was flung open by a frightened nurse.

"Dr. Parrish, it's Perino!"

Eric was already in motion, racing for the door.

Chapter Fourteen

Eric raced down the hall with Sam and David on his heels, then Jack behind. A Code Gray meant a security risk and the unit went into automatic lockdown, locking patients in their rooms because an outbreak of violence destabilized the entire unit. Some patients were already sticking their heads out to see what was going on, and a patient with a severe anxiety disorder, Mrs. Jelik, was coming down the hall from the opposite direction, wringing her hands. Eric could hear Donald Perino screaming in his room, then came a loud crash of something metallic hitting the floor.

"No! No! NO!" Perino raged at the top of his lungs. A blonde nurse and two orderlies were backing out of Perino's room in fear. "Get away from me! Get AWAY!"

"Get back, please." Eric reached the doorway to Perino's room and ushered the blonde nurse and the orderly out of harm's way. "Did you call security?"

"Yes," the nurse answered, shaken, and Eric knew she was relatively new, so he placed a steadying hand on her shoulder.

"Tina, stay calm and we'll be fine. What happened?"

"He was fine, at least I thought he was." Tina's brown eyes rounded with fear. "I went in to give him his meds and for no reason, he slammed his head into the bed table."

"Got it." Eric steered her to Mrs. Jelik, pointing. "Tina, please put Mrs. Jelik back in her room. We're in lockdown."

"Yes, okay." Tina hurried off, as Eric turned to face Amaka.

"Amaka, get me five milligrams haloperidol and two milligrams lorazepam."

"On it!" Amaka turned on her heel and rushed away.

Perino kept yelling, "No, no! NO! Get away! Get AWAY!"

The orderly shouted to Eric, "Doc, what you want me to do?"

"Nothing—no matter what happens, don't go in that room." Eric wouldn't consider endangering an orderly, and hospital procedures were clear in case of patient violence—utilize only trained professional staff, as few as possible, and stabilize the situation until security arrived. He turned to Sam, behind him. "You stay here, too."

"Eric, he's my patient and he trusts me. I should help. Plus, he's big. You're gonna need an assist. I should go in with you." Sam blinked, his grayish eyes grave behind his wire-rimmed glasses.

"No, stay. Pass me the syringes when Amaka gets back. Don't come in until security gets here."

"Understood, but be careful." Sam nodded, and they both knew he had to stay behind for safety's sake. Psychiatrists, psychologists, and mental heath workers in hospitals had an assault rate of 60 percent, six times higher than other healthcare professionals.

"Donald, please settle down," Eric said calmly, entering the hospital room where his patient stood raging on the other side of the bed. Donald Perino was in his mid-forties, six feet two inches and 350 pounds of paranoia. Perino had been admitted two days ago after a break, ironically caused not by his mental illness, but by the abrupt withdrawal from one of his medications for depression, Klonopin or clonazepam. It was psychiatry's dirty little secret that many antidepressants did more harm than good when the patient abruptly stopped taking them, which was unfortunately common behavior among the mentally ill.

"No, no, leave me alone!" Perino yelled, his dark eyes blazing in terror. Blood dripped down his forehead from where he'd injured himself, matting his brown hair and making a gruesome freshet. Fortunately, the wound didn't look serious, just bloody. The bed table lay on its side, and his breakfast tray, eggs, toast, and coffee cup were scattered on the floor.

"Donald, relax, please settle down." Eric kept his tone calm, remembering his training. He approached Perino from a forty-five-degree angle because it was less confrontational. He stopped before he violated Perino's personal space, which was a leg's length, because it would escalate his agitation. He made eye contact but he kept it like casual observation, not a fixed stare. He held his arms at his sides, not only because it was less threatening, but they'd be available to fend off a blow. He cleared the doorway so he'd have an escape route.

"No, no, no! Go away!" Perino backed up against the reinforced windows. He raised his meaty arms as if warding off a blow, his gaze so wild-eyed and unfocused that Eric wasn't sure Perino recognized him.

"Donald, it's Dr. Parrish, and I need you to sit down in the brown chair." Eric pointed to the chair, having been trained that simple commands would help him regain control of the situation. He couldn't let Perino hurt himself, the staff, or his fellow patients. "Please, sit down and tell me what's happening. I need to see that wound on your head."

"No, no! ARGGGHHHH!" Perino bellowed, throwing back his head, baring his teeth, and roaring like a raging animal. Blood poured down his face, a horrifying sight.

Eric stood his ground. Security still wasn't here. Perino was going from bad to worse. Eric didn't move or do anything that could be misinterpreted as aggressive. Paranoia among schizophrenics typically caused combativeness, and Perino had a history of childhood aggression and disturbing behavior, like starting fires.

"No, no, no!" Perino started shouting again. "I know who you are! You don't fool me! Don't you come near me! Don't come near me!"

"Donald, I'm Dr. Parrish. Please sit in the chair and tell me what's going on."

"You're not Dr. Parrish! You're a liar!" Perino hollered, spitting the blood that ran past his lips. Veins bulged in his neck.

"I am Dr. Parrish." Eric pointed to the chair again. He didn't know what was taking security so long. "Please sit in the chair. I need you to sit down. I've been treating you here. I remember that your wife Linda brought you in. You had stopped taking your medication, do you remember? You said it made you feel lethargic. You gained weight, almost thirty pounds?"

"You're a liar! You're with the CIA! You all are! So's that blonde! She said she's a nurse but she's a liar! She's trying to take the thoughts out of my mind! You give me pills! You poison my blood! You *make* me crazy!"

Eric glanced at the doorway. Jack's expression was oddly impassive, but David's young face looked stricken and flushed. Security was nowhere in sight. Amaka had returned and was passing the syringes to Sam, who held them discreetly in his left hand, waiting to slip them to Eric. But Eric couldn't subdue Perino and administer two injections without security to hold Perino down.

"That's why I'm here!" Perino took a threatening step toward Eric, advancing on him. "You make me angry! You make me want to kill somebody!"

"Donald, please sit down in the chair." Eric edged backwards toward the door, hiding his hand behind him so Sam could pass him the syringes. In the next moment, Eric felt a syringe in his palm, but it was only one, not two. Sam was sending him a signal. "Donald, please, sit down in the brown chair."

"No, no!" Perino kept coming, his face a blood-soaked mask. "You're *making* me a killer! You want me to kill for the CIA! Get out of my way! I have to get out of here, right now!"

"I can't do that, Donald. You need to stay here and talk to me." Eric stood in front of the door. He couldn't let Perino out of the room to harm his staff or other patients. He braced himself for a takedown. He couldn't wait for security. "Please sit down in the—"

"No, no, NO!" Perino screamed in Eric's face. "If you don't let me out of here, I'm going to *kill you!*"

"Donald, stop—"

"Move!" Perino lunged for Eric, and Eric reacted instantly, grabbing Perino's burly right arm at the wrist, forcing it down abruptly, then quickly stepping backwards, yanking Perino off-balance and simultaneously injecting him with the sedative.

"No, no, don't!" Perino howled, as Sam charged from behind, wrapping his left arm around Perino's beefy chest, injecting him and continuing to pull him backwards.

"Donald, it's Dr. Parrish and Dr. Ward, we're here to help you." Eric and Sam sandwiched Perino, taking him down in a controlled fall, with Sam protecting Perino's head with his hand so it didn't hit the floor.

"No!" Perino hollered, pinwheeling his arms, kicking his legs, and trying to get up, as Sam scooted from underneath him.

"Donald, please relax." Eric straddled Perino and held him down with a hand on each shoulder. Blood bubbled from Perino's head wound, dripping sideways onto the floor. "Be still. Calm down. You're going to feel the sedative starting to work."

Perino shook his head, his eyelids fluttering, already starting to lose consciousness. A commotion came from the hallway, and in the next moment, three security guards burst into the room, led by their captain, Jed Barneston. Grant, a security guard, rushed to Eric's side, the other helped Sam to his feet, and a third went to restrain Perino.

"Chief!" Jed called out in alarm. "You okay?"

"Fine, thanks." Eric got off of Perino. "He's out now. Let's get him into bed."

"Doc, we have to clear the threat zone." Jed shooed Eric and Sam out of the room, per procedure. Security guards hurried back in to help secure Perino, who would be treated for his head wound later, after it was safe.

"Thanks, buddy." Eric exhaled, smiling at Sam. "I couldn't have done it without you."

"Nah, you couldn't have done it without haloperidol," Sam shot back.

And behind him, grinning at Eric with evident relief, stood Kristine.

Chapter Fifteen

An hour later, Eric was trying to catch up on his paperwork when there was a knock on his office door. He looked up from his desk to see Amaka, with a slight frown. "Something up?" he asked.

"Chief, can you come with me a minute? I need to show you something, right away."

"Sure, is there a problem?" Eric rose, crossed to the door, and they left together. He felt concerned because she wasn't the type to exaggerate. "What is it?"

"It's personal. I need to discuss it with you in private." Amaka took his elbow and whisked them down the hallway, toward the conference rooms. They reached the conference room, where she opened the door and went inside, with Eric following her.

"Congratulations, Chief!" everybody shouted.

"Whoa, *what*?" Eric gasped, astonished. His staff filled the conference room, and everyone was grinning—Sam, Jack, David, the medical students including Kristine, nurses, nurse's aides, psych techs, social workers, occupational and art therapists, even the dietitian. Cupcakes, muffins, a sheet cake, cups, paper plates, and cans of soda covered the conference table, and in front of it like a banquet manager, stood their stout hospital administrator, Jason Kittredge, who was beaming at Eric.

"Congratulations, Chief!" Jason clapped him on the arm. "We're number two!"

"We're number two!" "We're number two!" "We're number two!" Everyone chanted, clapping their hands, and Eric realized he'd been so busy with Hannah and Max over the weekend that he hadn't even realized it was that time of the year.

"We're *number two?*" Eric asked, astounded. "We're getting ranked number two?"

"Yes, we are!" Jason practically shouted with happiness. "Our psychiatry service, *your* psychiatry service, just got ranked number two in the nation by *U.S. Medical Report*! It's still confidential. I got word through back channels."

"You're kidding." Eric could never have hoped as much. The highest ranking they'd ever had was eleven, and he'd been trying to break the top ten.

"Congratulations!" Jason applauded, and everybody joined in, clapping.

"Wait, quiet, everybody." Eric waved for the clapping to stop. "What about Mass General? They've been number two forever."

"We knocked them out of second place. Like that old car commercial, we try harder!"

"Are you *serious?* They own second place." Eric shook his head in disbelief.

"Not anymore! We scored a 29.6, almost a perfect 30. It put us ahead of every psychiatric service in the country but one, McLean. We came from behind! We're the dark horse, the underdog!" Jason's grayish eyes lit up behind his wire-rimmed glasses. "Thanks to you, your leadership, and your long-range planning. The changes that you've made over the past few years have come to fruition."

"No, it was all of us." Eric collected his thoughts, motioning around the room. "Congratulations, everybody. I'm so proud for all of you, and I appreciate everything you did to make this happen. We pulled together and it looks like—"

"We're number two!" Kristine shouted, stepping front and center, and Eric got the distinct impression that she was trying to get his attention, as everybody joined in, chanting again, "We're number two!" "We're number two!"

"Chief!" Jack pushed Eric playfully. "Come on, Jason's right. Take the credit. I've seen the changes you instituted—the formation of treatment-teams, the full multidisciplinary approach, especially liaising with the geriatric unit—they're all working."

Jason pumped his head, retaking the floor. "The other hospitals, they've been watching us, hoping we'll fall on our faces, but we proved them wrong. We proved them *all wrong*."

Eric couldn't help but smile. "Jason, that's a negative worldview. You might need a shrink."

Everybody laughed, including Jason, but he wasn't about to shut up. He turned to the medical students, with Kristine in front. "There are sixteen hospital specialties that are data-dependent for their rankings, but four specialties are ranked according to reputation only, psychiatry among them. That means that our ranking came from a reputational survey of physicians, who were asked to name the hospitals they consider the best in the specialty for difficult cases."

"Woohoo!" Kristine cheered, louder than the others. Eric thought she was more dolled-up than usual this morning, with brighter lipstick and her long, dark hair blown-dry, which he knew was a big deal, from Caitlin.

Jason added, "That means it's even *harder* to get because in certain respects, it's somewhat subjective."

Eric snorted. "*Somewhat* subjective? It's completely subjective."

Jack waved him off. "Chief, if somebody throws you a rose, don't bitch about the thorns."

Eric laughed, and so did everybody else.

"Not only that," Jason interjected, "we made the Honor Roll. We never made the Honor Roll before."

"Honor Roll?" Eric felt like the parent of a gifted overachiever. "How did that happen? Did we get the extra credit questions right?"

Everybody laughed except Jason. "Joke all you want to, but it's only for hospitals that rank high enough in at least six specialties.

The Board is over the moon. They extend their special congratulations to you, Chief."

"Jason, enough. So what happens next? You promote it out the wazoo?" Eric knew that medicine had become about marketing.

"The sky's the limit." Jason's enthusiasm bubbled over. "We have to wait to press-release it, but we can start priming the pump. There will be TV commercials, billboards, banners, radio ads, and targeted online ads on Facebook and Twitter, too."

Eric smiled. "Don't forget about the swag. We need pens that say We Try Harder, plus T-shirts."

David burst into laughter. "How about bottles of hand sanitizer? And beach towels?"

"Yes!" Jack clapped his hands. "Travel mugs!"

"Beer coolers!" yelled one of the nurses.

Kristine caught Eric's eye, saying, "Condoms!"

Everybody laughed harder as Eric looked away from Kristine, breaking eye contact. He didn't want to encourage her.

Jason waved off the laughter. "Okay, I know you're having fun, but this is a wonderful achievement, and it's because of Eric and your hard work. It will redound to the hospital's benefit for years to come."

Eric nodded, then he realized he had come in this morning thinking that he might quit his hospital job over the custody issue, but he didn't know if he could do that now. He'd never felt more a part of the team than he did at this very moment, when he realized he would have to leave it behind. But he couldn't say any of these things, so he pasted a smile on his face, and said:

"Jason, please thank the Board, on our behalf."

Chapter Sixteen

Eric shut his office door behind him, walked to his desk, and sank into his chair. He'd been crazy busy—a running joke on the psych unit—because the number-two ranking had thrown the hospital into a tizzy. He'd fielded phone calls and congratulations from administration all day, then he had treatment rounds. Donald Perino had stabilized, though his forehead had taken three stitches.

Eric checked his desk clock, a clinician's habit, which read 5:15; it made him think of Max, who was undoubtedly looking at the clock somewhere across town, then tapping his head. Eric worried about how he could help him, then about Renée Bevilacqua. Eric thought of what Arthur had said, that OCD patients rarely become aggressive, so he put it out of his mind, or tried to, as he swiveled to face his computer, palmed the mouse, and logged onto his email. He wanted to check it before he left to have drinks with the staff, most of whom had already gone to celebrate their number-two ranking.

He watched his email pile onto the screen, skimmed the senders and subject lines, and determined that none of it required an immediate answer. His gaze strayed to the late-day sun that struggled to make its way through the window, which had a view of approaching thunderstorms and the Medevac helicopters that rushed emergency cases to the rooftop landing pad. His was the best office on the floor, but even so, was a medium-sized box, barely big enough for an institutional desk of indeterminate wood across from two brown pleather chairs and a matching couch, on the side. The rug was a tweedy gray-green and the walls were painted a soothing green pastel, a color he thought of as Managed-Care Mint. His diplomas, board certifications, and professional awards blanketed them, although Eric wasn't the show off type. Caitlin had made him frame everything, showing off for him by proxy.

You have to toot your own horn, she would always say.

Eric looked out the window, trying not to think about Caitlin. He would normally have called her to tell her about being number two, but he'd stopped himself. His eyes fell on the bookshelves overflowing with medical and psychiatric textbooks, the professional journals and papers, the myriad volumes and memoirs on psychiatry, its history, and its neuroscience; Eric lived a life of the mind and it showed. His thoughts stopped at the familiar purple DSM, the volume that categorized the mental and emotional disorders that plagued human beings, and he wondered if being heartbroken was one of them. Or all of them.

Eric hadn't reached a final decision about whether to go for primary custody of Hannah, and though he knew he was overthinking it, he couldn't stop. He had to acknowledge that gaining the number-two ranking and even going through what they did with Perino had given him pause. He loved his job, and he had a purpose here at HGH. He owed Susan a call with his answer today, and it had been on the back of his mind all day. Suddenly he heard a knock, and he looked over to see Sam at his door.

"Hey, Chief. You're coming out with the gang, aren't you? We're celebrating."

"I suppose I should." Eric rarely went out with the gang, trying to keep his professional distance, but he was going to make an exception.

"Of course you should come." Sam frowned, surprised. "You're the guest of honor. Plus you're my excuse. I said I had to go to a party for the boss, so how would it look if the boss didn't go?"

"What did you get out of?" Eric logged out of his email. He would call Susan later tonight.

"T-ball. Seth plays on Mondays, but I can go late."

"How old is he these days?" Eric was thinking of Hannah, his allegedly abnormal kid who didn't like sports. He rose, checking his pants for his cell phone and keys.

"Five. It's young for T-ball but he loves it. I loved Little League, too. So did my brother. It's a Ward thing." Sam opened the door. "Come on, everybody's there but us."

"Okay, I owe you a drink, too. You saved my ass with Perino." Eric went to the door, with Sam following.

"No worries. I'll feel it in my back tomorrow."

"Ha! I feel it in my back right now." Eric locked his office door behind him.

"It had to be the new nurse that set him off. He didn't recognize her."

"Agree." They fell into step walking down the hallway, and the unit was quiet because the patients were in the dining room for dinner. Eric waved good-bye to the nurses as they passed the station. "I'm worrying about him. He's on risperidone for the psychosis and fluoxetine for the depression, correct?"

"Yes."

"But he's not responding to treatment, and if anything, he's getting worse. I'm worried that his agitation is a side effect from risperidone." Eric unlocked the interior door of the unit, letting them both into the airlock, then unlocked the outer door and locked it behind them.

"You think it's akathisia?"

"Yes," Eric answered, mulling it over. Akathisia was a common side effect from risperidone, involving agitation and extreme anxiety, which caused the patient to act out, even violently.

"I don't think so. We're not seeing any of the motoric movements, like marching in place, getting up and getting down, or tapping."

"He says he's anxious."

"Right, and he is, because of his delusions that the CIA's after him. He's still hearing voices, too. I really believe that the agitation is a result of the underlying condition, his psychosis, and not a side effect."

Eric could hear the conviction in Sam's tone. "So you want to keep him on the risperidone and fluoxetine?"

"Yes, I want to stay the course. I don't want to undertreat him. He's really sick."

Eric could hear the same concern he felt for Max. "Okay. He is your patient and you know him better."

"I worry about side effects, too. But we can't be so conservative that we don't do right by him."

"Agree." They walked ahead to the elevator bank, falling into a companionable silence as they stepped inside the arriving cab, not talking shop because of patient confidentiality. The other employees chattered away, the elevator reached the ground floor, and they left the building and hustled across the street to the strip mall that held the gym, liquor store, Wawa convenience store, and their local watering hole, Thatcher's, one of the last independents in a world of Chili's and TGIFs.

Eric took the lead through the glass door, and his eyes adjusted to the darkness. The place was long and rectangular with an old-school wooden bar, but he didn't see his staff at the bar area, which was crowded with employees from the Glencroft Corporate Center, scruffy middle managers and IT types in logo polo shirts chatting up women with freshened makeup and laminated ID lanyards.

"What a scene," Eric said to Sam under his breath.

"Suburban singles, eh?"

"Lord deliver me. Stay married, Sam." They made their way to a restaurant area in the back, and Eric spotted his staff, all of them in their red W lanyards, laughing around a table crammed with chicken wings, fried mozzarella sticks, sliders, and sweating pitchers of beer. Eric realized that his affection for them was tribal. After all, he was their Chief. They all began to look over at him, heads turning, each bursting into broad grins, clapping. He'd warned them not to say anything in public about their number-two status, but he got a better idea.

"Hey, kids!" Eric called out, holding up his right hand and extending the middle three fingers. "What's this?"

"What, Chief?" one called back. "I don't know!" another said. A third yelled out, "Are you giving us the finger?"

"It's a W!" Eric said, laughing. "For Wright because we are Wright!"

"We are Wright, We are Wright, We are Wright!" The staff started cheering, then they dissolved into laughter, speeches, and self-congratulation.

In time, Eric settled next to Sam, Jack, and David, avoided eye contact with Kristine, drank warm beer, shared mediocre buffalo wings, and entertained his staff with bad jokes, laughing harder than he had in a long time. He noticed Jack flirting with Kristine, their heads bent together, but he looked away. He let himself forget about Caitlin, his lawyer, Max, and even his beloved daughter, and he bought everybody all the food they could eat but only two rounds of drinks. And in the end, he bid them good-bye with a lump in his throat that couldn't be explained by a few watery beers.

He left the bar and breathed in the warm night air, acrid with cigarette smoke from a group on the sidewalk. It was growing dark, and he crossed the street, slid out his iPhone, and checked the time—8:48—so he had time before he called Hannah to say good night, at nine. He read his email as he walked to the hospital parking lot, a multilevel concrete affair. He reached the first level of the garage and the parking spaces reserved for department chiefs, where he put his phone on lock, slipped it back into his pocket, and dug in his other pocket for his keys.

"Hey, Eric," someone said, and he looked up, surprised to find Kristine standing beside his car. She looked lovely, even better though her makeup had worn off. She'd had a blazer on at work and at Thatcher's, but she'd taken it off and had on a black dress that outlined a gorgeous body, with black high heels, which reminded him he wasn't dead below the waist.

"Oh, hi, Kristine. Didn't I just leave you at Thatcher's? How did you get here?"

"I slipped out when you weren't looking. I wanted to see you. I've been trying to see you alone, all month." Kristine pouted. "I only have one week left on my rotation, but no matter what I do, I can't get you to notice me."

"Oh, I notice you." Eric caught himself. "I mean, I notice you."

"Then why didn't you answer my text?" Kristine took a step toward him, meeting his eye directly, her lips parting slightly, curving upward in a sly smile.

"Um, well," Eric started to say. "I thought we could talk about Jacobs today. I didn't get to it because Perino—"

"You knew I didn't really want to talk about Jacobs." Kristine took another step toward him. "I wanted to talk about us."

"Oh, no. There's no us." Eric stepped backwards.

"Not yet, but there can be."

"Kristine, no, there can't, it's not appropriate. It can't happen."

"Why not?" Kristine blinked, her smile amused. "You're single and I'm single. Don't tell me you're not attracted. I know you are."

Eric's mouth went dry. "That's not the point."

"What's the point?"

"The point is that you're on my unit."

"Only for a week, and do you know how many people are hooking up in that hospital? What difference does it make that we work together?" Kristine's smile didn't change and her sharp blue eyes searched his, as if she wanted an answer.

"There's an imbalance of power between us."

"I know, but there's nothing I can do about that." Kristine grazed his shirtsleeve with her fingertips. "I have power over you. Can you deal with it?"

Eric couldn't deny his reaction to her nearness, or touch. She smelled great, and he shouldn't have had anything to drink. "No, it's not right. This can't go any further."

"You're dismissing it out of hand, but you shouldn't."

"Yes, I should." Eric took a step toward his car, but before he knew what was happening, Kristine was on tiptoe, looping her arms around his neck, kissing him fully. He grabbed her arms, stopped her, and set her back on her heels. "Kristine, no, listen. This can't happen."

"Just think about it, is all I ask," Kristine called after him.

But Eric stepped to the car, got his keys, chirped his door unlocked, jumped inside, and drove off.

Chapter Seventeen

"Hi, Hannah." Eric drove through the garage with the phone to his ear, keeping an eye out for Kristine. There was only one pedestrian exit to the garage, and the reserved parking was on the first level, but he didn't see her.

"Daddy, I knew you would call!"

"I'm sorry I'm late. Are you in bed already?" Eric reached the exit, pushed the button to lower the window, and slid his pass card into the turnstile. He thought he would hear Kristine's high heels click-clacking somewhere, but the garage was stone quiet.

"Yes, I turned out the light but I kept the phone on. Mommy said it was okay for five minutes."

Eric felt his gut clench at the mention of Caitlin. He returned the pass card to his visor and waited while the turnstile arm rose. "I won't keep you too long. You sound tired, and I know you need to get to sleep. I just wanted to say good night and tell you I love you."

"I love you too."

"Tell me, how's your ankle? Does it feel better?"

"Yes. You're going to come and take me to school tomorrow, right?"

"Yes, of course, but don't forget I won't see you tomorrow night because your mommy is taking you to your cousin Rebecca's birthday dinner." Eric turned left out of the garage, checking the rearview to see if anybody was driving behind him, but there wasn't. His was the only car leaving the garage, and he didn't know if Kristine drove to work. Most people did, but not all the medical students had cars.

"Mommy said tomorrow is the last time."

"Wait, what are you saying?" Eric didn't know what Hannah was talking about. He'd lost the train of thought over Kristine.

"Mommy said tomorrow is the last time you're taking me to school."

"No, it's not." Eric stopped at the light. The strip mall was to his right, and he glanced over to see if Kristine was walking through its parking lot, heading back to Thatcher's, but it was too dark to see anything. "I always take you to school Tuesdays and Thursdays. Tomorrow isn't the last time."

"Mommy said it is." Hannah sounded a little crumbly, her voice thinning, the way she did when she got sad.

"Mommy said that?" Eric hoped Hannah had simply misunderstood, but his gut was telling him otherwise. He'd been taking Hannah to school Tuesdays and Thursdays ever since she started first grade, because her elementary school started late, at 8:20, and it gave Caitlin a chance to get into work early. He would make breakfast for Hannah, pack her lunch, the whole shebang. It had become a special thing they did together, and he wasn't about to give it up.

"Why can't you take me to school anymore, Daddy?"

"I'm not sure." Eric fought the impulse to throw Caitlin under the bus. "I'll talk to Mommy about it, okay? Is she around? Can you put her on the phone?"

"Mommy! Mom! Daddy wants to talk to you!" Hannah called out, and Eric could hear some commotion on the other end of the line, then some talking he couldn't understand, then Hannah got back on the phone. "Daddy, Mommy said she can't come to the phone and you should call your friend."

"My friend? What friend?"

"Susan. Isn't that your friend?"

"Oh, right. Susan is my friend." Eric simmered. Susan was his friend for $350 an hour. He hit the gas, entering the line of traffic. "Okay, don't you worry. I'll talk to Mommy about it, and we'll figure it out. I'll see you tomorrow morning, same time as usual."

"I like when you take me to school."

"I like it too." Eric suppressed a twinge. He wished for the umpteenth time that he and Caitlin had never split up. It was one thing to go through a divorce, but another to watch your kid get tortured.

"Can we have eggs and ketchup tomorrow?"

"Yes, it'll be special. We'll have eggs."

"Yay! Mommy says I have to get off the phone now. Good night, Daddy. I love you."

"I love you too, honey. Sleep tight."

"Aren't you going to say 'pleasant dreams'? That's what you always say."

"Whoops. Pleasant dreams, honey. Good night." Eric hung up, navigating with one hand while he pressed the number to call Susan. He kept his eye on the road, leaving the hospital campus, but his thoughts were racing. If he hadn't made the decision about custody yet, he had made one now.

"Eric?" Susan asked, picking up. "Glad you called."

"Hi, listen, I made a decision. I want to go for primary custody, but I don't know about quitting my job at the hospital yet. I might've jumped the gun on that."

"Whoa, you sound different."

"I'm furious, that's what I am." Eric stopped at a red light. "Hannah just told me I can't take her to school in the mornings anymore. Caitlin is seeing someone, by the way."

"I know, I talked to Daniel today. I was going to tell you when you called me. She was very unhappy that you came over uninvited."

"Did she tell you that she took Hannah to an emergency room without telling me? Because she hurt herself playing the stupid softball? I was worried and I called but they didn't answer." Eric stared at the red light, hearing himself and hating in his own voice the tit-for-tat fighting that he'd seen in couples he counseled. Almost uniformly, the wives found him first, looking for support. They didn't know it when they came, but they were all looking for the support to get a divorce. He realized that Caitlin must have been just like those wives, wanting out, looking for the opening, trying to find the courage.

"Okay, relax. Changes are coming, Eric."

"Like what?" Eric tried to keep his temper. "Like that all of a sudden I can't take Hannah to school?"

"That, for one."

"But why? I just want to take my kid to school. I've been doing it since she started school!"

"We didn't provide for your right to do that in the agreement."

"Seriously?" Eric hit the gas as the light turned green. "How many things didn't we prepare for in this agreement?"

"This isn't on me." Susan's tone stiffened. "We have a standard custody agreement, but you two have been ignoring it, as a past practice. Now Caitlin is reverting to the agreement, going to go strictly by the letter. In other words, your informal practices are going to be null and void. It's a fairly typical pattern."

"What do you mean, a pattern?" Eric switched lanes, newly angry. Eric drove home, and the neon signs of the CVS, Gap, Walgreens, McDonald's, and Wendy's became a suburban blur.

"You and Caitlin were working well together, having a pretty informal custodial relationship and keeping things in place, which involved your being around the house more. That's why you didn't exercise your right to have overnights during the week, correct?"

"Right. I wanted Hannah to sleep in her own bed during the week."

"Well, I spoke with Daniel, and Caitlin is taking the position that it's not going to work for her anymore for you to come by the house in the morning, be in her kitchen, make breakfast with her pans, and then take Hannah to school."

"What if I came by in the morning on Tuesdays and Thursdays, and took Hannah *out* to breakfast? I get up early. It's not a problem for me, and she likes to get up early too."

"That doesn't solve the problem."

"Why not? Why doesn't it?" Eric felt a tension around his chest he hadn't felt in ages. He realized he was driving distracted, so he turned into a CVS parking lot and braked, leaving the engine and air conditioning on.

"You have to look at the facts the way a court would, and what your ex is requesting is reasonable. We both know that she's seeing someone, and I don't think he's staying over there now, but one day he will. The current custody arrangement is conventional in every way—"

"I want to change it. I absolutely want to change it. I want primary custody."

"Don't do this rashly, Eric."

"Susan, I never do anything rashly. I've never done a rash thing in my entire life." Eric flashed on how he'd turned Kristine away, in the parking garage. Any other man would have had her against the car.

"So you considered it, over the weekend?"

"I did nothing *but* consider it. Every decision I make is the most endlessly well-considered decision you can ever imagine, analyzed every which way from Sunday, including relevant pros and cons, research data, family-of-origin, barometric pressure, bloodwork, and the status of my own bowel movements."

Susan chuckled. "You're funny when you're mad."

"I don't feel funny, I feel like I'm being shut out of my own daughter's life. If this is the shape of things to come, then I want to file for primary custody."

"Fine. I'll draft and file the papers quickly serve them on Daniel, and copy you. It's a form, and I want to move before the court approves the previous agreement we filed."

"Go for it." Eric knew it was the right thing to do. He didn't relish the combat for Hannah, but he would help her get through. Eric felt as if he had crossed a line, and there was no going back. "As for my hospital job, I don't want to give it up yet. What do you think?"

"It can wait. You offered to quit the job, and I agreed because it makes your case for custody stronger. It makes it a closer case if you have a big job, but I'm not afraid of a close case. If you only win the easy ones, what kind of lawyer are you?"

"Okay, good."

"After I file, we all go by the agreement. On your nights, you should take Hannah to your house to sleep over."

"Okay, good. So I pick her up when it says in the agreement and take her over to my house?"

"Yes, exactly. The agreement provides that you take her to school the next morning, so you'll get your mornings with her that way, eh?"

"Good point." Eric considered it. "So I'll have her alternating Tuesday and Thursday mornings, plus two weekends a month."

"Exactly. Meet all the terms and times of the agreement. Caitlin thought you would be the only one to lose time, but now, so will she."

"It sounds like a war, with Hannah in the middle."

"Get used to it, Eric. I'm advising you to take her because not only will it give you more time with her, but it would look better to the court. You don't want to be asking for more time when you haven't utilized the time you've been given."

"Right. I see, we're making a record."

"Exactly. You also don't want to be in a position where the fact that you haven't been taking her overnight is somehow used against you, suggesting that you weren't interested."

"True, and school is almost over anyway." Eric could envision it, and it eased his heart. "I already painted the room."

"Good. Tomorrow morning when you go over there, don't start any discussions with Caitlin about not letting you take Hannah to school. She told Daniel that she wants all communication to be between the lawyers, and that's right. You may have been able to work together before, but for now it's radio silence."

"Whatever, fine." Eric had founded his entire professional life on the notion that talking could heal people and solve problems, but now he had to *not* talk to his own wife, about the most important problem in his life.

"Finally, don't breathe a word to her that we're going to file for primary custody. Be nice to her. Act like you're working with her. In terms of strategy, I want to spring it on her. I'm hoping to file our papers and serve Daniel right away, to surprise her before the weekend."

"What's the thinking there?" Eric's stomach flipped over, his loyalties mixed. As angry as he felt at Caitlin, it was strange to be conspiring against her. He lost focus a minute, feeling himself enter uncharted emotional territory.

"Look, Eric, no more Mr. Nice Guy. This is litigation, and we want to win. If we file before the weekend, we give her the weekend to worry."

"But how does that help us win, if she worries?" Eric rubbed his face. Caitlin was becoming his enemy. He'd never had an enemy before, especially not one he loved to the marrow. His *wife*.

"We win when we have our adversary off-balance, off-kilter. Winning is not a passive act. You actually have to *beat* somebody and you beat them before you even enter a courtroom, by dominating them. Especially your ex. She's a prosecutor, for God's sake. She wins for a living and she loves Hannah, too."

"You're right, but she doesn't *like* Hannah, though she'll never admit that to herself, much less in court." Suddenly Eric knew the truth, one that he'd never faced before. "Hannah isn't the kid she wanted, it's as simple as that."

"There you go." Susan didn't miss a beat. "Right now she has the upper hand. She's calling the shots and shutting you out. We have to get the upper hand and do some shutting out of our own. Litigation is always about power. We're about to right this imbalance of power."

Eric flashed on Kristine, talking about how she had the power, and now here was Susan talking about how he needed to get the power. It struck him as strange that he'd never thought of who had the power in his own marriage. He'd analyzed it in the couples he counseled, but that was an abstraction. That was them, not *us*.

"It's your weekend with Hannah, isn't it?"

"Yes, it would be."

"So she'll be at your place for the weekend, overnights on Friday and Saturday and home Sunday by seven o'clock. When I file the papers, I'll let them know that, commencing immediately, you will be there to take her for your weekend with her. You don't have to communicate that, I will. Got it? Don't be late with the pickups or the drop-offs. Judges hate that."

"I'm never late." Eric didn't add, *for anything.*

"That's good for Hannah to be with you this weekend. When Caitlin is upset, she'll be insulated from it."

"Right." Eric felt reassured that Susan was concerned for Hannah's well-being. "I really want to minimize the effect on Hannah. It's bad enough I'm going to be her mother's adversary, and she picks up on things. That will really bother her."

"I'm aware. Finally, I want you to keep your nose clean."

"My nose couldn't be cleaner."

"You know what I mean. Imagine that a court will find out everything you do, every misstep, because it will. You're not dating, are you?"

"No."

"Don't. Let's keep the record clean."

"Okay." Eric thought maybe it wasn't the worst thing that he hadn't had Kristine against the car.

"You won't be lonely forever," Susan added.

And Eric thought, *Bingo.*

Chapter Eighteen

4. I grasp quickly what motivates others.
Circle one: Doesn't apply to me. Partially applies to me.
   Fully applies to me.

Okay, so not everything is going according to plan. I already threw my temper tantrum. I broke my best controller by throwing it against the wall, cracking the casing.

I feel angry deep down. It's eating away at me, gnawing at my gut like a pack of rats.

What is it they say about the Serenity Prayer? You have to learn what you control and let go of what you don't. Or something like that.

Okay, so I don't control everything.

Evidently I make mistakes.

I called it wrong.

I thought it would work, but it didn't.

I thought he would go for it, but he didn't.

It pisses me off so much. I'm pacing in my bedroom, walking back and forth across the floor, probably wearing a line in the wood. Maybe if I keep pacing I'll turn into a chain saw, destroying the floor, then butchering the earth itself, then falling to the center and burning alive.

I thought I understood what motivated him, but I guess I was wrong.

This is going to be tougher than I thought.

But part of me likes that. It gets my juices flowing. I'll try to focus on that part. The part that appreciates the challenge. The part that wants an adversary who is truly worthy, not one I can crush quickly.

There's no fun in that, and I'm in it for the game, too.

That's the weird thing about gaming, nobody likes it when it says Game Over, even the winner.

That's why we play the next game, try to get to the next level, hit the button for a rematch, playing hour after hour into the night.

We never want the game to stop.

Suddenly, I'm not pacing anymore.

I feel better, like myself again.

The game is still on, and I really am good at knowing what motivates people. I always have been. It was never hard for me, it always came easily even when I was little. That's why I did so well even in elementary school, especially at math. I'm smart enough that I didn't have to study that hard to get good grades, but that wasn't what got me great grades.

Being a sociopath got me great grades.

I was the kid who deserved the A-, but got the A. I was even the kid who deserved the A, but got the A+. If there were extra credit questions, I answered them and got all the points, not just partial credit. Every grade that could possibly be rounded up, got rounded up in my favor.

Why?

My teachers liked me. By fifth grade, I could see what the teachers wanted, because it was so obvious. They wanted us to shut up, sit down, and do what they said when they said it. In other words, they wanted us not to be kids.

I learned this in fifth grade math class from Mrs. Cushing, whose left arm ended at the elbow, so she always wore a jacket and tucked her empty sleeve into her jacket pocket, like a fake hand. That year there was a weird bulge in the school enrollment, so Mrs. Cushing had thirty-five kids in her math class, which was seventeen more kids than a teacher with even two arms could handle.

You do the math.

The classes were so big they overflowed the regular school, so they moved us to mods, or modular classrooms, a fancy name for trailers with no air-conditioning.

I remember toward the end of the school year, with a heat wave roasting the mods to eighty-five degrees after lunch and Mrs. Cushing even hotter in the jacket she couldn't take off because it was the holder for her empty sleeve, and she was trying vainly to control Ricky Weissberg, the ringleader of the bad kids, who called out constantly, shoved each other in their desks, or generally caused non-stop trouble. It was the same thing every day, which gave me a headache, and I never liked Ricky anyway.

Math, I liked.

So I stole some of my mother's Valium and dropped it in Ricky's Coke at lunch. He didn't show up to math that day, or any day after I did that.

Ricky stopped existing for Mrs. Cushing and me.

I didn't know what happened to him, but school ended before he came back to class. His friends shut up without him to tell them what to do, Mrs. Cushing got her classroom back, and the heat wave broke.

And me, I got an A+ in math.

Chapter Nineteen

Early Tuesday morning, Eric stood waiting outside his own front door, or rather his ex–front door, on the welcome mat that Caitlin had ordered from Williams-Sonoma. The doormat was made of coir, whatever that was, and he remembered that she'd thought it was a bargain at almost $200. He had disagreed, but he thought it was cute that she'd wanted it so badly. He used to think that everything she did was cute. He didn't think that anymore. But evidently, somebody else did.

"Good morning, Eric," Caitlin said, opening the front door abruptly. She looked fresh and pretty, and he tried mightily not to love her anymore. Her hair was blown-dry into a sleek ponytail, and she had on a navy blue dress with her coordinating blue-and-red jacket, an outfit he recognized as going-to-court-wear. He wondered if she would wear it to court the day they fought over custody.

"Good morning, may I come in?" Eric asked, like some sort of Best Behavior Robot.

"Yes, of course." Caitlin admitted him like his Best Behavior Robot Counterpart, then stood aside, picked up her fancy purse from the console table, and grabbed her car keys. Coolly, she said, "I'll be going, and Hannah said you were going to make eggs, so please don't leave the dishes in the sink."

"I won't." Eric had never left the dishes in the sink in his life, but let it go. He stepped around her, giving her a wide berth, as if they were fighters in a marital boxing ring, except that nobody was throwing a punch because they both knew the sole spectator was watching from the kitchen island.

"Hi, Daddy!" Hannah called out, but she didn't come running in to see him as usual, though she smiled at him, a little tiredly, from behind her orange juice. She had already poured his and hers, and set the table, which was her job.

"Get the ketchup, honey!" Eric called back with forced cheer, as Caitlin went to the door, her keys jingling.

"Don't forget to lock up. Use Hannah's keys and then put them in the lock box in the garage."

"Of course." Eric had no idea why she was telling him things he already knew.

"Have a good day, Eric," Caitlin said, then waved good-bye to Hannah. "Bye, sweetie, have fun at school! I'll pick you up at aftercare."

"Bye, Mommy!" Hannah was already climbing down from the stool, and Eric left the entrance hall, plastering a smile on his face that didn't waver as he heard the front door close and Caitlin left the house. He entered the kitchen, looking around quickly. He remembered choosing the rustic Mexican tile on the floor, the white-and-blue flecked granite countertops, the white cabinets, the light blue of the walls, the oversized window behind the sink. The kitchen had been the heart of their home, but that time had passed. He understood suddenly why it didn't make sense for him to come here and fix breakfast, as if he had never left.

"Hey, pretty girl." Eric went to Hannah, tousled her hair, and gave her a kiss on the top of her head. "Scrambled or fried?"

"Can we have scrambled eggs?" Hannah righted her glasses, blinking. Her eyes seemed troubled behind them, and her mouth made an unusually sad little line. Still she looked adorable in her little pink T-shirt, jean shorts, and pink Converse sneakers.

"Of course." Eric wondered what was bothering her. Maybe Caitlin had told her about the move. "You okay?"

"Yep."

Eric knew better than to rush her. "Are you cooking today or am I?"

"I cooked last time, so it's your turn." Hannah headed for the pantry off the kitchen, where they kept the ketchup.

"Okay." Eric went to the refrigerator, opened it, and got the egg carton, butter, and Half & Half. The latter was his secret ingredient, which made his scrambled eggs so delicious. Caitlin had never liked when he made them that way, not wanting the extra calories, but now he was free to get crazy. "How's your ankle?"

"Fine, no more bandage." Hannah retrieved the ketchup, closed the cabinet door, and brought it back to the island, where she set it down with finality.

"Does it still hurt?"

"Not really."

"How did you sleep?" Eric flipped his tie over his shoulder so he didn't stain it, took a knife from the silverware drawer, carved some butter, and put it in the pan, then turned on the heat.

"Okay."

"You ready for school?"

"Yes."

"Only one week left, right?"

"Yep."

"Good." Eric got a Pyrex bowl from the cabinet, cracked an egg into it, and held out the drippy shell for her. They liked to play Eggshell Golf, a game in which they tossed eggshells into the sink and scored a point if it landed in the garbage disposal. "You want to take a shot?"

"No." Hannah shook her head.

"Why not?"

"I just don't want to."

"Okay, then watch the master." Eric raised the eggshell, faced the sink, and tossed it in a perfect arc, so it landed in the garbage disposal. "Did you see that? A hole-in-one?"

Hannah giggled, and Eric smiled too, happy that he'd gotten her out of her mood.

"I'm on fire." Eric returned to cracking the rest of the eggs in the bowl, but tossed the shells into the sink. "Are you doing okay, munchkin? You seem quiet."

"I'm *trying* to be quiet."

"Why would you do that?"

"Because, well, just because." Hannah looked away, went back to the kitchen island, and scrambled up into her seat.

Eric returned to the stove, which faced him away from her. Something was going on, but he didn't want to push it, and he certainly didn't want to be accused of pumping her for information. He wondered if Caitlin had told her that they were moving, but he sensed he would find out soon enough. He retrieved a fork from the silverware drawer, scrambled the eggs, then poured in the Half & Half.

"Daddy, am I a whiner?"

"No, not at all. Why?"

"Michelle said that her daddy said that I am."

"You're not a whiner, honey." Eric kept his back to her, stirring the eggs needlessly, because he knew that if he turned around, his face would show the anger he felt.

"He thinks I am, he said so. We went to the carnival with Mommy and Michelle and Michelle's daddy, and he said that I was a whiner because I didn't want to go on the rollercoaster."

"That's not whining, honey. You're allowed not to want to go on a rollercoaster." Eric kept his tone judgment-free, which only an experienced psychiatrist could've pulled off. He had no idea when they'd gone to a carnival. It had to have been one of the nights since he'd seen her last.

"I was afraid, but they said there was nothing to be afraid of."

"Not everybody likes rollercoasters. I don't like rollercoasters."

"Brian likes rollercoasters. And video games, too. He plays them all the time."

Brian, Eric thought, simmering. *His name is Brian.*

"He goes to different rollercoasters on vacations. Michelle loves them and they do it together and they think it's really fun."

"That's good for them, but people have fun in different ways. For example, we play Eggshell Golf. Now *that's* fun." Eric glanced over his shoulder, to see Hannah idly twirling her juice glass.

"Mommy said I didn't have to go on, but she didn't want to leave me alone, so she didn't get to go on."

"I'm sure Mommy had fun other ways." Eric flushed suddenly, hearing his own double entendre. "Did you get her some cotton candy? You know she loves cotton candy."

"Yes, she got it stuck on her sunglasses."

Good. "So Mommy had fun, in the end." Eric stirred the eggs again, almost finished.

"I'm trying not to whine so much," Hannah said after a moment.

"You know what I think, honey?" Eric composed himself, turned off the heat, and grabbed a plastic spatula from the utensils drawer because he was trained not to use a metal spatula with a nonstick pan. He ladled eggs into Hannah's plate and his own. "I think that saying what you think is much better than holding it in. Do you understand what I mean?"

"Yes."

"I always want to hear what you're thinking, and I know that your mommy feels the same way." Eric couldn't vouch for that asshole Brian. "So always let me know what's on your mind, okay?"

"Okay." Hannah picked up her fork, tilting her head down and digging into her eggs, as Eric turned to put the pan in the sink. He knew that she was mulling it over, ruminating about it, but not in the clinical sense. She processed things, just like he did.

"How are the eggs, honey?" Eric crossed to the island, sat down in his seat, and picked up his fork.

"Good." Hannah looked up at him, her fork poised, its large tines oversized in her small hand. "Guess what, Daddy."

"What?" Eric swallowed some eggs, which were delicious. It was because of the Half & Half.

"Mommy and me are going to live in Brian and Michelle's house."

Eric didn't know what to say.

Hannah blinked behind her glasses. "But I'm not allowed to whine about it because they have a pool."

Chapter Twenty

Eric felt out-of-sorts during the entire drive into work, preoccupied with the fact that Hannah and Caitlin were already moving in with Caitlin's new boyfriend. It seemed way too soon for Caitlin and it wouldn't be good for Hannah, though he had to admit to himself that it bugged him for his own reasons, too. He couldn't stop stewing about it as he parked the car in the garage, entered the hospital, and went directly to the fancy first-floor conference room for a meeting of the Pharmacy Review Board. He had so much going on that taking a meeting felt like an interruption, but it came with the territory of being Chief.

Eric tried to put Caitlin and Hannah out of his mind as he and the other members of the Board took their seats around the long table in the paneled conference room, which they used only for important committee meetings. The Board was composed of eight other department chiefs, the hospital pharmacist, and Mike Braezele from Legal, as a non-voting member. Their function was to determine which drugs would be carried in the HGH pharmacy, and today was the second meeting about a new cholesterol-lowering drug, Rostatin, which had just received FDA approval. In front of each Board member, like a corporate place setting, sat a sealed bottle of no-name water, a handful of generic butterscotch candies, an open laptop, and the slick marketing packet from Wacher Labs, the drug company that had developed Rostatin.

Eric zoned out while Chief of Cardiology Morris Brexler began presenting the argument for Rostatin. Morris had practically memorized the data supplied him by Wacher, and it never ceased to amaze Eric how many HGH meetings were composed of people reading aloud information that he could read himself. While Morris droned on, Eric paged through the Rostatin PR packet, with its shiny cover the color of freshly oxygenated blood and the interior materials printed in matching rose-colored headlines. It was some of the most expensive literature that he'd seen, and Morris was doing almost as good a sales pitch as the drug reps themselves, who weren't permitted inside the conference room, but waited in the hallway outside. Theoretically, they were there in case the doctors had any questions during the meeting, but the real reason was to pressure the committee members into approving the drug.

Eric looked over at him, returning his attention to the meeting. Morris was about Eric's age but acted a lot older, with a fastidiousness about his appearance. His sandy brown hair was always perfectly groomed, and he had small hazel eyes set close together over a long nose, with a year-round golf tan that made him look permanently prosperous.

"In sum," Morris was saying, "Rostatin is a better statin than Rosuvastatin and Atorvastatin. The science behind it is better, and we need this new drug, no question, in Cardiology. Now, any questions?"

"Yes," Eric answered, trying to keep the annoyance from his tone. "I'm trying to understand why we need to carry yet another statin. Rostatin's more expensive than Rosuvastatin and Atorvastatin, and they have a longer track record. I don't know why we have to go for the latest and the greatest, when its side effects are unproven. I don't want to see us go out on a limb. I don't know why we would."

"I couldn't disagree more. Why wouldn't we?" Morris turned his palms up in appeal, glancing around the table. "I think it's important that HGH remain in the forefront of medicine. Why should HGH be prescribing yesterday's statin?"

"Because it's safer," Eric answered flatly.

Morris slipped on his black reading glasses, with a frown. "Eric, did you read the papers I sent you?"

"Yes, I have."

"Then I don't see how you could have any doubts about Rostatin."

"Really?" Eric turned to his laptop and scrolled through the notes he'd taken from the papers. "Even in the papers you sent, the data shows that Rostatin correlates with increased incidence of muscle atrophy, and on the macro level, I'm not sure I approve of the treatment goals for this drug. In my field, we know that the brain needs cholesterol for proper function. Yet here comes another drug company that decides cholesterol has to be lowered from 200 to 190, so they can count on the market share expanding. It's cholestrol points for dollars. They know the algorithm. It's only about the money."

Morris shook his head. "One can hardly fault Wacher for trying to make money. They have shareholders to answer to, as a public company. The only question before us is should we carry Rostatin, which was approved by the FDA with flying colors."

Eric knew that FDA approval didn't go far enough, in terms of safety. "Morris, we both know that only two positive studies are required for FDA approval, and an article I found, which I emailed to you all, said in a footnote that Wacher got two negative studies, as well." Eric gestured at the packet. "I didn't see anything about the negative studies in here, and all four of the studies were commissioned by the drug company in the first place. Why didn't they show us those negative studies?"

"That's proprietary information. It contains trade secrets and the like."

Morris pressed his reading glasses onto the bridge of his nose.

"If so, then why aren't the positive studies also proprietary information? In any event, they should produce them to us before we approve Rostatin for the HGH pharmacy. I'll warrant to them I'm not going to form a competing drug company."

Everybody except Morris laughed, and Eric was beginning to wonder if the gossip about Morris was true, that he was in Wacher's pocket—literally. The Cardiology Chief had just built a vacation home in Myrtle Beach and he was putting three kids through private school. Everyone at the table knew how much Morris made at the hospital and also that his wife didn't work. Nobody could say with certainty where the extra money came from, but they couldn't say it didn't come from big pharma, either.

Eric continued, "We all know that data can be manipulated. In my field, for example, when studies showed a few years ago that certain antidepressants created suicidal ideation in adolescents, the FDA required black box warnings on them. More recently, the drug companies who manufactured the antidepressants studied the impact of the black box warning, and it should come as no surprise that they concluded the black box warnings are a disaster because fewer antidepressants are being prescribed and more teenagers are dying from suicide. It's a superficially persuasive study, but it's totally manipulated data. When you look at data underlying the studies, it shows that the suicidal patients included heroin addicts. That's just a faulty proxy."

"I don't see how that's relevant."

Eric let it go. He had made his point, and he could see heads nodding around the table. He would be damned if they'd get steamrolled into approving an unsafe drug and he loathed the corruption in the drug-approval process. Physicians at HGH ordered only those drugs stocked in the hospital pharmacy, and patients preferred to continue whatever medication they were on, after discharge. HGH was only one of the hospitals being lobbied to carry Rostatin, as the first wave of the drug's rollout across the country, and hospital approval could make or break a drug in the marketplace.

Dr. Sharon McGregor, Chief of Orthopedic Surgery, looked over. Her eyes were grayish behind wire-rimmed glasses, which set off her silvery hair, clipped in chic layers around her ears. "Morris, I agree with Eric. I feel as if we're rushing to trend on this drug. I don't want to approve it merely because it's the latest and greatest. It's not a Chanel jacket. It's okay if it's last season's."

Eric smiled. "What she said. Something about Chanel."

Everybody but Morris laughed again, even the three committee members who never said anything.

Sharon continued, growing serious. "Morris, do you need me to remind you that we did the right thing when we voted no on Calcix, that new osteoporosis drug? You see now, reports are coming out that it encourages excessive bone growth. Women are showing up with tumors in their jawbones. It's unconscionable. This committee is the last line of defense for HGH."

Otto Vinki, the diminutive Russian-born Chief of Internal Medicine, closed his laptop, which was what he did when he reached a decision. Otto was the oldest member of the committee, close to seventy-something, but his eyes retained their acutely brilliant blueness, though his bald head was covered by a network of fine white strands that looked more like bacterial spores than hair. "I also share Eric's doubts," Otto said, in a Slavic accent that would've sounded authoritative even ordering take-out pizza. "I believe that we're jumping the gun and I have an issue with the underlying theory. Statins don't treat a disease, they treat a *risk factor* for a disease. We can convince people that if they lower cholesterol, they have fewer heart attacks, but I quarrel with that treatment goal, too. I have my vote."

Everyone at the table turned, as, at the far end, the hospital pharmacist motioned for attention, raising an elegant hand with slender fingers. Mohammed Ibir was one of the most talked-about pharmacists in the system; African-American, hard-working, and only in his thirties, he was already developing ways to save HGH money. "The merits of Rostatin aside, I can tell you that it is much more expensive than Rosuvastatin and Atorvastatin. It's a third more costly, and I might add, that's typical for Wacher Labs. For example, the prices for their chemo agents are completely out of sight, and they have a new hep C drug in the pipeline that is projected to cost $84,000 per treatment cycle for one year."

"For one patient?" Eric recoiled, appalled.

"Yep." Mohammed lifted his dark eyebrows comically.

Sharon chuckled. "They have no shame!"

Morris pursed his lips, unhappy. "We're not discussing the hep C drug today, Mohammed. We have an agenda for a reason. Let's follow it."

Otto started shaking his head. "I've heard enough, and my patients await me. Shall we put this to a vote?"

"Yes," Eric answered.

Morris shook his head. "No, this is an important decision, and we allotted three meetings to discuss it before we vote."

Otto scoffed. "We don't need three meetings, Morris. We should vote."

Morris caught Mike's eye. "Mike, legally, we can't put it to a vote yet, can we? Donna's not here." He gestured to an empty chair, and Eric realized for the first time that the Chief of Pediatrics was missing.

Mike shook his head. "You're right, Morris. We can't vote without a full committee. People, we have to table discussion until next week."

Otto rolled his eyes.

Sharon groaned.

Eric sighed inwardly, then Morris turned to him.

"Eric, I hope you keep an open mind and review the studies in the meantime."

"Fine," Eric answered, wondering about that house in Myrtle Beach.

Chapter Twenty-one

Eric had just returned to the unit and tossed his messenger bag on his office chair when Amaka came to his door, with a frown. "Good morning, is something up?"

"Yes. Trouble. Perino's wife is here and she wants to take him home."

"Oh boy." Eric had been concerned there would be fallout with Perino after yesterday's incident. He headed with her down the hall toward Perino's room. "Where's Sam?"

"With Perino and the wife." Amaka fell into step beside him.

"Good. Did he call the wife after yesterday?"

"I don't know."

"Did he call Mike in Legal?"

"Yes, and they're standing by."

"Okay."

"I called security just in case, and they promise they'll be quicker this time."

"Security, really?"

Amaka shot him a confident smile. "No more instant replays of yesterday, not on my watch."

"Thanks." Eric arrived at Perino's room, immediately taking in the scene. Sam stood on the near side of the bed, looking relieved to see him, and Mr. Perino sat on the edge of the bed in his hospital gown, leaning forward slightly, staring down at the floor. His wife Linda was a short, round woman whose bleached-blonde hair was pulled back into a bristly ponytail, and she had on wide jeans and a pink sweatshirt with an iron-on dreamcatcher. She whirled around when Eric entered the room.

"Oh, here comes the big muckety-muck," Linda said, her brown eyes flashing with anger. Her forehead furrowed, and wrinkles lined her thin lips like a lifetime smoker. Her features were somewhat coarse, and she frowned in anger, stepping forward, holding Perino's streetclothes and sneakers.

"Good morning, Mrs. Perino." Eric extended his hand, but Mrs. Perino scoffed.

"You want me to shake your hand? I don't think so. You're the one who attacked my husband. I'm getting him out of here. He's not staying another minute."

Eric remained calm. He wanted to set the record straight, but he also understood how she could be upset. "Mrs. Perino, I didn't attack your husband. Here is what happened—"

"You did, too! He's got a big bump on his head because you *tackled* him. You're supposed to be taking care of him. We came here because we thought you would take care of him."

"We are taking care of him and we will continue to do so."

"He's only been here three days, and this happens? I'm taking him out of here."

"It would be against my medical advice for you to try and leave with him—"

"What do you know? You're not even his doctor. He is." Mrs. Perino pointed at Sam, who came forward, holding up a calming hand.

"Mrs. Perino, Dr. Parrish is my boss and he's fully up to speed on your husband's case."

"Oh yeah?" Mrs. Perino spun on her sneakers to face Eric again. "What were you doing when he hurt himself on the table? How did that happen?"

"I'm sorry, Mrs. Perino," Eric said, though Legal had told him that he should never apologize, because it could be construed as an admission of liability. "You're right, that shouldn't have happened—"

"How do you explain it then? Everybody here's asleep at the switch. Nobody's paying any attention to him. You just stick him in the room and ignore him."

Sam interjected, "Mrs. Perino, I explained it to you on the phone last night. You said you understood how this came about. It was your husband's reaction to an unfamiliar nurse."

Eric joined in, "Mrs. Perino, I assure you that we are giving him the treatment he needs. He wasn't being ignored, and he never would be. We work in teams and his team is absolutely dedicated." He turned to Perino, who slumped on the edge of the bed and still hadn't looked up. "Mr. Perino, how are you feeling?"

"I want . . . to go home," Perino answered, still staring at the floor. "You're not . . . helping me. Nobody here is helping me. I want to go home."

"Mr. Perino." Eric touched Perino's shoulder gently. "I'm sorry about what happened yesterday, but I can't let you go home, not until—"

"My wife wants to take me home . . . and she'll take good care of me, like before we started all this, in and out of hospitals, and I can go back to work—"

"Donnie, you don't have to talk to him." Mrs. Perino stepped closer, backing Eric away with a steady glare. "Doc, don't you dare speak to him. You're the one who could've broken his neck. He could have split his skull!"

"Mrs. Perino, please, listen to me." Eric faced her, undaunted. He could see that she was angry but underneath that, concerned for her husband's welfare. "As I've explained to your husband, his abrupt withdrawal from his meds can cause adverse and even violent reactions. That's why he hit his head on the tray, and we had to subdue him before he could hurt himself any further. That's why he needs to stay here—"

"No way," Mrs. Perino shot back, waving the streetclothes at him. "Now get out of this room so I can get him dressed and out of here."

"I can't do that, Mrs. Perino. Neither can you—"

"You can't tell me what I can and can't do! Who the *hell* do you think you are? *God?*"

"No, not at all." Eric kept his cool.

"I brought him to the hospital. I can take him out of here anytime I want. You can't stop me."

"Mrs. Perino, your husband was admitted under Section 201, after we evaluated him in the emergency room and decided to admit him. That's considered a voluntary admission, but that doesn't mean that the discharge is voluntary, as well." Eric had been unhappily surprised to learn that as a doctor, he spent too much time acting like a lawyer. The admissions and discharges of mental health patients were governed by a myriad of state laws, on top of the rules and regulations that the hospital imposed.

"What are you talking about? How could it *not* be? If I got him in, I should be able to get him out."

Eric knew it was counter-intuitive and Mrs. Perino wasn't in a listening mood. "If you recall, you were asked to sign a form agreeing to give seventy-two hours' written notice before leaving the hospital, if you are leaving against medical advice—"

"I don't have to follow your rules!"

"It's not our rules, it's state law. It says you can't take him out of the hospital today, and it's designed for your husband's well-being. You signed the form and—"

"I don't remember that! It musta been in the fine print! I didn't think I wasn't gonna be able to get him out again!"

Mr. Perino began rubbing his face, still hanging his head. "I want to go home. You can't keep me here against my will. I'm not a prisoner."

Eric addressed them both. "You have to think about what's best for him." He gestured to Perino, who by now was eyeing them both unhappily. "Please, think about what happened yesterday. Without warning, he started slamming his head into his bedside table—"

"So *you* say! Did you see it with your own eyes? Who knows what happened! I want him *out!*"

"I have no reason to disbelieve my nurse." Eric heard the sound of talking in the hallway, which told him that security was arriving.

"But legalities aside, how would you feel if you took him home and he got out of control? You wouldn't be able to help him. As you say, he could split his skull. You would never forgive yourself if something happened to him."

"Dr. Parrish?" called the security guard, as he entered the room with two other uniformed security guards. "Can we be of any assistance?"

"Not yet, thank you," Eric answered, holding up an open palm like a stop sign. "I think we will be able to figure this out together—"

Mrs. Perino gasped, then laughed derisively. "What the *hell* is this? Are you guys gonna *arrest* me? You gonna *handcuff* me? All I'm trying to do is take care of my husband!"

Eric turned to her, trying to defuse the situation. He wasn't about to have Mrs. Perino thrown out, even though it was within his power. "Security is here only in case we need them, but we're not going to need them."

"Doc, *you* might! I used to play women's softball, fast-pitch. I have a hell of an arm."

"Good to know." Eric managed a smile. He sensed the dynamic change as soon as security arrived, if only because Mrs. Perino probably felt embarrassed in front of them.

"Listen, I want to take him home, right now. He'll be fine at home with me. My sister's husband could help if I need it. They live around the corner. He works construction."

"In an emergency, you might not have time to call him. Your husband could hurt you without meaning to." Eric remembered the family history from Perino's file. "Your nieces and nephews come over a lot, don't they? What if he hurt one of the kids? Think about that."

"He would never do that," Mrs. Perino shot back, but less strident. "He never raised a hand to me or the babies. He loves those babies."

From the bed, Perino stared down at the floor, shaking his head. "I would never do that. Those kids, they're the world to me."

Eric put a hand on Perino's shoulder. "Mr. Perino, I know you wouldn't mean to, but that's not the point." Then he turned to Mrs.

Perino. "I agree with you, he would never do that when he's act-ing like himself, but he's still under the influence of these medica-tions. He's a threat to himself and his family until they're corrected and balanced in his system."

Mrs. Perino threw up her hands, her frustration plain. "That's just what Dr. Rockwell said. You guys keep telling me he's crazy because of his medication. Klonopin. Where do you think he got the medication? Valley Forge Memorial, that's where. A doctor just like you, he came in and told me my husband needed to be on those drugs. And now you're telling me that that's what made him crazy. What *is* it with you guys? Why should I trust you?"

"Because we care," Eric answered, simply. "We've been treating him and giving him the best medical care possible, and I know we can continue to help him through this transition—"

"Why can't I take him to another hospital? Can't I do that? Can't I get him transferred?"

"I think Dr. Ward has been making good progress with your husband, but that is your right, absolutely. You are free to go ahead and try to get him transferred; in that event, we would need the other hospital's confirmation that he has been admitted."

Sam looked from Eric to Mrs. Perino. "Mrs. Perino, we really have been making progress. We're following a treatment plan. It would be best for your husband if we could stay the course—"

"No, I'm leaving, I'm going to see a lawyer." Mrs. Perino glow-ered at Eric as she stormed to the door. "I'll have your license, I swear I will."

"Linda?" Perino asked, bewildered, and she stopped, putting her hand on his shoulder.

"I'll get them for this, I promise."

Chapter Twenty-two

Eric finally had a chance to sit down at the end of the day, stealing a few minutes to deal with the incident with Mrs. Perino, which he'd have to document, per hospital procedures. He was searching his system's vast internal website for the proper e-form when he heard a knock on his doorjamb.

"Eric?" Laurie appeared, dressed to go running in a white singlet and gray shorts, her long brown hair up in a clip. She grinned crookedly. "You forgot, right?"

"Right. Sorry. I can't go, I'm busy. Go without me."

"The hell I will. We're going. You need the exercise."

"I'm behind on my paperwork."

"There's not a doc in this hospital that's up-to-date on paperwork, and it's never about patient care, just insurance, and more regs, and more updates to regs to put in our binders, then a notice to throw out all the binders because we're going paperless."

"This is important. I want to log in this incident—"

"Oh, what happened? A crazy person did something crazy?" Laurie came around his desk, palmed Eric's computer mouse, and glanced at his monitor. "Bye, work."

"No, leave it." Eric reached for the mouse, just as Laurie closed out the website. "Arg."

"Get up and let's go."

"Go without me." Eric didn't feel like running. He felt like logging in Perino, answering his email, and worrying about Max, Renée, Perino, Hannah, and Caitlin.

"What's up? You look bummed."

"Remember Max Jakubowski, with the grandmother?"

"Oh, yes. How are they?" Laurie's face fell into grave lines. "I called her to follow up yesterday, but there was no answer."

"She's in hospice, and I'm worried about Max."

"The poor kid." Laurie clucked. "He was sweet."

"She appears to be hanging in there, but I know it's going to crush that kid."

"Let's get going, it will give us a chance to catch up and talk about it. Come on, you need cheering up." Laurie gave him a gentle shove on the shoulder. "You're too big a deal to run with me, now that you're number two?"

Eric smiled, leaning away from the computer keyboard. "Is this your way of saying congratulations?"

"Yes, how charming am I, on a scale of one to ten? Twenty-two?"

"I don't know, what's your ranking? Forty-something? Oh, wait. That's your age."

"Whoa, that's harsh." Laurie wrinkled her nose, comically. "We dropped to eleven."

"Ruh-roh, somebody needs to work harder."

Laurie burst into laughter. "Whatever, we're a great service, and you're not weaseling out of running."

"I can't run with you. I can't be seen with you anymore. You're bringing down my curve."

"You're milking this for all it's worth, aren't you?" Laurie grabbed his elbow, and Eric let her yank him out of his chair.

"I can't run, I have various and sundry number-two-type things to do. Things you wouldn't understand, things it would take you eleven times longer to understand."

"Oh, shut up. It's a nice night, almost no humidity, and we're going for a run."

"I didn't bring any stuff." Eric was on his feet, brushing down his pants.

"Oh please, I know where you keep it." Laurie crossed to his credenza, rolled open his bottom drawer, and pulled out a pair of wrinkled running shorts, which she held up. "Ta-da!"

Eric groaned, busted. "They have three months of crud on them."

"Please, I know what a dirtbag you are. Here, get dressed." Laurie tossed the shorts at him, and Eric caught them and threw them back at her, but they fell to the floor.

"Go away. Leave me alone."

"Your sneakers are in the drawer. I'll be waiting outside. Hurry up." Laurie left his office, closing the door behind her, and Eric picked up the shorts, crossed to the credenza, and rummaged around for a T-shirt, socks, and his sneakers. He changed quickly, then grabbed his old gym bag from the drawer, stuffed his clothes and his wallet inside, and zipped it up as he walked to the door and pulled it open, only to find Laurie facing Kristine in the hallway.

"Oh . . . hello, Kristine," Eric said, taken by surprise. He'd avoided her the entire day, but she'd managed to catch him at the exact wrong time.

"Dr. Parrish, do you have a minute?" Kristine turned to him, her lovely features arranged in a professional mask, undoubtedly for Laurie's benefit. "I need to speak with you about the Johnston case."

"Johnston?" Eric blurted out, before he had time to catch himself. There was no patient named Johnston on the unit. "Let's talk about it tomorrow—"

"I remember you, Kristine," Laurie interrupted him, arching an eyebrow. "We met Friday night in the ED. You're a medical student, correct?"

"Yes, why?" Kristine's eyes narrowed.

"If you have a question on a case, you should go ask an attending. You're not supposed to go directly to the Chief. He's not your colleague, he's your boss."

Eric put a hand on Laurie's arm. He didn't know what was going on between the two women, but it was time to cut it off. "Laurie, we should be going. Kristine, we can talk about it another—"

"Dr. Fortunato," Kristine shot back at Laurie, her resentment undisguised. "You don't know how we do things in Wright. Dr. Parrish doesn't care about hospital hierarchy. He's very accessible and he'd never let his ego get in the way of patient care. Maybe you do things differently where you work—"

"Stop right there." Laurie cut Kristine off, pointing at her. "I'm Chief of the Emergency Department, so I do more than work in the ED, I *run* it."

Kristine sneered. "Anybody can run a chop shop."

Laurie's mouth dropped open. "*What* did you say, child?"

Eric stepped in, facing Kristine. "Kristine, check yourself, please. Dr. Fortunato is entitled to your respect and so is her ED. Understand?"

"Yes." Kristine looked hurt, but Eric wasn't about to cater to her when she was so clearly in the wrong. He gripped Laurie's arm and moved her bodily down the hall.

"Laurie, let's go."

"Are you frigging *kidding me*?" Laurie looked back at Kristine as Eric dragged her away. "I cannot believe she said that! I want an apology."

"Forget it." Eric kept Laurie moving.

"I won't forget it! How dare she!"

"She's just a kid."

"She's way out of line! What's her problem? Talk about *grandiose*."

Eric steered Laurie past the nurses' station, where Sam and Amaka looked up curiously. "Good night, everybody," he called to them, waving good-bye.

"Good night, Chief!" Sam called back, and Amaka waved.

Laurie tugged her arm from Eric's grasp when they reached the locked exit door to the unit. "Seriously, Eric, that girl needs to be schooled."

"I know, and that's why I called her out on it." Eric dug in his pocket for his keys, found them, and unlocked the door to the unit, letting them both into the airlock.

"What is her deal? I'd fire her ass."

"We don't employ her, remember? She's on rotation, she'll be gone in a week." Eric unlocked the outer door, suddenly hating that he was always behind locked doors, feeling boxed in by the psych unit, the weirdness of the situation with Kristine, the dispute over Perino, the dilemma presented by Max and Renée, even his legal trouble with Caitlin over Hannah.

"I wouldn't give her a good recommendation, that's for sure. You should ding her ass."

"I just did." Eric unlocked the door, let them both into the hallway, and went ahead to the elevator, where the waiting crowd was talking, looking at their smartphones, or plugged into earphones.

"I mean give her a bad recommendation."

"Let's talk about it on the run."

"Okay." Laurie curled her lip. "I'll nag you for all six miles."

"*Six miles?*" Eric croaked, just as the elevator arrived.

Later, the sun was dipping and the air was cooling as they hit the trail that wound behind the hospital, strip mall, and Glencroft Corporate Center. Eric huffed and puffed, struggling until his body remembered that he was in decent shape even if his wind was terrible. He had yet to go running in his new neighborhood. He hadn't been ready to replace his beloved run on his old street.

"So what are you going to do about that medical student?" Laurie ran easily, swinging her long, lean arms and pumping her strong, well-muscled legs, barely breaking a sweat.

"Ignore her." Eric decided not to confide in Laurie about Kristine. He knew she'd just give him grief.

" 'Chop shop' my *ass.*"

"You made your point."

"What difference does that make?" Laurie glanced over with a grin. "If I stopped talking after I made my point, I'd never say anything."

Eric laughed, and the two old friends fell into an easy stride. He reminded himself that he had to start running again, though he doubted that this new trail would fit the bill, since it was the antithesis of nature unspoiled: a strip of paved asphalt congested with corporate running teams, cyclists in full spandex regalia, and middle-aged women walking fluffy dogs. Park benches bearing memorial plaques lined the route, as well as tall kiosks with trail maps, metal turnstiles at the end of each segment, and pushbutton traffic lights with speakers that spouted incomprehensible recorded messages.

"Nice trail, isn't it?" Laurie said, swinging her arms as she ran.

"Are you joking?"

"No, not at all. I think it's the only thing I've said in recent memory that wasn't a joke." Laurie chuckled. "In fact, I just surprised myself. Who knew I could play it straight?"

Eric smiled. "I did."

"Aw, thanks. Aren't you nice?"

"I'm a number-two kind of guy."

"Ha!" Laurie shoved him playfully, and behind her a pair of female runners jogged past, followed by a teenage skateboarder spreading his arms like wings, a carefree blur of tattooed arms.

Suddenly Eric heard a phone ringing and they both checked their pockets, but it was his phone. He stopped running and slid his phone from his pocket. "Excuse me."

"No worries." Laurie ran in place, keeping her heart rate up.

Eric checked the screen, but he didn't know the number, so he pressed Answer Call. "Eric Parrish here."

"Dr. . . . Parrish?" said someone, crying hard. "Oh no . . . oh no . . ."

"Yes, who is this?" Eric asked, alarmed. He didn't recognize the voice through the hoarse, choking sobs.

"It's . . . Max and . . . my . . . my grandmother, she just . . . *died*."

Chapter Twenty-three

"Max, oh no," Eric said, stricken. Laurie stopped running in place. A cyclist looked over with a neat swivel of his helmeted head as he sped past.

"She was just . . . talking to me." Max's sobs choked his words. "She was fine . . . then all of a sudden . . . her eyes got really . . . wide and she . . . she . . . made a sound, a really *scary* sound . . . it came out of her mouth . . . like a gurgle . . . and her eyes stopped and she just . . . *died*."

"Oh my God, this just happened? I'm so sorry." Eric could imagine how awful it must've been for Max, who had probably never seen death before.

"There's nobody here . . . but me . . . and her . . . it happened after the nurse left for the night . . . I called the hospice . . . and she's going to call the funeral people . . . but I just don't know what to do . . . I just don't understand, she was right there . . . she was *looking at me*."

"So you're there, alone? With her?"

"Yes, they said to wait . . . and they'd come, they'd call . . . but this is horrible . . . I can't believe it . . . what am I gonna do?"

"Max, if you want, you can come to my office." Eric wished he could reach through the phone and calm the boy. "We can talk about it. I can help—"

"No, no, no . . . I don't want to see anybody . . . I mean, we were talking about *Golden Girls,* and she was saying how funny Estelle was . . . I don't know what to do . . . it's just so horrible . . . I can't even deal."

"You can come later tonight if you want." Eric glanced at Laurie, who was listening, alarmed. "Anytime at all, you can call me and come to my office, or we can talk over the phone. I'm completely available to you—"

"It won't help, nothing can help . . . now she's gone, she's really gone, like . . . It's like, how can anybody's last words be about Estelle . . . that's just *not right,* and if I told her that now, she would laugh and laugh, and I shook her but it's the weirdest thing . . . I mean, I never saw . . . and she just looks so, she's like herself but she's *not herself* . . . she looks like she's asleep but she's not, *she's not.*" Max wailed, emitting a cry of grief so raw that Eric felt it rattle his very bones.

"Max, I promise you, you will get through this, and I will help you—"

"No . . . I don't want to see you anymore . . . I don't want to see *anybody* anymore . . . I don't have anybody, there's nothing . . . I just want to die. I wish I were dead—"

Suddenly, Max's voice cut off, and they were disconnected. Eric pressed End and Recall with a shaking hand.

Laurie puckered her lower lip. "I feel so bad for him," she said quietly.

"I don't like what he just said, that he 'wanted to die.'"

"Oh no."

"I don't want him to be alone right now. At this point, he's a suicide risk." Eric heard the ringing stop, but the call went to voicemail, so he said into the phone, "Max, it's Dr. Parrish calling you back. Please call me. I'm here and I can help you. Good-bye, and call anytime, no matter how late." Eric hung up, his thoughts racing. "I don't have the mother's number. I think he told me she works at an insurance company. God, I thought I'd get more time with him before she passed."

"How many times have you seen him, since Friday? Once?"

"Twice, but still." Eric pressed Recall, to try to get Max back again.

"Don't beat yourself up. You couldn't have mitigated this." Laurie rested a hand on Eric's shoulder.

"I could have, I should have." Eric listened to the phone ring. Three cyclists powered past, their bike chains whirring.

"How? You saw him both days of the weekend. What more could you have done?" Laurie squeezed his shoulder. "That's more than anybody else would've done."

"I knew he was in trouble, I've been worried about him." Eric heard the call go to voicemail, but didn't leave another message. He exhaled, trying to expel the tightness from his chest. "I almost wish he'd been sick enough to admit. Then I could've kept an eye on him. But I couldn't, honestly."

"He wasn't sick enough, even I could tell that."

"Not at that time, but he couldn't withstand her death."

"You can't admit him because he'll *become* a candidate for admission. It doesn't work that way. That's the law, and you know it as well as I do."

"He fell between the cracks, and I let him fall."

"You worried about suicide?"

"It's possible."

"Oh boy." Laurie frowned. "I'd send the crisis team out from the ED, but they're already on a call. Did you prescribe him anything?"

"I gave him a script for fluoxetine, twenty milligrams, a starting dose. There are thirty pills in a bottle."

"That's not dangerous, is it?"

"No," Eric answered, tense. "It won't kill him even if he takes the whole bottle. He'll just feel like crap. Fluoxetine is safer than the older antidepressants. Even the higher dosages, like forty or sixty milligrams, won't kill you either, even if taken all at once."

"That's good."

"I'm going to send the police over there." Eric raised his phone and called 911. The phone was answered immediately, and he said,

"Hello, this is Dr. Eric Parrish of Havemeyer General Hospital and I need a welfare check on a minor patient named Max Jakubowski, whom I regard as a suicide risk. He's a seventeen-year-old, and his grandmother just passed away at their home of natural causes. I need you to send someone to the house to check on him."

"We will, Doctor," the female dispatcher answered. "Do you have the address, and what is his name again?"

Eric scrolled to the contact list and gave her the information. He realized Max must have called from a house phone, which was why his phone hadn't recognized the number.

"What is your address and phone number, Dr. Parrish?"

Eric gave her his information. "Please get a cruiser over there, right away. Don't wait."

"They're on their way as we speak."

"Did they leave from the police station? Because I think that's about twenty minutes from the house."

"Dr. Parrish, I only work in dispatch. I can't tell you where they left from but I promise you, they'll be there as soon as they can."

"Can you ask them to call me when they get there?"

"That's not procedure—"

"Please, have the uniformed officer give me a call, it's a matter of life and death." Eric wasn't about to take no for an answer. He'd met many of the uniformed police of the surrounding townships when they'd brought his patients to the hospital ER. They would be happy to help him if they could, procedure or no.

"Okay, I'll have them call, Dr. Parrish."

"Thanks so much. Good-bye." Eric hung up the phone, his mouth dry. The next few hours would be critical for Max's safety, and he'd be on tenterhooks until he heard the boy's voice again. "We should get a call."

"Good. Why don't we sit down? There's a bench right there."

"I'm fine." Eric wanted to remain standing. He felt more in control, God knew why. He tried to imagine Max, sitting by himself in the empty house, alone with the corpse of his beloved grandmother, the only true mother he'd ever known.

"You don't look fine, you look pale. Come on, let's sit down." Laurie gestured to a cedar bench with a memorial plaque on the back.

"I'm trying to think what else I can do."

"There isn't any more you can do. You have to wait for him or the police to call back. Come on, we're in the bike path, standing here." Laurie crossed to the bench and motioned him over.

"I wish he would call back." Eric followed her and sat down, checking his phone reflexively.

"He will, don't worry."

"He's not ready for this." Eric rubbed his face, self-soothing. "I just wish I'd had more time with him. A week, maybe two. I could've gotten him stabilized."

"It wouldn't have helped. He wouldn't be more prepared to lose her two weeks from now than he is now."

"That's not true. I could do a lot in two weeks, especially if I saw him every day."

"You're not being rational. You're just upset." Laurie looked over, her gaze calm and practical, accustomed to crisis without drama.

"I'm upset but I'm not wrong. I can build the foundation for a therapeutic relationship quickly if the patient is motivated, and Max was motivated. If anything, he was needy."

"Eric, you can't do everything. You're not Superman."

"Still." Eric tried to shake it off, but couldn't. "I'll never forgive myself if he hurts himself."

"You really care about this kid, don't you?"

"I care about all my patients."

"I know, but this one, it seems different." Laurie cocked her head. "That's called enmeshment, isn't it, when you get too close to the patient? Do you think that's happening?"

"No," Eric answered, vaguely defensive. "I admit that I like him. You do, too."

"I do, but not like you." Laurie softened, and Eric realized in that moment that his eyes had filmed.

"I feel for him, what can I say?" Eric knew that he felt differently about Max, more sympathetic. Maybe because Max was fatherless and Eric had no son, and lately he even felt as if he were losing Hannah. Or maybe because Max was so alone, having lost someone he really loved. "The term isn't 'enmeshment.' As a technical matter, it's more like countertransference."

"I know I'm supposed to know what that means, but I don't."

"For example, transference is when a patient with father issues treats you like a father. Countertransference is when a psychiatrist begins to treat a patient a certain way, because of issues in his own life." Eric paused, challenging himself. "I suppose I treat Max in a fatherly way, maybe because of what's going on with my divorce, but I don't think it's gone as far as countertransference. But I'll monitor it, in any event."

"I'm not faulting you. I'm just saying that it's unusual, even for Captain Emotion."

Eric managed a smile at the old nickname. It had been a long time, since medical school, that they'd confided in each other, and it felt strange now that he was single. He tried to move past the awkward moment. "I wish I could go over there and check on him. I wish I could tell him it's going to be okay, that he will get through this, and that his grandmother would want him to get through this."

"I understand, you want to fix it but you can't."

"Right." Eric raked his fingers through his hair. He checked his phone, willing it to ring. "I can't stand just sitting here *not* doing anything. You can't solve a problem by remote control."

Laurie nodded. "I get that. Docs are born to fix things, or at least to try, as you say. I fix things all day long. I sew it, patch it, debride it, suture it. I know that people think ED docs are like high-end plumbers, but at least I get to fix it, if it's humanly possible. I tell my staff, if we lose anybody, it can never be because we didn't try hard enough."

Eric looked over. "Since when did you get so insightful?"

Laurie grinned. "Not just another pretty face."

Eric laughed, realizing, maybe for the first time, that Laurie really did have a pretty face. Best of all, she exuded a relaxed air, and her comfort in her own skin had always made him feel comfortable, despite her get-to-the-point bluntness.

"I have an idea." Laurie leaned back in the bench. "Forget the run. Let's sit here until they call back, then after that, we can have dinner. I'll make it for you, and you can see my new apartment. You still a G & T guy?"

"Yes." Eric smiled, surprised she remembered his drink.

"Good. I have Tanqueray and I might even have a lime or two. What do you say? You up?"

Eric managed a smile. "You had me at 'forget the run.'"

Chapter Twenty-four

Eric followed Laurie inside her apartment, checking his phone. He'd driven his car behind Laurie's, his worry about Max intensifying. Neither Max nor the police had called him back, and he'd called the 911 dispatcher asking if the cops had been at Max's house yet, but the dispatcher didn't know.

"Still no word?" Laurie called over her shoulder, tossing her keys and purse onto a pine console table.

"No, I called the police and also left another message for Max, but I haven't heard from him, either."

"I'll make dinner, and you try to chill out. I'm sure we'll hear from them soon." Laurie gestured around the room. "What do you think of the place?"

Eric tried to rally, looking around the boxy two-bedroom on the first floor of a brick complex of low-profile, garden-type apartments. The living room/dining room was a large white rectangle filled with a dining set of dark wood that coordinated with a big tan sofa, over-sized chairs, lacquered black bookshelves, and a matching entertainment case. There was a sisal rug, and two windows at the far end of the room that overlooked a tall green hedge meant to hide the parking lot. The windows had actual curtains, which was more than Eric could say for himself. Vibrant modern art lined the walls, with colorful abstract shapes that looked like Rorschach tests, but he kept that thought to himself. He answered, "The place is great."

"Really?" Laurie flashed him an uncertain smile, and Eric realized that she wanted reassurance, a vulnerable side to her he hadn't seen before.

"Yes, I like the art. I don't have any art up yet."

"Thanks. They're old-school Matisse prints. They're my favorite. Aren't they so pretty?"

"Yes." Eric realized he'd inadvertently said the right thing.

"Do you want water or a gin and tonic?" Laurie walked into a pretty, clean kitchen with sunny yellow walls and butcher-block countertops.

"Just water, please. I have to keep my wits about me."

"Okay." Laurie opened the door to the refrigerator, which was stocked to the gills. Green kale, romaine, and beets in plastic bags stuffed the shelves, next to strawberries, blueberries, and plastic tubs of chopped pineapple and cantaloupe.

"Your fridge looks like a produce section. You have all this, for yourself?" Eric stopped short of asking, *why?*

"Of course. I count, don't I? I love to cook." Laurie gestured at the food comically, like a game show hostess. "What would you like for dinner? I can make salmon with dill, sole with butter and capers, or a nice, big salad."

"Whatever's quickest and easiest."

"A salad, okay? That'll be quickest."

"Perfect. Great." Eric glanced at the phone, and the time read 7:32. It had been almost an hour since Max had called him, and he couldn't imagine what must be going on. Maybe the police had been delayed in getting there or maybe they'd come and gone. Eric thought about Hannah, realizing that he might be too busy later to call her. "Laurie, do you mind if I make a quick call? I want to call Hannah."

"No worries, go ahead." Laurie finished pouring him a glass of water from a Britta pitcher and brought it over to him. "You can go in my girl cave if you want privacy. If you stay here, the reception is best by the door. I think there's a cell tower down or something."

"Thanks." Eric walked to the door, scrolled to Favorites, and pressed Call. The phone rang, then a recording came on saying, "This number is no longer in service. Please call customer service between the hours of nine and five, Monday through Friday." Eric hung up. He must've dialed wrong or maybe it was the faulty reception. He pressed Hannah's number again, the phone rang, but again, it was picked up by the recording, which said, "This number is no longer in service . . ." Eric hung up, angry. "Unbelievable."

"What's the matter?" Laurie looked over from the kitchen, where she was chopping romaine lettuce on a white cutting board.

"Hannah's phone's been disconnected. I think Caitlin is playing games."

"Why would she do that?"

"We're fussing over custody. In fact, we're about to have a custody battle."

"Whoa, I didn't know." Laurie paused in her chopping.

"It just happened, I decided." Eric's gut tensed. "I'm calling my lawyer. Bear with me."

"Go for it." Laurie resumed chopping.

Eric scrolled to find Susan's cell number and pressed Call. The phone rang but went to voicemail, and he left a message: "Susan, please call me as soon as you can. I think Caitlin has disconnected Hannah's phone." Eric hung up, then scrolled back to Favorites, where Caitlin's cell number was still listed. He pressed Call, and the phone rang and rang, then went to voicemail. "Damn it!"

"She's not picking up?"

"No. We have to talk through lawyers now." Eric rubbed his forehead, listening to his ex-wife's cheery outgoing message, which tonight was making his blood boil. When the beep sounded, he reminded himself to sound calm, for the record: "Caitlin, I'm trying to reach Hannah to say good night, like I do every night, but for some reason her phone has been disconnected. I'm sure this must be just a mistake. Can you please ask her to call me to say good night? Thanks so much." Eric hung up, exhaling.

Laurie looked over. "You should have that gin and tonic."

"No, I'm fine," Eric said, getting his bearings. His marital issues paled in comparison to what was going on with Max. He prayed to God the boy hadn't hurt himself. "I don't know what's keeping the cops. Would your staff call you if he were brought into the ED?"

"Yes, I called and asked them to on the way here. The cops are probably handling the situation, they're pretty good in Radnor." Laurie brought two blue-patterned plates to the table and set them down.

"I could call one of the higher-ups in the precinct." Suddenly, Eric's cell phone started ringing. He looked down, didn't recognize the number on the screen, and answered it immediately. "This is Dr. Parrish."

"Dr. Parrish, Officer Charles Gambia. We are at the Teichner residence on 310 Newton Road, in Berwyn."

Eric recognized the address as Max's. "Yes, how's the boy, Max Jakubowski? Can I speak with him?"

"He's not here, Dr. Parrish."

"What?" Eric asked, surprised.

"He's not here. His mother is here, and the body of the deceased has been taken away by representatives from the funeral home."

"But where's the boy?" Eric felt more worried than ever.

"He wasn't here when we arrived. We did a walk-through but the house is clear."

Eric's thoughts raced. "Does his mother know where he is?"

"No."

"When did you get there?"

"We arrived at approximately 6:45 P.M., Doctor. We were in the vicinity and came over directly."

Eric pieced it together. So the police had gotten there quickly, but too late to stop Max from leaving. Still that was forty-five minutes ago. "Why did you wait to call me? Were you looking for him?"

"We've been dealing with the mother since then, Marie Jakubowski. She's in quite a state."

"She must be, with her mother just having passed. Could I speak with her?"

"Uh, well—" Officer Gambia hesitated. "I'll ask her. She's right here."

"Thanks." Eric heard a commotion on the other end of the line, then the voice of a crying woman, saying something he couldn't understand.

"Dr. Parrish?" Officer Gambia said, back on the phone. "She doesn't want to take the call. Excuse me, but my partner and I have to go. We got another call."

"Okay, but what about Max? Is there anything you can do to locate him?"

"He's not a missing person, so we can't put out an APB."

"But isn't there anything else?"

"No. Check back later, give us a call."

"I understand. Thanks."

"Good-bye." Officer Gambia hung up the phone.

Eric pressed End, his thoughts churning. He turned around to see that Laurie had set the dining-room table for a great dinner. In a wooden bowl in the center of the table was a huge romaine salad with sliced avocado, roasted peppers, and crumbled feta on top, next to a plate of crusty seeded bread and a block of butter. Beside one of the plates stood a glass of water and a tall, icy gin and tonic.

"Any luck?" Laurie rested a hand on the table, eyeing him with concern.

"No." Eric felt a twinge of regret, but he had to go. "Dinner looks amazing, but will you forgive me if I can't stay?"

Chapter Twenty-five

It was dark by the time Eric reached the warren of half-stone split-level homes in the downscale, seventies-era development, and he cruised up a curved street that had no streetlamps, dark except for the lights, flickering television sets, and glowing computer monitors inside the houses. He pulled up opposite Max's house, parked, and cut off the ignition, scanning the scene.

Max's house was two stories tall and so low-profile that it was barely visible behind the wildly overgrown hedges. A dark Toyota sat parked in the driveway; it had to belong to Max or his mother. The house had no outside light fixture, but the glow of the curtains told him that someone was home.

Eric got out of the car, pocketed his keys, and hurried across the street, walking up the driveway. He reached the small porch in front of the house, which had a narrow roof that did little to shelter a few white PVC chairs, a tattered beach chair, and a grimy white ashtray shaped like a cigarette that read Butt Out! There was a large picture window in the front of the house, but the curtains were completely drawn, though he could hear the sound of a television inside.

He knocked on the weathered front door and waited a few minutes, but there was no answer. He knocked again, harder, then waited again. He wasn't worried about whether coming here constituted a boundary violation; on the contrary, now that he feared Max was suicidal, Eric had an obligation to inform his mother of that fact. Abruptly the door opened to reveal the outline of a short woman in a bathrobe, whose features he couldn't see because she stood in silhouette. He assumed it was Eric's mother. "Mrs. Jakubowski?"

"Yeah. I'm Marie."

"I'm Dr. Parrish, a psychiatrist who's been treating your son Max. Please accept my condolences on the loss of your—"

"What psychiatris'? I don't know anything about a psychiatris.'"

"May I come in and talk with you, about Max?"

"Okay." Marie pulled the door open, edging backwards unsteadily, trailing the hem of her bathrobe, and Eric stepped inside the house. The air smelled like chilled cigarette smoke, and in the light, he could see in Marie the telltale signs of an alcoholic: jowly cheeks, watery bloodshot blue eyes, deep-set lids at half-mast, and broken capillaries on her cheeks and nose. She was probably in her late forties but looked a decade older.

"Marie, I'm concerned about Max. He's not here, is he?" Eric glanced around the small living room, with the curtains shut tight on the front window and covering the top half of another window, which held a rattling air conditioner. An oversized brown couch sat pressed against the paneled wall next to a brown plaid recliner, matching a faded brown-patterned rug. Brown and blue prescription bottles cluttered a heavy end table, which also held a full glass ashtray, dirty plastic cups sweating circles onto the wood surface, and an open bottle of Smirnoff's. Eric sensed the house was otherwise empty, because the rooms beyond the living room were dark and quiet.

"No, he's not here. Like I *told* the cops, he's not here. He's gone, vamoosed, see ya later, alligator." Marie slurred her words, her gaze unfocused, and Eric, who had seen so many impaired patients in the ED that he was almost as good as some of the police at accurately assessing the level of alcohol impairment, placed her at twice the legal limit. He doubted she'd be able to understand him, but he had to try anyway.

"Marie, I came because I'm worried about him. I'm very concerned that in the aftermath of your mother's death, he may try to harm himself—"

"Are you really Max's psychiatris'? Who pays for *that*?" Marie snorted. "Don't tell me, lemme guess. My *sainted mother*, right?"

Eric was appalled, if not completely surprised, by her reaction. "Yes, your mother did pay, but do you understand what I'm telling you? I'm telling you that Max could be suicidal. It's important that we find him, right away. Was he here when you were here?"

"Yeah, until I tol' him to call whoever and get the damn commode and bed outta the room." Marie made a vague motion, flapping her hand at the room in general. Her blue chenille bathrobe fell open, revealing that she was nude underneath, but the prospect was hardly appealing. "I didn' wanna look at a *toilet* in the damn living room, every time I come in the damn house. I'm the lady of the house, but they never treated me that way, especially him, and he started yellin' and he lef', he ran right outta the door, just took off without another word, just like his dad, you know what they say about the acorn and the tree."

Eric felt a pang of sympathy for Max, imagining the boy grief-stricken and his mother talking about toilets. "Do you have any idea where Max could be? Any places he liked to hang, like Starbucks, the library, the mall, anything?"

"Starbucks? Are you kidding? God knows where he goes, ever. Only place in the mall he ever goes is that damn video game store. You wanna know where he is, ask my mother. Oops. Oh, right." Marie cackled, a darker echo of her mother's mischievous cackle. "I tell you this, those two were peas inna pod, and she took *good care* of him in that will of hers. She always told me she wasn't leaving me *a dime*, it was all going to him." Marie frowned suddenly. "Now, what kinda thing is that to say to your only daughter, your *only child*? You're the psychiatris', isn't that *toxic*? That's a *toxic person* right there. Same with the life insurance, she already told me he was her beneficiary. The only way *I* get any money is if he *dies*."

Eric ignored her talk, which struck him as profoundly ugly in the circumstances. "You need to think and help me—"

"Max, Max, Max, that's all I ever hear, everybody's worried about Max. My mother, all the time worried about Max, he has no friends, he spends too much time on the computer, that's all I ever hear."

"Marie, time is of the essence here. Did he have any friends at all, at school or at work, even from the neighborhood, that you know of—"

"Nobody needs to worry about Max, believe me. I can tell you right now, he's a liar, a what-do-you-call-it, a *pathological* liar. You can't trust him." Marie pushed a stray strand of light brown hair from her face, trying to smooth it back into a long, messy ponytail. "He says he doesn't have friends, but I hear him on the phone at night, talkin' to somebody."

Eric's ears pricked up. "Who, do you know? Another kid from school? Or work? A gamer?"

"God knows, you can't believe *anything* he says, I know. Nobody knows him better than I do, *nobody*. I nursed that boy and he looked at me funny from the minute he was born. There's something really weird about that kid and there always was. He's not like everybody else. He's not normal—"

"But who was he talking to? Did you tell the police about that?"

"No, he coulda been talkin' to himself, for all I know, or trying to fool me." Marie waved him off, seeming to take it back. "You think you know Max, but you don't. He got you fooled. That kid is *crazy*. His father was the same way, but he wasn't as smart, didn't hide the crazy as well, just had a weird look in his eyes. Max pulls that little-boy-lost routine, but believe me, I know better. That kid is a master manipulator. He manipulated my mother and got everybody at that school fooled. He's so damn smart. He was in gifted from third grade, and if he's a genius, he's an evil genius."

Eric doubted that Max went to the mall, so there had to be another place. "Did he go to the school, to the park, a ballfield, or a place like that?"

"No, no, no no, he should be here, but he's nowhere to be found. Do you think he cares about me? It's *my* mother who died, not his. *His* mother is alive and sitting here by herself, all by my lonesome. Zack had to go out of town, and Max knows that, but does he care?

Is he here to take care of me in my hour of need? I ask you, what about me? Why doesn't *anybody* worry about me? Why doesn't *my own mother* worry about me? They don't show me any respect, they *kick me when I'm down,* they don't know what it's like, they don't know my pain, they have no idea." Marie seemed to pause, focusing on Eric anew, with a deep frown. "I want to know who the *hell* you think you are, *Doctor.* Where you get off seeing my son without my permission, without me even *knowing.* He's not eighteen yet, do you know that? How is *that* legal? You tell me."

"It is legal," Eric answered, calmly. "Even though Max is a minor, he can seek counseling without parental consent."

"I don't believe that for a single minute, that can't be legal, that's definitely *not* legal!"

"It is, but I have an obligation to speak with you if he becomes suicidal, and that's why I came tonight. I'm concerned that—"

"What does he talk about when he sees you, huh?" Marie sniffed, arching a thin eyebrow. "He probably tells you all about me, they always blame everything on the mother, don't they? What does he say about me?"

"I'm not permitted to tell you what we talk about—"

"What do you mean you're *not permitted* to tell me? He's my son, my only child. I'm his mother. I have every right to know." Marie folded her arms, bouncing on the balls of her barefeet but almost tripping on her hem. "I want to know what he said about me, or I'm not telling you a *damn* thing."

"Marie, if we can cooperate we can help him—"

"How'm I gonna live now? What am I gonna live on? My salary, it sucks! Max knows where her money is, like three different accounts, plus she gets Social Security. I looked through his room and his desk but I couldn't find it. I tried to get into his laptop, too, but he has it under a password. Did he talk to you about the money? Did he tell you where the money is?"

"I can't answer what he did or didn't talk about in therapy," Eric answered, but he was starting to form a plan.

"Then how did they pay you, by check? I want to know that account number. I have every right to know where that money is, every penny of it. I'm going to get what's coming to me and I'm not going to let that kid, or *her,* do me out of what's mine." Marie gritted her teeth in anger. "God knows where they hid her checks, you'd think there would be one around, but that kid is such a *sneak.*"

"You know, if I could see his room, I might be able to find the accounts, or something that can lead to the accounts." Eric thought that if he could look around in Max's bedroom, maybe he could find something that would tell him where the boy had gone. His professional instincts told him that it might be a boundary violation, but he wasn't going to stand on technicalities if it could save Max's life.

"Why the hell not? Follow me." Marie walked away, somewhat unsteadily, lifting her bathrobe so she didn't trip.

Eric followed her to the left, where there was a short stairwell.

"Let there be light." Marie clawed the wall, hitting a light switch on the second try. A frosted glass fixture went on overhead, illuminating a brown carpet in a stairwell in need of vacuuming. Scuffmarks marred the off-white walls, and nothing was hung on the wall going up the stairs.

"Here let me help." Eric worried Marie would fall even though she put a hand on the banister, so he guided her by the elbow, climbing the stairs.

"Aren't you such a gentleman?" Marie chuckled under her breath, and they reached the second-floor landing together, where she flipped on the other overhead light. There was a short hallway with three closed doors, but only one had a large black poster of a robot/camera, which read Portal. It looked like it had come from a video game, and Eric didn't know if it was a pun, but he followed Marie as she opened the door and went inside.

Eric crossed the threshold, though red flags started waving. He had never been in the bedroom of a patient and sensed that his colleagues, and maybe even Arthur, would have disapproved, but a life was at stake. The air smelled fresh, the white walls unscuffed, and Eric sensed that Max's bedroom was probably the neatest, cleanest room in the house, an oasis amid the clutter, chaos, and grime.

It was a small room, with two windows on either side of a queen bed with a gray-and-white striped comforter, neatly tucked in around the sides. On the left was a wall-mounted metal bookshelf that held school books, lined up, and underneath that, a black computer desk with two large monitors, a keyboard with a plastic cover, and an array of video game joysticks and controllers, one shaped like a gun. The floors were hardwood, uncovered except for a blue rag rug beside the bed. Eric didn't see anything that would lead him to know more about where Max could be or who he had been on the phone with.

Eric walked to the desk. "Marie, would you mind if I looked in his drawers, just to see if there's anything that can help?"

"Suit yourself," Marie answered, seeming to have forgotten Eric's pretense for searching the room, that he was looking for bank accounts. Maybe she'd realized that he'd wanted to snoop or maybe she didn't care.

"Thanks." Eric opened the desk drawers, one by one, and inside them were school supplies, Bubblicious, Skittles, comic books, manga books, and old boxes of Magic cards. Eric drew the line at going into the computer and he didn't know the password anyway.

"You see he keeps everything neat, he always did, even put his toys away when he was little, stacked up all the blocks, the crayons in the right holes in the box, he dried off all his own paintbrushes, all by himself. He never gave me any trouble, not really."

"He painted?" Eric straightened up, remembering the water-paints that Max had described and his ritual of saying the colors.

"Loved to paint, painted all the time, I stuck the pictures somewhere, I saved a lot of them."

"I'd love to see them." Eric eyed the video game posters that lined the far walls, neatly tacked up in a row like an alternative art gallery of robots, zombies, transformers, and paramilitary types, with anonymous masks for faces, above Sine Mora, Assura's Wrath, The Walking Dead, World of Warcraft, Game of Thrones, Diablo III, Tomb Raider, Dark Souls 2, Wolfenstein: The New Order.

"Video games, right? We *get* it." Marie snorted. "I'll tell you, once that boy latches onto something, he latches onto something. He's obsessed with these games, I tell you that. He used to try to explain it to me, what the plots were like, when he was a little boy. He used to talk to me, we got along good then, just him and me."

Eric heard the tone of her voice changing, softening, and her gaze had strayed from the posters to a single photograph, on the night table. It was of Marie herself as a lovely young mother holding a giggling baby boy, who must've been Max. Mother and son were looking into each other's eyes, and Marie was smiling at her baby boy, who reached his pudgy hand toward her face.

"He was so cute then, so smart, even then, he was a good baby, really good baby, he never cried or fussed, wherever you put him, there he stayed, looking at books or DVDs, he would watch anything, even then."

"How old was he, in that photo?"

"There, he was one, just cut his teeth, had a full set, that's a sign of intelligence, you know." Marie's eyes filmed. "We were close then, even 'til he was five or six or seven. When he first started school, I used to read to him at night, and he loved that."

Eric thought of Hannah, roughly the same age.

"I gave this to him for his birthday." Marie walked over to the bookshelf, and next to the trig textbook sat a small plush rabbit of threadbare yellow, folded over on itself, collapsed. She picked it up.

"Which birthday, do you remember?" Eric asked, to get her talking.

"Sure, his third, we lived in Delaware then and we rented a nice place, a studio apartment near Lewes. That was our bes' time, our *best* time together, just him and me."

"When did you move from there?"

"When he was four, almos' right after, I remember this bunny was all he wanted for his birthday, he saw it in the Kmart and he had to have it, and he loved it." Marie returned the toy to the bookshelf and tried to make it sit up, but it doubled over again, his ears flopping forward. "Right after then, I met Bob, and he drank, and I started drinking with him, and I moved to Aston with him, then we broke up, but in the meantime, we los' our way together, Max and me, we los' each other. I didn't know you can lose people but you can, you lose your way and you lose the people on that way, and I think I became a bad mother." Marie turned to Eric suddenly, her eyes brimming. "I know you think I'm a bad mother. I am, I know it too."

"I don't judge," Eric said, though he had been. He tried to tap into his professional self. "I know it's hard to be a parent, and we all make mistakes."

"Do you have kids?"

"Yes, a seven-year-old girl."

"Nice, what's her name?"

Eric realized he'd never had a patient ask his child's name, then he reminded himself that Marie wasn't a patient. "Hannah."

"You get along, spend time with her?"

"Yes." Eric felt his throat catch. He didn't want to lose his way with Hannah, ever.

"That's good, don' make the mistakes I did, you gotta hold him close, you gotta always stay in touch with him." Marie blinked tears from her eyes, and though she seemed to be sobering up, Eric wasn't sure she was addressing him anymore, but her former self.

"Tell me what happened with Max."

"I tried to be a good mother, and I was for a long time, but then I turned bad, and okay, so maybe I drink, I admit it, and I'm not proud of it, I'm not, I went to rehab once but it didn' work." Marie smoothed her hair back into its ponytail, then tugged her bathrobe closed in front. "But that's normal, everybody says it, relapse is a part of recovery and all that, everybody has trouble now and then, that's when we moved up here with my mother, and she did such a good job with him, and he loves her so much, he does, more than me, I know it." Tears welled in her eyes, and she sank onto the bed, hanging her head. "Now it's too late to change it, to get it back, he's grown up, it's over."

"It's not too late, it's never too late." Eric crossed to her and put a hand on her shoulder. "We need to find him, and if we find him, I promise you I can help him. I can get you some help, too."

"No you can't, it's not possible." Marie shook her head, wiping her eyes with the cuffs of her overlong sleeves.

"Yes, it is possible. All you have to do is want it, Marie. I've seen people turn their lives around, people in a lot worse shape than you."

"For real?" Marie looked up, her eyebrows lifting, her aspect newly hopeful, and Eric heard Max's voice in hers, remembering he had said the same phrase, during session.

"Yes, for real." Eric told her, but first he had to find Max.

And he had only one move left.

Chapter Twenty-six

Eric left Max's street, driving with the phone to his ear, leaving yet another message for Max, who hadn't answered the call: "Max, it's Dr. Parrish calling you again. Please call me, no matter how late. I can help, so please call." He hung up as he drove, then dialed 911.

"What is the nature of your emergency?" asked the female dispatcher, and Eric recognized her voice from before. Radnor was a small township, so it wasn't completely unexpected.

"This is Dr. Parrish calling. You remember, I called you about my minor patient, the suicide risk. Max Jakubowski. I still can't locate him. Have there been any calls from him or in reference to him?"

"Not to my knowledge."

"You would know if somebody was going out on a call regarding him, wouldn't you? It's not that large a police force, and you can't get that many calls."

"Dr. Parrish, it isn't procedure to discuss the calls that come in."

"Just tell me this, you're the only dispatcher, aren't you?"

"No, there is one other. May I put you through to the squad room so you can ask them your questions? This line is for emergencies only."

"Thank you, please do." Eric sped through the darkened streets, planning his next move, driven by an urgency that was more than professional. Partly he felt responsible for Max, and partly he knew that the boy had no one else to rely on. Eric pressed the gas and accelerated forward into the darkness.

"This is Officer Melanie Nathan. How can I help you?"

"Officer Nathan, I am Chief of Psychiatry at Havemeyer General and I'm trying to locate a minor patient named Max Jakubowski, who I believe is a suicide risk. His grandmother died tonight and he disappeared. Officer Gambia went to look for him at the house, but he wasn't there, only his mother."

"What is the location of the residence?"

Eric told her. "He lives there with his mother and grandmother but his mother doesn't know where he is, either."

"What is her name?"

Eric told her that too. "I spoke with his mother and she's not much help."

"When was he first reported missing?"

"I called at around six thirty but I don't know if he's been officially reported missing yet. I'd like to do that right now, if I could."

"When was he expected home?"

"He wasn't expected at any time. He was home. His grandmother died and he was home with her alone, then he left abruptly and no one knows where he went."

"And what time was that, Dr. Parrish?"

"Around six o'clock," Eric repeated, tense.

"This evening?"

"Yes."

"That's too soon for him to be considered a missing person, as you probably know."

"I understand that, but time is of the essence with a patient under this kind of stress. I need to know if he called or if any of the other officers got an emergency call involving him."

"I have no knowledge of that, Doctor."

"But you would know if Max called or a call came in about him, wouldn't you? He's a teenage boy. How many calls about a teenage boy can you get on a weeknight in Radnor?"

"I will ask around the squad room and get back to you. May I have your number?"

"Thanks." Eric gave her the number, they both said their good-byes, and he hung up, then dialed Laurie's cell phone and waited for her to pick up.

"Eric?" Laurie asked, concerned. "What's happening?"

"Max still hasn't shown up, and I need your help."

"You want me to see if he's in any of the other EDs?"

"Yes, please." It was just what Eric had been thinking. "I'm assuming he didn't come into ours?"

"No, he didn't. I would've called you. I checked in twice and told them to call me if they had any word of him. Did you try the police?"

"Yes, in Radnor Township, but so far, no word."

"I know a lot of uniforms in Chester County and Delaware County. Let me see what I can find out."

"Thank God for you," Eric said, meaning it. It felt good to have help.

"Where are you? What are you doing?"

"Looking for him."

"How? Where? Do you want company?"

"No thanks," Eric said, touched. "You're helping me more by making those calls. I have one last move."

"What is it?"

"Tell you later, if it pans out. Got to go."

"Sure thing, call me later. I'm up watching Jimmy Fallon. He's my new television crush. That's how pathetic my life is lately."

"Bye." Eric smiled as he hung and turned into the parking lot and pulled into the first available space. SWIRLED PEACE, read the multicolored sign; it was where Renée Bevilacqua worked. Eric was following a hunch that the only lifeline Max had was Renée, and it was possible that the boy would find his way here. Max could be sitting here in his car this very moment—crying, grieving, and every fifteen minutes, tapping his forehead.

Eric cut the ignition, knowing that being here was a boundary violation. Still, he couldn't *not* come, given that he'd tried everything else and the downside risk could be Max's suicide. He twisted around, grabbed his old blue ball cap from the backseat, and popped it on, an improvised disguise. He didn't want Max to recognize him or he might take off.

He looked over at the frozen yogurt stop, which was a free-standing box in the middle of the asphalt lot. Cars parked in an upside-down U-shape around its sides and back, leaving both the right and left aisles for entrance and exit. Most of the parking spaces in the front lot were full, and a crowd of teenagers hung in front of the shop, which had a concrete patio with picnic tables and rainbow-striped umbrellas.

Eric kicked himself for not asking Marie what type of car Max drove, but he looked around to see if there was anybody sitting in a car, in the driver's seat. He looked to his right, and there was no one in the line of cars next to him, but he couldn't see the farthest car clearly, probably eight away. There were two shadows in the front seat in the seventh car, a couple.

He adjusted his outside mirror and used it to see the single line of cars parked down the middle aisle, but nobody was in them. He swiveled his rearview mirror and aimed it at the cars on the right-most side of the lot, but it was too dark to see inside them. He realized that if Max had come here to follow Renée home, he could be parked behind the shop, in order to wait without drawing suspicion.

Eric could wait until closing time to see if Max would flush himself out, but the closing time was eleven. He'd never forgive himself if Max hurt himself between now and then, in a car parked only yards away. He slipped the keys from the ignition, unclipped his seatbelt, and got out of the car, closing the door behind him. He double-checked the parking lot out front, but didn't see anybody sitting in the cars on the rightmost row. He kept his head down and walked past the cars and teenagers, then kept going beyond the shop. Cars were parked against the back fence, rear-bumper side out, and they ended in a blue Dumpster on the right.

Eric walked along the rear bumpers, and nobody was sitting in the cars, except for a couple in the middle car, making out in the driver's seat. He kept going and turned right around the shop, walking the rightmost side of the upside-down U, and the only occupied car was a minivan full of kids, eating frozen yogurt while they watched a DVD glowing from the back of the seats. Eric turned and looked inside the shop. Families and teenagers milled around inside, and the store was brightly lit. Max wasn't inside, but there were three shop girls behind the counter and a fourth at the cash register, in tie-dyed long aprons over SWIRLED PEACE T-shirts and jeans. One was a redhead. It had to be Renée.

Eric found himself opening the door to the shop. Stainless-steel self-service frozen yogurt machines gleamed in an area to the right, next to stacked bowls and cups, and except for the cashier, the employees circulated among the crowd, helping customers work the self-serve fro-yo machines. Eric zeroed in on Renée, who fit Max's description of her: a petite young girl with a moptop of short dark red curls pulled back from her face with a skinny pink ribbon. She was naturally pretty, with a fresh-faced charm, blue eyes, and an easy smile. She must have felt Eric's eyes on her, because she turned to him and made her way over.

"Do you need help, sir?" Renée asked, cocking her head.

"Uh, yes." Eric tried to get his act together. If he looked up "boundary violation" in the dictionary, there would be a picture of him talking to Renée. He spotted the gold necklace around her neck, the one Max liked.

"You haven't been here before, have you?"

"No, I haven't."

"I figured, because new people get intimidated on their first time. The prices are by weight, and it's all self-serve." Renée gestured to the lineup of machines, each with a double spout, labeled Vanilla, Belgian Chocolate, Banana, and Blueberry. "Which flavor would you like? You can mix two of them, we call that the Swirl-Away, and you can even mix three, which is called the Swirlwind Romance. Four flavors is the Tilt-A-Swirl." Renée rolled her eyes in a goofy way. "The manager makes us say that. He thinks it's really funny."

"It is, kind of." Eric could see why Max had a crush on her because she was so warm and relaxed, and it must have put the boy at ease.

"So what flavor would you like? And do you want a large, medium, or small?"

"Medium, vanilla." Eric was thinking of Hannah, who loved vanilla ice cream and could make distinctions between Ben & Jerry's, Haagen-Dazs, and Turkey Hill.

"You want me just to do it for you?" Renée took a medium cup from the stack. "We're not that busy."

"Thanks, yes, I appreciate it." Eric took a flyer. "You look familiar to me. I drop my daughter off at PerfectScore and I think I've seen you there with your mother."

"I go there! They're the best!" Renée held the cup under the spout, grabbed the lever, and twisted it up and over.

"I think they have a few different tutors, but she gets tutored by a guy named Max."

"So do I!" Renée grinned as she twisted the yogurt dispenser, his Styrofoam dish in hand. "He's so smart. He's, like, a genius!"

"That's what my daughter says, too. She likes him."

"I like him, too. He's shy and super-nerdy, but he's a nice guy."

Eric felt reassured to think that Renée liked Max, then realized that was probably inappropriate. It struck him that maybe it was countertransference, after all. "What days do you go to tutoring?"

"Wednesday and Saturday."

"Oh, so you haven't seen him today?"

"No." Renée turned the cup as frozen yogurt coiled inside. "What's your daughter's name?"

"Hannah," Eric blurted out, because he was a terrible liar.

"Where does she go to school? I go to Sacred Heart."

"She goes to public school." Eric wanted a story Renée couldn't verify.

"Sweet! You want toppings, don't you? Follow me, sir." Renée led him to the toppings case, where there stood another employee, a tall young African-American woman with bright blue hair and a nose ring. Renée waved her down happily. "Trix, incoming!"

"Cool!" Trixie smiled.

Renée turned to Eric. "Sir, this is Trixie and she's in charge of toppings. She goes to PerfectScore too, but she doesn't have Max."

"Oh, hi," Eric said, surprised, though he shouldn't have been. PerfectScore was only five minutes away, and it made sense that local girls worked here.

Renée continued, "Trix, we were just talking about Max and how smart he is." She turned to Eric. "We don't think the tutor she has is as good he is."

Trixie stuck out her lower lip. "Totally, my tutor's all about the practice tests, but I can do the practice tests myself. Max is way better. He teaches Renée tricks, like, for the problems."

"That's what my daughter says," Eric said, before anybody asked him any more questions.

"Okay, well, I'll leave you to it," Renée said, waving a hand airily.

"Thanks," Eric said, as she went to help other customers.

Trixie smiled at him. "Sir, you can choose as many toppings as you like, and the price list is there on the wall."

Eric chose strawberries and M&Ms, also Hannah's favorite, paid almost seven dollars, left the shop, and walked to the car, his head wheeling around to see if Max were here. So far, it didn't look like he was, and Eric went back to his car, chirped it unlocked, got inside, and ate the yogurt while he considered his next move. Max hadn't come yet, but he could still show up. Eric had nothing else to go on, no other idea where Max could be, and just like Max, nothing was waiting for him at home. He ate his yogurt absently, and his gaze fell on the parking lots of the other stores on this side of the street: a Walgreens, a drive-through Dunkin' Donuts, and a Hill's Seafood. Max could be in any one of those lots, waiting for Renée to get off work. In fact, it was probably likelier that Max was in one of those lots because it would be easier to go unnoticed.

Eric decided to wait it out, until eleven o'clock. The cars came and went, minivans and pickups, newer models and old, and as darkness fell completely, it was impossible to keep track or to discern anybody sitting in the cars, waiting. He felt increasingly worried, wondering where Max could be. He sensed it would shake out closer to eleven o'clock. He would have to bide his time.

He replayed his conversation with Max, then with Marie. She had been worse than Eric had imagined, and it was easy to understand how Max's life would fall apart now that his grandmother was gone. Eric could help Max if he could get to him before it was too late, and it made him sick to think that all he could do was sit in a car and wait, but it was his only bet.

Eric picked up his phone, thumbed to the Internet, and typed in white pages. He went to the site, plugged in Renée Bevilacqua and Berwyn, and a short list of addresses popped onto the tiny screen. None of the listings was under the name Renée, which he had expected, but there were plenty of Bevilacquas and the site listed their ages: they all were men or women aged forty-five and up. One of them had to be Renée's mother or father, and Eric skimmed the addresses to see which were the closest, since they would be the likelier. There were three Bevilacquas that were possible candidates: Trianon Lane, Sunflower Road, and Gristmill Road. So he wouldn't be able to tell where he was going until Renée left.

The dashboard clock went from 8:30, to 9:30, to 10:30, and Eric put his phone away and focused complete attention on the store. The crowd of teenagers had thinned, and only a few customers were in the store. Renée was wiping down the countertops, Trixie scooping the toppings into white tubs, and the cashier taking money from the drawer and stuffing it into a cloth bag with a zipper.

Eric could count on one hand the cars in the parking lot, and most of those were in the back, probably the employees' cars. He scanned the Walgreens and the Dunkin' Donuts lots, but he didn't see Max anywhere. In time, the lights of the Swirled Peace went off, and the girls left the shop, chattering and laughing. Eric shifted up in his seat, coming to alertness. Renée was easy to spot because of her red hair, and he watched as she hugged the other girls goodbye and walked toward the back of the parking lot. The leftmost car was a cobalt blue Honda Fit, and Renée made a beeline for it. In a few moments, the Honda's engine started, the headlights went on, and the Honda zipped forward.

Eric looked around to see if any headlights came to life in any of the parking lots, but no dice. He turned his head away as Renée steered toward the exit of the parking lot, and as she passed behind Eric's car, she was yapping on the phone, pressed to her ear. She barely braked at the exit before entering traffic on Barrett Street, then she turned left, and Eric still didn't see anyone else around that seemed to be in pursuit. Traffic was light, the day winding down, and Renée sped to the traffic signal, which was red.

Eric turned on his ignition, reversed out of the space, and took off after her, trailing her at a safe distance.

A guardian angel to the guardian angel.

Chapter Twenty-seven

Eric followed Renée down Barrett Road, which was a well-lit main drag, two lanes going both ways with traffic lights at regular intervals. He stayed a car length away, traveling behind a burgundy Cadillac that tailgated her, but its driver was a smoker, leaving his hand with the cigarette outside the car. Eric eliminated him because Max didn't smoke.

The traffic cruised forward after the light, nobody in a hurry except for Renée. The Cadillac took a right onto one of the side streets, so Eric lost his buffer car and he moved up directly behind Renée. Her driving made it a job to keep up with her in a way that wasn't obvious, but Eric figured she was probably talking on the phone, oblivious to the fact that she was being followed.

Eric kept a sharp eye on the traffic. Renée's aggressive driving served his purpose because after five blocks or so, it flushed out the only two other cars that stayed with her; one was an older black Toyota sedan, and the other was a blue VW Cabriolet. Eric could tell from their silhouettes that both drivers were short men, but either could have been Max. He didn't want to get close enough to risk being seen by either of them and he didn't have to, if he just bided his time.

Eric trailed them all, watching them jockey for position, the three cars like moving pieces of the same puzzle as they traveled. He kept in mind the potential Bevilacqua addresses as they sped eastward; he eliminated Trianon Lane because that was to the right, so only Sunflower Road and Gristmill Road were left. Renée zoomed forward, and an orange Horizon Plumbing van joined the mix, giving Eric some temporary cover from the black Toyota, which was getting dangerously parallel to him in the slow lane. He shifted his gaze underneath his cap to see if Max was driving the Toyota, but the Horizon van accelerated at the last moment, pushing the Toyota forward and ruining Eric's view.

The van turned off after a few blocks, but the black Toyota and the VW Cabriolet stayed, and suddenly Renée put on her left blinker, turning unpredictably onto Wheatfield Drive, another main drag running south. Both the Toyota and VW signaled left and turned onto Wheatfield after her, and Eric had to brake to let the VW into the turn lane ahead of him, catching a glimpse of the driver in shadowy profile.

The driver looked like Max, and Eric felt the start of recognition, but he couldn't be sure. He followed the traffic with renewed determination, turning left onto Wheatfield. He'd traveled these roads before and realized that Sunflower Road wasn't in this direction. That left only Gristmill Road, but he wasn't familiar with it, in any event, and there was always the possibility that he'd picked the wrong Bevilacqua address.

He fed the car gas as Renée accelerated and narrowed his focus to the VW. It was a younger person's type of car, and though he hadn't figured Max for the convertible type, the boy could've bought it used. Renée's car, the Toyota, and the VW barreled down Wheatfield, which was also two lanes both ways, with side streets off of both sides.

Eric switched into the slow lane to keep everyone in his view. The terrain changed, the trees taller and leafier, the houses set farther back, and the streetlights fewer and farther between. There were some traffic lights, and Eric kept an eye on the VW as it stayed slightly behind Renée's car next to the Toyota. Wheatfield Drive wound left and right, and slower cars joined the trio but dropped off, and the VW stayed with Renée's car. Eric bet that the driver was Max.

He felt his heart beat faster as Renée put on her right blinker, switched into the right lane, and slowed just enough to make a right turn. Renée turned into a side street, but the black Toyota kept going on Wheatfield, leaving only the VW. Eric held his breath as he watched the VW put on its right blinker, switching to the right lane, and turn right after Renée. It had to be Max.

Eric shifted forward in his seat. He turned left behind the VW and spotted the street name, Harvest Road. Harvest was a quiet residential street with no traffic lights, and the three cars traveled in the darkness together in a line—Renée first, the VW, then Eric. Renée decelerated only slightly but suddenly the VW slowed considerably, which Eric realized would be just what Max would do if they were approaching Renée's house.

Eric braked, shifting up in the seat. He'd never tried to intercept anybody in a car, but it couldn't be that difficult. Renée had put on her right blinker, and he was sensing they were getting closer to Gristmill Road, especially given the Wheatfield/Harvest motif of the street names. Eric flashed his high beams, signaling to get Max's attention, but the VW didn't speed up or slow down.

Harvest Road curved sharply to the left, and Renée zoomed ahead, turning left off of Harvest without her blinker. Max slowed, but instead of following Renée, put on his right blinker and braked to a stop, confusing Eric, who braked as well. In the next moment, the VW turned right into a driveway of one of the houses, #212 Harvest.

Eric groaned, watching as the VW's ignition went off and its lights out. He'd been wrong. The driver couldn't have been Max. It was somebody who lived here, and unless Eric stepped on it, he was going to lose Renée. He accelerated, taking the first left that Renée had taken and catching a glimpse of the street sign, Gristmill Road. Her red taillights glowed at the end of the street, and he slowed, braking when he realized that the beginning of Gristmill looked like a regular road, but ended in a large cul-de-sac.

Eric pulled over to the curb on the right. He put the car in park and watched as Renée zoomed into the driveway of a large house in the middle of the cul-de-sac, then her engine and taillights went off. So Renée lived on Gristmill Road, but Max hadn't followed her home. Eric switched off the ignition so his engine noise didn't draw attention. He exhaled, puzzled.

He realized that maybe he was jumping the gun. There was still a chance that Max was on his way and he knew where Renée lived. Max could be on his way, right now, just to make sure that Renée was home safely. Either that, or the boy was somewhere out there, doing away with himself.

Abruptly, Eric's car filled with light from the headlights of a car that was turning onto Gristmill Road. The headlights finished their turning arc, straightened out, and headed down Gristmill Road. The car was a dark coupe, and Eric tugged the brim of his cap down as the coupe drove by, but he spotted a male driver. Eric waited to see if it was Max, and since it was a cul-de-sac, Max would probably drive forward, follow the cul-de-sac to check Renée's car, then drive out again. Eric would be able to stop him at the bottleneck. It was perfect.

Eric watched the dark coupe drive slowly down Harvest Road, enter the cul-de-sac, drive along its curb, and exit the cul-de-sac, driving toward Eric in the opposite direction. Eric shifted up in his seat, in anticipation. If the driver was Max, he would come eye-to-eye with Max, and the boy wouldn't be able to avoid him.

Suddenly, the coupe switched on its high beams, temporarily blinding him, and braked beside Eric's car, so that the driver was only a foot away. Eric looked over to see that it wasn't Max, but a middle-aged man, his eyes narrowed behind his horn-rimmed glasses.

"Excuse me, pal," said the driver, sternly. "I live on this cul-de-sac. I know my neighbors. You're not one of them. What are you doing here?"

"Oh, sorry." Eric reached for his cell phone and held it up. "I just got a text and I pulled over to answer it."

"Why were you on the street in the first place?"

"I didn't realize it was a cul-de-sac. I was on Harvest when I got the text and I turned onto the street, but I didn't know it dead-ended. I must have missed the sign."

"Oh, okay." The driver eased back in his seat. "You didn't miss the sign, there isn't one. Most people around here know this is a cul-de-sac, but if you're not familiar, I can see how you could make that mistake. I didn't mean to jump down your throat, pal. These are the days of 'when you see something, say something.' "

"Understood, completely."

"I'm not saying you're a terrorist or anything. I mean, obviously, you're not a terrorist."

"No, of course not. I'll be on my way. The text can wait." Eric started the engine and put the car in gear.

"Good. We have an active town watch here, and sooner or later, somebody's going to call the cops."

"Of course, good night now." Eric hit the gas, cruised slowly forward, and turned around in the cul-de-sac, glancing over at Renée's house, which was a large brick Château type, with the lights on downstairs. He steered to the exit of the cul-de-sac and waved goodbye to the coupe driver, who flashed him a thumbs-up.

Eric didn't exhale until he reached the top of the street.

Chapter Twenty-eight

Eric headed south, his chest tightening, an unhappily familiar sensation. He remembered back when he was in the throes of his disorder, tension like steel bands would squeeze his chest, lungs, even his windpipe. He controlled his breathing and drove ahead, wondering where Max could have gone. He passed the closed, dark strip malls in Devon, the Whole Foods parking lot finally empty, the Brewster's ice cream just closing, and the last of the independent mechanics, the one he used. It occurred to him that PerfectScore wasn't far away and there was an off-chance Max could be there.

He took a left turn, then two rights, and he could see PerfectScore. The sign glowed crimson, subliminally suggesting Harvard, which was the right color to affluent parents giving their kids every advantage to get into the best colleges. The store was brick and single-story, and he pulled into the small parking lot, but it was empty. He drove around the back of the lot, but it was completely empty.

He left the lot and took a right turn, heading home and sensing the tension in his chest wouldn't be leaving until he had found Max safe. He drove past the darkened houses and found himself thinking about the families within, the children tucked in on a school night and the mothers and fathers climbing into bed together, too

tired for sex, but spooning like he and Caitlin, the very compan-
ionship a comfort. Eric loved being married, loved having a home
base in the family, loved being taken into the same place every night.
It struck him that he wasn't really missing Caitlin, but a wife, a
home, a family, security. Maybe he had been as guilty as she of falling in love with a cardboard cutout, not a person. Looking back,
they never got along that well, and their bickering was about who
took the trash out last time, or who forgot to record which check,
or who went out to Staples for school supplies, and by the end, they
were both keeping score—and both were losing.

Eric realized that he was driving on automatic pilot toward
his old house on Mill Road, not his new home. He braked and
made a U-turn. He didn't live there anymore. He wasn't about to
drive by and see if Caitlin was alone, or if there was another car in
the driveway, Brian's. He hit the gas heading home, then realized
with a start that Max could be there waiting for him.

Eric accelerated, driven by a glimmer of hope. The traffic lights
had been switched to blinking yellow and it took only five minutes to reach his street. He craned his neck to see if there was a
car parked in front of his house or in his driveway, but there wasn't.
The fixture next to his front door cast a white cone of light onto
his front step, where something was sitting.

"Come on, son," Eric said to himself, trying to see as he drew
closer. From two doors away, he could see that it wasn't a person
but some sort of shape on the doorstep. He pulled into the driveway, turned off the ignition, and got out of the car.

He crossed the lawn, pocketing his keys. A brown shopping bag
sat on his doorstep, and he looked inside. There was a handwritten note on top, which read ***Here's the dinner you didn't get to
have. Call if you need to. Love, Laurie***.

Eric picked up the bag and went inside.

Chapter Twenty-nine

**5. I perceive the emotions of others but I do not feel those
   emotions.**
**Circle one: Doesn't apply to me. Partially applies to me.
   Fully applies to me.**

I love funerals.

I love funerals the way normal people love parades, fireworks, birthday parties, or barbecues.

I suspect I'm not the only sociopath who feels this way.

Why do we love funerals?

Not because we're evil, though we are.

Because they're so damn easy.

Look, most of my life is me playing a role, picking up on the social cues, trying to read people to know what to say. I'm very good at it, as I've said, I was born this way, and I've only gotten better at it over time.

But to be real with you, it gets old.

It gets tiring.

It's an effort to always be putting on an act, because you're trying to figure out how to act.

You know how you feel at a party, when you're trying to show everybody that you're cool, or smart, or make good conversation, or look good? You're giving them your party face, and you probably can't wait to get home, when you can take it off.

Well, that's how I feel all the time. I can never take my face off, except when I'm alone.

But when somebody dies, like at a funeral, it's obvious what I'm supposed to do.

Act sad.

That's easy, so easy.

I haven't been to a lot of funerals, but I'm looking forward to more.

I don't even try the full-on cry, because honestly that is a little tough for me, to try to muster up some tears when I have absolutely no idea what sadness feels like.

Plus my mother is the master of the full-on cry, a fact I didn't even know until I was in high school and my Uncle John died. We were at his funeral on a cold and cloudy morning, standing in the cemetery in a small group, all of us wearing black, which I didn't even have when I was thirteen so I had to take the bus to the shopping center the day before and spend my entire birthday savings, $189, on black clothes, a total waste of money.

Anyway, my mother made a fool of herself that day, crying like a baby at the graveside, her face turning all kinds of pink, snot pouring from her nose, the sobs interrupting whatever the priest was saying, and when the time came that we were supposed to put the roses on the wooden casket, she threw herself on top of the thing and started hugging it, like it was a tree.

What a scene.

Can you say, "over the top"?

That's when I learned how *not* to behave at funerals, because later when we went to the restaurant, I could hear my older cousins gigging about what a drama queen my mother was and how she didn't like her brother anyway. My grandmother even told my other uncle that she probably owed him money, that's why she cried crocodile tears.

That was the first time I heard the expression "crocodile tears," and I had to go look it up to see what it meant, obviously not tears that crocodiles cry.

Whatever.

What I learned was that when somebody dies, or whenever you hear any really bad news, the trick is to just get a glimmer of wetness in your eyes. This way, everybody will think you're holding back tears, that you'd be crying your eyes out like Niagara Falls if you really let it rip, but you won't, because nobody needs to see you making a fool of yourself when, let's face it, people die.

Even nice people, like Uncle John.

Who my mother really did love.

Anyway, sometimes at night, in the bathroom, I practice in front of the mirror, trying to get the glimmer going. I bought some Visine that does the trick, and it helps if you touch the plastic tip to your cornea, which irritates it. But I'm trying to see if I can do it without the Visine, on my own.

I can't really think of anything to make the tears come, except sometimes, I think back to Uncle John's funeral. I think back to that morning, and I pretend I'm thirteen years old again and a really nice guy died.

Then I think about the 189 bucks I wasted.

And it makes me cry.

Chapter Thirty

It was a humid morning, and Eric walked toward the hospital from his car, feeling raw and distracted, since Max was still missing. He'd hardly slept last night and ate only some of the delicious food that Laurie had left him. He'd called Max two more times, then called the Berwyn and Radnor police, but Max hadn't been picked up or seen. He called the local emergency rooms, but Max hadn't been brought in there, either. He'd called Marie from the car this morning, but she hadn't picked up, and he was guessing she was hungover. Still, knowing Max, home would be the last place he'd go.

"Congratulations on the new ranking, Dr. Parrish," said one of the hospital accountants, materializing beside him as the automatic doors of the breezeway whisked open and employees and visitors entered the hospital.

"Thanks," Eric said reflexively, coming out of his reverie. The number-two ranking was undoubtedly the worst-kept secret in the Western Hemisphere. He'd always thought that the myriad HIPAA regulations governing privacy were unnecessary, but he was starting to think everybody in the hospital was a blabbermouth.

"We're so jazzed about it in Accounting. We think it will do a lot for business. It's profile-raising."

"Yes, hope so." Eric's pager went off, and he reached reflexively for his holster. Employees flowed around him to their various elevators and wings. "Excuse me, I should get this."

"Sure, bye." The accountant headed to the elevator bank, and Eric paused to check his pager. **Please come up before you go to the unit**, read the page, and it was from Brad Farnessen in hospital administration. Eric was in no mood for hospital bureaucracy, but he had no choice and now he was going to the same floor as the accountant, who was already stepping into the elevator cab.

"Hold the door!" Eric ducked inside, the doors closed, and they rode up together.

"Isn't Wright in the other side of the hospital?"

"I have to stop up and see Brad."

"Prepare to have your ass kissed," the accountant said with a sly smile, smoothing out a patterned tie. "I heard some scuttlebutt they're afraid you're gonna leave. You can write your own ticket."

"Oh, come on."

"Be real. You think we're the only hospital that heard about the rankings?"

"I'm not going anywhere." Eric smiled as the doors to the elevator rattled open, and both men stepped out.

"See ya," the accountant said, with a short wave.

"Take care." Eric heard his phone alert that he'd gotten a text and he slid it from his pocket and checked it. It was from Laurie: **You okay? Any word on Max? Call anytime.** He took a second to reply, **I'm fine no word re max. thx for the grub ttyl.**

He entered the lobby, a circular room with an airy domed ceiling, located in the oldest wing of the hospital, which dated back to colonial Philadelphia. White plaster filigree covered the walls, brass sconces lit the space, and the floor was black-and-white marble parquet, polished to a high sheen. There were three arched exits, leading to the financial, personnel, and executive departments, respectively, a power rotary controlling the operations of the entire seven-campus medical system of The PhilaHealth Partnership.

Eric took the middle exit, for executive. The hallway was hushed and empty, unlike the rest of the hospital, which bustled with activity. Currier & Ives foxhunting prints lined the walls, their green and blue hues fading. Offices lined the hallway, belonging to the many functionaries employed by the system, and Eric peeked through the open doors to see them in incongruously modern carrels, retrofitted to squeeze into the historic dimensions of the space.

He passed office after office, which mirrored the complexity of hospital bureaucracy. A maze of regulations governed the system, especially in the employment area, and it was a little-known fact that not everyone who worked at the hospital was an employee, especially on the medical staff. Eric was one of the minority of doctors employed by the hospital, and it gave him better benefits, even if it required him filling out three hundred more forms. He had once looked at the organizational chart in his employment manual, pleased to see his own name near the top, reporting only to the Chair of Psychiatry of the entire multi-campus system, Tom Singh, who in turn reported to the Chief Medical Officer, the CMO of the system, Brad Farnessen. Eric liked and respected Tom and Brad, but he never wanted their jobs. Both were physicians, but neither got to practice anymore, and that was no fun at all.

Eric turned left onto the hallway with Tom's and Brad's offices, the two closed mahogany doors at the end of the hall, each with female assistants out front, sitting in carrels they had made homey by covering the low fabric walls with thumbtacked photos of their children, gardens, cats, and dogs. Both assistants were working on their computers.

"Hey, Eric." Brad's assistant, Dee Dee, an attractive African-American woman with long hair, smiled at him. "Congratulations on making number two."

"Thanks. How have you been?"

"Good." Dee Dee slid off her colorful reading glasses and let them hang from a chunky beaded lorgnette around her neck. "They're ready for you, you can just go in."

"They?" Eric crossed to the door and opened it, surprised to find that not only was Brad inside, but Tom and Mike Braezele from Legal, the three of them standing around the small conference table opposite Brad's large, uncluttered desk. Medical textbooks, regulatory manuals, and family photos lined bookshelves behind the desk, next to a lineup of framed diplomas. "Hi, I didn't know we were all meeting."

"Hello, Eric." Mike crossed the room, extending his hand, and so did Tom and Brad, and they all smiled stiffly through the bureaucratic ceremony of saying hello and shaking hands. Tom, Brad, and Mike struck Eric as corporate clones but for the fact that Tom was of Indian descent: they all were balding with graying hair and they wore similar steel-rimmed glasses that coordinated subtly with gray lightweight suits, white shirts, and ties of patterned silk. Eric felt oddly underdressed in his oxford shirt and khakis, and instead of a tie, his lanyard bearing its red W like a scarlet letter.

"Eric, please, sit down." Brad gestured to one of the side chairs, and he took the head of the table. "Congratulations. That's an achievement to be proud of."

Tom sat at his right hand. "It sure is, congrats."

"Yes, well done!" added Mike from Legal, who sat a few chairs down, sliding a Mont Blanc from his breast pocket and a legal pad from the center of the table.

"Thanks, and my staff deserves a ton of credit." Eric pulled out a chair and sat down. There was a polished sheet of glass on top of the mahogany table that reflected the divided squares of light from the mullioned windows.

Brad smiled. "Our service in Exton has thirty-five beds. They're an excellent service, but I know that the bigger units get the most attention. So your achievement is doubly impressive, given that the odds are stacked against you."

"I completely agree," Tom interjected, then patted his graying hair. His progressive lenses bisected his large, round brown eyes, magnifying their bottom half. "You should know that I was very pleased to see us get the ranking in psychiatry. I know we don't always get the respect we deserve as a specialty, but your efforts will go a long way toward remediating that, within our system."

"Great." Eric felt closer to Tom, who knew that their profession was stigmatized, so they were fellow underdogs. Still, he couldn't understand why the atmosphere felt so tense for a congratulatory meeting. He turned to Brad. "So, is this what you called me up to talk about?"

"Not exactly," Brad answered. He shifted forward in the seat, stroking his tie as if it were out of place, which it wasn't. "Unfortunately, I received a call this morning from the Dean of Jefferson Medical School, and it seems that a third-year medical student on your service, Kristine Malin, is making an allegation of sexual harassment against you."

"*What?*" Eric asked, shocked.

"Of course, Eric, we're not accusing you of anything, but you know the procedure in the event of an allegation like this—"

"That's not true! What did she say? What is going on—"

"We will know more details soon. She filed something in writing with the Dean, and he called me." Brad hesitated. "The Dean told me that, in general, she alleges that you have been making sexual advances on her, which culminated two nights ago, after you had been out drinking with her—"

"I wasn't *out drinking with her*! After we got the number-two ranking, I bought drinks for my staff on the unit, my *entire* staff. I met them at the bar, they were all there, not just her!"

"I'm sure. You don't have to defend yourself with us, Eric."

"But this is outrageous!"

Brad held up a hand. "She also told the Dean that these advances culminated in an incident in the parking garage, in which you attempted to force yourself on her, taking advantage of the fact that you knew she had been drinking—"

"No!" Eric exploded. "That's *insane,* that's a lie—"

"Of course it is. We know that such conduct would be inconsistent with your character—"

"*She's* the one, *she* waited by my car, *she* tried to kiss *me*, not the other way around! *She's* the one making advances, and I turned her down."

Brad opened his mouth, then shut it again, and Eric realized that he had said the wrong thing. Brad, Tom, and Mike had believed there was no substance to the allegations and now they were hearing differently. Mike began making notes with his gleaming pen, his head down.

"Brad." Eric tried to control his tone, but wasn't succeeding. "She made advances to me and I rejected them, that's why she filed the complaint."

"She made the advances?"

"Yes." Eric flashed on Kristine's expression when she'd had the fight with Laurie, but he didn't tell them about it, because it would've added fuel to the fire. "Brad, I swear to you, I did not make any advances to her. I would *never* do anything like that."

"Of course you wouldn't, you're a happily married man. We know Caitlin."

Eric's mouth went dry. "In fact, Caitlin and I are filing for divorce, but that has no bearing here. I would never do anything inappropriate with a medical student or anyone on my staff."

"Well now." Brad lifted a graying eyebrow. "How are you doing with the divorce? Is it affecting your work? Or your performance?"

"No, of course not."

"There's no shame in it, Eric. I'm divorced myself. I know how difficult it can be. It wouldn't be surprising that it would affect your work."

"I'm not bothered by the situation to the level where it affects my work, and this sexual harassment claim is absurd."

"What about this event the other day, where security was called, involving a patient? A Mr. Perino? I understand that you took it upon yourself to subdue him?"

"I was protecting my staff," Eric answered, off-balance. "How did you even know about that?"

"We got a notice from the Board that the patient's wife is filing a complaint. She alleges you committed a battery against her husband."

"Are you kidding?" Eric groaned. "My attending, Sam Ward, was there and he knows the truth. So was my charge nurse. There's nothing to it, nothing whatsoever."

"I'm sure. Hundreds of these are filed a year, and very few have any merit. The Board of Medicine in Harrisburg will send an investigator, usually an ex-cop, to investigate the matter. It's just unusual, because you've never been the subject of even a single charge."

"This is meritless, absolutely." Eric felt mortified.

Brad blinked. "Eric, you need not explain yourself to us, and in fact, you mustn't."

"Why not? How am I supposed to defend myself? You're sitting here, making outrageous allegations, and I can't let them go unrefuted."

"Excuse me," Brad said, raising his finger. "Let us be clear. We are making no allegations against you. We know you have a spotless record and we're following procedure. We have had one or two such complaints, as regards the students on rotation, and the procedure is clear. There will be an investigation, which will be dealt with within a matter of days, because these things are taken very seriously."

"Who investigates?"

"An independent investigator, usually outside counsel, performs the investigation. He meets and interviews with the complainant, any witnesses to any of the incidents which she makes allegations about. Were there any witnesses in the parking lot that night, that you recall?"

"No, there was no one."

"What about to the other advances, for example, the ones she made against you?"

"No, there were no witnesses."

"Did you tell anyone?"

"No." Eric was kicking himself. He thought of the text Kristine had sent him, but it would look innocent, on its face.

"Fair enough." Brad cleared his throat. "As I was saying, after the investigator meets with her and any other witnesses, he will then meet with you. Concurrent with the factual investigation, our procedure also provides for a 'collegial intervention.'"

"What's that?"

"It will be held today, at one thirty, and it's an inquiry to determine whether there is an impairment issue that we should know about."

"What impairment issue?" Eric blurted out, then it dawned on him. "You think *I* have a *drug issue?*"

"No, Eric. Again, this is merely our procedure, and Mike can tell you"—Brad gestured generally in Mike's direction, but the lawyer kept making his notes without looking up—"that we have to follow procedures for liability purposes. The purpose of the Physician Impairment Committee is to examine if there's any drug, alcohol, or mental health issue."

"But there isn't." Eric's head started spinning. He had heard rumors of impairment issues in the Anesthesiology Department, which made sense because they had easy access to pain meds like Oxycontin and Vicodin, but it was a rarity in psychiatry. "And what's the Physician Impairment Committee? Who's on it? I never heard of it."

"It's *ad hoc,* formed for each specific case. In your case, there will be three committee members—myself, Tom, sitting as Chair of Psychiatry, and third, your attending, Sam Ward."

"Sam? He reports to me, for God's sake. I'm his *boss.* Isn't that a conflict of interest, besides the fact that it's completely humiliating?"

"I understand, but those are the rules and regulations."

"What rules and regulations? Where are you getting them from?"

"Eric, please keep your voice down." Brad glanced toward the door. "This is confidential, for your own protection."

"Eric, by the way," Mike added, "I'm advising you not to discuss this matter with anyone."

"Of course I wouldn't," Eric shot back. "Do you think I want to give it more currency than it already has?"

"It goes without saying that you won't raise the subject with the complainant."

"Of course not—" Eric stopped himself, to clarify something. "Wait, Kristine's going to work on my unit, after this?"

"Yes, she has another week in her rotation, according to our records."

"But why would she still want to work for me, someone who supposedly has been sexually harassing her? Forcing myself on her in parking lots? Doesn't that prove how false these allegations are? What a liar she is?"

"Not necessarily." Mike pursed his lips. "If I may play the devil's advocate, she would say that she has no choice. If her allegations were true, she shouldn't have to quit."

"But they're *not* true!"

"Even so," Mike continued calmly. "It's common in any employment context for a complainant to keep working after they've filed a sexual harassment or discrimination lawsuit."

"So we can't fire her?"

"No. First, she's not our employee. Second, firing a complainant for filing charges of sexual harassment or other discrimination is unlawful retaliation. Don't take any action vis-à-vis her at all, not even a reprimand, in the time she has left."

"Well that's just great, isn't it?" Eric felt blocked in. "How am I supposed to have someone work for me who's utterly dishonest? Whom I can't trust at all? Who would do something like this? I wouldn't let her near a patient now. The woman is delusional at best, and a liar, at worst."

"It can't be helped. My advice is to have as little to do with her as possible and never be alone with her, for any reason." Mike picked up a folder from the seat beside him and extracted a photocopied booklet, about seventy pages long. "Now, in answer to your question, the pertinent rules and regulations are in the medical staff bylaws, and in case you don't have a copy, we Xeroxed one for you. Let's take a moment to look together at Appendix F, which are the guidelines for addressing disruptive behavior."

"Disruptive behavior?" Eric repeated in disbelief.

"Bear with me." Mike was already opening the pamphlet, flipping toward the back, and finding the page, then he turned it around to show Eric. "Look, here. 'Disruptive behavior' is defined as 'conduct that undermines a culture of safety and adversely impacts the quality of patient care or continued effective operation of the hospital' "—Mike pointed to the paragraph, moving his index finger as he read aloud—"and includes, without being limited to, 'verbal or physical abuse of colleagues or staff; threatening or intimidating behavior exhibited during interactions with colleagues; offensive conduct; and sexual harassment.' "

Eric tried to follow, but the words swam before his eyes.

Mike continued reading, "'The aforementioned disruptive behavior interferes with operations and as such, is adverse to our mission and will not be tolerated and renders the employee subject to discharge.' "

Discharge? Eric could lose his job because of these lies? His reputation would be ruined. What effect would it have on his custody case if he were found guilty of sexual harassment? Or if he were even *suspected* of sexual harassment?

"Eric," Mike said, setting the pamphlets aside. "You do not need a lawyer to go with you before the Physician Impairment Committee. I will not be present at the Physician Impairment Committee, that's why it's called a collegial intervention. It's strictly physicians only."

"But it has a legal impact." Eric struggled to think clearly. The whole thing was surreal. "You're telling me I could lose my job depending on what they find."

"No one has ever taken a lawyer into a Physician Impairment Committee, and in my view, you do not need one. This is a factual investigation, and if your side of the story is correct, as I'm sure it is, you will prevail."

"My side of the story is the truth, and of course it will prevail." Eric rose. "I assume the meeting is over. I'm holding up my staff meeting."

"Eric, you can't leave just yet." Brad rose, gesturing to Tom. "Tom, uh, has something left to say."

Tom got up, his hand in his pocket. "Eric, the procedures call for one last thing."

"What?" Eric asked, trying to stay in control.

"You have to take care of this, right now." Tom withdrew his hand from his pocket and set a clear plastic jar with a screwtop lid on the glistening conference table.

Eric couldn't believe his eyes.

"Sorry, Eric. We need a urine sample."

Chapter Thirty-one

Eric got off the elevator on Wright, still stunned. He had never in his life been asked to pee in a cup, though he'd ordered it every day on his unit, from drug abusers and the like. The notion humiliated him, and he'd barely been able to hide the shame he felt when he'd left the men's room on the administrative floor and had to palm his urine sample, so that Dee Dee didn't see it while he discreetly passed it to Mike. Eric had had the crazy thought that he should throw it at him, but it wasn't Mike's fault, it was Kristine's.

Eric walked to the door of the psych unit, swiped his ID card, got his keys from his pocket, and unlocked the door. It pissed him off no end that he had to deal with bogus personnel problems when Max was still missing, perhaps even dead, and there were real patients on his unit who needed him. It was even ridiculous that he had to start his day late for such nonsense, and that they had to delay the staff meeting. It would back him up on his treatment rounds and for the entire day. He entered the security airlock, then unlocked the other door.

He let himself into the unit, passed the nurses' station and TV lounge, and spotted Amaka striding toward him, holding a stack of files, so he plastered a smile on his face. "Honey, I'm home," Eric said, then realized he probably wasn't allowed to joke around that way anymore.

"Did they give you a bonus or at the very least, a knighthood?" Amaka asked, with a spreading smile.

"Not quite." Eric knew she would expect a report because a meeting upstairs was a big deal. "They wanted to talk over the details about the marketing campaign, the rollout, and things like that."

"The rollout?" Amaka chuckled softly. "Listen to you."

Eric didn't even know where he had heard that term. He didn't even know why he'd said it. "Yes, I'm a marketer now. I sell healing."

"So when is the rollout?"

"I forget. It was the usual blah blah blah. Let's get the day started." Eric walked down the hallway, and Amaka walked with him.

"By the way, did you hear the rumor? Everyone's saying that you're going to renegotiate your contract after the rankings, and you'll leave if they don't meet your terms." Amaka looked over with a mild frown. "You wouldn't leave us, would you?"

"Of course not, don't worry about it."

"I'm only telling you this because I'm your friend."

"I know, thanks." Eric smiled again at Amaka. "Why don't you go assemble the troops?"

"You mean herd the cats."

"Ha!" Eric said, heading into his office, dropping off his messenger bag, and trying to get his act together. But when he came out, he spotted Sam in the hallway, walking ahead of him toward the conference room.

Eric stiffened, assuming Sam already knew about the sexual harassment claim because the Physician Impairment Committee meeting was scheduled for 1:30 today. The thought mortified him, but he had to hold his head high and keep going. He had a meeting to hold, patients to serve, and a unit to run. He'd always liked Sam, and he'd thought it was mutual, but he wondered what Sam would think of him, now.

"Good morning, Chief," Sam said, turning to him with a smile. "Everything okay?"

"Yes, fine." Eric could barely look Sam in the eye. "How's everything on the unit?"

"Everybody's fine and finishing breakfast."

"How's Perino?"

"I checked on him, and he's stable."

"And Leah Barry?"

"I'm worried about her and I discussed it with David. Amaka will tell us what the nurses said last night, but she seems stuporous to me. Her dosages are too high."

"Good to know." Eric fell into step beside Sam and they walked into the conference room together. David and Jack filed in after them, talking to each other, then the psych techs came in with two of the caseworkers. Eric became aware that even though he stood with Sam, he kept checking the door, waiting for the moment when Kristine walked in. "So. What else is new?"

"Nothing." Sam blinked.

"How was your son's game the other night?" Eric was showing he was still the Chief, a sort-of family man, and never the subject of a valid sexual harassment claim.

"They won, actually." Sam smiled, his eyebrows lifting in mild surprise, because they rarely talked about anything but the unit and the patients.

"Good." Eric was too distracted to make small talk, and his mouth felt dry. "We should have a coffee machine here, don't you think? Why is there only one on the unit?"

"I know, right?"

"We meet here every day, yet we get the coffee from the coffee room and bring it here." Eric wondered if Kristine would show up for work.

"Come to think of it, we should, Chief. We can make our own lousy coffee here. We don't have to import it."

"Agree." Eric forced a smile. He hoped that Kristine had called in sick.

"Then it's a plan. Now, how many forms do we have to fill out to get a new coffee machine?" Sam chuckled at his own joke.

"I'll treat us, how about that? Cut through the red tape."

"I'll split it with you."

Just then Kristine walked in the door, talking quietly with the other medical student, and Eric had to hide his astonishment at her appearance, which had completely changed. Gone was her perfect makeup and the glossy hair that even he could tell was blown-dry. She had on a pair of oversized tortoiseshell glasses, so she must've been wearing contacts lenses during her entire rotation, and her hair was pulled back into a messy ponytail. She wasn't wearing her usual dress, but a navy blazer with a white shirt underneath and khaki pants. Even though she was still attractive, it was in a daughterly way, like the smart-girl next door.

Eric's thoughts raced. He didn't know what she was doing or why she was doing it, unless they were interviewing her today for the investigation. He kicked himself for not asking when that was taking place. He didn't know how she thought she would get away with it, anyway. Everybody on the unit knew the way Kristine dressed; she was famously the pretty one, the Girl Who Dressed Too Hot For Work. But no one on the Physician Impairment Committee would know any of that, except Sam. Meanwhile, Eric turned back to Sam, who was saying something about choosing the best coffee machine.

". . . it does taste better, and you get a hot cup that way, but it's terrible for the environment. All those plastic cups, they end up in landfills. Did you read about that garbage island in the Pacific? It's twice the size of Texas. It's been there a hundred years, and if this keeps up, we'll ruin the entire ecosystem . . ."

"Right." Eric kept his eyes pointedly from Kristine, who took her customary seat with the other medical student, their heads bent in unusually earnest conversation. It struck him that Kristine could have told the medical student about the sexual harassment claim. They talked about juicy gossip all the time; Caitlin called it girl drama when the female lawyers in the D.A.'s Office did it. Certainly the Dean of Jefferson Medical School knew and others on his staff.

Amaka took her seat, motioning to Eric to get his attention. "Chief, you said you wanted to get started."

"Right, yes, of course." Eric realized that he and Sam were the only ones left standing. He fled to his chair at the head of the table, pulling it out. "Amaka, talk to us."

"Good news, to begin with." Amaka opened the first folder on the top of her stack. "It appears that Mr. Echeverria had another good night's sleep and continues to improve."

Eric noticed that Kristine was still whispering to the other medical student. He would usually let that slide, especially among the staff in the back row, but today it unnerved him.

"He slept seven hours, was compliant with medication, and had another nice visit with his family, including his young son. The child drew a very nice picture. He hung it up."

Jack snorted. "I saw it. My dog could do better."

David snorted. "My cat could do better."

"That's enough," Eric snapped, on edge. Silence dropped like a stage curtain, with gazes shifting around the table. The attendings joked around at every meeting, but he was displacing his anger. It was Kristine he wanted to tell to shut up, but he caught himself. If he told her to stop, would it draw more attention to them both? Would it piss her off? Would she use it against him? Was it retaliation under the sexual harassment law?

Amaka glossed over the awkward moment. "Mr. Echeverria has one day left on his insurance. Jack wants to discharge him today. Chief, approve?"

"I'll take a look at him on treatment rounds and decide then." Eric was punting, but he couldn't think clearly enough with Kristine still whispering, a continuing hiss like a steam kettle, building up pressure.

"Moving on," Amaka continued, shifting her file to the next patient, running through the vitals, the particulars, and the nurses' notes . . .

Eric zoned Amaka out, her clipped words drowned out by Kristine's hissing. All he could think of was how many people in addition to Sam or the other medical student knew about the sexual harassment claim. If one person told another person and they told three other people, then by noon today, twenty-five more people would know. It could ruin his reputation, even if he was cleared of the claim. People would always wonder whether he, the newly single top doc, had harassed young Kristine.

"Kristine, stop it!" Eric blurted out, his head swiveling to look at her, and she met his eye behind her glasses, apparently guilelessly. The room went silent again, with everyone looking at him curiously. Eric realized from their bewilderment that Kristine had already stopped whispering. He'd been responding to the hissing in his head, as if he were one of his patients suffering from delusions, not their doctor, here to heal them.

"Chief? Pardon?" Amaka frowned, puzzled.

"Excuse me, go on." Eric kept it together as Amaka continued, giving the overnight status update on patient after patient, and he replied when it was necessary, managing to make it through the remainder of the meeting by focusing on his patients, who deserved as much, and Max, whom he'd have to call about later. The meeting concluded, and Eric got through treatment rounds with Sam and the team the same way, by staying focused on the care of his patients.

At noon, Eric grabbed a yogurt and a soda from the vending machine and fled to his office, closing the door behind him. He knew he was hiding but he needed the breather, and he had the Physicians Impairment Committee meeting at 1:30. He slid his phone from his back pocket, scrolled to Contacts, found Marie's phone number, and dialed it, listening to it ring as he went to the desk and sat down. It rang twice, then was answered. "Marie, it's Dr. Parrish."

"Hello, Dr. Parrish," Marie answered, her voice sounding vaguely boozy. He had no idea if she'd gotten his earlier phone message.

"Did Max come home?"

"No, I haven't seen him. Have you heard anything?"

"No. Doesn't he work today?"

"He's supposed to, but his boss called looking for him. They said he didn't come in. He didn't call either. They don't know where he is."

"Oh no." Eric couldn't pull any punches. "I'm very concerned about his mental state and whether he's done himself harm. I haven't heard from the police, have you?"

"No."

"Does he ever stay out at night? How typical is this?" Eric could guess the answer from what he knew about Max.

"To be honest, I don't know how typical it is." Marie hesitated. "I . . . don't always . . . stay here."

"But it's not like him, is it? He's a responsible kid. Has he ever even missed a day of work?"

"I don't know, I doubt it."

"Marie, last night you mentioned that Max talks on the phone to somebody, maybe a friend of his. Do you have any idea who that person could be?"

"No, I don't know. I just know he talks to him a lot on the phone at night."

"It's a he? How do you know it's a boy? Did you hear him say a name?" Eric wondered if it could be Renée.

"I didn't hear him say a name, but it *has* to be a boy. I don't really think Max had a girlfriend, do you?" Marie chuckled, and Eric heard ice tinkling in a glass, which troubled him.

"Marie, it's not my business, but it would help a lot if you could stick to Diet Coke. This is about Max, and we have to work together to find him. It doesn't get more—"

"It's just that it's so crazy, and it's a lot to deal with, all of a sudden the house is empty, and the funeral home wants to schedule the service for my mom, and I don't even know where Max is, and it turns out she paid for the whole thing, but they want to know what kind of flowers I want and things like that . . ."

"I understand," Eric said, when her voice trailed off. "I know this is a hard time for you, but Max has to be the priority now. We have to find him."

"Okay, okay, I hear you."

"Good. I have to go now because I want to call the police. Call me if he contacts you, would you?"

"Yes, fine, thanks. Thanks so much for helping. Don't think I don't appreciate you, because I do. I know you really care about him, I can tell. Bye now."

"Okay, good-bye now." Eric hung up, got the non-emergency number of the Radnor police, and pressed Call.

"Squad room, Sergeant Colson speaking. How may I help you?"

"Hello, this is Dr. Eric Parrish, a psychiatrist at Havemeyer General Hospital, and I'm calling about one of my private patients. I'm concerned that he's a suicide risk after his grandmother's death yesterday, and he's been missing since then. His name is Max Jakubowski."

"How old is he?"

"Seventeen, a senior at Pioneer High. He works at PerfectScore but he hasn't shown up for work today and his mother doesn't know where he is, either."

"So how long has he been missing?"

"Since six o'clock last night, but it's very unusual for him to be out at night, especially overnight." Eric was going with his hunch.

"Can you give me a brief description of the boy?"

Eric told him generally what Max looked like. "Is he considered a missing person yet?"

"We don't stand on technicalities, Dr. Parrish."

"Good, because it's a matter of life and death. I called last night, and Officer Gambia went to the boy's house for me. He knows the case."

"Hold on, please, Dr. Parrish. It may take a few minutes."

"Okay, I'll wait." Eric moved his mouse to wake up his computer, entered his passcode, and watched email pile onto the screen. He skimmed the senders' names and subject lines distractedly, but one jumped out at him. He moved the mouse to click it open.

"Dr. Parrish?" Sergeant Colson said, abruptly back on the line. "I talked to one of my patrolmen, and they are aware of the situation from last night. We will keep an eye out for the young man and notify you if we hear anything. We have your cell number from last night."

"Thank you."

"Good-bye, Doctor."

"Bye." Eric stared at the computer screen. The email was from Susan and it read: **Dear Eric, Attached please find a copy of Husband's Petition for Primary Custody, which was filed and served** today. **Please feel free to call if you have any questions. Best, Susan.**

He opened the attachment and tried to read it, but the terms tumbled all over one another, **MINOR CHILD, WIFE, HUS-BAND, PRIMARY RESIDENCE**, all the stuff of his personal life, bollixed up in boldface. He studied it until it was time to go to the Physician Impairment Committee meeting.

He didn't eat the yogurt.

Chapter Thirty-two

Eric took a moment to compose himself before the Physician Impairment Committee meeting, standing outside the closed mahogany door in the empty hallway. He had to get his head in the game, so he pressed his custody petition and Max to the back of his mind, so he could focus. He braced himself, opened the door, and entered the conference room, but Brad Farnessen, Tom Singh, and Sam Ward were already there. They had water bottles and fresh legal pads, and Eric realized they must have been told to arrive much earlier. They sat in a panel on the far side of a Formica table with a fake wood surface, shaped like an upside-down U.

Brad smiled at Eric and rose abruptly, gesturing to his right. "Eric, come on in. Please, sit down."

"Thanks for coming, Eric," Tom said, rising from the center seat, his voice falsely light.

Sam rose last, meeting Eric's eye with obvious discomfort and pursing his lips. He actually gave Eric a little hippie-wave, then shoved his hand into his pocket. "Hey, Chief."

"Hello, everyone." Eric sat down in the black mesh chair to their right, and while everybody resettled, he looked briefly around. The room was small, rectangular, and windowless, and there was a large flat-screen television mounted on the wall, a futuristic pod-type conference phone in the center of the table, and a whiteboard on the wall that read at the top, HGH Patient Safety Communication Board.

"Eric, thanks for coming." Tom cleared his throat, easing back in his chair in the center seat. "We would like to begin by making a statement on behalf of the committee. We want to make clear, at the outset, that we appreciate your hard work for the past fifteen years."

"Thank you." Eric kept a smile on his face, but it unnerved him to look into Tom's chilly gray eyes, so he shifted his attention to the whiteboard on the back wall. Underneath the title were various columns and notations, written in thick black Sharpie.

"We appreciate your cooperation in this meeting, which we hope you understand is a formality."

"Understood." Eric read the whiteboard's left side, which was headed Employee Injury Report, and under that, a column of Last Splash Exposure, Last Stick Exposure, Last Physical Injury to Employee by Patient, and Last Slip/Fall. There were June dates written in Sharpie next to each category except for Last Slip/Fall, so evidently May had been a good month for hospital employees' staying upright.

"Let me briefly explain the procedure, which is informal. There will be no audio or video recording of this meeting, though we may take notes." Tom gestured at the legal pad sitting before each of them. "If you would like to take some notes, too, we can get you a pad."

"No, thanks." Eric kept his eyes on the whiteboard and read a column that had no heading: Last Mislabeled Specimen, Last Preventable Harm Event, Last Fall with Injury, Last Serious Event, Last Sentinel, Last CLABS, Last CAUTI, Last C.DIFF. There was a date written next to each one, and he realized midway through that he was reading a list of employee mistakes, which made him wonder if this was the Liability Conference Room. If so, he'd come to the right place.

"This meeting will last about an hour, and during it, we'll be exploring the allegations made in a sexual harassment claim filed against you by Kristine Malin, a medical student on rotation in your service."

Eric cringed inwardly, to hear the words said aloud in Sam's presence. If his attending didn't know about it before, he knew it now, and it would probably explain Eric's wacky behavior in the staff meeting this morning.

"I'll be asking the questions here. It's not as if you have to field questions from the three of us, as if we were a Roman triumvirate. You won't be sworn in. We know you are honest and we trust you to tell us the truth."

"Thank you." Eric forced himself to look away from the whiteboard in case it made him look false, like an actor reading cue cards.

"Finally, you should feel free to ask any questions you have. This isn't an inquisition, it's a discussion. Do you have any questions about procedure, before we move on?"

"Yes." Eric told himself to remain calm. "What happens after this? You listen to me, then you decide if I'm credible or not? The three of you make a judgment?"

Tom nodded. "Generally, that's true, but that's only part of the decision. The investigator will meet with the complainant, Ms. Malin, and he will make a recommendation as to the veracity of her allegations. We will review his recommendation and reach a final decision within the week."

Eric saw his opening. "Is Kristine, uh, Ms. Malin, being interviewed today?"

"Yes, I believe she is, this afternoon."

"I knew it!" Eric leaned forward, urgent. "Look, I don't know why she's telling these lies about me, but she looks completely different today than she's ever looked during her entire rotation. She usually wears contacts and dresses up, lots of makeup and skirts, but today, she's wearing glasses, pants, a blazer. Her hair is back in a ponytail. She's not wearing any makeup."

"What's your point, Eric?" Tom frowned, recoiling.

"I think she's trying to fake it for the interviewer today. I think she's trying to create a false impression that she doesn't dress nice or is overly attractive." Eric knew it sounded like he was blaming the victim, so he tried to explain. "Not that the way she dresses would excuse any harassment on my part, but I swear to you, I didn't harass her." Eric faced Sam. "Sam, you work with Kristine every day. Don't you know what I'm talking about? Didn't she look different today in the staff meeting?"

"Honestly, she did." Sam nodded, turning to Tom. "Tom, Eric is completely right. I never saw Kristine look like that before. Not that that would justify harassing her or anything, don't get me wrong, but Eric is totally right. Kristine's very cute, if I'm allowed to say that . . ." Sam hesitated. "I can say that, right, Tom?"

"Yes," Tom answered.

"Okay," Sam continued, "she's pretty and she dresses up every day. All the nurses talk about her, they all think she wears her skirts too short. Anybody in the unit would tell you the same thing. But today, she was definitely dressed down. In fact, I thought she was sick when she walked into the meeting, like she had the flu."

"Thank you!" Eric blurted out. "Sam, thanks, that's *exactly* what I mean." Eric turned to Tom, in appeal. "Tom, you hear that? That's *proof.* I swear to you, I did not harass her. I would never—"

Tom raised a palm like a traffic cop. "Eric. You made your point, and Sam, thank you for the corroboration." Tom nodded in Sam's direction, then returned his attention to Eric. "But we haven't gotten to that point yet, and Eric, you're mistaking the purpose of this meeting. This is to determine and discuss, in a collegial way, whether you have any impairment issues. The procedure begins with the drug testing this morning. None of us was surprised to learn that you tested negative for alcohol or drugs in your system."

"Of course I did. I'm not impaired in any way."

Suddenly the mechanical crackle of the loudspeaker filled the conference room. "Code Gray, Drs. Parrish and Ward to Wright. Code Gray, Drs. Parrish and Ward to Wright."

"Oh no." Eric jumped to his feet just as his pager went off, and in the next second, so did Sam's, beeping simultaneously. Eric reached for his pager on the fly, but Sam beat him do it, with a gasp.

"Chief, they called police to the unit. Must be Perino." Sam got up and headed around the table toward the door, but Eric was closer and he reached the door first, flinging it open

Brad frowned, rising. "Code Gray, that's a security issue, right? Is it an elopement? It'd better not be, and they shouldn't have called the police. That's not procedure."

"Tom, Brad, we have to go!" Eric called over his shoulder, with Sam on his heels.

"Sure, go." Tom rose, startled. "We can do this later."

Eric hustled down the hallway, his thoughts racing. He prayed to God Perino hadn't hurt one of the nurses. "What's the matter with Perino, Sam?"

"Sorry, Chief, I'll figure it out." Sam hustled through the double doors leading to the Wright Wing.

"Let's take the stairs." Eric took a left turn to the stairwell, pressed open the door, and took the stairs two-by-two with Sam at his side. They reached the first landing, and Eric heard the stairwell door opening downstairs behind them, followed by voices. "Is that Brad and Tom?"

"Yes," Sam muttered under his breath. "Somebody has to make sure we follow procedure."

"I hear you, brother." Eric didn't have to say another word. The last thing they needed during a crisis were two bigwigs trying to prove they knew what was going on in the trenches.

"Eric, Sam!" Tom hollered up the stairwell, his voice echoing. "Right behind you!"

"See you up there!" Eric hollered back, and he picked up the pace as they passed the third floor, then the fourth, and finally burst through the door on five, which emptied them next to the elevator bank outside the unit. They could see through the glass airlock that a cadre of blue-uniformed security guards and two men in suits stood with Amaka, who looked stricken. A ring of nurses and residents stood behind her, uniformly concerned, and Kristine stood, faking a frown, but Eric didn't have time for her games because everything happened at once.

"Oh God." Sam swiped his lanyard ID for them both, and Eric got out his key ring and unlocked the outer door.

Brad and Tom caught up with them. "What the hell is going on?"
Eric rushed to Amaka. "What happened? Is it Perino?"
Sam craned his head over the crowd. "Did he hurt somebody?"
"Dr. Parrish, hello, I'm Detective Rhoades," said one of the men
in a dark suit, stepping forward. He was a tall beefy man about
Eric's age, with brown eyes and a wide, fleshy face. His hair was
shorn close, so his scalp showed. "Dr. Parrish, we're sorry to inter-
rupt you, but it can't wait. This is my partner, Detective Pagano."
He gestured to a skinnier, younger man who stood behind him.
"Yes, what is it?" Eric asked, alarmed. "What's happening?"
"We'd like you to come down to the administration building and
talk with us. We think you might have some information that can
aid a current investigation."
"What investigation?"
"It's regarding the murder of Renée Bevilacqua."

Chapter Thirty-three

"Renée is . . . dead?" Eric stood, stunned. He couldn't believe it. It couldn't be true. He felt shaken to his very marrow.

"Who's Renée, Eric?" Brad asked, surprised. "Is Renée a patient on the unit?"

"No, it's about one of my private patients." Eric was reeling. His heart banged against his chest wall as if it were trying to escape.

"Dr. Parrish," Detective Rhoades said. "Will you come help us out?"

Amaka touched his arm. "Eric, go if you have to. We can hold the fort."

"Okay, then, yes." Eric tried to collect his agonized thoughts. Guilt overwhelmed him. His first clear thought was that Max must have done it, and Eric had made the wrong decision in not warning Renée or the police. But in the next moment, Eric felt torn by profound confusion and ambivalence. He still couldn't really believe that Max would do Renée harm, or that Max was capable of murder.

"Thanks, let's go." Detective Rhoades went to the door, and Eric numbly left the unit with the detectives, then got into an elevator and they rode downstairs in silence. The elevator doors opened onto the hospital lobby, and they hustled through the crowd of employees with HGH lanyards and visitors carrying Mylar balloons and gift-shop stuffed animals. They left the hospital, and Eric went outside with them, where the bright sunlight brought him from his reverie and the questions started to come.

"Detective, how was Renée killed? When did this happen? Where was she found?"

"We'll discuss that when we get there, Dr. Parrish, if you don't mind." Detective Rhoades motioned him to a gray Taurus sedan with darkened windows, parked in the no-parking zone in front of the hospital entrance. When they reached the Taurus, Detective Pagano opened the back door, and Eric slid into the backseat, surprised to see the stainless-steel divider between the front and the back. There were no inside locks on the doors. The detectives got into the front seat, and the car lurched off.

Eric sat in the backseat, stricken. The awful news begin to sink in. So Renée, that adorable curly-haired redhead, was dead, so young. Murdered. It didn't seem possible. Eric did and didn't believe it. He wanted to know how it had happened, even as he couldn't believe it had happened. He prayed she wasn't strangled. He didn't know if that would make it more likely that Max had killed her; Eric still couldn't believe that Max would do such a thing. He knew from his experience and training that OCD sufferers rarely acted on their fantasies, and even Arthur had agreed with him. So what had happened to Renée?

He looked out the window at the passing traffic, but all he could see was Renée's fresh face, how cute she was, how bright her eyes, and how sweet her manner. He mentally gathered the few facts he knew about her; she wanted better SAT scores, she lived in a nice house on a cul-de-sac, she talked on the phone too much when she drove, she had a lot of friends, she was popular.

Eric felt confounded. He didn't know enough about Renée to begin to answer who would have killed her, if not Max. Her boyfriend? Someone else at school? Someone in her family? Or was it a random act of violence? How had she died? Eric realized he didn't have to guess. He slid his iPhone from his pocket and scrolled to the Internet. He started to type Renée Bevilacqua into the search window, but the signal was bad. His eyes filmed. He stopped. He didn't have the heart for it right now.

The car was nearing the police station, and Eric had to compose himself. He assumed that Max hadn't been found yet, because if he had, the police or Marie would have called him. Ironically, whether Max had killed Renée or not, the boy would be in agony— if Max killed her he would want to die, and if somebody else had killed her, he would still want to die.

Eric felt more fearful than ever that Max would kill himself; the boy had nothing left, neither his beloved grandmother nor the girl he was fixated on, the one he had worried so much about, the one he feared he would kill, the one that he had actually killed. If he had.

Eric wasn't sure that Max had committed murder, so he didn't know what justice would mean right now, but he was a psychiatrist and a physician. As such, he could do no harm. He had taken an oath. It clarified his next steps. He had to do what he could to save Max. He had to help the police find him and he would have to tell them what they needed to find him, but *only* what they needed to find him, because Eric's communications with Max were confidential. Eric was permitted to breach his confidentiality only that much, if it would save Max's life.

The Taurus turned right onto Iven Road and traveled past the softball field toward the administration building, where the township had its offices and the police station. Iven was usually a quiet street lined with a handful of stone homes, but it didn't look that way right now. Cars and white news vans with colorful NBC, ABC, CBS, and FOX affiliate logos were parked all along the street to the township administration building, their microwave towers sticking up like spikes.

Suddenly his phone started ringing, and he looked down to see the call was from Laurie, so he answered, "Hi."

"Eric, what's going on?" Laurie sounded tense. "I heard cops came and want to see you about some investigation. What's the matter?"

"I'm okay, don't worry." Eric couldn't tell Laurie about Max because he didn't want to say too much in front of the police.

"But what's going on? What did they tell you? Where are you?" Laurie asked the questions staccato, like an emergency doc wanting to get the vitals: BP, respiration, check, check, check.

"I should go. We just got to the police station."

"You're going to a police station without a lawyer? Don't you need a lawyer?"

Eric knew Laurie's brother was a criminal lawyer in Philly. "Of course not, it's not about me. I have to go, we're here. Fill you in later."

"Eric, but—"

"Bye, talk soon." Eric hung up as they turned into the grounds of the administration building, which was a new, modern, glass-and-red-brick box, landscaped with mulched specimen plantings, next to a two-level parking lot. Media thronged in front of the building, and as soon as the Taurus turned left into the long driveway, the reporters sprang into frantic motion, grabbing microphones, hoisting videocameras to their shoulders, taking still pictures with cameras held overhead, and holding cell phones and tape recorders aloft.

Detective Rhoades groaned. "Dr. Parrish, you can see we got company. You don't have to talk to them, and I would advise you not to. They're like cockroaches. There's armies of 'em and if they get a crumb, they'll come back for more."

"Right, of course," Eric said, as the car pulled up in front of the station. He realized that he still had his HGH employee lanyard on, so he took it off swiftly and stuck it in his pocket. He didn't want the reporters to know his name or where he worked.

"Sit tight. We'll get you inside nice and easy. The only way to do this is orderly." Detective Rhoades turned around, his face hardly visible through the perforated grate. "We're going to come around to the backseat. Stay with us and walk straight to the door. They're going to yell questions. My advice would be not to comment."

"Right." Eric pocketed his cell phone.

"Stay seated until we come around the back." Detective Rhoades turned off the engine, then both detectives got out of the car and walked quickly to the backseat. Detective Rhoades came around, reached in a meaty hand for Eric, and practically lifted him bodily out of the car.

The media erupted in noise, everyone calling out at once. "Sir, who are you?" "Are you family?" "Are you here in connection with the Bevilacqua murder?" Reporters held up microphones, cameras, and cell phones. "Are you related to the victim?" "What information do you have?" "Did you know Renée Bevilacqua?"

The detectives hustled him to the entrance, and Eric kept his head down. They reached the entrance, the smoked glass doors slid open, and they found themselves inside a boxy hall with gray carpets. Detectives Rhoades let go of his arm. "Well done, Dr. Parrish. Come this way."

"Thanks. Call me Eric."

"Okay, Eric. I'm Jerry. My partner's Joe."

"Great." Eric followed the detectives through another glass doorway. To the right were segmented windows that divided the entrance from a sort of office space, and next to that a Coke vending machine and a white box that read Delco Medicine Drop, Help Prevent the Abuse of Prescription Drugs. They turned into a sleek, clean two-story lobby with rust-colored couches, recessed lighting, paneled walls, and an orange-carpeted spiral stairway that curved to the right.

"Is this the police station?" Eric tried to orient himself.

"Yes. We're lucky, we wouldn't have so much space if we didn't share with the Township."

"It's nice." Eric thought it looked nothing like the crappy ones on TV.

"Thanks. Right this way." Detective Rhoades bypassed the staircase, led them to a set of doors, and they entered a large, empty office that had a glass wall on the far side and a side wall lined with beige file cabinets, a printer, a copier, and some file accordions. Several desks occupied the middle of the room, each holding neatly stacked files next to their blotters, and around the edges were kids' school photographs, Little League pictures, and Phillies, Eagles, and Sixers regalia.

Eric thought it looked like a generic corporate office until he noticed a large bulletin board that read Cleared Cases, and underneath that hung thirty eight-by-ten mugshots of men and women of all shapes, sizes, ages, and races. Their expressions varied—lost, defiant, drunken, vacant, stricken, and damaged—and next to their names were their crimes—Robbery, Burglary, Ag Assault, Simple Assault, Criminal Mischief, Terroristic Threats, Home Invasion, Assault with a Deadly Weapon. Any one of them could have been the patients whom Eric saw at the hospital, brought by cops into the ED. There was so much mental illness among the criminal population, and so much mental illness being criminalized, that it was impossible to see where one problem ended and the other began.

"Here we go, Dr. Parrish. Would you mind stepping through the metal detector?" Detective Rhoades gestured him toward a metal detector in the back of the room.

"Not at all." Eric walked through it, and Detective Rhoades met him on the other side.

"Would you like something to drink? We got coffee, soda, a bottle of water." Detective Rhoades smiled, showing remarkably even teeth.

"Water, thanks."

"How about something to eat? Lotta sandwiches upstairs. Cookies, too. It's leftover conference food, but it's good."

"No, thanks." Eric hadn't eaten since the morning, but he wasn't hungry.

"This is the place." Detective Rhoades opened the door to a small room. "Why don't you go in and sit down, and we'll get you that water?"

Chapter Thirty-four

The room was a small beige rectangle, and the outer wall was a floor-to-ceiling glass covered by white blinds, while the wall on the right was a massive black sheet of glass, obviously an observation window. Eric could see a fuzzy silhouette of himself ghosted faintly in its dark reflection. He sat perched on the edge of a black mesh chair at a narrow table with a fake-wood top, pressed against one wall. He set his phone on the table, which otherwise held only a black landline telephone and, inexplicably, a roll of toilet paper.

"Here you go, Eric." Detective Rhoades returned and eased heavily into the chair catty-corner. He set two bottles of water down on the table and slid one to Eric.

"Thanks." Eric uncapped the bottle and drank thirstily as Detective Pagano entered the room with a water bottle and took a chair at the other end of the table. Eric could see, in the indirect light from the window, that Pagano was maybe ten years younger than Detective Rhoades, probably in his early thirties, with cheeks that bore the faint pitting of adolescent acne. His face was long and narrow and his small, dark eyes were set too close-together, which gave him an unfriendly aspect.

"So, Eric, thanks for coming down. We really appreciate it."

"I'm happy to help."

"This is a new investigation, and we like to dot our i's and cross our t's. That's why we videotape our interviews. You don't mind, do you?"

Eric hesitated. "Uh, no, but where's the camera?"

"Behind there." Detective Rhoades waved at the black glass. "So, tell me about yourself. What's it like to be the head doctor on the psychiatry department? No pun intended." He chuckled. "Get it? Head *doctor, head* doctor."

"Funny." Eric managed a smile.

"You like it?"

"My job? I love it."

"How long have you been at HGH?"

"Fifteen years."

"What are the hours like?"

"It's basically nine-to-five."

"Must be nice."

Eric felt defensive, for some reason. He sensed the detective's demeanor change, becoming less friendly. "I have private patients, too. I see them at my house."

"You're allowed to do that? Moonlight, like that?"

"Yes. It's not atypical. Why?"

"Just curious. I moonlight too. Do security at parties." Detective Rhoades shrugged his heavy shoulders. "You weren't just getting in to work when I saw you, were you?"

"No. I was at a meeting." Eric wasn't about to elaborate.

"You got a family? Me, I have a wife, three kids."

"Uh, I mean, yes."

"But you live alone, right? I looked you up. You live in the Township."

"Right, yes." Eric was surprised the detective had looked him up, but he shouldn't have been. Everybody Googled everybody nowadays.

"So you're not living with your family?"

"Do we need to talk about my family?" Eric didn't want to talk about Hannah or Caitlin. The detective could know Caitlin was an A.D.A. "I'd like to talk about Renée Bevilacqua. That's why we're here, isn't it?"

"Okay, yes, no problem." Detective Rhoades eased back in his chair and crossed his legs. His fleshy face fell into grim lines. "Tell me what you know about her. It's such a sad case. Her parents are beside themselves. Her father just lost it when we were out at the house."

"I'm sure." Eric could only imagine what Renée's family was going through. He had treated families who had lost loved ones to violent crime and he'd even treated victims of violent crime. They worked impossibly hard in therapy to come out healthy and whole. The process took years.

"So how do you know Renée?"

"I don't know her, exactly." Eric had to choose his words carefully.

"Oh, I thought you knew her."

"No, I don't."

"I thought you said at the hospital that she was one of your private patients."

"No, I didn't say that," Eric answered, uneasily. It was uncharted professional territory, trying to decide what he could divulge and what he couldn't.

"Then I musta heard wrong. When that other doctor asked who Renée was, I heard you say she was one of your private patients."

"No, I didn't. I'm not allowed to divulge the identities of my private patients or my patients at the hospital."

"So you can't tell me whether or not Renée was your patient?"

"No, wait, I'm not making myself clear." Eric shook his head, unnerved. "I can't tell you who my patients are, but I can tell you that Renée wasn't one of them."

"You can't tell me who your patients are, but you can tell me who they *aren't*?" Detective Rhoades smiled, scratching his shorn head.

"Exactly. The identities of my patients are confidential. Does that explain it?"

"Yes." Detective Rhoades paused, eyeing him. "You okay, Eric? You seem kind of upset."

"No, I mean, yes. Obviously, I am upset, a young girl was murdered."

"How did you know she was young, if you didn't know her?" Detective Rhoades pursed his lips. "I got the impression you hadn't heard she was murdered until I told you."

"Detective, let me explain. Whom I treat and what they say during treatment is strictly confidential, as a matter of doctor-patient privilege. You must know, that's a matter of Pennsylvania law." Eric knew that much about the law, though he couldn't cite chapter and verse.

"Right." Detective Rhoades nodded.

"But I can breach that confidentiality, to a certain extent, when I believe that one of my patients is a danger to themselves or someone else." Eric felt like such a hypocrite saying the words. He hadn't told the police when he had the chance. He hadn't saved Renée. But maybe he could still save Max. "And if I breach it, I'm allowed to tell you only the barest minimum to prevent that patient from harming himself or anybody else."

Detective Rhoades listened intently. "So tell me."

"I have a private patient, a seventeen-year-old, Max Jakubowski. I reported him missing last night and I told the police that he disappeared after the death of his grandmother at about six o'clock."

"You called here?"

"No, Berwyn. I called 911 and asked the Berwyn Police Department to go to Max's house, and they did, but they couldn't find him."

"And the name of this patient is Max Jakubowski?"

"Yes. Have you seen a report come in about him today?"

"No. Give me a description of him."

"As I told the officers last night, he has light brown hair, blue eyes, and goes to Pioneer High School." Eric glanced over at Detective Pagano, noticing for the first time that he was taking notes on a skinny pad. "That's the most I can tell you, except for his home address, which Officer Gambia knows."

"He's with the Berwyn PD. They're not this jurisdiction."

Eric tensed. "Okay, it's 310 Newton Road in Berwyn. That's all I can tell you."

"What does Max Jakubowski have to do with Renée Bevilacqua's murder?"

Eric hesitated, his heart pounding. He was the only person who knew the link between Max and Renée, and he hated divulging even a part of it. It was the only way to save Max's life, but it could also put the boy on the hook for Renée's murder. There was still a part of him that believed in Max. He wasn't about to give the police information that they could use to convict him of a murder he didn't commit.

Eric answered, "All I can tell you, within the limits of my confidentiality, is that I have information that suggests that Max might know something about Renée Bevilacqua's death."

"What information do you have?"

"I can't tell you more than I've already told you. He's missing and you need to find him. As I told the officers last night, I believe he is a suicide risk."

"Why do you believe that?"

"I can't answer that question."

"Does that have to do with Renée Bevilacqua?"

"I can't answer that question, either."

"Does he know her, go to school with her?"

"I can't answer any of those questions."

Detective Rhoades frowned. "How long have you been seeing Max as a patient?"

"I can't answer."

"Did you tape your sessions with him?"

"No."

"Did you take notes?"

"Yes." Eric knew what was coming next.

"Will you produce those notes for us?"

Eric hesitated. "No, not even under subpoena. It's strictly confidential. I'm telling you what you need to know now. Find Max."

Detective Rhoades's frown deepened. "Where do you think Max is?"

"I don't know."

"You have *no* idea?"

"No."

Detective Rhoades paused, his eyes narrowing. "I'm not going to play footsie with you. A young girl is dead. *Murdered.* I looked her parents in the eye, nice people, they were beside themselves, grief-stricken, trying to understand why their daughter was killed walking through a nice, safe park behind their house, choked to death."

"She was choked?" Eric kept his expression neutral, trying not to betray the shock he felt. Renée had been strangled, just like Max had obsessed over.

"Yes, no signs of a ligature, just bare hands. Their dog came running home alone, that's how the parents knew something was wrong. The father had gone to work, but the mother hadn't left yet. Her name is Margaret, a nurse. She went to the park and found her daughter, lying there dead. She called 911, hysterical."

Eric didn't say anything. His throat constricted, his chest felt tight. He prayed to God that Max hadn't killed Renée.

"I told her parents that I'm going to find whoever killed her and lock him up. Nothing makes me madder than somebody like you, who might be able to help me find that killer, but who won't. Who *refuses* to help. Who doesn't care about justice."

"It's the law," Eric said, stricken.

"It's a *technicality.*"

"I don't make the law."

"You live around here, so you know that we don't get a lot of murders, less than a handful in the ten years I've been here. And I will level with you, it feels horrible. It feels horrible to lose a human life. It feels horrible to see a young girl lying facedown like that." Detective Rhoades clenched and unclenched his jaw. "I'm never going to get that sight out of my mind. That's got to stay with me forever, like a *brand.*"

"Yes." Eric realized that his wasn't the only profession with a case you couldn't forget, the Ghost.

"There is nothing more important to me or to this department right now than locking up that girl's killer. You follow me?"

"Yes."

"So? You're not going to come clean?"

"I've done what I can."

"I'm trying to get justice for that girl. Doesn't that matter to you?"

"I'm not stopping you from getting justice for her, and we could be out looking for Max. I'm telling you he's a suicide risk."

"But you won't tell me why."

"Yes, I did, and I told the police last night too. He was very close to his grandmother and she died yesterday. He's been missing since then."

"You won't answer my questions."

"I've answered the ones I can."

"Fine, two can play that game. Now I'm going to tell you what *I* can." Detective Rhoades leaned over, his eyes newly hard. "I know that last night you visited Renée Bevilacqua at the frozen yogurt place she worked at. I have two witnesses who placed you there and they told me you talked to her."

Eric felt his stomach flip. He flashed on the girls last night. Trixie at the toppings, the other one at the cash register. The police would have gone there today. The girls would have told them everything.

"I also know that you followed Renée home last night. I have your car on three different street cameras, from her work to her house."

Eric thought of the drive. Of course there would be traffic-light cameras, all kinds of cameras.

"I know that you were parked on her street around midnight. I have an eyewitness who placed you there, and your car was positively identified by a member of the town watch."

Eric thought of the man who had stopped him on the cul-de-sac. The man had even mentioned the town watch.

Detective Rhoades bore down. "That means you were the last person to see Renée alive."

"So?" Eric recoiled, aghast. "You can't believe I had something to do with her murder. Are you *serious*? That's absurd!"

"The coroner is performing the autopsy as we speak, but he places time of death between seven and nine in the morning. Where were you at that time?"

"I was getting ready for work," Eric shot back, incredulous.

"You live alone, and unless you were sleeping with somebody, you can't corroborate your alibi."

Eric's mouth dropped open. "What *alibi*? It's not an alibi, I don't need an alibi!"

"You had time to kill Renée and still get to the hospital."

"Of course I didn't kill her." Eric couldn't believe the words coming out of his own mouth. It was surreal. "I would never do such a thing."

"Then why were you following her?"

Eric wanted to tell, but he couldn't breach confidentiality to that extent. "I can't answer that."

"Why did you go in the store to talk to her?"

"I can't answer that." Eric felt stricken, remembering that he had pretended that he had a daughter who went to SAT tutoring. The girls in the shop must have told the police that, too.

"Did you wait for her to get off work?"

"Yes." Eric could answer that because it had to do with his actions, not something that Max had told him in session.

"Why were you waiting for her?"

"I can't answer that."

"You can, but you *won't*!" Detective Rhoades slammed his heavy hand on the table, with a *bang*. "Then who killed her? Are you telling me Max Jakubowski killed her?"

"No, I'm not." Eric felt his throat catch. It was exactly the inference to be drawn from his words, but it wasn't his intent. "I'm telling you that you need to find Max before he kills himself."

"Don't try to deflect. We'll run down that lead, but right now, you're my guy."

"No, that's not possible." Eric's mouth had gone bone dry.

"Why did you stalk her?"

"I didn't."

"How did you even know her?"

"I didn't, I told you that."

"Then why did you tell her you had a daughter her age—when you have a little girl?"

"I can't answer that." Eric felt his face aflame.

"It was a lie, wasn't it? It's not true."

"I didn't kill her or anybody, I swear it." Eric thought of what Laurie had said on the phone about a lawyer. "I'm not answering any more questions without a lawyer."

Detective Pagano rose, walking over to Detective Rhoades with a frown. "Jerry, take it easy, buddy."

"I'm fine, Joe." Detective Rhoades glanced at his partner, then returned his attention to Eric as he reached inside the breast pocket of his sport jacket, pulled out some papers, and tossed them onto the table. "This is a search warrant. Your home is being searched right now and so is your office at the hospital."

"*What?*" Eric said, outraged. "Wait. You can't do that."

"Yes, we can."

"But there are patient files, medical information protected by HIPAA—"

"We won't search patient files. They're not in the scope of the warrant. Read it." Detective Rhoades stabbed the warrant with his finger. "We're also in the process of impounding your car from the hospital parking lot."

Eric gasped. "Why do you want my car?"

"Why do you think?" Detective Rhoades slid a Kleenex tissue from his breast pocket and used it to grab Eric's phone from the table. "By the way, I'm confiscating this."

"But you *can't*! I didn't do anything."

"I'm taking your clothes, too." Detective Rhoades motioned to Eric's chest. "You'll be changing under the supervision of two uniformed officers, so the chain of custody stays intact."

"I want to call a lawyer, right now."

"Fine, we'll shut off the camera. Talk here." Detective Rhoades grabbed the landline from the table and banged it in front of Eric. "And say hi to your wife for me."

Chapter Thirty-five

Eric waited until Detectives Rhoades and Pagano had left the room to pick up the receiver of the landline. He didn't know what Detective Rhoades had meant by the last remark, this was an emergency and she was an expert, who might also have an in with Detective Rhoades. Eric pressed in the numbers of her cell phone and she picked up immediately.

"Caitlin Parrish, Assistant D.A."

"Caitlin, it's Eric."

"Eric?" Caitlin asked, angry. "I never would have answered if I knew it was you. My caller ID says Radnor Police Department."

"I know, that's where I am. This is going to sound crazy, but they think I'm involved with the murder of a young girl, Renée Bevilacqua. I don't know if you heard about it—"

"*What?* Of *course* I heard about it. The whole office is in a tizzy. Jason and Michaela are all over it, and I think the brass is giving a press conference today."

"Well, there are two detectives questioning me, and one is named Jerry Rhoades. I think he knows you. They're searching my house and office. They want to confiscate my clothes."

"What are you *talking* about?" Caitlin asked, incredulous. "That's what they do to suspects."

"They think I'm a suspect."

"That's not possible. Is this some kind of joke?"

"No, it's real, but it's crazy." Eric took heart, not completely surprised that Caitlin was able to put her personal feelings aside and understand the seriousness of the situation.

"They really think you're a *suspect*? *You*?"

"Ridiculous, right? One of my private patients might be a suspect, but I can't tell them anything because of confidentiality." Eric knew she would understand what he meant, because even with their pillow talk, they kept certain things confidential, about each other's professions.

"So what are you going to do?"

"I need a criminal lawyer, or maybe you could call Detective Rhoades and tell him that this whole thing is ridiculous. Or can you talk to somebody in your office?" Eric remembered that Caitlin always got along great with the higher-ups. "Talk to Bob or Scott, one of the bosses. I mean, talk sense into *somebody*. Tell them that I would never commit a murder—"

"Wait. Just so I understand. So you're at the station now and you need a criminal lawyer?"

"Yes."

"And you want me to talk to Rhoades or my boss for you?"

"Yes, please. I would really appreciate it."

"Tell you what, Eric." Caitlin paused. "I'd love to help you out, but I'm too busy dealing with the custody petition you filed against me this morning."

"Caitlin, look, I know you're pissed, but—"

"*Pissed*?" Caitlin raised her voice, her tone turning frosty. "*Pissed* doesn't begin to describe how I felt when I opened that email and saw my own name on the *caption*. I've been wishing awful things on you ever since. I can't even *work* for how distracted I am, how *furious* I am at you for *suing me* for custody."

Eric should've known. He should never have called her, no matter what Detective Rhoades had said. She was a human being, and she was angry, hurt, and a lot of other emotions that weren't working in his favor right now. "Caitlin, please listen—"

"You want my *help*? Ha! Fat chance. You're a suspect in the investigation of the Bevilacqua murder and you want me to make some calls for you? Stick my neck out for you? Pull some strings? Engage in a potential conflict of interest, after what you're trying to do?"

Eric could hear she was just warming up. He didn't even try to interrupt her.

"You want me to call Detective Rhoades and vouch for you? I'm laughing my *ass* off. Let me tell you something about Detective Rhoades, I can give you the inside scoop. Would you like to know something about Detective Rhoades?"

"Yes," Eric answered, though he gathered the question was rhetorical.

"He's one of the smartest detectives working the job. He looks kinda like a bulldog, doesn't he? They call him Dog, short for bulldog. That's his nickname. You know why? Hint—it's *not* because he looks like one."

Eric's stomach did a backflip. Meanwhile, he hadn't realized it before, but Detective Rhoades did kind of look like a bulldog.

"How else can I help you, Eric? You want me to call one of my buddies in the criminal defense bar and get you out of this situation you've gotten yourself into? I'll send you a lawyer, all right. I'll send you the worst criminal lawyer I know."

"Caitlin, I get it."

"Good. Bye." The phone went dead.

Eric inhaled stiffly, trying to figure out whom to call next. He needed a lawyer and he was concerned about his patient files at the hospital, so it made sense to call Mike Braezele in Legal. Eric pressed in the hospital's main number. The phone rang once and was picked up by an operator, then he asked to be put through, and the call was answered after a few clicks.

"Legal Department," said a businesslike female voice, which Eric recognized as Dee Dee's.

"Dee, it's Eric Parrish. Is Mike there?"

"Oh my God, Eric," Dee Dee said, instantly concerned. "Are you okay? What's going on? I heard there were cops in your office."

"I know. Can I speak to Mike?"

"He's not here. He's on your unit with Brad and Tom."

"Can you transfer me?" Eric visualized the scene, sickened. He could imagine Amaka and the shocked staff, standing by helplessly while the unit was invaded by police. He prayed it didn't destabilize the patients and that Perino didn't have another violent break.

"Sure, yes, hold on."

"Thanks, will do." Eric waited on hold until there was a click on the phone as it was picked up.

"Eric, what the *hell*?"

"Mike, they're on the unit?"

"Yes, it's unreal!" Mike sounded shocked, which Eric had expected.

"Are they in the file room?"

"No, there's six cops, swarming all over your office. Going through your drawers, putting your things in boxes. They took your computer!"

"Put the unit in lockdown, Mike."

"We did, right away. What's going on? This is insanity!"

"It's a long story." Eric's doctor-patient confidentiality extended to everyone, even Mike, and he didn't have time to explain now anyway. "Can we stop them, legally? I don't want them going through any patient files. We don't have to let them do that, do we?"

"No, that's not an issue. Patient files aren't within the scope of the warrant."

"What does that mean, 'scope of the warrant'?" Eric remembered that Detective Rhoades had used the same term.

"I'm not going to give you a lecture on the search and seizure clause of the Fourth Amendment, Eric. Are you involved in this murder case? Is that true?"

"No, I had nothing to do with it, at all. It will get straightened out."

"What do you mean 'straightened out'?" Mike lowered his voice, as if he were trying not to be overheard. "Was this girl one of your private patients?"

"No, she wasn't."

"Then what? How do you know her? The police don't search offices unless they suspect you of a crime."

"Mike, I'm not accused of anything—"

"Are you a person of interest? Are you a *suspect*?"

"Yes." Eric wasn't going to lie. "Mike, is there any way you can come down here or send somebody on your staff?"

"Come where? Where are you?"

"I'm at the Radnor police station. They're searching my house and car, they want my clothes—"

"Eric, listen, I don't know what you're involved in, but I'm not about to come down there, nor will I send anybody else from Legal. You're suspected of the gravest possible crime."

"Mike, I didn't do it. You can't really think I did it. You know better than that. You *know* me." Eric had known Mike for fifteen years. The lawyer had started only a week before Eric had.

"That's irrelevant, and I shouldn't have said that because that's not the point, as a matter of law. If she was one of your private patients—"

"She *wasn't* my patient."

"Was she a patient on the unit?"

"No."

"If that's true, then HGH has no connection with the matter." Mike's tone turned officious. "Any wrongdoing by you would be outside the scope of your employment at HGH. Therefore, neither I nor my staff can represent you. Furthermore, the insurance that the hospital purchases for you under your employment contract does not cover legal expenses incurred outside the scope of your employment at HGH, whether they be civil or criminal."

Eric hadn't even been thinking about insurance. He already knew where this was going.

"You need to get your own lawyer to represent you and you need to pay for it on your own dime. I'm assuming you have malpractice coverage or similar coverage for your private practice. You do, don't you?"

"Yes." Eric did maintain additional insurance, at the cost of ten grand a year, but Renée hadn't been his patient, so he doubted it was covered.

"Eric, if I were you, that would be my first call, my malpractice insurer."

Eric checked his watch, and it was already three thirty. He hadn't even gotten to make treatment rounds today. "Is everything okay on the unit?"

"Yes, Amaka and Sam have everything in control."

"Good. I'm not sure if I can make it back today. I have to stop by the house and—"

"Eric, don't come back to work. I have to talk to Tom and Brad, but you can't return if you're a *murder* suspect."

"Wait. *What?*" Eric couldn't believe what he was hearing.

"We have no choice, Eric. This is a PR nightmare." Mike groaned. "We just got the number-two ranking, you were our poster boy."

"No, that's not right, that can't be!" Eric raised his voice. "I'm not charged with anything, they didn't arrest me. It's just speculation, and I'm going to call the lawyer and get it cleared up. You can't tell me not to come back, just because it's bad PR. It's my job, my *unit*. I have a contract!"

"Eric, I'll tell you the way this is going to play out. Any misconduct by you, especially criminal misconduct rising to the level of murder, nullifies your contract with HGH."

"You can't do that. How can you do that?" Eric's head started spinning.

"I'm going to recommend that you be put on indefinite suspension, pending the outcome of the investigation and/or trial."

"What trial? You're firing me? I'm *fired*?"

"No. Suspended. Indefinitely. I'll see if I can make it with pay."

"I don't care about the money! I have patients, they're counting on me."

"They'll be fine."

"No, you can't!"

"We can and we will. Sam will run the unit with Amaka until you get back."

"But when can I come back? How long will that be?"

"It's up to the cops, Eric." Mike clucked. "What the hell's going on with you, lately? The incident with Perino? The sexual harassment claim? Now, *this*? Is it the divorce? Wait, hold on." Mike covered the phone with his hand. "I have to go. Tom's calling me."

"But Mike—"

"Get a lawyer, Eric." The phone line went dead, and suddenly there was a knock at the interview room door.

"Dr. Parrish, this is Detective Rhoades. I have two patrolmen here to assist you with your clothes."

Eric thought fast. He didn't know the number of his malpractice insurance company, but he knew someone who was great in any emergency, whose brother was a lawyer.

"Give me five minutes," he called to the police.

Chapter Thirty-six

An hour later, the door to the interview room was opened, and Eric rose to meet his new lawyer, Laurie's brother Paul Fortunato. In medical school, Laurie used to regale him with wild Paul stories, as if her younger brother were the id to her superego, but on first impression, Paul reminded Eric of Laurie; he had her curly black hair, strong face, and animated features—flashing espresso-brown eyes, fleshy lips, and a quick smile. Paul was in his mid-thirties, of short stature but fit, dressed in an expensively tailored dark suit with a shiny purplish print tie. He wore too much aftershave.

Eric extended a hand. "Hi. Eric Parrish."

"I'm Paul. Good to meet you."

"Heard a lot about you."

"You, too. Please, siddown." Paul gestured to the mesh chair and set a Footlocker bag and a slim metallic briefcase on the table. "Let's talk first, then we'll call in the local constabulary. They already gave me the 411. They have you talking to the girl at the yogurt place, following her home, and parking in front of her house. You want them to find your patient, but you're not giving them any information and they think you're stonewalling. I'll have you out of here in fifteen minutes."

"How?" Eric sat down, surprised.

"You'll see." Paul flashed a quick smile, evidently enjoying himself. "Laurie said you have questions for me. Ask away."

Eric blinked. "I do have questions, but don't you want to ask me whether I murdered Renée Bevilacqua?"

"Why would I do that?" Paul looked at him like he was crazy, rounding animated brown eyes.

"It's a logical question."

"Not for me, I'm a criminal lawyer."

Eric hoped he was kidding. "Well, I didn't do it. I had nothing to do with her murder."

"Thank God. I only represent innocent clients."

"Are you serious?"

"No." Paul snorted.

"I want you to know I'm innocent."

"I don't care."

Eric recoiled. "Really? How can that be?"

"Are you asking me about legal philosophy? We need to discuss this, why?" Paul shook his head, chuckling softly. "Laurie said you're a typical shrink, yakkety-yak. I love my big sister, don't you? She's cute, right? I think she has a thing for you. Don't tell her I said that."

"No, she doesn't. We're friends." Eric couldn't smile. "Don't be ridiculous."

"I kid you not." Paul nodded. "She talks about you a lot. She told me you were divorced. Why don't you ask her out? What are you waiting for? She's dyin' on the vine."

"How is *this* a more appropriate conversation than legal philosophy?"

"Good point! Touché!" Paul chuckled. "Okay, I never ask my clients if they did it. Why? It's legally insignificant. I'm not a dirtbag, I'm a purist. I represent the Constitution, it's the purest law we have, not bought and paid for, like now. Our forefathers were geniuses, not thieves. Lofty enough for you? The Constitution guarantees your rights, but cops and prosecutors cross that line all the time. My job is to push 'em back, shove 'em back, wa-a-a-ay back!" Paul did a cheer. "Go, team! Feel better?"

"No."

Paul seemed not to hear him. "You need somebody to stand up for you. You're the little guy, you just don't realize it yet. The Commonwealth has all the aces, and you don't even know you're playing cards." Paul rubbed his hands together. "Just so you know the legalese, you can stand on your privilege, which is codified by statute in Section 5944. In Pennsylvania, you can't be examined in any civil or criminal matter as to any information acquired in the course of your professional services on behalf of your client. It's a very strong privilege, and it can't be waived without the written consent of your client. The only exception is for future harm and that isn't interpreted to prove past conduct. Now ask me your questions. The Keystone cops are waiting for us."

"Don't underestimate these guys. They seem to be moving really quickly."

"They have nothing else to do."

Eric remembered what Caitlin had told him. "My ex-wife says Detective Rhoades is very tenacious. She's an assistant district attorney."

"Oooh, I'm scared. Meanwhile, why'd you marry an A.D.A.? Was she pregnant? Do prosecutors even *have* sex? Or maybe they do, but they don't enjoy it?"

Eric couldn't get a bead on this guy. "Are you having fun? Because it seems like you are."

"Yes, I am. I love my job. I protect people and I win. Watch me. Let me do my stuff." Paul threw up his hands. "Now ask me your questions already! This is the worst date ever! Too much foreplay!"

Eric smiled, despite himself. It actually felt good. "Okay, the police are searching my office at the hospital and my house, and they took my car. Can they do that?"

"Yes, but it's grabby. Next question."

"Paul, I run a psychiatric unit, and what the cops did at the hospital jeopardizes some very sick people. My patients need routine and calm. Disruption like that can set them back days, and their insurance companies only allow them a limited number." Eric thought of Perino. "For example, I treat a schizophrenic who thinks the CIA is after him. It doesn't help that uniformed police arrest his psychiatrist and search the unit. Can the cops really do that?"

"Yes, they can, and if you ask me, the schizophrenic is right. The CIA really is after us. So's the NSA and the rest of the alphabet."

Eric let it go. "What about my patient files? The cops told me it wasn't within the scope of the warrant, but I don't know what that means."

"When police obtain a search warrant, they have to specify what they're searching for and what they intend to seize. The cops aren't requesting patient files because they know the hospital would take them to court. They'll do it later, but not yet."

"They took my phone. Can they do that, too?"

"Yes, buy a new one. You're probably a week away from an upgrade. Whenever I need a new phone, I'm always a week away from an upgrade." Paul rolled his eyes. "You want to see some real criminals? Look at AT&T. Verizon. Sprint. Bankers, mortgage companies, the Fed. Then move on to Congress. *Those* are the guys that belong behind bars, not you. The law is made by people who are bought and sold, but that wasn't true in 1776, in my hometown. Next question?"

"They want me to give them my clothes. Can they do that?"

"Eric, they're doing you a favor. You dress like a middle-aged lesbian."

"Okay, enough." Eric smiled again. "I see where Laurie gets it from."

"Any other questions?"

"No."

"Excellent! I'm going to call in the locals." Paul pointed at Eric. "Clam up, Ralph Mouth. I'm going to make a speech and try not to say the F word. I'm doing great so far, right?"

"Great."

"My wife's idea. Because of the kids. We have a swear jar, like a TV family. All we need is a laugh track."

"My ex-wife curses all the time."

"Really? Maybe she was okay." Paul held up the Footlocker

bag. "By the way, I brought you sweats and a new phone, and I'll give you a ride back to work."

"They suspended me. Can they do that?"

"Prolly. See what I mean? *Criminals.*" Paul scowled. "We'll discuss it later. I'll drive you home. Give them your Amish outfit, we're leaving." He turned around, crossed to the front door, and opened it. "Detective Rhoades?"

"Right here." Detective Rhoades appeared at the door, a sour expression on his face, with Detective Pagano behind him.

"Step into my office." Paul gestured them into the interview room, deadpan.

"Thank you." Detectives Rhoades shifted his gaze in Paul's direction. "I'd like to resume the discussion, since you two have had a chance to confer."

"Thanks, but no." Paul shook his head, neatly. "The interview's over. You're not charging him, and he's not answering any more questions. Don't tell me, let me guess—you didn't Mirandize him."

"He's not in custody."

"I take it that's a no. You didn't read him his rights?"

"Correct. He's not being arrested."

"You may not have arrested him, but we both know he was in custodial interrogation."

"It wasn't." Detective Rhoades folded his beefy arms, but Paul looked him directly in the eye, unintimidated.

"You didn't read him his rights because you didn't want to tip him off. You knew he was a suspect when you picked him up, yet you neglected to inform him of that fact. He's a respected doctor, and he's trying to do the right thing. You tricked him."

"We didn't read him his rights because it wasn't required by law."

"The judge will disagree with you. If you move against my client, I'll file a motion to suppress your videotape." Paul gestured at the black window. "Plus you picked him up at work, for maximum terroristic effect. You didn't even care about the mental health of the patients on his unit, all of whom are straight-up nuts, if not right about the CIA. That's bullying and intimidation. How do you sleep at night?"

"I don't like your attitude." Detective Rhoades frowned.

"Neither does my wife." Paul gestured to Eric. "My client is happy to leave you with his dorky shirt and Mom jeans. I'm embarrassed by the way he dresses—and I've represented pimps."

Detective Rhoades cocked his head. "You know, every lawyer from Philly is just like you. Smart-assed."

"And every cop from the sticks is just like you. Needs a mint." Paul motioned the detectives out the door. "Let's leave our baby boy in the dressing room, shall we? He's old enough to find his own zipper."

"I'll send in a patrolman to preserve the chain of custody," Detective Rhoades said, leaving the interview room.

The room emptied, and Eric glanced at his watch, with a start. It was almost six fifteen, and he saw patients at home tonight, starting at seven o'clock.

He'd have to hurry.

Chapter Thirty-seven

Eric emerged from the police station with Paul, and the two men barreled through the media blanketing the sidewalk. There were more reporters than before, holding up cell phones, microphones, and videocameras. Photographers raised portable metal grids of klieglights and used camera flashes, which went off like so many tiny explosions. The reporters dogged the two men, filmed their every step, and shouted questions:

"Mr. Fortunato, who's your client?" "Sir, who are you?" "What's your name?" "Why did you change clothes?" "Is this in connection with the Bevilacqua murder?" "What were you doing in there for so long?" "Come on, give us a comment!"

Eric kept his head down, hiding his face. The media knew that Paul was a criminal lawyer, and unfortunately that identified him as a suspect, unlike when he'd entered the building. Then he could've just been someone giving information, which was what he'd thought he was. But the reporters smelled blood and chased them to the parking lot.

"Paul, is he a person of interest or suspect?" "Did they confiscate his clothes?" "Why didn't they arrest him?" "Is there any new information in the Bevilacqua case?" "Do the police have any leads?" "Come on, please, give us a quick statement. Tell us who he is. This is your chance to get out in front of this!" "Sir, sir, what's your name? Do yourself a favor and make a statement before the police do!"

Eric and Paul broke into a light jog toward Paul's black Mercedes SUV, which was parked illegally in the packed parking lot. Paul chirped it unlocked on the fly, and they reached the car and jumped inside the front seat. Paul started the engine, and the reporters surrounded the SUV.

"This is awful!" Eric recoiled, shocked. Camera flashes popped all around, and a massive set of klieglights switched on, flooding the SUV with white-hot light. He turned instinctively away.

"Don't hide your face. Hold your head high and look forward. Don't look at them." Paul threw the car into reverse and backed out, honking the horn.

"Be careful not to hit anybody."

"Why? That's my favorite part."

"I took an oath. Do no harm." Eric faced forward, forcing himself not to make eye contact with any of the reporters. He'd seen scenes of the media like this in movies, but he never realized how chaotic it was in reality.

"I took an oath too. But I crossed my fingers." Paul kept reversing and honking, scattering the reporters. "You know, the cops could come out and do crowd control, but they won't."

"Why not?"

"Because they want the pressure on you. They want you to be film at eleven. Like I told you, they got the aces and you're just figuring out there's a card game." Paul put the car into forward gear and hit the gas, steering toward the exit.

"They're not going to follow us, are they?" Eric could see in his peripheral vision that reporters were running to their cars and news vans parked along Iven Road.

"Don't worry, I'll lose them. You're riding in eight cylinders of a tax-deductible getaway car." Paul took a quick left, zooming past the picket fences and privet hedges in front of the tasteful homes on the back street, then took another right turn through the lovely neighborhood behind Lancaster Avenue.

"I'm supposed to see patients in my private practice tonight." Eric glanced at the dashboard clock, which read 6:32. "I have the first appointment at seven o'clock, at home."

"Get the new phone and cancel them. You can't see patients to-night. I need to get the facts of your case." Paul glanced at the rear-view mirror, taking another right turn.

"I can't divulge confidential information to you, either." Eric slid the phone from his pocket, hating what he had to do. He never canceled an appointment, and his private patients needed him, too.

"I have to know as much as you can tell me. The boy, the girl, and the frozen yogurt." Paul pulled the Mercedes into the bumper-to-bumper traffic, heading west.

"My house is in the other direction." Eric looked down at the new phone, missing his old phone, which contained his entire life, plus a cute picture of Hannah on the home screen. He'd missed talking to her last night and he'd have to make sure he spoke to her tonight.

"I'm leading them the opposite way, just in case. But I actually think we did lose them." Paul checked the rearview again, with a grin. "See, criminal law can be fun!"

"Way to go," Eric said, grateful. Suddenly the ringing of a cell phone reverberated inside the car, and the lighted GPS screen on the dashboard changed to read Laurie Calling . . .

"It's big sis!" Paul hit a button on the steering wheel, answering the call. "Hey, honey! Mission accomplished! The *Eagle* has landed! Tell me how much you love me."

"I love you, Paul." Laurie's voice sounded amplified and mechanical over the speaker system. "You're smart, you're not dumb, like everybody says."

"'I can handle things! I'm smart! Not like everybody says. I'm not dumb! I'm smart and I want respect!'"

"'You broke my heart, Fredo. You broke my heart.'"

Eric didn't know what they were talking about. "What are you guys saying?"

Laurie chuckled, over the speakers. "It's *The Godfather,* the extent of my brother's cultural literacy."

Paul nodded, driving. "I'm Fredo, she's Michael. She gets to be Michael because she's older."

"Because I'm smarter," Laurie shot back.

"Way harsh, sis." Paul grinned. "Anyway I'm rolling home with your boyfriend. Keep it up and I'll take him back to the hoosegow."

"Paul, he's not my boyfriend, he's my colleague."

"Yeah, right, he said you were *friends.* Ha!"

Eric ignored the awkward moment. "Laurie, thanks for calling Paul. I don't know what I would have done without him."

"Yes!" Paul hit the steering wheel in delight. "Another satisfied felon!"

Laurie groaned. "Paul, calm down. Where are you guys? Eric, aren't you coming back to the hospital?"

Eric tasted bitterness on his tongue. "I can't. Believe it or not, I'm on indefinite suspension."

Laurie gasped. "Are you kidding me?"

"I know."

Paul clucked, *tsk-tsk.* "They dissed my boy here! What kind of crap is that? You can't get a more dedicated employee, all he talks about is his patients. That's why he's perfect for you, Laur. Workaholics should be together so they can breed more workaholics, which will boost the economy and save the country. And when America does well, Europe does well, and the rest of the world follows. It all begins with you two, Laurie. You and Eric. Save the universe—or don't. Your choice."

Eric smiled, against his better judgment. "Laurie, we're going to my house. We're almost there. I'm going to cancel my private patients."

"Text me the address. I'll meet you. Bye, guys. Gotta go." Laurie hung up.

Paul hit the button, looking over. "I did good, right? I'm quite the matchmaker."

Eric wasn't about to talk about his love life, or lack thereof, anymore. "Excuse me, I have to call my patients."

"Go ahead, I won't listen."

"If so, I have a diagnosis for you." Eric pressed in the phone number of his seven o'clock appointment, Jean Carfoni, whose number he remembered because it was similar to his own. He held the phone to his ear, waiting for the call to connect. He adored Jean, a middle-school teacher he'd been treating for depression caused by a long battle with CLL, a chronic blood cancer.

"Hello, who is this?" Jean said, picking up.

"Jean, hi, it's Dr. Parrish. I'm afraid I'll have to cancel our appointment tonight. I'm sorry it's such short notice. I'm hoping you haven't left the house yet—"

"Dr. Parrish? Thank God! I've been calling you. Are you okay?"

Eric didn't like the worry in her voice. "I'm fine, and I'm sorry I didn't call you back."

"You know, this is going to sound crazy, but I thought I saw you on TV. They didn't say your name but I swear it was you, at the Radnor police station. The news was about the murder of that girl from Sacred Heart. It wasn't you, was it?"

Eric couldn't bring himself to lie. "I'm sorry, but I can't explain. May I call you later to reschedule?"

"Yes, of course," Jean answered, her tone puzzled. "Call when you can, Dr. Parrish."

"Thanks, and I will. I have to go, good-bye." Eric hung up, shuddering. "Damn it."

"Don't stress. Hang in."

"Thanks." Eric looked out the window, as twilight was taking over. People were driving home from work, talking and texting on their cell phones, but they were separate from him, in other vehicles, behind glass. He wasn't *of* them, not anymore. The police suspected him of murder, and he might have been responsible for the death of a young girl. He had a suicidal patient, who had to be more desperate than ever. He didn't have a job or a wife; he didn't even live with his own child. Eric felt apart even from himself, wearing clothes someone else had picked out, generic gray sweats.

"Call your patients," Paul said, softly.

Eric raised the phone to his ear, called information and got the number, then canceled on his other patient, who, mercifully, had not yet heard that he was suspected of strangling a young girl to death. When he finished the call, he filled Paul in within the confines of his confidentiality, and Paul listened carefully, dictating notes into his cell phone.

They took the back roads to Eric's house, turning onto his street. As they got closer, Eric looked ahead to see that his front door had been broken, the wood splintered in two. "They broke the door down?" he asked, appalled.

"Sorry, bro. That sucks."

"Is this more bullying tactics?"

"No, they were just trying to get in."

Eric didn't smile.

"No, really. That's how they execute a search warrant. How else are they going to get in?"

"How about they call the landlord? And they *leave* it that way, with a broken door? That's not secure."

"It's the Main Line, Eric." Paul cruised to a stop in front of the house and turned off the ignition.

"Still." Eric got out of the car and closed the door, noticing the silhouette of his neighbors at their front window, the entire family watching him. He wondered what they'd think of him, having seen cruisers pulling up to his house, cops busting down the door, and carrying out his personal belongings. He stalked to the front step and ran his fingers along the crack in the door, which zigzagged like lightning down the length of the wood panels. A sharp shard splintered in his hands. He hadn't realized he felt proprietary about the place until this very moment, so he gained a home at the same time that he lost it, with a wrench in his chest.

Paul came up beside him, placed a hand on his shoulder, and started to say something, but Eric looked over.

"Don't make a joke," he snapped, more harshly than he intended.

"Let's go inside. I'll help you clean up."

Eric felt a regretful pang. "Sorry I snapped."

"Dude, if you don't snap after what you've been through, then *you* need a shrink." Paul clapped him on the back, and Eric smiled, and together they moved the broken door aside, entered the house, and walked through the entrance hall into the living room.

"Oh no." Eric scanned the mess with a sinking heart. Couch cushions had been turned over, and professional journals, reference books, and novels had been torn from the bookshelves and scattered on the rug. The drawers of the entertainment center hung open, and the DVDs had been dumped. A bag of laundry beside the door, which he had intended to drop off at the dry cleaners, had been turned upside down on the hardwood floor.

"Before you ask me, the answer is yes, they can do this."

"Why do they?"

"I'll play devil's advocate and say that they're being thorough." Paul picked up a plaid shirt from the laundry pile and held it up. "May I burn this?"

"I had my laptop on the coffee table. They took my laptop. They just take everything I own? Invade my privacy, just like that?" Eric crossed to the coffee table where his laptop used to be, but all that was left was the gray power cord. Ugly blackish soot covered the table in patches, which he assumed was fingerprint dust.

"They would typically get a computer in an investigation like this, and I read your warrant, it was included in the scope."

"They see everything I have? The papers I'm working on, my work and personal email, all my pictures?" Eric thought of the pictures of Hannah and Caitlin he'd taken, the albums of beach vacations, trick-or-treating, and birthdays. He'd backed them up in the cloud, wherever that was, but even if he didn't lose them forever, he couldn't stand the notion that strangers would be pawing through them, seeing the most personal moments of his life. "Paul, it's my *life*."

"I know."

"Let's go to my office. It's this way." Eric hustled from the living room, glancing into the kitchen on the way, which was also a mess. Blackish fingerprint dust marred the counters. All of the cabinet doors had been left open, and the drawers had been pulled out. Pots and pans sat willy-nilly on the counters, and the freezer door had been left open. "They search the *freezer*?"

"To see if you're hiding drugs. Or Häagen-Dazs."

Eric stormed ahead to his office. "Paul, if the patient files aren't included in the scope of the warrant, does that mean they can't look at them? They're not even allowed to look at them, are they? That's a violation of my patients' rights, and I won't have it."

"No, they're not."

"I keep them in a locked cabinet." Eric opened the door to his office and flicked on a light. His desktop computer was gone, leaving only the surge protector. His desk and end tables had been dusted for fingerprints, leaving more dirty black patches. His bookshelves had been emptied, and his books, papers, and journals scattered all over the rug. He crossed to the wood file cabinet where he kept his patient files and tugged on the brass handle, but it was locked, the way he left it.

"Still locked. Exhibit A, the silver lining." Paul smiled.

"Guys, you here?" said a voice behind them, and they both turned to see Laurie standing in the threshold. She had on a blue cotton sweater, khakis, and running sneakers, with her hair twirled up in a tongue depressor. She was holding two boxes of pizza. "The cavalry is here with carbohydrates."

"Yes!" Paul went over to Laurie and kissed her on the cheek. "Mom would be so proud of you. What's better than a nice Italian girl? There's a reason it's a stereotype, people."

"Thanks for coming," Eric said, walking over. He took the warm pizza boxes from her and set them on his desk amid the clutter.

"Eric, I can't believe they did this to your place." Laurie's expression looked strained as she eyed the office. "I can't believe any of this is happening. You have to tell me what's going on."

"I'll fill you in."

"I'll help you put the house back together. We can clean it up in no time."

"That's just what I said! We must be related!" Paul went over and opened the pizza box. "Please tell me this is double cheese, triple sauce."

"It is, and the one underneath is mushroom."

"I'm a mushroom guy," Eric said, suddenly hungry.

"Eric, get with it." Paul opened the top box, releasing an aromatic steam. He slid out a gooey slice of pizza, bending over to hold it away from his suit. "She knows you're a mushroom guy. She remembers. You might be the dumbest smart guy I ever met. Anyway, I'm out of here."

"Now?" Eric asked. "I thought you wanted to talk about the case."

"I got what I needed in the car." Paul went to the door and stopped in the threshold, biting off a strand of melted mozzarella. "You can fill me in tomorrow. I'll call."

Laurie turned to Paul. "Why are you leaving? I just got here."

"Exactly. I'll leave you two *friends* alone." Paul turned neatly around and walked away, down the hall.

Eric and Laurie fell briefly silent, listening to Paul's footsteps on the hardwood as he left the house, and Eric sensed that they were newly uncomfortable in each other's presence, since Paul had said the unsayable. Eric didn't know if Laurie really did have a thing for him, and in any event, there was no romance in the air, only tomato sauce.

"Thanks for the pizza," Eric said, reaching for the second box. "I really do love mushroom."

"I do, too," Laurie said quickly. "I didn't really remember that you liked it, I got it because I like it. I mean, who doesn't like mushroom pizza? It's awesome."

"Right. I'm starved, I can't remember the last time I ate." Eric opened the pizza box and was sliding out a hot slice when the landline phone started ringing on the desk. He held the slice, leaned over quickly, and picked up the receiver. "Hello, this is Dr.—"

"What have you done, Doctor?" a woman yelled, slurring her words. "What have you done to my son?"

Eric recognized the voice, instantly alarmed. "Marie? What's the matter? Is Max back?"

"Get over here right now!"

Chapter Thirty-eight

Eric sat in the passenger seat of Laurie's white BMW, and she pulled up across the street from Max's house and cut the ignition. The street was dark and quiet except for the yapping of dogs in one of the houses. He and Laurie had gotten here quickly because she drove almost as fast as her brother, and Eric had updated her on the way over.

"Thanks for the ride, I won't be long." Eric reached for the door handle.

"Eric, can't I come?" Laurie hung on the steering wheel.

"No, we agreed." Eric didn't have time to fuss. He wanted to get inside the house. Given what Marie had said on the phone, he knew it wasn't likely that Max had come back, but he held out hope. "It's too weird a situation. There's too many variables."

"You think I can't handle variables? Do you know what I do for a living?"

"You agreed you would wait."

"You knew I wouldn't keep my word."

"I don't want to argue with you. I have to go." Eric opened the door, climbed out of the car, closed it behind him. He hustled across the street, and Laurie did the same thing, sprinting to catch up with him on the sidewalk.

"I'll be helpful, you'll see."

"This is not helpful. This is worrisome." Eric hurried up the front walk with Laurie at his heels.

"You used to like me."

"That was before."

"I really remembered that mushroom was your favorite. I just didn't want to admit it before."

"I know that. Now once we get inside, stand behind me. Understand?" Eric knocked on the metallic screen door, but the front door was open and he could hear a reality show on the TV, inside the living room. The TV went suddenly mute, and Marie appeared at the doorway.

"Get in here right now. Who is that with you?"

"Hello, Marie, this is Dr. Laurie Fortunato. She treated your mother in the emergency room, last week—"

"Whatever, don't try to change the subject. Come in." Marie backed up, and Eric let himself in through the screen door and entered the living room, stepping protectively ahead of Laurie.

"Is Max here? Did he come home?" Eric looked around, but the house was dark and quiet, like before. The end tables showed the usual signs of clutter, with the same plastic glasses and half-finished vodka bottle. The big-screen TV played on mute, the air conditioner rattled away.

"No, he didn't, as if you didn't know that!" Marie folded her arms, standing in the middle of her living room.

"I didn't know that." Eric could smell the alcohol on her breath. Her eyes were at half-mast again, but this time she was dressed in a boxy cotton shift, stained on the flowery print in front.

"Okay, so why don't you explain to me why the police were here today! They were asking all kindsa questions about Max, if he knew that girl who got killed, Renée, whatever her last name—"

"Bevilacqua," Eric said, reflexively.

"I told them, I have no *idea* how Max knew that girl, or even if he knew that girl, there's no way in the world Max would kill anybody, he would never *kill* anybody."

Eric realized that Marie didn't know that Renée had been one of Max's students at PerfectScore. He wasn't surprised by that, but he couldn't tell her because he'd learned it in session.

"I kept askin' them, why are you askin' me this? Why are you comin' to me? They went upstairs, they searched his room. They turned it upside down! My son didn't know that girl!" Marie's droopy eyes filmed, but then her rage returned. "They won't tell me what's goin' on because it's a police investigation, and that's all they keep sayin', it's police information."

Eric understood her confusion. Both he and the police were following their own rules about confidentiality, leaving Marie on the outs, bewildered and angry.

"I tell the cops, I've been askin' you to find my son and his *shrink* has been tellin' you to find him, and they say that was the other police station. I tell them there's no way he knew that girl and they won't tell me why they think he knows her."

Eric didn't interrupt her, trying to follow what she was saying, but her words were tripping all over each other, between the emotion and alcohol. A cell phone rang from her pocket, but she ignored it.

"So they ask me if they can look around, like in his bedroom and whatnot like you did, but I say 'hell no,' and they make some noise about going to get a warrant." Marie raised her voice, spitting. "I say 'go get your freakin' warrant' because my boyfriend will be home soon and he can stick your warrant up your ass for you."

Eric could imagine how well that was received, if it was Detectives Rhoades and Pagano doing the questioning. Marie's cell phone stopped ringing.

"So then I turn on the TV, and who do I see on the news but *you*! You comin' from the police station, they showed you! I saw you, even though you had on some disguise or something! You looked like a guy off the street, not a doctor! Not a psychiatrist!"

Eric realized she was talking about the sweat suit.

"At first I thought you were there about Max, trying to find him, but then they said on TV that it was to do with the murder of the girl, and then I realized the connection. *What's* the connection?

You're the connection!" Marie pointed at him, stabbing the air with her finger. "*You* went to the cops and you told them that my son killed that girl! Why did you do that? How could you? How dare you! He was your patient!"

"Marie, I didn't. Anything Max told me in session I kept completely confidential." Eric felt like a hypocrite telling her that, even though it was true. The practical effect of what he had done was to put Max on the hook and he knew it, but he'd done it to save the boy's life.

"He trusted you and you betrayed him! He would never kill anybody, he didn't even know that girl!"

"I didn't betray him."

"Then what were you doin' there? Why do they even know about you? You know what I think? I have it *all* figured out." Marie pursed her lips. "I think *you're* the killer. I think *you* killed that girl and you're trying to blame it on Max! You framed Max! You're framin' my son for *murder*!"

"No, Marie, that's not what's going on—"

"That's exactly what's going on!" Marie shouted, her gaze slipping in and out of focus. "And you know what else I think? I think *you* killed my son! He's not missing, he's *murdered*. You killed them *both*!"

Eric stepped back, shocked. "Marie, no, I've been doing everything I can to find Max, to save his life. I care about him, and—"

"I don't believe you! You must've been screwin' that young girl and she probably told her parents, or something like that, and you shut her up! You killed them both! You murdered them both!"

"No. Marie—"

"You're just like those guys on the *First 48,* who act like they're all upset that their wife's missing, but really they killed her! The whole time, it's been you! You killed her and you killed Max, and he's never coming back home, he's never coming home *again*! I lost my mother, and now I lost my son. I don't have any family left, no family at all!"

"Marie, let's sit down and I can explain—"

Suddenly, the screen door opened, and a large bearded man

entered the living room in a blue Montgomeryville Motorcycles T-shirt, grimy jeans, and worn workboots. His dark eyes zeroed in on Eric behind his wire-rimmed glasses that kept sliding down a bulbous nose. His fleshy lips contorted into a scowl, buried in a dark unruly beard. "Marie, is this the guy?" he asked, glowering at Eric.

"Yeah." Marie turned on Eric. "This is Zack, my boyfriend I was telling you about, and he's been on the road two straight days, trying to get home. You tell Zack what you did to my son, and you tell the truth, the whole truth and nothing but or he will beat it out of you. Zack loves my Max as much as I do, he's going to be his stepfather someday. This ends here and *now*!"

"Zack, I'm Dr. Parrish." Eric stood his ground. "I'm Max's psychiatrist and I'd never do anything to hurt him. I'm trying to find him and I fear he could harm himself."

"Oh really?" Zack came over, frowning with menace. "We had no trouble until Max started seeing you, then he disappears, and I gotta tell you, it just doesn't sit right with me, you showing such interest in him, coming over here and looking in his room—"

"Wait, *Archie,* is that *you*?" Laurie asked from the doorway, stepping into the room, but the big man whirled around to face her.

"Dr. *F*?" Zack broke into a grin, showing yellowed teeth. "What're *you* doing here? How've you been?"

"I'm fine, thanks!" Laurie reached up and gave Zack a big hug. "How are you? You look great!"

Eric had no idea what was happening, but he was going with the flow. He glanced at Marie, who seemed vaguely deflated that there wasn't going to be a cage match in her living room.

"Dr. F, I'm almost a hundred percent! The neurologist you got for me did an awesome job, and Bryn Mawr Rehab was great. I learned my lesson. I always wear my helmet now."

"Terrific! You're not even limping. That's excellent."

"Thanks." Zack turned to Marie. "Babe, this is Dr. F, the one I told you about from my accident. We should invite her to the wedding."

"For real?" Marie asked, surprised. "*That* Dr. F?"

"Yes, she's the best little doctor I ever had." Zack seemed to address the room, expansively. "I got in a motorcycle accident about nine months ago, some teenager ran a stop sign, and man, it didn't look good. They had to Medevac me to the hospital. Dr. F fixed me up, then she got me an appointment with this big-time neurologist. He only took me because she said so." Zack threw his arm around Laurie, tugging her to his side like the prom picture from hell. "He knew his stuff, but he wasn't a sweetheart like Dr. F."

"Wow," Eric said, nonplussed. He met Laurie's eye, receiving her I-told-you-so message.

Marie frowned. "I don't understand something. I get that she's Dr. F, but who the hell is Archie?"

Zack frowned, sheepish. "Archie's my real name, babe. I never told you. I mean, do you blame me?"

"*Archie?*" Marie repeated, incredulous. "Like Archibald?"

"No, like Archie Andrews." Zack shrugged his heavy shoulders.

Laurie looked up at Zack. "Archie, I know that you and Marie are upset about Max, but hear me out. Eric is one of my oldest friends at the hospital, and I vouch for him. I swear to you, he has Max's best interest at heart."

"Hmph." Marie frowned, more deeply, and Marie's cell phone started ringing again.

"Don't you think you should get that phone?" Eric asked Marie, gingerly. It went against his every instinct not to check a phone. "Someone is really trying to reach you. You never know, it could be Max."

"It's only bill collectors, they call all the time." Marie waved at the air. "Anyway, I'm glad you're having an old-home week but that doesn't change anything, not for me. I still haven't heard why Dr. Parrish was at the police station today, and how all of the sudden the cops think Max murdered that girl."

Zack looked over at her. "Marie, we should sit down and talk, try to figure it out together. Try not to be prejudiced or talk smack. We need to cool our jets and get you a nice cuppa coffee. Huh, babe? What do you say?"

"I don't know," Marie answered, uncertain. "I think we need to go have a little kitchen talk."

"Fine." Zack motioned Eric onto the couch in front of the television. "Doc, sit down with Dr. F, and we'll go get coffee."

"Great idea," Eric said, heading to the couch.

"I agree, Archie, uh, I mean, Zack." Laurie sat down next to Eric on the couch, just as Marie's cell phone started ringing again.

Zack turned to her. "Babe, maybe you *should* get that. It could be Max, you never know."

"All right, fine." Marie slid her phone from her dress pocket.

Eric glanced at the muted TV, then did a double-take. "Oh my God, no!" he cried out, in shock and horror.

"What?" Laurie asked, but then she turned to the TV and saw what he meant, gasping aloud. "Marie, Zack! Look!"

But Eric was struck dumb. He stared at the TV, which showed a live-action nightmare unfolding in real time.

STUDENT BOMBER AT MALL, read the bottom of the screen. Above it was a videotape of the King of Prussia Mall, surrounded by arriving SWAT vehicles, police cars, and fire trucks, their lights flashing.

Next to the video was a grainy cell-phone picture.

There was no doubt about who was in the photo.

The student bomber at the mall was Max.

Chapter Thirty-nine

"Give me the keys!" Eric ran, with Laurie beside him, to the BMW while Zack and Marie hurried to his red pickup truck in the driveway.

"Eric, I'll drive."

"Let me." Eric had to be in control of something. He had to make this mission his own.

"Drive safe." Laurie tossed him the keys and he caught them, jumped into the driver's seat of the BMW, shoved the key in the ignition, and took off as soon as Laurie was in the seat beside him.

"Don't worry, we can fix this," she said, but Eric knew it was his problem to fix.

"I can't believe how wrong I was. I still don't believe it," Eric gunned the powerful engine and tore down the dark street. The high beams of Zack's truck appeared behind him. They hit the end of the street together, and Eric hit the gas around the turn.

"Take it easy."

"There's no traffic, and I'm fine." Eric gripped the steering wheel, holding it hard. "Why don't you try to get the cops on the phone? Tell them we're on the way. Ask for Detective Rhoades or Pagano."

"Okay, but what do you think you're going to do at the mall?"

"I'm going to try to talk to him, I'm gonna try to talk him out of it."

"Who? Max?"

"Of course, Max." Eric steered past the smaller homes that dotted the neighborhood. Lights shone from the windows. The streets were quiet and dark. A man walking a German shepherd stopped to look as the BMW and pickup sped past, going too fast.

"Why you?"

"He's my patient."

"It's not like at your office. He's at a mall, taking hostages, and he's got a bomb."

"All the more reason he needs to talk to me." Eric steered into the darkness, taking a right turn. He didn't need GPS. He knew the back roads to Route 202, which led directly to the mall.

"How? What would you say?"

"I don't know, I'll figure it out. I know this kid, he's doing this out of desperation. He doesn't want to kill anybody."

"Eric, he killed Renée."

"We don't know that for sure."

"You can't seriously doubt that, can you?"

"Part of me does."

"Even now? Sure as hell it is him at the mall."

"I know that." Eric had been right about the repeated calls to Marie's cell. It hadn't been bill collectors or Max, but the cops telling her to come to the mall. "Part of me knows him and has faith in him. He's not a violent guy. It's not in his psyche."

"So he snapped, isn't that possible? Isn't that exactly what you were afraid of the first night in the emergency department? That when his grandmother died, he'd have a psychotic break?"

Eric didn't say anything for a minute, concentrating on driving at speed. He sensed Laurie was right, but he couldn't bring himself to concede. There was something wrong, something that didn't fit. Eric hadn't assessed Max as a bomber, even after any break.

"Eric, I understand why we're going there, to see if we can help. To be there if we're needed. But you can't take this on."

"I took it on when I took him on." Eric accelerated past the fancier homes, circular driveways, and ADT Security decals.

"No, you didn't."

"Yes, I did."

"What's happening here? You trying to vindicate yourself? Redeem yourself for not turning him in to the police?"

Eric couldn't think clearly enough to answer her questions. His heart hammered. He knew Laurie was trying to help, but he wished she would be quiet.

"Eric, the police called Marie. She's the one they think can reach him."

"That's because they don't know her or the family history." Eric steered onto the main drag and whizzed past Chili's, Target, and Cold Stone Creamery with Zack's truck behind him, running red lights. The traffic was light, and there was no police presence. He assumed the surrounding jurisdictions had been called to the mall.

"They met her today. They saw her. They saw that the place is a mess, even if she wasn't drinking, it's not hard to figure out. They're detectives."

"So what's your point?"

"They called her because she's the mother."

"They called her because they had nobody else to call."

"They could've called you."

"How?" Eric spotted the turn that lead to Route 202 up ahead and accelerated smoothly. "How would they reach me? They have my cell phone, and we weren't in the office. Besides, they suspect me of Renée's murder. They probably suspect both of us at the same time, either individually or together. Like Marie with her crazy theory that I killed both Max and Renée. Laurie, do me a favor and try to reach the police. I can't talk. I want to concentrate on getting there."

"Okay, okay." Laurie reached for her phone, and Eric checked the dashboard clock: 9:13. He imagined Max watching the second hand on his watch, in the throes of his compulsion. Max was at greater risk for suicide than he had ever been, now that his grandmother and Renée were dead.

"Laurie, I just realized something. Max doesn't want to kill those kids. He's committing suicide. This is going to be suicide by cop."

"You think?"

"Yes. A patient like Max would be likely to commit suicide by cop. He's desperate and scared. He wants to die, but he's not able to bring himself to pull the trigger. So he's going to put himself in a position where the cops will pull the trigger for him."

"How grim." Laurie sighed. "It must be so awful to be in that kind of despair."

"Exactly, and there's a part of him that is angry at Marie, too. If I had to suss it out, he wants her to see how much he's hurting, because she ignores him."

"That makes sense."

"And at seventeen years old, he lacks the empathy to realize that he's ruining that cop's life, too. Nobody in law enforcement wants to shoot a kid, but Max isn't going to give them any choice."

"Yikes."

"I know." Eric gripped the steering wheel and aimed the car like a bullet through the dark night. They flew down Route 202 to the mall, passing trucks and tractor trailers. The speedometer went from seventy-five to eighty to eighty-five. Ahead were the lights of the Costco, Best Buy, and movie multiplex. The green exit sign popped into view, and they followed its curve with Zack's truck behind, powering together onto the four-lane road that ran past the massive King of Prussia Mall complex, the Plaza first and the Court behind.

"We're here." Eric slowed to a safer speed and lowered his window. The entire Plaza area was being cordoned off. Traffic was being detoured. Cops with orange flashlights were waving traffic onto one lane, farthest from the scene.

"I can't reach the detectives." Laurie looked over, phone in hand. "They won't give me any cell numbers."

"Keep trying."

"They're not gonna let us drive through to the mall."

"We'll see about that." Eric stopped at the last red light before they cordoned off the street. TV news vans with network logos lined the road, their spiky microwave towers puncturing the black sky. Police cruisers, ambulances, and other first responders barreled past them in the far lane, sirens wailing and red lights flashing. The traffic light turned green, and Eric cruised to a cop directing traffic. "Officer, we need to get to the mall—"

"Sir, no, move it out, move it out!"

"Officer, the red pickup behind me is the boy's mother, the bomber's mother." Eric made himself say the words. "I'm the boy's psychiatrist, Eric Parrish. The police called us and said to get to the scene, right away. You have to let us through."

The cop frowned under the patent bill of his cap. "Sir, I've had reporters lying through their teeth to get closer to that mall."

"Officer, you can verify this information. We were called by Detectives Rhoades and Pagano of the Radnor Police. We've been calling to tell them that we're on the way."

"We don't know those guys. We're Upper Merion P.D."

"Officer, there's going be a lot of different jurisdictions here, but we have to get through. You want to be the one who stops us, when we were summoned here?"

"Okay, go." The cop waved them into an open lane to the left, behind a line of smoking flares.

"Thanks, Officer." Eric hit the gas and signaled to Zack to follow him.

"Pretty fancy footwork." Laurie smiled, tense.

"Beginner's luck." Eric drove down King of Prussia Road, got in the left lane, and turned onto Mall Road, which bisected the mall complex, dividing the older Court on the right from the newer Plaza on the left. "Where's the video store, in the Court or the Plaza? Can you look that up on your phone?"

"Hold on." Laurie looked down, touching buttons on the phone. "It's in the Plaza. Right downstairs, next to the Starbucks."

"So which mall entrance do I want? The first one on the left?"

"Yep." Laurie pointed. "That'll be the closest."

Eric steered down Mall Road, craning his neck as he drove, trying to see the large parking lot in front of Lord & Taylor, which was controlled chaos. Police were hurrying terrified shoppers from the mall, a stream of men, women, and children running for their lives. Shouting, crying, and screaming wafted through the car window. Cops and other personnel were erecting a large white tent for a command center. Fire trucks were pulling up with firefighters, and boxy white ambulances idled, at the ready. Black Humvees unloaded black-helmeted SWAT teams. Official personnel ran this way and that, in uniforms of all types, including dark FBI and ATF windbreakers. Lights and portable generators were being connected, and sawhorses unloaded from the back of municipal trucks to set up a barricade.

Eric felt horrified to think that the person causing the terror was his own patient. "This is a nightmare. These poor people. I pray nobody gets hurt. Max doesn't know what he set in motion here."

"Eric, I'm so sorry I got you into this." Laurie sighed, eyeing the scene.

"No, it's okay. Max needs help. This is proof, as awful as it is."

"But somebody else could've helped him, another psychiatrist. I got you into it, and look what happened. The cops, your job."

"I wouldn't want anybody else to do it," Eric said, realizing he meant it once it was said aloud. "I want to be the one to help him, and in a way, he's helping me."

"Now you're talking crazy."

"Who better?" Eric turned left onto the uphill ramp that led to the Plaza. The Neiman Marcus was to his right and the main entrance straight ahead. The ramp was blocked at the top by a line of uniformed police in front of sawhorses. Eric drove slowly toward them, with Zack's truck behind, and cops broke out of line and started running toward him down the ramp, motioning for him to stop, waving flashlights or their hands.

"Sir, you're not permitted on his road!" shouted one heavyset cop, as he reached the car, and Eric braked.

"Officer, I'm the bomber's psychiatrist and I'm here with his mother. We were called here by Detective Rhoades of the Radnor Police. You have to let us through."

"I didn't hear anything like that." The heavyset cop peered into the BMW at Laurie. "She the mother?"

"No, she's an emergency physician. The boy's mother is in the truck behind me, with her boyfriend. You have to let us through."

"Sir, you two are just medical personnel, and we have all the first responders we need. The mother and the father might be getting through, but you and the other doc aren't going anywhere until I check with the brass." The heavyset cop turned around, jogged back to the other cop, and they spoke, their caps bent together. Another cop ran back to Zack's truck, while the heavyset cop took off, hustling away to the line of cops.

"Eric, oh my God, look. Snipers." Laurie pointed, and Eric looked up at the flat roof of the Neiman Marcus, where SWAT members in black gear were taking positions at the corners of the building. He could see that the position offered the best angle on the mall entrance, which was a panel of four doors set in a massive glass wall, but he couldn't see through the entrance.

"Laurie, where exactly is Video City?"

"Hold on." Laurie looked down at the mall map on her phone, the bright blue light illuminating her face from below. "The first store at the entrance is the bank, the second is a Sunglass Hut, then the third is Video City."

"Damn, I wish I could see what was going on." Eric squinted, eyeing the mall. It was impossible to see farther inside, over the police and other personnel, running this way and that.

"Wait a minute, hold on." Laurie tapped away on the touch screen of her phone.

"What are you doing?" Eric shifted over.

"Here we go, it's a live feed. There are so many news vans around, I knew one of them would have the video uploaded already."

"Of course." Eric watched the video, a close-up of the inside of the mall shot from the outside. The lights were on the first floor, and the camera angle was trained on the video game store, which had a glass front wall. The image was indistinct due to its amplification, and the camera angle didn't show the store in its entirety, but Eric could see enough to fill him with dread. Video City was empty in the front but there was a counter in the back, and behind it stood a dark silhouette, small in stature, which he recognized as Max in a hoodie. Eric realized that if he could see Max that easily, then so could the snipers.

Laurie looked over. "Hey, the cops are letting Zack and Marie through."

"They are?" Eric turned around as Zack's truck zoomed past them, heading alone to the mall entrance, where the cops parted and the truck was waved through. The pickup moved at a crawl toward the white tent, then stopped and was swarmed by uniformed police. Eric couldn't see Zack and Marie because of the crowd and the darkness, but the police hustled them toward the white tent, so he knew Zack and Marie had gotten to somebody in command.

"That's good." Laurie returned to watching the live feed on her phone.

Eric scanned the scene, troubled. He hoped Marie had sobered up enough to talk to Max, but her very presence would remind him that there was nobody left to whom he was close. Max could have seen the TV news report about his being at the police station and believe that Eric had put him on the hook for Renée's murder, betraying him. It would leave Max feeling even more alone, hopeless. Suicidal.

"Sir, sir!" The heavyset cop came jogging back to the BMW. "Sir, please leave immediately. Turn your vehicle around. You're not being permitted access."

"Officer, please, I know I can help. Let me show you some ID." Eric reached for his ID lanyard, then remembered it had been in his pocket when his clothes were confiscated by the police.

"Eric, we should go," Laurie said, just as her phone rang. She answered the call, "Dr. Fortunato here. Zack, hold on." Laurie turned quickly to Eric. "Zack wants to talk to you."

"Sir, move it out, move it along!" The heavyset cop waved him to turn around.

"Officer, give me five minutes," Eric said to the cop, taking the phone. "This is the mother and her boyfriend." He put the call on speaker. "Zack, what's going on?"

"Marie is freaking the hell out," Zack said, tense. "She can't stop crying. They called Max on his cell but he's not answering."

"Can you get me in there, Zack? Ask the powers-that-be in the tent. I can go talk to him."

"I tried that. They say no."

"Can you give the phone to whoever's in charge? Let me talk to him."

"Okay." There was some noise, then an authoritative voice came on. "This is Lieutenant James Jana. Who am I speaking with?"

"Dr. Parrish, I'm Max's psychiatrist. I know I can help if I can talk to Max. Is there any way you can patch me through to him?"

"No, I couldn't even if I wanted to. He's not answering the phone. He made the one call and that's it. He won't even pick up for the mom. We left messages on his cell and the store landline."

"What did he say when you spoke with him? How did he sound?"

"Cool, calm, and collected. You're this kid's psychiatrist. What's his problem?"

"I can't discuss his diagnosis."

"You're kidding, right? This kid has a bomb and you're playing games, Doc? What about those kids he's holding hostage? What about them?"

"Lieutenant, what did he say to you, exactly? What does he want? Does he have any demands?"

"That's confidential police business. We're not even releasing that to the hostage families. We don't want it in the media."

"I'll keep it confidential, I swear. Please tell me. It will help me understand his mental state, and I can help you reach him."

"Fine, only because of your relationship to the boy and the mother. But if this comes back to me, if I see this online or anywhere else, there will be hell to pay."

"That won't happen, you have my word. Please tell me."

"He has five hostages, all kids. Four boys and a girl. He said he's going to kill the first one in fifteen minutes and kill another one every fifteen minutes after that."

Eric felt his blood run cold. It was horrific, coinciding with Max's tapping ritual, but something about it didn't make sense. "What about the bomb? Why the bomb?"

"Then he's going to blow himself up and everybody with him."

Eric wasn't buying the story, not from Max. "Lieutenant, ask yourself. How is this a plan? If he really wanted to kill those kids, why wait? Why give you so much notice? If he really wanted them dead, they'd be dead already. And why the bomb?"

"Dr. Parrish, you tell me. The kid's a head case."

"His plan tells you that he's not going to kill those kids. He's not going to set off a bomb. He wants to commit suicide by police. He wants your guys to kill him."

"That possibility ran through our minds. We have a top-notch terrorism negotiator here from Homeland Security who said the same thing."

"Homeland Security?" Eric glanced at Laurie, who looked grave in the dark car. "Lieutenant, this kid is not a terrorist. Nothing like that is going on. He's just a—"

"I don't have time to yammer, Doc. We got to save mass lives."

Eric knew what that meant. They were going to kill Max before he got a chance to kill anybody else. The snipers were already getting into position. "Lieutenant, isn't there any way I can get in there and talk to him?"

"No, sir, there is not. Out of the question. It's unsafe."

"But I think I can convince him to stop. You can save his life and the lives of those hostages."

"Sorry, I have to go. Good-bye."

"Damn it!" Eric gritted his teeth, handing Laurie back the phone.

The heavyset cop clapped his hands together. "Sir, you heard the lieutenant. Please turn the vehicle around and exit the area."

"Eric." Laurie touched his arm. "We have Marie's cell phone number, and if he calls her, she can put you through to him. You tried your best, but we should go."

"Sir, listen to your wife. Turn it around, immediately." The cop edged backwards to give the BMW room to navigate. "Immediately, sir!"

"Okay. Will do. Thanks, Officer," Eric said, waving him off, and the cop turned away to jog back to his post.

Eric turned to Laurie, kissed her on the cheek, and opened the BMW door. "Wish me luck," he said, then jumped out of the car.

And hit the ground, running.

Chapter Forty

Eric bolted to the curb, jumped the short hedge, and ran straight into the melee in the parking lot, knowing the heavyset cop wouldn't be able to find him in the darkness and confusion. Uniformed police, EMTs, FBI agents, ATF agents, and militaristic SWAT teams with military gear hustled this way and that. The night air filled with crackling radios, Nextel phones, people shouting, kids crying, and police barking orders. Snipers on the top of Neiman Marcus dropped into lethal crouches.

Eric kept his head down, running toward the mall, ducking behind a parked ambulance, then a fire truck, hopscotching his way closer to the entrance. He moved steadily forward, looking for a way to get into the mall. Police in tan, black, and blue uniforms hustled stricken shoppers from the entrance, and nobody was entering except for cops, firefighters, and other first responders, an all-hands-on-deck effort to evacuate people before shots were fired or a bomb detonated. The command center was to his left, about a hundred feet away, so Eric ducked behind a fluorescent green fire truck.

Firefighters stood on the other side of the truck, toward the back, talking in a small group, and Eric noticed something. A few of them had taken off their overcoats on this hot summer night, standing in their T-shirts, suspenders, and flame-retardant pants. Their jackets hung on the truck itself, and Eric knew it was his only chance. He grabbed one of the jackets, which read Campbell on the back, slipped it on, and ran toward the mall. He kept his head down, raced for the entrance, and joined the line of first responders dashing into the mall.

Eric crossed the threshold, glancing up at the second-floor balcony, horrified to see that snipers in black military uniforms were taking positions along the railing. They'd have a clear shot at Max inside the video game store, through the glass front wall. The firefighters took off in all different directions, hurrying shoppers outside as police officers relayed them forward, but Eric ran straight, streaked toward the video game store, and ran inside.

"Max!" Eric called out, and Max turned around, standing behind the counter in Oakley sunglasses and a black hoodie.

"Dr. Parrish." Max raised a hunting rifle.

Eric tried not to look at the muzzle of the rifle. He couldn't see Max's eyes behind the sunglasses. "You don't want to shoot me. You don't want to shoot anybody."

"You sure about that?" Max's voice sounded chilled, a tone Eric had never heard coming from the boy.

"Yes."

"Why?"

"Because I know you, and I know you don't want to shoot me or anybody else." Eric's mouth went dry. "That's not who you are."

"You don't know me that well, Dr. Parrish."

"Can I put my hands down? Will you lower that rifle?"

"No. Keep your hands up."

"Max, what are you doing?"

"What does it look like I'm doing? I have five hostages. They're locked in the storeroom." Max checked his watch, then looked up, his expression obscured by the sunglasses. "In five minutes, I'm going to take one out and shoot him. I'm trying to decide which one."

Eric absorbed, rather than merely heard the sentence. He felt it penetrate his skin, sending shockwaves through his body, to his very marrow. He didn't know this Max, this faceless terror behind sunglasses and a weapon. This wasn't the Max he had in his office, talking about feeling invisible. Eric could almost believe that this Max would kill kids and blow up a mall. But part of him still had faith.

"You don't believe me, do you?"

"I believe *in* you, Max. I believe in you." Eric spoke from the heart, not as a therapist, not even as a father, but just as a man with his hands in the air, praying he could get everybody out alive.

"What does that mean? That you believe in me."

"It doesn't mean anything. It's just a feeling. It's an emotion. You can't parse it or analyze it. It's pure." Eric felt as if he was channeling something that had been in him for a long time. "I'm here for you. I want to get you out of here, alive. I can't stand the idea that you could die, you're too good for that, you're too young." Eric nodded over his shoulder, toward the balcony. "They have snipers, Max. They're going to shoot you before you kill anybody, and I think that's why you're here. I think that's what you want. And I'm here for you, to tell you it doesn't have to be that way. That it can't be that way. I want you to let the kids go and walk out with me."

"It *does* have to be this way. The kids have to die, and I have to die. The bomb has to go off and everybody has to die."

"No," Eric said softly. "Can I put my hands down, please?"

"Okay," Max answered, after a moment.

"Thank you." Eric lowered his arms slowly, but he stayed in the same position, aware that he was blocking Max from the snipers' rifles. They wouldn't shoot if Eric was in the way. At least he hoped they wouldn't.

"You should just go, Dr. Parrish. You don't need to be here. You don't want to see what happens."

"I'm not leaving without you."

"Renée's dead, Gummy's dead." Max checked his watch. "Everybody's dead."

"I don't think you killed Renée."

"Really?" Max snorted. "Four minutes."

"If you killed her, tell me you did. Because like I said, I don't believe you. I believe in you."

"That's catchy, Dr. Parrish but"—Max paused, swallowing

visibly—"if you want to know the truth, I don't know whether I killed her or not. I probably did. It probably was me. That's what we're both worried about, isn't it? You were worried, you asked me all those questions."

"Why do you say that you don't know if you killed her?"

"I was drunk." Max lowered the weapon slightly.

"What do you mean, you were drunk?"

"I started drinking. Vodka. My mom always has plenty of it around and I took some. After Gummy died, I was upset, I called you, remember?"

"Yes, of course." Eric heard Max's voice soften, and he sounded a little more like the boy who'd been in session.

"I just wanted to drink, I didn't want to think about it. I parked near the school and nobody saw me, I just sat there drinking. I fell asleep in the car and when I woke, I just started drinking again. I wanted to see if you could really drink yourself to death."

Eric became aware that there was movement behind him. He saw in his peripheral vision the black shadow of a sniper on the balcony, in front of Tiffany's. He stood his ground, between the sniper and Max. "Where were you yesterday morning, when she was killed?"

"I woke up in the Giant parking lot, I was hungover. It's, like, I don't remember anything."

"Where's the Giant parking lot? Is it near Pickering Park?"

"Fifteen minutes away. I passed out, and when I woke up, I didn't even know where I was. I musta driven there drunk."

Eric listened, pushing his awareness of the sniper from his mind. Sweat formed under the heavy jacket.

"When I woke up, it was, like, three o'clock in the afternoon, and I threw up, and I turned on the radio and they said . . . Renée was . . . dead." Max faltered, as if the words lodged in his throat. "I don't know if I did it or not, but I probably did. So now I have to pay, and now everybody has to pay."

"Max, what if you didn't do it? What if somebody else did it?"

"Who? Who would've done it?" Max's voice turned almost pleading. "Answer me that. Tell me. I'm the crazy one, I'm the one with the tapping, I'm the one who fantasized about killing her and now she's dead. I think I did it, and it doesn't matter anyway because there's nothing anymore. There's nothing for me. Everybody's dead." Max checked his watch. "Three minutes."

"Your grandmother wouldn't want you to do this. Your grandmother would want you to let those kids go and walk out with me."

"My grandmother's dead. I don't have anybody."

"That's not true. You have a yellow rabbit."

"What?"

"A yellow rabbit, I saw it in your room. Next to your bed, by the photograph." Eric was improvising, but let himself talk, hoping to strike a chord. "It was interesting to me, to see that. In a room covered with all kinds of video game posters, a little yellow rabbit slumped over. I'm curious why you saved it."

"Oh please."

"Tell me, tough guy with the sunglasses, not to mention the rifle." Eric let a note of humor filter into his tone. "Why the rabbit?"

"It's just a toy, is all."

"A toy from a better time of your life."

"Right."

"You were happy then?"

"Yes."

"What if you could be happy again?"

Max didn't answer.

"You can be happy again. Even after all you've gone through, you can be happy again, and I can help you. Give me a chance."

"So?" Max said, after a moment.

"So we figure this out together, just like therapy. It's the same thing, just you and me, walking into the cave together. You have the flashlight, and I have your hand."

"No, sorry. Too late."

"What about the bomb?"

"What about it?"

"Where is it?"

Max nodded toward a Whole Foods bag sitting on the counter, and Eric swallowed hard.

"Is it going to blow up?"

"No, that's not how it works."

"Where did you get it?"

"I made it. It's not hard, you can just look on the Internet."

"Really." Eric had read that, but it was hard to imagine Max making a bomb. And the boy hadn't been home. Where did he make a bomb? How did Max get the ingredients? The time? "I want to see it. I want to see what a bomb looks like."

"You can't see it, really. It's wrapped up."

"I still want to see it. Show it to me."

Max stayed still, then shrugged. "Why don't you go see it for yourself then?"

"I can't move."

"Why not?" Max checked his watch. "Two minutes."

"Because of the sniper. I'm covering you. I'm blocking his shot."

"What?" Max tilted his head up, but Eric couldn't tell if he saw the sniper behind his dark glasses.

"The sniper behind me, he's moving into position, and these guys are experts. He's going to shoot you right over my shoulder—or he's going to shoot through me."

"So you should move, Dr. Parrish."

"No, I'm standing here. If they want to shoot you, they're going to have to shoot me."

"Are you *serious*?"

"Yes."

Max said nothing, biting his lip. "Please. Move."

"No."

"Then *I'll* move." Max moved a step to the side, and so did Eric, mirroring him. Max moved a step to the right, and so did Eric, mirroring him again.

"I'm here for you, Max. I'm not going anywhere."

"So you're standing here, like, you're gonna save me?"

"No, I'm standing here as a placeholder. Do you know what that means?"

"No."

"It means I'm holding your place, until you are ready to stand

for yourself. You don't need me to save you. I can help you, and you can save yourself." Eric sensed that Max was listening, so he continued. "I'm not going to let them kill you. I'm not going to let you kill yourself. I'm going to show you an alternative. That's my job, to get you over the times when you believe there aren't any alternatives, to help you through the time you don't have any hope. To make you know that you can be happy again, and that you will be."

"That's not possible."

"Yes it is. I'm sure of it."

"How do you know that?"

"Because it happened to me." Eric thought that if there was ever a time for self-disclosure, it was now. "I used to be anxious, I had an anxiety disorder. I kept it secret, and it keep me apart from everybody. I thought it would never end, and I thought about ending it all, more than one time. But then I got into therapy and I got better. It was hard work, but I had the help of a great therapist. He's still in my life, and he always will be. He's a father I never had."

"This sounds like bull."

"It's not, it's absolutely true."

"And you think you can do that for me?"

"Not for you, but with you. You and me, we can do it together."

"You want to be the father I never had."

"No, I want to be the psychiatrist you never had. I want to be the help you've never had. I want to give you the attention and the time you never had. I want to give you a chance you never had. Will you let me do that? Give us both a chance, Max. This isn't you, not the real you. The gun, the bomb, the hostages." Eric nodded at the Whole Foods bag. "Do you know what? I don't think it's a real bomb, at all. I think you dressed like a bad guy in a video game and you got some old rifle, and you told the clerk it was a bomb and they believed you. But I don't think it's real. I don't think any of this is real. Am I right?"

Max didn't reply, impassive behind the sunglasses. He checked his watch but said nothing.

"Do you even have any bullets?"

"No," Max answered softly.

"Thank God. So now we have to get out of here, and we have to get these kids out of here safely, because this is a very dangerous situation. Anybody could get shot, everybody's on edge, and you're not gonna believe what it looks like out in the parking lot." Eric nodded at the landline. "Just pick up the phone and call your mother. Tell her to tell Lieutenant Jana that you're letting the kids go. That the bomb was a hoax. That you and I are coming out with no guns. Unarmed. Tell her that it's over."

"I said no." Max stayed very still. "No."

"Yes." Eric couldn't stop now. It was time. "I'm going to walk toward you. I don't want the snipers behind me to get trigger-happy."

"No, don't." Max edged away. "I don't know—"

"I'm coming toward you now, Max." Eric began to walk toward the end of the counter.

"Stop, no."

"Don't do anything quickly, just walk to the end of the counter, meet me, and set the weapon down."

"No."

"Yes, please, do it!"

Max finally moved, met him at the end, setting the weapon down on the counter, then seeming to buckle at the knees, collapsing. "I'm sorry, I'm so sorry."

"I know." Eric caught Max and held him close, keeping his own back to the sniper. "Good job, Max. Good boy. It's over now."

"I didn't mean to, I didn't want to."

"I know, I know. Call your mother." Eric slid the phone to Max, still shielding him, and Max sniffled, beginning to cry, then pressed the number into the phone and held the receiver to his ear.

"Mom?" he said, dissolving into tears.

Chapter Forty-one

Eric and Max walked down the hallway, both of them holding their hands up, as directed. Eric had told Lieutenant Jana on the phone that Max was unarmed and the bomb a hoax, and the lieutenant had given them explicit actions on how to get out of the mall safely. Armed snipers lined the balcony, faceless under black helmets. He and Max had released the hostages, a terrified store clerk and four boys hiding embarrassed tears, all from a soccer day camp. The authorities weren't worried about danger anymore, but Eric sensed they were mad as hell, rightfully so.

"I'm scared," Max said, walking toward the exit with his hands in the air.

"Stay calm, it's okay." Eric walked him past the lighted billboards on the wall, with beautiful women showing Almay makeup and holding costly leather handbags conspicuously, Nordstrom evidently having a sale.

"What do you think they're going to do to me?"

"We're going to get through this, you'll see." Eric didn't want to say more because anything could happen. Max could change his mind and make a run for it, trying to draw gunfire and get himself killed.

"How long do you think they'll put me in jail for?"

"Keep your hands up and walk slow, you're doing great." Eric squinted against the klieglight outside, and all he could see were the silhouettes of the crowd through the mall entrance, about a hundred feet back from the door. Behind them, fire trucks, ambulances, and Humvees made massive hulking shadows. Shouting, talking, and crowd noise filtered through the glass doors.

"Dr. Parrish, how do we open the door if we have to hold our hands up?"

"I think they're going to do it for us, pal." Eric could already see a phalanx of uniformed police rushing the door. He held his hands high. "Max, get your hands up, and do whatever they say."

"I'm so scared," Max blurted out, and it was the last thing Eric heard him say because the police surged forward toward them like a massive wave, bursting through the doors and swarming over them both.

"We're unarmed, we're unarmed!" Eric shouted, and he heard Max cry out, but his voice was drowned out in the orders shouted by the police.

"Get down! Get down on the floor!" the cops hollered, and before Eric could comply, police officers were in his face and more were grabbing him from behind. They tackled him and shoved him bodily to the floor, wrenched his arms behind his back, cuffed his wrists together tightly, and pressed his face into the concrete, banging his cheek hard.

"You're under arrest, sir! Anything you say can and will be used against you," one of the cops started to say.

Eric lost the end of the sentence as his head pounded; he'd had his bell rung on the floor. They yanked him to his feet, surrounding him.

"This way, come this way!" the cops shouted, hurrying him out of the mall. He twisted around, trying to see Max, and the boy was engulfed in uniformed cops rushing him toward a cruiser parked at the curb.

"Eric, I'll call Paul!" somebody shouted to him, and Eric looked over to see Laurie being held back by a line of uniformed police, waving to get his attention.

"Come with us, come this way!" the cops hollered, everybody

shouting at once, practically picking Eric up by his arms, rushing him to a waiting cruiser, and opening the door. They stuffed him inside, pressing down on his head, then closed the door behind him. The backseat of the cruiser was dark, with bucket seats of hard plastic and a thick metal grate that separated it from the front seat. There were two uniformed cops in the front seat, and the cruisers lurched off in tandem.

Eric shook off his headache. His shoulders arced in pain, as did his wrists. He perched forward slightly, not to lean on them. He looked out the window and noticed a crowd of teenage shoppers crying as they clutched their Abercrombie and Nordstrom shopping bags. His gut wrenched at the terror that Max had caused, but at the same time, he felt relieved nobody had gotten hurt, including Max himself, though the boy still wasn't out of the woods.

The cruisers steered toward Mall Road and stopped while the cops moved the barricades, permitting them to pass. FBI, ATF, uniformed police, EMTs, and firefighters tried to see inside the cruiser, and Eric began to process the enormity of what had just happened. "Officers," he said, raising his voice to be heard through the grate. "Where are we going? What happens now?"

"Sir, we're taking you to the Upper Merion station house."

"So you're from Upper Merion Police?" Eric knew the Upper Merion Police Department was bigger than Radnor Police, owing to the major businesses and industries in the King of Prussia area.

"Yes."

"What am I being charged with? What will the boy be charged with?"

"The A.D.A. will answer your questions. We'll be there in fifteen minutes, with this traffic."

"That kid will need to be on a suicide watch, Officers."

"We'll tell them."

The rumbling cruiser left the vast mall complex, with Eric in the darkened backseat, his shoulders and wrists throbbing. The streets were congested with police cruisers, fire trucks, ambulances, and other official vehicles, driving bumper-to-bumper with cars, press vehicles, camera trucks, vans with microwave towers, and television news vans bearing the shiny logos of NBC, ABC, FOX, CBS, as well as CNN. The route to the Upper Merion police station cut through the thriving business district of King of Prussia, lined with McDonald's, Chili's, Sleepys mattress stores, chain stereo installers, and a myriad of other shops, crisscrossed by a disorderly network of double-lane roads rendered virtually impassable by the fracas at the mall.

Abruptly, the sirens on Eric's cruiser screamed to life, blasting his eardrums. Instinctively he reached up to cover his ears, but the handcuffs prevented him. He grimaced, pain reverberating from his wrists up his arms, setting his nerves jangling. He craned his neck to see Max, but they had been joined by two other cruisers as a police escort, traveling as a motorcade.

Suddenly, bright lights filled the interior of the cruiser, and Eric turned around to see a no-logo news van, its highbeams on, driving alongside, taking videos inside the cruiser and aiming the lens at him like a gun.

"You believe this knucklehead?" muttered the cop driving Eric, and the other cop cursed softly under his breath.

They lost the news van, and traffic parted as the cruisers sped past, and drivers gaped at them, press filmed videos, and teenagers in backseats held up cell phones, taking photos. The motorcade turned onto King of Prussia Road, and Eric could see all the way down the street the white-hot klieglights surrounding the station, so many that they illuminated the dark night sky like a cumulus cloud of light, haze, humidity, and cigarette smoke.

They zoomed toward the police station and slowed to turn into the packed parking lot, with cars and news vans parked everywhere, willy-nilly. A massive crowd of media came running toward them but were pressed back by double lines of Upper Merion police officers in black uniforms, standing in tight formation. Beyond their barricade, Eric had never seen so many TV videocameras, cameras, tape recorders, boom mics, regular mics, and every type of reporter, photographer, or TV anchor.

The cruisers stopped at the same moment, pulling up in front of the police station in a protected slot formed by the barricade.

Eric looked over, and unlike Radnor, Upper Merion had its own large, aging redbrick building with an institutional white portico in front. Police jumped out of the cruisers at the same time, as if it had been coordinated, and Eric boosted himself up in the seat, to see more uniformed police emerging from the police station and splitting into two groups, one hustling to Max's cruiser and the other to his cruiser, then flinging open his car door.

"Sir, come with us, quickly, come!" A police officer in a black uniform stuck his head inside the backseat.

"Sure." Eric was tugged out roughly by the officers, who surrounded him in a tight cluster as he tried vainly to see Max. Eric knew that the boy had to be terrified, not only by the consequences of what he had done, but by the military police presence and the chaos of the scene, with sirens blaring, reporters screaming questions, and bright lights everywhere, blinding.

"Max!" Eric called out, but Max was engulfed by police, who swept him forward through the doors and inside the police station. Eric didn't see Marie or Zack anywhere, and he feared for Max.

"Officer," he said to the cop, hustling him inside and through the bright waiting room packed with police, "that boy needs help. He needs to be on a suicide watch in his—"

"I'll tell the sergeant, sir, keep it moving, keep it moving."

"I am, but he really needs help—"

"Gotcha, sir," the cop said, his face showing the strain as he propelled Eric forward down the hallway to the right, while Max was taken to the left

Eric turned to catch one last glimpse of Max, but all he saw was a sea of black caps and uniforms. He felt a deep wrench in his chest, knowing that he had done the only thing he could do for Max, but wondering what would happen next for the boy.

Chapter Forty-two

"Another fine mess!" Paul entered the large interview room with a smile, but it seemed a little forced.

"Thanks for coming." Eric looked up from where he sat, in an institutional mesh chair. They'd taken off his handcuffs, but his wrists still hurt. They'd taken the firefighter's jacket and his cell phone, again.

"Thank God for Laurie, but don't tell her I said so. You don't know what it was like to go through school after that brainiac. Talk about a tough act to follow." Paul set his metallic briefcase on the table, a grimy grayish Formica.

"Where is she? Is she here?"

"No, she had to go back to work. Some car accident on 202, which doesn't surprise me. Traffic was nuts, and it's a freaking circus out there."

"I know." Eric could feel the police station buzzing outside the interview room, which was a long rectangle with beige walls and a large window to the left, with closed blinds through which he could hear the noise of the media thronging outside. Inside, the redbrick station house was packed to busting with Upper Merion police, FBI, ATF, and Homeland Security, in windbreakers with acronyms on the back. They'd all stared at him as he was brought in, his hands cuffed behind his back, his head down.

Paul eased into the chair catty-corner to him, tugging up his neat slacks. "So my sister told me the whole story, you went into the mall to save the kid. I have a crush on you, too, now."

Eric smiled. "I just wanted everybody to get out alive."

"They did, and you ended up in handcuffs. They should be thanking you, not arresting you. No good deed, eh?"

Eric wasn't interested in personal glory. "So what do we do now?"

"You and I have a pep talk. The big game is in half an hour. They'll interview you, right here."

"I'm arrested, but what for? Does this mean I have a criminal record?"

"Not yet, you haven't been arraigned, and I'm hoping if we play ball with them, we can get them to drop the charges."

Eric breathed a relieved sigh. "How?"

"Let me explain. They want to question you, and we're going to answer as many questions as you feel comfortable answering."

"Okay," Eric said, confused. "But how is this different from today, at Radnor? You told me I didn't have to answer any questions, that I have a privilege that's protected by statute."

"That was then, this is now. It's a complex legal situation, unlike earlier today." Paul paused. "The first thing you have to understand is that this is a turf war between three armies. It's like three street gangs fighting over the same block. You're the block."

"I figured."

"The feds got their panties in a snit because what happened at the mall runs afoul of several federal statutes, mostly new antiterrorism laws, like those against the threatened use of bombs and other explosive materials, as well as hostage-taking. Upper Merion P.D. has skin in the game because the mall is in Montgomery County and state criminal laws were broken, namely kidnapping, kidnapping of a minor, unlawful restraint, simple assault, and reckless endangerment. The third jurisdiction involved is Radnor because the girl is still dead."

"Renée Bevilacqua."

"Yes. Here's how I see this play out." Paul leaned over, intense. "The feds should drop out because it wasn't a real bomb or real gun. Politically, they have no margin in keeping pressure on you, or even on Max. If anything, they look like horses' asses because it turned out to be a kid with an empty shoebox. Follow me so far?"

"Yes."

"The real players, believe it or not, are the junior varsity, Upper Merion and Radnor. Upper Merion has a solid beef because Max took those kids hostage, which is a felony no matter how you slice it, and against kids, which as you know, is a definite no-no."

"Max is a minor, himself."

"They won't necessarily charge him that way. The good news is that Upper Merion will go after Max, not you."

"That's not good news." Eric's heart sank.

Paul frowned. "Stop worrying about Max. Right now."

"I can't, he's my patient. In fact, he needs a lawyer and I'm hoping you can represent him."

Paul's dark eyes flared. "Are you insane? He's got a mom and a father figure, that's good enough. That kid has to get a lawyer on his own. I can't represent him and you."

"Why not?"

"Because there's a conflict of interest between the two of you. Those cops are trying to figure out what the hell is going on here. They still suspect you of the murder, and given what Max pulled tonight, they think he's straight-up crazy. Right now, they're putting their heads together, trying to figure out which of you did it and if you acted alone or together."

"I'm not going to desert him. He still needs help. He should be on a suicide watch. Do you know if he is?"

"Eric, that kid put you right where you are now." Paul leaned forward, placing his hands facedown on the table. "We don't have time to talk about it because you're about to get heat like you've never had in your life."

"What do you mean?"

"You still have information that they need on Bevilacqua. They want to know what Max told you about Renée in his sessions, why you sent the cops to find him, and why you followed her to work and home. They want to know everything you know about Max and his involvement with her murder."

"*If* he was involved." Eric wasn't about to tell Paul what Max had told him in the video game store. It was still privileged, and just because they weren't in his office didn't mean it wasn't confidential.

"Yes, *if* he was, but they have a lot of questions and they know you have the answers."

"I don't know who killed that girl."

"But you know more than they know, don't you? You know things that you won't even tell me, right? I can tell by the look on your face. The live legal issue is Renée's murder, and they're going to pressure you to give them the information."

"I have a privilege to respect, and nothing's changed since earlier today." Eric thought about it. "In fact, the stakes are only higher. My patient tried to commit suicide tonight. He has nobody in the world but me, and I can't betray him now, or I tell you, he will kill himself."

"Today, at the Radnor police station, you claimed your privilege and they let you walk out. That's not what's going to happen tonight, not after the fiasco at that mall. As you say, the stakes are higher now."

"What do you mean?"

"Remember what I told you today, about the power of the Commonwealth? And how they have all the aces when you don't even know you're playing cards?"

"Yes."

"As a legal matter, whether you get charged with a crime, and the extent to which you are charged, lies completely with the discretion of the prosecutor. The D.A. herself would be here if she weren't in the hospital, and I promise you, she's calling the shots. Anyway, the state is gunning for you. Why? You have information they need and they have a way to get it."

"How?"

"They're going to try to squeeze you. You give up what the kid told you in therapy about Renée, and they will make *everything* go away—the feds will drop any federal criminal charges against you arising out of the terrorism statutes, Upper Merion will drop any charges against you for obstructing the administration of the law by going into the mall, and Radnor will drop the potential murder or conspiracy to murder investigation against you in connection with Renée."

"So if I give him up, I save myself."

"Yes."

"I should trade his life to save my ass?"

"You got a problem with that?" Paul didn't crack a smile.

"I still won't violate my privilege. If I divulge, he'll see it as a betrayal. He'll lose the only person he has left. He could kill himself."

"Then we'll play it by ear, at the meeting." Paul exhaled, slowly. "Let's move on to a related point. My defense for you will be to delineate you from Max. To try to distinguish how what you did tonight is very different from what he did. That makes a big difference, legally."

Eric hated the turn the conversation was taking.

"Pennsylvania doesn't have a good statute concerning interference with the police, which is basically what you did. The most they could charge you with is obstructing the administration of law and other governmental functions, but that's only a misdemeanor of the second degree. Normally, charges could come from your actual misconduct, but you didn't assault anyone, disturb the peace, cause a riot, or physically resist arrest. A case like yours, where your conduct didn't harm anyone and caused a good outcome, the most I think they could throw at you would be a minor charge, like disorderly conduct and with an ARD disposition, which is arbitration. It's the best-case scenario."

"They have to charge me with something?"

"Yes. You can't disregard their orders in a hostage situation. The consequences can be too dire. They won't do nothing—unless we give them the information they want."

Eric's head was spinning. "So what's the bottom line?"

"If you stick to your guns, then you're going to spend the night in jail."

"Can't I bail myself out? How much will it cost?"

"You haven't been arraigned yet, and these things take time. I can guarantee you they're going to drag their feet, but that's not even the big gun."

"What is?"

"Their next move is to call you before the grand jury. You have a right to refuse to answer questions of the police and prosecutor, but you *have to* answer questions before the grand jury unless you have a valid privilege, like the Fifth Amendment or your statutory privilege under Section 5944."

"So then, I'm good, right?"

"Wrong. The prosecutor could then bring you before the supervising judge of the grand jury and he will determine if you can lawfully refuse to answer questions. The prosecutor would argue to him that you should divulge because of the state's interest in the health, safety, and welfare of its citizenry. And they're going to win. The court order will force you to reveal the information."

"That can't be the law."

"That can be the politics, and it's close enough on the law. Judges have discretion, like I told you, and it's not just about that girl's murder anymore, it's about shutting down the King of Prussia Mall. K of P is the biggest mall in the country, bigger than the Mall of America since the expansion, 2 million square feet. Employs seven thousand people and it's a major tourist attraction, bringing money into the county."

"How do you know all this?"

"I looked it up, and my wife shops until *I* drop. As I was saying, if you think that the King of Prussia Chamber of Commerce and the economic clout behind the mall are not going to influence the supervising judge of the grand jury, you're mistaken. And state judges are elected, not like merit appointments. Those judges get the gig because they have coin and juice, not because they look good in black. And let's be real, who doesn't?"

Eric's thoughts raced. He sensed where Paul was going.

"The judge will give them an order that compels you to divulge, maybe not all of what you know, but a lot more than you're willing to divulge now. If you don't obey that order, you're going to jail for contempt of court."

"For how long?"

"Until you comply. A contempt of court sentence can be open-ended. Judges have the same kind of discretion that district attorneys do. They all work for the same boss. The almighty dollar."

Eric tried to wrap his mind around the details, but he knew he was in deeper trouble than before. "They can't send me away forever."

"They can—until you comply. There's not a lot of law on the subject or cases about shrinks, but do you want to be the one who makes new law?"

"How can you go to jail if you don't commit a crime?"

"The crime would be failure to comply with a court order. If you don't divulge after the court orders you to, you're in contempt. Do you see what you're up against?"

The scary part was, Eric did.

Chapter Forty-three

Ten minutes later, Eric found himself seated at the table next to Paul, and the interview room brimmed with personnel getting settled in mesh chairs and along the wall. Several FBI and ATF agents stood at the back of the room, next to someone from Homeland Security, and they had introduced themselves to Paul when Eric was brought in, nodding at him briefly as they gave Paul their business cards. The federal agents hadn't introduced themselves to Eric, and he got the gist that he had become a lesser life form, a prisoner. The *them,* in the us against them.

On the wall facing him was an observation window like the one at the Radnor police station, but its surface was more reflective. Eric avoided his own reflection. He didn't want to see the way he looked in police custody. They'd taken the firefighter's jacket, which afforded him at least some cover, and he felt more vulnerable than ever in the generic gray sweat clothes, without his phone, pager, and employee ID lanyard. He'd become generic himself, a forty-something white guy, of average height and build, a common criminal.

Eric and Paul sat across from Detective Rhoades of the Radnor Police, as well as Captain Alan Newmire of the Upper Merion Police, who looked to be in his forties and was remarkably tall, maybe six-five, with bristly salt-and-pepper hair that refused to stay in place and hooded bright blue eyes in a longish, lined face, with a fresh sunburn. He had on a black uniform, his chest enlarged by the bulletproof vest underneath, which made a thick rim at his collar like a turtle's shell. To his left sat A.D.A. Pete Mastell, whom Eric could identify on sight as a junior prosecutor, still in his thirties, with dark, gelled hair and sharp brown eyes that were always on high alert. Eric felt a residual kinship with him, flashing on the D.A.'s Office picnics and softball games he'd gone to with Caitlin, but they were his friends no longer. On the contrary, he considered himself lucky that Caitlin wasn't from the same D.A.'s Office. The thought led him to Hannah, with a wave of sadness. He hadn't talked to her last night and felt oddly cut off from her, too.

Paul clapped his hands together. "Folks, Dr. Parrish has consented to meet with you to cooperate and resolve this matter. It goes without saying that he doesn't have to do any such thing. That said, let's talk procedure. I'm not going to have a panel of top brass interrogating my client. So you folks need to appoint somebody to be your designated driver, and we will answer questions from him."

Everybody on the other side of the table reacted—lips pursed, eyes narrowed, and a gentle snort of derision emanated from the assistant district attorney.

Captain Newmire raised his index finger, as if he were summoning a waiter. "Fair enough, I'll be the point man."

"Thank you. Also, is there a reason the *federales* are in the room?" Paul gestured at the federal agents standing along the back wall. "It's intimidating, but I'm sure that's not your intent."

The agent on the end answered, "I'm Special Agent Sorenson of the Philadephia bureau, and we have an interest in these proceedings."

Paul waved airily at the observation window. "I feel you, but why can't you go stand in whatever room is behind there?"

"We'd just as soon stay, if you don't mind."

"I do mind, but I'll see if Dr. Parrish does." Paul turned to Eric. "Can you deal with a studio audience?"

"It's fine," Eric answered, sensing that there was a method to Paul's madness. The lawyer was establishing a jokey, though com-

pletely serious, dominance, and by asking Eric if he agreed, it made him feel more powerful. He shifted in his chair, sitting straighter.

"One final point, before we begin." Paul's tone turned conversational. "Dr. Parrish doesn't want me to toot his horn, but he risked his life tonight to save others. He ran into that mall because it was the right thing to do. His actions resulted in the hostages' being released unharmed and the shooter being in your custody. I think that my client is a hero. So do they." Paul nodded out the window, toward the media. "Those guys tomorrow, they're going to say the same thing. They saw him run in, saw the kids run out in their cute little soccer jerseys, saw him escort the shooter out and save the day. Dr. Parrish deserves your thanks, and the fact that he is sitting here before you, treated like a felon or even a terrorist, is beyond me."

"Mr. Forunato—"

"Please, call me Paul. I'm trying to make nice."

"Fine, Paul." Captain Newmire smiled, less tightly, and turned to Eric. "Dr. Parrish, your counsel and you take the position that you did the '*right thing*' "—he made air quotes with his fingers— "but we disagree. You were expressly prohibited from entering the mall. You proceeded irregardless. You violated state and federal law, interfered with an emergency police action, impersonated a first responder, and recklessly endangered the lives of others."

Paul interjected, "Please tell me you're kidding. If not for Dr. Parrish, you'd be at the morgue tagging toes. That mall was a powderkeg."

"Powderkeg?" Captain Newmire turned to Paul with a frown. "It was a hoax. The bomb was a shoebox and the perpetrator's rifle was non-functional."

"You're missing the point, Captain," Paul shot back. "The firepower didn't come from a kid with a musket, but from you and every other police precinct in the tri-state, loaded with AR-9s and all the other toys the feds gave you as surplus from Iraq, not to mention armed SWAT teams, ATF, FBI, and whatever else. It was a military action with assault weapons, Humvees, and I even saw a SERT tank."

"It wasn't a *military* action."

"It was overkill, plain and simple."

"It was a reasonable reaction to a threat situation." Captain New-mire stiffened, but Paul didn't back down.

"You have the toys and you're dying to use 'em. It was you and your men who created a potentially dangerous situation, and all Dr. Parrish did was make sure nobody got hurt. A bigger man would be able to thank him, but I won't hold my breath."

Eric remained silent, watching the reactions, especially to Paul's last line. The FBI agent on the end folded his arms, and everybody stiffened. Eric cleared his throat, sensing that he needed to soothe some egos and dispell the bad vibes. "Gentlemen, I may not be a lawyer, but I'm enough of a therapist to tell you that we should move on. Counseling doesn't always work, and not every marriage can be saved."

Captain Newmire and Detective Rhoades chuckled unexpect-edly, and there were tense smiles around the room, so Eric felt as if he had diffused the situation, which he was coming to think of as his hobby.

Captain Newmire nodded, easing back in his chair. "Fair enough, Dr. Parrish. I speak for everyone here when I say that we appreci-ate your cooperating with us and answering a few questions."

"Thank you." Eric managed a smile.

"The first question concerns your relationship to Max Jakubowski. How long has he been your patient?"

Eric braced himself to make his case. "Captain, as Detective Rhoades has probably told you, I take the confidentiality between me and my patients very seriously. I can't answer questions about my therapeutic relationship to Max, anything he told me in ther-apy, anything relating to his diagnosis, or things of that nature."

Captain Newmire pursed his lips, which were thin. He had a five o'clock shadow, salted with whitish hairs. "Let's begin with what you *can* tell me. Max is your patient, correct?"

"Yes, although I revealed that to Detective Rhoades only because I'm permitted to reveal that when a patient is at risk for suicide.

I divulged that information so they could go and find him, since he had been missing." Eric paused. "Where is Max now?"

Captain Newmire hesitated. "In custody."

"Here?"

"Yes."

"I don't know if anyone told you, but I am concerned about his mental state. There's a substantial risk he might harm himself. He needs to be on suicide watch."

"I got the message, thanks."

"So you're watching him?"

"Yes."

Somehow Eric didn't feel relieved. Captain Newmire said the right words, but his tone remained brusque and cool, unlike the hotter-headed Detective Rhoades, who now sat quietly, his meaty hands folded in front of him. "Have you questioned Max yet?"

"No."

"Does he have a lawyer?" Eric felt a sharp kick to his right leg under the table, evidently from Paul, trying to shut him up.

"Not to my knowlegde, though his mother is trying to find him one."

Captain Newmire eyed him.

"What about a psychiatrist?"

"Why do you ask?"

"Because practicalities prevent me from counseling him right now, and he needs psychiatric help. I can give you some numbers of my colleagues in private practice. You need to get him some help."

"Oh, we do, do we?" Captain Newmire's tone curdled, but Eric wasn't surprised.

"Yes, you do. You have legal obligations to care for those in police custody. If he were bleeding from a wound, you'd get him a physician. He's in obvious emotional distress, so he needs a psychiatrist." Eric felt Paul kick him under the table again.

"Let's move on." Captain Newmire cleared his throat. "Now, you reported Max missing after he telephoned you on Tuesday night, is that correct?"

"Yes, that's true."

"What is your relationship to the deceased girl, Renée Bevilacqua?"

"I had no relationship to her. I didn't know her."

"But you met her at her place of business, isn't that correct?"

"Yes, that is true."

"You can tell me that because it doesn't involve Max or your treatment of him, is that correct?"

"Yes, you just asked me a question about my whereabouts and I answered it."

"Why were you at the frozen yogurt shop Tuesday night, speaking with Ms. Bevilacqua?"

"I can't tell you that."

Captain Newmire lifted a graying eyebrow. "You know, I think of myself as a logical man. Methodical. It drives my wife nuts. And if you can't tell me why you were at the yogurt shop, then it's a logical conclusion that the reason involves Max Jakubowski. Now, we have learned that Max Jakubowski was Renée Bevilacqua's SAT tutor at PerfectScore. Your being there at the shop was because of Max Jakubowski, correct?"

Eric started to answer, then stopped himself. "I can't answer that. I can't confirm or deny that."

"Did Max introduce you to her?"

"I can't answer that."

"Did you introduce Max to Renée?"

"No."

"Who knew her first?"

"I didn't know her."

"Except for the night you went to the yogurt shop, for a reason you won't explain."

Paul sighed theatrically. "Captain, Dr. Parrish has been consistent on that confidentiality issue, and I respect that, as should you. Without waiving my attorney-client privilege, I'll volunteer that he hasn't told me that either."

Captain Newmire faced Eric. "Were you involved with the murder of Renée Bevilacqua?"

"Absolutely not."

"Did you conspire with Max Jakubowski to murder Renée Bevilacqua?"

"Absolutely not."

"Did you ever suggest to Max that he murder Renée Bevilacqua?"

"No, of course not."

"Were you engaged in a romantic relationship with Renée?"

"Of course not."

"Was Max?"

"I can't answer that."

"Do you know why Max would be in possession of Renée Bevilacqua's cell phone?"

"I can't answer that." Eric tried not to let his shock show. They must have found Renée's phone in Max's bedroom. He doubted that they'd told Marie, or she would have told him.

"Did there come a time during your counseling with Max that you became afraid he would murder Renée?"

"I can't answer that question." Eric tried to keep his expression impassive, betraying none of the pain the question evoked in him.

"Dr. Parrish, if you think that a patient is homicidal or suicidal, you have a duty to warn the intended victim and the police, don't you?"

"Yes, I do." Eric remained stoic.

"Yet tonight, you told Lieutenant Jana that you were concerned that Max was trying to commit suicide by police, didn't you?"

"Yes, I did." Eric swallowed hard.

"If you thought Max was suicidal, why didn't you admit him to Havemeyer General?"

"I can't answer that question." Eric would be asking himself that same question for the rest of his life.

"Did you think Max was suicidal tonight?"

"Yes, and you didn't have to be a trained psychiatrist to know that. It was common sense." Eric was trying to rely less on the privilege. "When the lieutnant told me what Max had threatened on the phone, it was clear the threat didn't make sense. Max intended only to bring harm to himself, not anybody else. The fact that he had a fake bomb and no bullets proves as much."

"Your attorney said that you risked your life tonight. Did you believe you were risking your life when you ran into the mall?"

"Yes, but I wasn't thinking of that. I was thinking I had to get Max out before he got hurt. I knew if I could talk to him, I could convince him."

"And you knew that how?"

"I'm not going to elaborate because it would compromise my confidentiality." Eric glanced at the clock on the wall, which read 10:55. He wondered where Max was in the station house, knowing he'd be counting off to his tapping and colors ritual.

"Dr. Parrish, earlier in this interview, you spoke very strongly on Max's behalf, asking questions about his welfare and whereabouts, and you breached a police barricade to save his life. It sounds as if you have a personal relationship to him."

"No, I have a professional relationship to him."

"But Max called you on your personal cell phone after his grandmother died, isn't that correct? That's not confidential, because you told it to the Radnor Police."

"Yes, Max did do that."

"Does he call you frequently on your cell phone?"

"I can't answer that." Eric remembered the police had his cell phone, so they had undoubtedly checked his phone logs. They were trying to catch him in a lie.

"Do other patients call you on your cell?"

"Yes, my private ones do, in emergencies."

"Is your relationship with Max intimate?"

Paul sighed. "God. Really?"

"Of course not," Eric snapped.

Captain Newmire blinked. "You went to Max's house and spoke with his mother about him, is that correct?"

"Yes."

"Is that a practice of yours, with your private patients?"

"No."

"Have you ever done that with any patient, previously?"

"No." Eric had to admit it.

"It's also true that you spent some time in his bedroom, isn't that correct?"

Eric hesitated. The fact wasn't properly within the privilege. His boundary violations were coming back to haunt him. "Yes, that's true."

"Why did you do that?"

"That I can't answer."

"Was it the first time you had been in Max's bedroom?"

"Yes, absolutely," Eric answered, disliking the implication.

"Did you see Max in your private home, for his counseling session?"

"Yes, in my home office."

"Was he in any other room of your house, in addition to your home office?"

"No."

"Has he been in your bedroom?"

"No." Eric remembered the fingerprint dust he had seen on the first floor of his house. He hadn't even had a chance to go upstairs and see if it was on the second floor.

"Did you ever go anywhere with Max? Whether in his car or yours?"

"No." Eric imagined that the police had already dusted inside his car. He wondered when he'd get it back.

"Do you believe you have an unusual amount of influence over Max?"

"No."

"Even given the events of this evening?" Captain Newmire paused. "You were able to go into that mall and bring him out in suprisingly short order."

Eric sensed he was moving into dangerous ground. "Do you have a question?"

"As a psychiatrist, aren't you trained in ways to influence your patients?"

"No, that misunderstands the therapeutic process. We help them to influence themselves."

"Doesn't that involve, for want of a better word, manipulating them?"

"No, not at all."

"Funny, because you seem to manipulate Max."

"No, I don't."

Paul interjected, again, "Is that a question?"

Captain Newmire cocked his head. "We have to understand what's going on here, and what is the extent and nature of the relationship between Dr. Parrish and Max. Dr. Parrish won't explain to us what the relationship is, so we're left to draw some logical conclusions. One is that Dr. Parrish has a great deal of influence over Max, so much so that he could single-handedly end a stand-off and hostage situation. That corroborates my theory about what kind of control, influence, or manipulation that Dr. Parrish exerts over this young boy, whose father is out of the picture. There is more than ample evidence to infer that Dr. Parrish exerts, shall we say, a Svengali-like influence over this boy."

"That's ridiculous!" Paul snorted.

"That's not true," Eric added.

"Because we aren't getting any information from Dr. Parrish, we can't agree that it's ridiculous. We have to investigate because a girl is dead, and it is not inconsistent with these facts that Max committed that murder at Dr. Parrish's bidding."

"Also absurd," Paul snapped.

Captain Newmire continued coolly, "Nor is it inconsistent with those facts that Max entered the mall tonight with his fake bomb and gun, staged a hoax that he was going to kill people and blow up the mall, also at Dr. Parrish's bidding."

"What?" Eric blurted out, flabbergasted. "Why would I want him to do that? Why would I want kids taken hostage? Or the mall blown up?"

"To make yourself look good."

"What, how?" Eric felt a tingle of fear. He hadn't seen this coming and he guessed Paul hadn't either. The cops were assigning him primary responsibility and painting Max as his puppet. Eric didn't know how to defend himself without putting Max on the hook or breaching his privilege.

Paul waved Eric into silence. "Captain, what are you saying? Why would Dr. Parrish do something so heinous? Order kids taken *hostage*?"

Captain Newmire faced Paul. "Dr. Parrish was taken in for questioning today, in connection with the murder of Renée Bevilacqua. Perhaps he used Max Jakubowski to make himself look like a hero, less like a murder suspect." Captain Newmire swiveled his head around to Eric. "Did you send Max into the mall with a fake bomb and old weapon? Was it your plan he was following?"

"No, wait, are you saying I knew it was a hoax?"

"Yes, it certainly is possible, and we're not left with any other logical inferences, because you won't provide us any information that would enlighten us and convince—"

"This is blackmail!" Paul interrupted, his disgust undisguised.

Captain Newmire ignored him, glaring at Eric. "In addition, we've investigated and we have learned that you were placed on indefinite suspension at the hospital."

Paul threw up his hands. "What does that have to do with anything?"

Eric felt instantly mortified, saying nothing.

Captain Newmire ignored Paul again. "Hospital officials tell us that the reason for their action was confidential, but perhaps that was part of your motivation. It's not unreasonable that you would stage a hoax to rehabilitate your reputation with the hospital and get reinstated. Did you send Max into the mall to do your bidding? Then run in to save the day?"

"Of course not!" Eric shot back.

"Okay, we're done!" Paul interjected, pushing his chair away from the table. "Captain Newmire, you're arguing with my client, despite the fact that he is cooperating with you to the fullest extent possible. He's not answering any more questions about your inane and wild theories." Paul turned to Eric. "Please, not another word, Doctor. We're done here."

Captain Newmire pursed his lips. "Then he's going back to his holding cell. We have enough to hold him and will do so."

"What are you charging him with?"

"We'll have to discuss that with the district attorney." Captain Newmire glanced at the assistant district attorney, who kept making rapid notes. "We'll let you know what the charges are as soon as possible, then he will be arraigned, unless he reconsiders his decision not to cooperate fully. Dr. Parrish has a choice to make and he can think about it in his cell."

"You should be ashamed of yourself."

Eric tried to suppress the fear he felt. He was going to jail. It didn't seem possible, or real. He was going to be charged with a crime; he'd have a criminal record. He looked at Captain Newmire. "Captain, I'm entitled to a phone call, aren't I?"

Captain Newmire blinked. "For what? You already have counsel, Dr. Parrish."

"I want my phone call," Eric answered, without elaboration.

Chapter Forty-four

The interview room emptied, leaving Eric to make his phone call, so he pulled the landline phone over and pressed in the number, suppressing his worries. He didn't want to let another night pass without talking to Hannah. He didn't have her new cell-phone number, so he called Caitlin at the house, wondering if she would pick up. The caller ID would show up as Upper Merion police station, and she would know exactly who it was. He prayed she would pick up anyway, and in the next moment, the ringing stopped.

"Caitlin, thanks for taking the call," Eric said, with relief.

"Who is this?" asked a male voice, which took Eric aback. He thought he'd dialed the wrong number, then he realized that he was talking to Caitlin's boyfriend, Brian. It was one thing to know that she was sleeping with another man, but quite another to hear his voice, which was deep, strong, and undeniably hostile. Eric felt a stab of sexual jealousy, as well as anger. He couldn't ignore the irony that Brian would spend the night sleeping next to Caitlin, while he would be sitting in a jail cell.

"This is Eric Parrish, Hannah's father and—"

"You're not allowed to be calling here. You're not allowed to communicate with Caitlin directly. Have your lawyer call her lawyer."

Eric wanted to punch him through the phone. He was tired of

defusing situations, or maybe he was just at the end of his rope. "I want to speak to Hannah."

"Then you should have called her phone number."

"You know full well that Caitlin disconnected Hannah's cell."

"She's asleep."

"I don't want to wake her up, but Caitlin could check and see if she's really asleep. Is Caitlin there?"

"Hannah's asleep."

"You don't know that. The phone is downstairs, and she's upstairs. I know the house, I was there before you." Eric heard the words come out of his mouth, realizing they weren't talking about the house anymore.

"Take my word for it."

"I'm not taking your word for anything. I don't have to talk to you to speak to my own daughter." Eric raised his voice, feeling himself lose control. "And by the way, if you ever call my daughter another name, much less a *whiner,* I'm going to beat the living crap out of you."

Brian snorted. "You're a trip, you know that, buddy? Where do you get off filing for custody? You act like it's about Hannah, but it's about you. You want Caitlin back but she's done. You're jealous she's with me. You're trying to hurt her and you know the way to hurt her is through Hannah, so that's what you're doing."

"That's not true, and I don't have to discuss it with you."

"Caller ID says you're at Upper Merion police station. You're under arrest. That's going to look great to the court, don't you think? Good luck trying to get custody. You'll be lucky if you get unsupervised visits."

"Put my daughter on the phone." Eric would have to call Susan as soon as he got out.

"You really want to talk to your daughter now? You want to tell her where you are? You know what it does to a kid to be ashamed of her own father?"

Eric knew exactly what it was like to be ashamed of his father, but he didn't need this jerk to psychoanalyze him. "I'm not going to fight with you. Go see if my daughter is asleep—"

"Dude, you make me laugh. Do you have any idea what your daughter's going to go through at school? How the kids are gonna bully her?"

Eric had thought the same thing, which was the reason he wanted to speak with Hannah. "If anything, I got those hostages freed."

"Bully for you. Thing is, kids don't know the difference. All they know is her dad's in jail. That's what they're going to say. We don't want her to have to face those bullies."

"*We?*" Eric shot back, angry. "Listen, *dude,* don't parent my child. Ask Caitlin to check if Hannah's sleeping, and if she's not, put her on the damn phone."

"I don't take orders from you."

"Put my daughter on the phone! She needs to hear the truth from me so she can hold her head up high at school tomorrow."

"We're not sending her to school tomorrow."

We, again. "Why not? She has to go to school. You can't keep her out of school forever. That's not the way to deal with this situation."

"Sorry, we're not as smart as you. That's why you're calling from jail. Because you're so smart."

"Let me talk to her!" Suddenly Eric heard Hannah's voice in the background, but he couldn't make out what she was saying. The phone went silent, but it didn't sound as if Brian had hung up but was covering the receiver with his hand. Eric could hear some muffled noise and Hannah talking, and in the next moment there was a shuffling on the line.

"Eric?" Caitlin came on, her voice clipped. "I hope you're happy. You woke her up and she's here. You can speak to her for a few minutes, then that's it."

"You don't have any right to limit how long I talk to her."

"Discuss that with your friend Susan. I'll put Hannah on the phone now. Hold on."

"Daddy?" Hannah asked. "Is that you?"

"Hannah!" Eric felt his heart leap at the sound of her voice, in its charming little-girl register. "Honey, it's so good to hear you!"

"Are you okay, Daddy? I'm worried. What's going on? Where are you?"

"I'm fine, everything's fine." Eric hated the thought that he had caused her any anxiety.

"I miss you."

"I miss you, too. I'm so sorry I woke you up."

"I wasn't asleep, I was waiting for you to call. I heard Brian and Mommy, and I knew it was you on the phone. I wanted to talk to you."

"I wanted to talk to you too—"

"Daddy, they showed you on TV. They said that bad guys had guns at the mall and there was a bomb! It's *our* mall, where I got my cleats. You didn't get hurt, did you?"

"Not at all, I'm fine, sweetheart. It wasn't really a bomb, it was a fake bomb. Nobody tried to hurt me or anybody else. It's all over now and it's fine."

"Who's the bad guy? Was the bad guy your patient? Was that him on the TV? He had on a hoodie, he looked kinda scary. What's wrong with him?"

"Honey, yes, that's my patient, but he's not a bad guy."

"Then who's the bad guy? The police were there, so many, I saw, all over the mall."

"There were no bad guys tonight." Eric wanted to say, *except for Brian*, but held his tongue. "Everything is fine. I went to the mall to help my patient and now he's fine too."

"I miss you. When can I see you? I heard Brian say you were in jail. You're not really in jail, are you?"

Eric never lied to her, but he was tempted to tonight. He decided against it, because he couldn't control what Caitlin and Brian would tell her. "I am at the jail because I'm helping them figure out some things."

"Why are you at jail? You didn't do anything wrong. Did they make a mistake? Only people who break the law go to jail."

"I didn't do anything wrong."

"I know, but on TV you came out of the mall and there were police all around and you were holding your hands up, like *you* were the bad guy, like on *Cops*." Hannah sounded mixed-up, her voice thin and shaky. "Did you tell them you didn't do anything wrong? Do they think you did? Why did they think you did?"

"They were confused because I was at the mall, too."

"But why did you have your hands up? Were the police going to *shoot* you? Mommy said no, but I saw them, they took you and put you in the police car, then Mommy turned the TV off. They weren't going to shoot you, were they? I started crying but Mommy said you were okay."

Eric's heart broke for her. "Honey, you don't have to worry about me. I'm fine. I was helping, not doing anything wrong. I'll be home tomorrow—"

"Aren't you going to work, tomorrow? You didn't get fired, did you? From the hospital?"

"What makes you say that?" Eric didn't understand how Hannah could have known about what had happened at work.

"Mommy said you don't have your job anymore, I heard her tell Brian. She told him that her friend Daniel called the hospital and the hospital said you got fired."

Eric rubbed his forehead, frustrated. Hannah heard everything that went on in that house. So Caitlin and Brian knew about his suspension. He prayed the hospital hadn't said why.

"You didn't get fired, did you? You're good at your job, aren't you?"

Eric punted. "I don't want you to worry about any of this, please. It's not your problem—"

"Daddy, wait a minute. Mommy says I have to go to bed. I better go. Good night. I love you."

"I love you too, hon—" Eric said, feeling a pang, but the phone went dead.

He hung up after a moment, eyeing his reflection in the observation window. He looked lost, he felt lost, and he was losing everything that mattered to him: his child, his job, his freedom, even his reputation.

He could only bear his own reflection for a minute.

Then he looked away.

Chapter Forty-five

Eric leaned back against the wall of his holding cell, having changed into a prison uniform, which was like hospital scrubs except for the orange color. His cell was hot and humid, the size of a large closet, with grimy white cinderblock on all sides except for the front, which had a locked door of thick Plexiglas, so that he could look out onto an empty hallway, also of cinderblock. The cell contained only an undersized stainless-steel toilet that reeked of urine, because it had no lid, and a stainless-steel wedge built into the wall, which made a seat for him. He had no handcuffs on, though there was a large metal ring welded onto his seat for leg shackles.

The lights were dim, and the entire area quiet, and Eric felt a wave of fatigue wash over him. He closed his eyes and tried to clear his head, but couldn't. He thought about Hannah, the hospital, and the questions they'd asked him in his interviews. Always in the back of his mind was Max and what was going to happen to him. Eric knew that Paul was right; he'd have to separate himself from Max from now on, given that there was a criminal proceeding. If the police were casting Eric as a Svengali in Max's life, then any controlling role he took would only fuel their suspicions, even as his questions had.

He flashed on Max in the video store, saying that he couldn't remember if he killed Renée, but nevertheless blaming himself. Max

Chapter Forty-six

6. I am cunning.
Circle one: Doesn't apply to me. Partially applies to me.
   Fully applies to me.

Well.
   Remember how I said that not all sociopaths are killers?
   That was true.
   I was right about that.
   For once, I wasn't lying.
   By the way, I've never killed anybody before.
   But now, it looks as if I'm going to have to kill somebody.
   Because I refuse to be thwarted.
   Because I have to get what I want.
   I know how to get what I want, and I'm not going to stop until
I get what I want.
   I have to win, and I fully intend to win.
   By the time this is all over, there are going to be a lot of dead
people, but the last body on the ground will be his.
   Eric Parrish's.
   He's proven that he's an adversary worthy of me, and he's fought
back with a single-mindedness that I suppose I could admire, if I
knew what admiration felt like.

took responsibility for Renée's i
feared harming her, but Eric kne
complex of symptoms. Even Arthu
couldn't bring himself to believe th
could he be totally sure Max was guil

Eric raked back his hair, praying that h
in standing on principle. If he ended up g
lose custody of Hannah, so he was tradin
other. He couldn't do that, but he couldn't mak
either. It was no-win, wherever he turned.

There was only one way to make things right.
Eric had to find out who killed Renée Bevilacq
And he had to do it before he went to prison for

But mostly, it's time for him to go down, and it looks like I'm going to have to do it myself.

I feel supremely confident.

I know I can do it.

I don't have a doubt.

He's actually perfectly positioned, he just doesn't realize it. He thinks he's making progress, but he's only getting himself in deeper. He thinks he's succeeding, but he's failing.

He's trying to win, but he'll lose to me.

I'm already setting a new plan in motion, shifting in response to his moves, and developing new moves of my own.

I will win in the end.

I will crush him.

I will destroy him.

I will be the worthier adversary.

I have set so many schemes in motion, pulled so many scams, tricked so many people that I couldn't begin to detail them all.

My life so far has been a series of lies, or maybe one big long continuous lie, it doesn't matter.

I've lied to everyone, even you.

I've fooled you, even here.

You'll see what I mean, by the time it's over.

What's to come is my biggest lie yet, my biggest scam yet, and my best scheme ever.

It will be deadly and bloody, and in the end, I will emerge victorious.

And the game will finally be over.

Until the next one.

Chapter Forty-seven

The next morning, Eric stood with Paul in the large processing area, getting ready to leave. Two uniformed police talked quietly on the far side of the room, which had beige file cabinets, a long counter covered with wire baskets of multicolored forms, and stacked manila files. It had taken all night for Eric to be booked and arraigned for obstructing the administration of law, a misdemeanor under the Pennsylvania Crimes Code. He'd posed for a mug shot and didn't need to see it to know that he looked mortified. His finger-pads bore black ink from the old-school inkpad used to fingerprint him. He'd changed into new clothes that Paul had brought for him: a fresh white shirt, gray slacks, and new loafers, so he was a well-dressed criminal.

Paul turned to him, straightening his tie of navy silk, which he had on with a slate gray shirt with a cutaway collar and another closely tailored suit, of lightweight charcoal wool. "Eric, let's bounce. I parked facing out so we can make a clean getaway. By the way, I got you another cell phone, but if you don't hold on to this one, I'm taking it out of your allowance."

"Thanks." Eric managed to smile.

"I'm cheering you up."

"I know. I'm acting cheered up."

took responsibility for Renée's murder because he knew that he had feared harming her, but Eric knew that was only part of the OCD complex of symptoms. Even Arthur had agreed with him. Eric still couldn't bring himself to believe that Max had killed Renée, nor could he be totally sure Max was guiltless.

Eric raked back his hair, praying that he was doing the right thing in standing on principle. If he ended up going to prison, he would lose custody of Hannah, so he was trading off one child for another. He couldn't do that, but he couldn't make the opposite choice, either. It was no-win, wherever he turned.

There was only one way to make things right.

Eric had to find out who killed Renée Bevilacqua.

And he had to do it before he went to prison for good.

Chapter Forty-six

6. I am cunning.
Circle one: Doesn't apply to me. Partially applies to me.
   Fully applies to me.

Well.
   Remember how I said that not all sociopaths are killers?
   That was true.
   I was right about that.
   For once, I wasn't lying.
   By the way, I've never killed anybody before.
   But now, it looks as if I'm going to have to kill somebody.
   Because I refuse to be thwarted.
   Because I have to get what I want.
   I know how to get what I want, and I'm not going to stop until
I get what I want.
   I have to win, and I fully intend to win.
   By the time this is all over, there are going to be a lot of dead
people, but the last body on the ground will be his.
   Eric Parrish's.
   He's proven that he's an adversary worthy of me, and he's fought
back with a single-mindedness that I suppose I could admire, if I
knew what admiration felt like.

But mostly, it's time for him to go down, and it looks like I'm going to have to do it myself.

I feel supremely confident.

I know I can do it.

I don't have a doubt.

He's actually perfectly positioned, he just doesn't realize it. He thinks he's making progress, but he's only getting himself in deeper. He thinks he's succeeding, but he's failing.

He's trying to win, but he'll lose to me.

I'm already setting a new plan in motion, shifting in response to his moves, and developing new moves of my own.

I will win in the end.

I will crush him.

I will destroy him.

I will be the worthier adversary.

I have set so many schemes in motion, pulled so many scams, tricked so many people that I couldn't begin to detail them all.

My life so far has been a series of lies, or maybe one big long continuous lie, it doesn't matter.

I've lied to everyone, even you.

I've fooled you, even here.

You'll see what I mean, by the time it's over.

What's to come is my biggest lie yet, my biggest scam yet, and my best scheme ever.

It will be deadly and bloody, and in the end, I will emerge victorious.

And the game will finally be over.

Until the next one.

Chapter Forty-seven

The next morning, Eric stood with Paul in the large processing area, getting ready to leave. Two uniformed police talked quietly on the far side of the room, which had beige file cabinets, a long counter covered with wire baskets of multicolored forms, and stacked manila files. It had taken all night for Eric to be booked and arraigned for obstructing the administration of law, a misdemeanor under the Pennsylvania Crimes Code. He'd posed for a mug shot and didn't need to see it to know that he looked mortified. His finger-pads bore black ink from the old-school inkpad used to fingerprint him. He'd changed into new clothes that Paul had brought for him: a fresh white shirt, gray slacks, and new loafers, so he was a well-dressed criminal.

Paul turned to him, straightening his tie of navy silk, which he had on with a slate gray shirt with a cutaway collar and another closely tailored suit, of lightweight charcoal wool. "Eric, let's bounce. I parked facing out so we can make a clean getaway. By the way, I got you another cell phone, but if you don't hold on to this one, I'm taking it out of your allowance."

"Thanks." Eric managed to smile.

"I'm cheering you up."

"I know. I'm acting cheered up."

Paul looked him up and down, eyes narrowing like a custom tailor. "You look damn good. You should dress like that from now on."

"I look like you."

"Exactly." Paul chuckled softly, then his smile vanished. "Before we leave, let's talk a game plan for the media. They're still out there, more than before because—"

"Wait a second. Where's Max? Where are they keeping him?"

"I don't know, and you don't care. Get it?"

"I'm just asking. There's only one wing with holding cells, isn't there? I kept expecting them to bring him in last night, but they didn't. Did they take him to some juvenile detention center or something?"

"Eric, really?" Paul flared his eyes meaningfully. "What about Max is-not-your-business don't you understand?"

Eric forced himself to voice his fear. "I just want to know he's alive."

"Oh. He's fine." Paul's expression softened. "Sorry. He's alive."

"Did they get him a lawyer and psychiatric help?"

"I have no idea."

"Have they charged him yet?"

"Again, I don't know, but I doubt it."

"I know that you want us to be officially separate, but is there a way we can find out?"

"If you're good. Maybe." Paul rolled his eyes, then picked up his briefcase. "Now can we get going?"

"Did Newmire say what he's going to do? Does he know if the D.A.'s Office is going to court?"

"I told you, I think that's about to happen, but they don't preview their sneak attacks."

"So, how long do you think it will take?"

"For what?"

"For them to go to court and get the order?"

"It's Thursday, and I'm thinking maybe Friday or Monday at the latest."

"That soon?"

"Yes. They'll want to keep the pressure on you." Paul motioned him toward the door. "The A.D.A. and Newmire are giving a press conference out front in fifteen minutes."

"Really." Eric was surprised, though he guessed that was naïve.

"Yes, and I want you out of here before it starts. I think they timed it this way on purpose. And so it begins, the war of the press releases."

"What do you think he'll say?"

"We'll listen in the car while Howard Stern is on break. Now, I told the press we wouldn't make a statement and I let that be known around the station house, too."

"Good, I don't want to make a statement."

"That's what I figured, that's why I'll be making the statement."

Eric felt confused. "I thought you said we weren't making a statement."

"No, I said I let them *think* we weren't making a statement, but we are. I am."

"What will you say?"

"I don't know yet. Something incredible. I speak extemporaneously, so it looks like it's coming from the heart."

"But it is."

"Yes, plus it looks that way."

Eric let it go.

"I look slick, but I'm really not. You know, Eric, Harry Truman never said 'Give 'em hell.' He said, 'I just told him the truth and they thought it was hell.'"

"He said that?" Eric almost didn't believe him.

"Yes, he did. Don't you read? You should read more, Eric. Enough talk, let's roll."

Eric and Paul strode out the exit doors, stepping onto the concrete entrance area, in the bright sunlight. There was no barricade to protect them from the media, and a mob of reporters raced at them, brandishing videocameras, cameras, tape recorders, and microphones, and shouting questions.

"Dr. Parrish, how did you end the standoff last night?" "Dr. Parrish!" "Doc, is Jakubowski your patient?" "Were you trying to save his life or the hostages?" "Did you know any of the hostages, are any of them your patients?" "Tell us the way it went down!"

"Quiet, folks! Quiet, please!" Paul waved his hands for order, then commandeered the podium. "I'm Paul Fortunato, and I'd like to make a brief statement on behalf of my client Dr. Eric Parrish. Actions speak louder than words, and you saw Dr. Parrish's actions last night. You saw him run into the mall during a hostage crisis, allegedly perpetrated by Max Jakubowski, and after Dr. Parrish went in to the mall, you saw the children being held hostage in the storeroom being released, running out happily into their parents' waiting arms. After that, you saw Dr. Parrish escort Mr. Jakubowski from the mall, and Mr. Jakubowski voluntarily surrendered to police."

Eric noted the subtle way that Paul described his role, setting him up from the outset as not only separate from Max, but as someone helping him.

The crowd interrupted, the reporters shouting questions: "Dr. Parrish, come on, is it true that you disobeyed direct police orders?" "What are you charged with?" "How did you do it, Doc?" "Give us a comment?" "Do you have negotiation training?" "Is it true that Max Jakubowski is your patient?" "Would you like to make a statement?"

"Folks, quiet please!" Paul, waved his hands for order, then resumed, "So who is Dr. Parrish? By way of background, he's a local boy, raised in Chadds Ford, risen to Chief of Psychiatry at Havemeyer General and is presently on indefinite leave from the hospital, dealing with this situation."

Eric felt his face flush, while a few reporters shouted random questions. He hadn't realized that Paul was going to discuss his suspension, but then understood the lawyer was preempting it coming out later. It was a risk, but the hospital would probably back him up, because the reason Eric was on suspension was confidential and HGH had as much interest in keeping it quiet as he did.

"Folks, let me get to the point. We all love this country, but we can't deny its recent history has been marked by tragic shootings in malls, schools, and any other place where good people gather.

Many of these dangerous acts are perpetrated by people who are in serious need of psychiatric help, the kind of help that Dr. Parrish provides. The only way to stop these tragic events is to get at the root of mental illness and treat these individuals, not only for their own sake, but for the safety of all of us and our children."

Eric couldn't have said it better himself, but he was pretty sure he wouldn't have, under the circumstances. The reporters quieted, holding up tape recorders and cameras to record Paul's statement.

"These people cannot be helped without professional counseling, such as Dr. Parrish provides, and essential to the therapeutic process is confidentiality. Patients will not open up about their emotions, fears, and thoughts to a psychiatrist, unless they can be sure the psychiatrist will not betray them and reveal those thoughts. Dr. Parrish takes his oath of confidentiality very seriously because he cares about his patients, and also because he cares about the common good."

Eric looked down, embarrassed. The camera lenses swung toward him, their lenses capped with rubber shades.

"You saw no better representation of that last night, at the mall. He will not be taking any questions today because of the very same confidentiality, which he follows so strictly that he cannot even confirm or deny whether Max Jakubowski was his patient." Paul paused. "Now. I understand that it's in your blood, as members of the press, to want answers to your questions. But every one of you has a reporter's privilege, and you would protect that as well, so you should understand. Therefore, Dr. Parrish will not take any questions today, nor will he take any in the days to come, so please don't harass him. In fact, Dr. Parrish divulged no confidential information to the police last night, which set their badges spinning, as you can imagine."

The crowd laughed in response, and Eric realized Paul's joke was perfectly timed.

"Furthermore, folks, I'll go out on a limb and predict that the D.A.'s Office is going to take Dr. Parrish to court, to try to force him to break his confidentiality and compel him to divulge a patient's innermost thoughts, or face contempt of court."

The crowd erupted in shouted questions, "Which patient?" "You mean Jakubowski?" "It's Jakubowski, right?"

Eric remained calm, with effort. He hadn't realized that Paul was going to go there, either, but he understood why the lawyer was doing it. Now the A.D.A. and the police would be in a defensive position when they made their statement, because Paul had gotten to them first.

Paul waved the reporters into calm. "No matter what the D.A. throws at him, Dr. Parrish will continue to protect the principles that safeguard the integrity of the therapeutic process. We will never solve the problems of lethal violence at our malls and schools until people stand up like Dr. Parrish does, not only risking life and limb, but even personal freedom. Thank you." Paul turned to Eric, taking his arm. "Dr. Parrish, let's go."

Eric turned to the lot, and he and Paul hustled to the black Mercedes SUV. The press chased them, calling out their questions and pleading for a comment. Eric jogged, making a fist with his hands, hiding his inked fingertips, maybe for himself. They reached the car, and as Paul chirped it unlocked on the fly, they both jumped in.

Paul cranked the ignition, hit the gas, and steered straight out of the parking lot with Eric in the passenger seat, holding his head up the way he was supposed to, trying to act like a hero when he'd just been booked as a criminal. A few of the news vans gave chase, but Paul ignored them, entering the thick traffic in King of Prussia.

"Well, Eric?" he asked, glancing over "Like the statement?"

"Yes."

"The best thing is, it was all true." Paul steered up the street, stopped at a red light, and lowered the radio, which was playing Howard Stern's distinctive voice. "I'll drop you off at home, then I have to get to work."

"Sure, thanks."

"Anyway, I'm glad you're pleased with the statement. I went off script when I got to the part about the motion to compel, but I think it was a good idea. I always think my ideas are good ones, in retrospect."

"Why was it a good idea?"

"I like when we get the jump. The law is so scant on the issue, and if the judge is going to decide it in favor of business interests, our only counter to that is public opinion. If most people think you're a hero, making Abercrombie & Fitch safe for Americans, then the judge is going to think twice before he issues an order compelling you to divulge."

"Good, and at the very least, I would think it buys me a little more time."

"What do you need the time for?"

Eric hesitated. He wasn't sure he wanted to confide in Paul, but it might help to have a sounding board. "I guess I'm wondering who really killed Renée Bevilacqua."

"That means you don't think Max did it?"

"Right, I don't. I'm not sure, anyway, either way."

"You're aware that the police think he did. After last night, the suspicion is much greater on him than it is on you. At bottom, they're only leveraging you to get the information they need to convict him."

"I know, but because they think they have the killer, they're not looking for him anymore. I can't stand by and let the kid get convicted for a murder he didn't do."

"Not your problem."

"I can't just ignore it."

"Yes, you can. Like this. Watch me." Paul drove on, singing a little song under his breath. "See? It's easy. This is me, living my life, motoring along, not taking on the problems of the world. You think too much, anybody ever tell you that?"

"Only everybody who's ever met me."

"If you're not gonna listen to them, listen to me." Paul pursed his lips. "If you start snooping around, like you did when you showed up at the frozen yogurt place, you're going to deep-six the beautiful defense case I'm building for you. I'm advising you against it, strongly."

"I hear you."

"The question isn't whether you hear me, but whether you heed me, and if you don't, I'm *telling*."

Eric looked over, confused. "Telling who? The cops? The judge?"

"No, worse. *Laurie.* She'll smack you upside your head."

Eric smiled, thinking about her. "You're probably right. And I've seen her with a scalpel."

"Ha! She has a dark side, my sister. Nobody believes it, but she used to torture me when I was little." Paul reached for the radio and turned it on. "Let's see if we can hear any report about what the cops are saying. We're the big story, and I bet KYW has it, or NPR. I don't care about their canned statement, but if they take questions, I want to know. I predict that your ears will be burning in three, two, one . . ."

Eric braced himself, and Paul punched a few numbers on the console and turned up the volume.

Captain Newmire's voice came on the radio, saying: "To sum up, I would like to respond to the statement by Dr. Parrish's attorney. We understand how much the doctor values his confidentiality, but we have reason to believe that Dr. Parrish has information concerning the murder of Renée Bevilacqua, a sixteen-year-old girl who was found strangled to death yesterday morning in Radnor."

The reporters started murmuring, and Eric felt the impact of the statement like a body blow. It was the first time he had heard it enunciated so clearly, in public. It made him sound like he was protecting a murderer, and that's what they would all think.

"We in law enforcement never forget the victims of a heinous crime or their grieving families. We are following all leads on the Renée Bevilacqua murder. Dr. Parrish's lawyer is right when he said that when he claimed his privilege, our badges started spinning. That is because we do not take the murder of a young girl lightly."

Paul winced. "Maybe you had to be there."

Captain Newmire went on, "We want justice for Renée Bevilacqua. We do not appreciate it when our efforts to find out who murdered her are thwarted. Justice for Renée Bevilacqua far outweighs the legalities and technicalities. I'm not a lawyer, and I know there are statutes that protect Dr. Parrish's confidentiality, but speaking as a father, I do not know how the man sleeps at night." Captain Newmire paused, evidently composing himself.

Paul shook his head. "He's not crying, is he? If he cries, the terrorists have won."

Eric wasn't laughing. The line about him sleeping at night had struck home. He had barely slept since this whole thing had happened.

Captain Newmire cleared his throat. "I'll end my statement now and take a few questions, time permitting."

The reporters responded by hollering their questions, but they weren't on the microphone, so it sounded like a frantic cacophony, impossible to understand over the radio.

Captain Newmire came back on. "Okay, I'll repeat the question, which is, 'Don't we give Dr. Parrish any credit for ending the standoff at the mall?' Well, yes, while it is true that Dr. Parrish was involved in the effort to get the hostages out unharmed last night, I would point out that the heavy lifting was accomplished by law-enforcement personnel from the surrounding six counties, SWAT and Special Emergency Response Teams, or SERT, in addition to first responders such as firefighters and EMT personnel, and federal representatives from Homeland Security, ATF, and the FBI."

Paul chuckled. "Deputy Dawg here reminds of my five-year-old. If it's a truck, fire engine, or police car, he loves it. Scratch him and he's Bob The Builder."

Eric heard a new warmth in Paul's tone, talking about his son. He thought of Hannah with a stab of guilt. He would have to call Susan as soon as he got home.

On the radio, Captain Newmire continued, "Finally, in answer to your question, we absolutely discourage citizens from interfering with emergent situations such as presented by the mall. It is for that reason that Dr. Parrish was charged with obstructing the administration of law, a misdemeanor. Upper Merion has a talented and well-trained police department, and King of Prussia is not the Wild Wild West. We don't need any cowboys. Thank you very much, and now I'll take the last question."

Paul snorted. "Cowboys. Nice. Good analogy. I should've thought of that."

On the radio, the reporters shouted questions, then Captain Newmire said, "The question, which is, 'Does the District Attorney's Office plan to compel Dr. Parrish to breach his doctor-patient privilege regarding any information he might have from Max Jakubowski regarding the Bevilacqua murder?' "

"Nice restatement," Paul said, with a sly smile. "Sounds like the press got on board with us."

Captain Newmire answered, "That is an excellent question, but unfortunately, that is not my expertise. That question can best be answered by the District Attorney's Office, and as you all know, the D.A. is in the hospital at this time. Thank you very much, ladies and gentlemen."

"Aha!" Paul lowered the volume on the radio. "We learned something. We know the A.D.A. was supposed to be at the press conference. So why wasn't he there? Because they heard what we said about the grand jury and they didn't want to answer the question. The A.D.A. is the guy to answer the question, so they disappeared him. He went out for a glass of milk. That's what they drink. Milk, no rocks."

"So it's good for us or not? Are they going to make me go to the grand jury?"

"It's good for us, because it shows that they think we scored a hit. We backed them down, but they won't stay down forever. They'll regroup, get their ducks in a row, and go to the grand jury later, after everybody's forgotten that you're Wyatt Earp and they've spun you into the shrink who's protecting a crazed murderer."

"Damn," Eric said, and Paul looked over, as he turned onto Old Gulph Road, heading toward home.

"So you're taking my advice? No digging into that murder, right, cowboy?"

"Absolutely," Eric said, looking out the window into the sun. "By the way, you need to bill me one of these days, don't forget."

"Geez, you are squeaky clean, aren't you? I'm doing this as a favor to big sis."

"The hell you are. Bill me."

"On the other hand, if you marry my sister, I'll pay *you*." Paul smiled. They cruised along the winding streets, near his old house, passing the graceful stone homes of the Main Line, behind the fresh green stretches of perfect lawns and the mulched beds around the landscaped plantings. Both men fell silent, each to his own thoughts.

After a while, Paul broke the silence. "Eric, don't take what Deputy Dawg said to heart. It's basically the difference between procedure and substance, and the fact is, the procedure protects the substance."

"What do you mean?"

"I know I sound geeky, but that's where I live." Paul wet his lips, warming to his topic. "Like I told you in the beginning, I represent the Constitution, and the procedure in the Constitution is there to protect everybody's rights to its substance, that is, our individual freedoms—the right to live free, the right to pursue happiness, the right to free speech, the right to religion, and the right to be free of oppressive government. Follow?"

"Yes."

"For example, we don't want government to search our homes whenever they want, so we place restrictions on the procedure— the search warrant has to be specific, limited, has to itemize what they want, has to be served at a certain time, has to meet a bunch of requirements. They're all so-called technicalities, but they protect the right to live your life, in your home, the way you want. That's a freedom that our forefathers protected for us. That's the beauty of the Constitution and the Bill of Rights. *Capisce?*"

"Yes." Eric nodded. They had reached his neighborhood and were almost home.

"Just because somebody calls it a technicality, that doesn't mean it doesn't matter. Nobody thinks about it in a nuanced way, especially not Deputy Dawg, and to be fair, ours isn't a nuanced culture. We paint everything in broad strokes, we don't stop and analyze." Paul turned to Eric, frowning. "I care about justice for Renée, too, don't think I don't. But screaming for justice isn't how you get justice. You get justice *because* of the technicalities, not *despite* them."

Eric looked over, surprised at his vehemence. "I get it, that makes sense."

"Feel better?"

"No," Eric answered, because they turned onto his street and he could see a commotion at the middle of the block, in front of his house, "What the *hell*?"

"Reporters. They must've looked up where you live. You're not that hard to find."

"Damn." Eric scanned the scene as they got closer. Two TV news vans sat parked in front of his house, next to a long lineup of cars, disrupting the peace of the street.

"Okay, no problem, you know the drill. Don't feed the trolls."

"What does that mean?" Eric tried to estimate the number of reporters and stopped counting at fifty.

"It means we gave our statement, and now, it's radio silence. Don't talk to them. I'll get you into the house, no comment all the way, and then you ignore them."

"My neighbors must love this."

"Get used to it. They're there for the duration. Just say nothing and hold your head high. They're not allowed on your property, that's why they're at the curb."

"Got it." Eric realized something, as they slowed to approach the line of cars. "They must have seen the front door, broken. They probably know the police searched my house."

"There's nothing you can do about that, so don't sweat it."

Eric felt an odd swell of shame. "I need to fix the door."

"What is it with you and the door? Look on the bright side, you won't get broken into with them there."

Eric rolled his eyes.

"Again, cheering you up. Here we go." Paul cruised to the line of news vans, slowing to turn into Eric's driveway, and the reporters wheeled around, spotting them. "You have a back door, right?"

"Right."

"How about a hammer and some nails?"

"For the door?"

"No, for the reporters." Paul winked, as he slowed to steer into Eric's driveway.

And the reporters came running.

Chapter Forty-eight

"Susan, thanks for taking my call," Eric said into his new phone, as he hurried into his home office. Paul had left after he'd helped him nail the front door shut. He'd use the office entrance for now.

"Eric! I saw the news. That's incredible, you saved those kids! I couldn't believe it when I saw it on TV!"

"Great," Eric tried to sound happy. Sunlight filtered through the panel of windows, sending luminous shafts on the papers, books, and purple DSM, scattered all over the floor. He opened his file cabinet and began thumbing through the patient files for Max's, while he planned his next move.

"My son showed me YouTube videos of you, there's like twenty of them so far, running past the cops. It already has thirty-two hundred views!"

"Susan, last night, I called home to talk to Hannah, and—"

"I know, I heard from Daniel." Susan's tone changed, her enthusiasm disappearing. "We have a problem."

"I'll say we do." Eric thumbed through the patient files, toward the J's. "Caitlin's boyfriend tried to keep me from talking to Hannah, and she saw me on TV, she thought I was a bad guy. They wouldn't let me explain it to her. Now it has to wait until I see her tonight."

"Sorry, you're not getting her tonight. They're refusing in view of the Bevilacqua murder case. They filed a petition with the court today, for emergency relief. They want an order saying that Caitlin doesn't have to let you have Hannah tonight."

"Damn it! Caitlin knows I'm not guilty of any murder. She's using it as an excuse. I'm not charged in connection with Bevilacqua." Eric found the manila file labeled Max Jakubowski and pulled it out of the cabinet. He was going to review his notes to see what Max had said about Renée and refresh his memory of their sessions.

"Weren't you just charged by the Upper Merion Police with obstruction of justice?"

"Well, yes, but because I went into the mall." Eric shut the cabinet, went to his desk with the file, and cleared the debris to make a work space for himself. There had to be something that would give him a lead to follow up on.

"Eric, bottom line, you were arrested on CNN. Caitlin will get her order. We'd look like idiots if we oppose it. Besides, you've seen their papers from today, so you know the bad news."

"Wait, what papers from today? What bad news? I haven't seen anything." Eric looked up from Max's file, alarmed. He'd study it after the call.

"You haven't seen what they filed? I thought that was why you called. I emailed them to you an hour ago."

"Emailed? Oh no, I didn't see them. The police confiscated my computer and my phone." Eric scanned the disaster area that was his office.

"Well, this morning, they filed their response to our petition for primary custody."

"Already?"

"Yes, I know, it's even early, but it was a strategic, aggressive move. They're striking while the iron is hot, and it doesn't get any hotter. You just got out of jail and you're a murder suspect."

"Susan, *you* can't really believe that I committed a murder."

"I know, I understand that you're protecting that patient, that Max. The papers are calling him Mad Max, you know."

Eric winced. He didn't confirm or deny what she'd said about Max because he couldn't.

"Your patient killed that poor girl, and I totally understand that you have to keep it confidential. It's like attorney-client privilege —"

"Susan, please, don't editorialize. They're just keeping me on the hook to try to get information out of me." Eric knew he was losing the argument. He felt it slipping away from him, all over again. He had made his move for Hannah and he was going to lose his own daughter.

"Eric, it's public record that you were taken in for questioning and are a suspect."

"I won't be a suspect much longer—"

"But you are now. It was a true statement when they filed. That's why they didn't wait. Their argument is strongest now."

"Do I get any points, because of the mall thing? I don't really think I'm a hero, but if it gets me Hannah, I'll take it."

"No, not in a custody case. You keep forgetting that it's not a nice-guy contest, it's all about the best interests of Hannah. Plus their papers are really good, and so is their argument."

"So what do they say?"

"I can sum it up for you. Max Jakubowski is your patient, and he's clearly a dangerous character. He took kids hostage and imprisoned them in the video store." Susan paused. "By the way, my son and his friends shop in that store, all the time. If that *nutjob* had hurt one hair on my son's head—"

"Max wasn't going to hurt anyone. He had no bullets, no bomb." Eric let the *nutjob* go.

Susan scoffed. "Oh, that makes it okay? Do you know the *trauma* those kids must have gone through? You, of all people!"

"Susan, let's stay on point. What does that have to do with my custody petition?"

"Everything, and I was getting to that. Max is your private patient, isn't he? You hold your sessions with him at your house, don't you?"

"Yes, right."

"This would be the same house where you want Hannah to live with you?"

Eric grasped the implication of what she was saying.

"You're asking them to award you primary custody at a home where, under the same roof, you treat patients so dangerous they take children hostage—at *gunpoint?* Make bomb threats? Cause the largest police action this area has seen, like, *ever?*"

"Oh no." Eric rubbed his forehead. "But I curate my private clients. They're harmless."

"Then how did Max get into your private practice?"

"Max came in through the hospital, but that's not the point. They're safe."

"We can't convince a court of that, not now, after the mall. It only takes one kook to hurt Hannah. Hold on, let me read you Caitlin's response." Susan paused, and there was the sound of computer keys. "Here, it says, 'Petitioner Husband has a list of ten private psychiatric clients whom he treats during regular therapy sessions, which are held at his home, in a small room attached to the back. The office is directly connected to the home through a door, which doesn't even have a lock, and there is no security to prevent these mentally ill patients, including many on psychotropic medications, from entering the house at will.' "

Eric groaned. "I treat depressed people, anxious people, people in deep grief. It's not *Silence of the Lambs.*"

"Let me continue. 'In addition, Petitioner Husband treats these mentally ill patients during the evening hours, when the likelihood of dangerous assaults on the couple's seven-year-old daughter is far greater, and the possibility of sexual assault is ever-present—' "

"Enough," Eric said, his stomach turning over.

"To be honest, it's a winning argument."

"I could move. Get a new place that has a separate building for my office, like an outbuilding. I have a lease, but I guess I could break it." Eric thought of Hannah's bedroom, which he'd just painted Primrose Pink. "Or I could rent an office that's not in my home."

"Okay, now we're talking. Those are two possibilities."

"Do we tell the court that?"

"Eric, hold that thought. I have an appointment, I have to go."

Susan paused. "We have ten days to respond. Do you think you'll be clear of this murder investigation by then?"

"I hope so." Eric looked down at Max's file.

"Good. I'll send you their papers in hard copy, so you can read them yourself. In the meantime, keep me posted."

"I really don't get Hannah tonight?"

"No, you don't. I'm going to write the judge a self-serving letter, saying that he needn't issue an order and we'll agree not to see her tonight, in view of the extraordinary circumstances. I'll play up your actions at the mall, how brave you were."

Eric sighed, temporarily defeated. "Maybe it's better for her tonight. I have reporters on the front lawn."

"It's the right way to go. Pick your battles. Let this cool down before you start making demands."

"Okay, thanks." Eric hung up, and his attention returned to his notes from his first session with Max. He pressed Hannah to the back of his mind and started reading. The landline on his desk rang a few moments later, and he answered it reflexively, in case it was a patient. "Hello, this is Dr. Parrish."

"Dr. Parrish, my name is Tyler Choudhury and I'm calling from *The Philadelphia Inquirer,* and I'd like to ask you a few questions about the Bevilacqua murder—"

"I'm sorry, I have no comment."

"But Dr. Parrish, this would be a chance for you to tell your side of the story. You can try to explain whether you're standing on the confidentiality laws, or hiding behind them—"

"No comment. Good-bye." Eric hung up the phone, opened Max's file, and got busy.

Chapter Forty-nine

An hour later, Eric had read his notes thoroughly, and though they jarred his memory for many details, they didn't give him any thoughts or clues about who could have killed Renée. His gaze strayed out the window to the leafy butterfly bush, and orange monarchs and yellow swallowtails flitted here and there. It would've been a restorative sight if not for the reporters out front, who talked constantly, laughed, and sent clouds of cigarette smoke wafting through the screened windows.

He felt distracted, and it struck him how odd it was that he was at home, when he should've been at the hospital. His life, like his house, had been turned upside down. His thoughts reverted to his patients at the hospital, as if his mental processes followed the track during the workday, and he found himself wishing he could hold the morning meeting and hear from Amaka how everyone's night had been, then make treatment rounds, go through each of his patients, wondering how they were doing, expecting Sam was up to the task, hoping that Perino was improving. He thought then of Perino's wife, wondering if she believed that Eric was the bad guy she'd pegged him as, now that he was officially protecting the secrets of a murderer, or maybe was one himself.

Eric realized that Kristine would probably have a good laugh over his troubles, delighted to see that her attempt to ruin him was being done even more efficiently by the police. He still had no idea why she'd filed the sexual harassment charge, unless it was out of some jealousy of Laurie, but if that were so, Kristine had a level of pathology that Eric hadn't detected, undoubtedly because he wasn't paying any attention to her. To him, she was just another medical student on a psychiatric rotation, even though she was an exceptionally pretty one, but it struck him that Kristine was unusually skilled at hiding her emotions, as well as bizarrely focused on harming him. But she and her bogus harassment charges were the last thing he had to worry about right now.

Eric heard the reporters out front burst into laughter, so he got up and closed the windows, his thoughts churning. It was almost impossible to try to understand who had killed Renée, because he knew almost nothing about her. He went back to the desk, thinking more clearly now that the room was quieter. It was also possible that Renée's murder could've been an instance of random violence, so that the murderer would be unrelated to Renée. That was a possibility about which he would have no information, exclusively within the knowledge of the police, but Eric doubted they were even exploring those avenues, now that they had Max in custody.

The phone rang again, and Eric knew it was probably a reporter, but he couldn't not answer. There was no other way for anyone to reach him, either his patients or his staff from the hospital. "Hello, this is Dr. Parrish."

"Dr. Parrish, my name is Nancy Steinman, I'm calling from *USA Today* regarding your patient, Max Jakubowski. We're doing a think piece on the relationship of gun laws to mental health laws, and I was wondering if you would comment—"

"I'm sorry, no comment."

"But your experience would really illuminate—"

"No comment." Eric hung up. He thought a minute, wondering again about Renée. She was a teenager, so she had to have a Facebook page. He hardly spent any time on Facebook; so much of his work was confidential and Caitlin was the one in their household who kept it up. She spent time on Facebook at night, reading her feed, keeping her status updated to her network at the D.A.'s Office, and posting their family and vacation photos.

He returned to his phone, opened the Facebook app, and out of curiosity, went first to check up on Caitlin. He typed her name in the search field, but **Add Friend** popped up next to her name. Eric blinked, stung. Of course, he was already Caitlin's Facebook friend, but he realized that Caitlin must have unfriended him, which was evidently the Facebook version of divorce. He tapped to double-check and could see only a limited version of Caitlin's profile. He stalled a moment, eyeing the screen, which showed only thumbnails of their Facebook friends, noticing that there were a few new ones. He scanned quickly and found the one he was looking for. Brian Allsworth, it read beside his name.

Eric was about to touch the profile picture, but stopped himself, realizing it was a vortex he didn't want to enter. Caitlin had moved on, he would have to as well, and in any event, his personal life wasn't as important as Renée Bevilacqua.

So he typed Renée's name into the search function, and a long list of Renée Bevilacquas appeared, their thumbnail pictures difficult to see on the tiny phone screen. He scrolled past older women, women from Australia and Italy, and clicked on a few that looked a little like Renée, but weren't her. Finally, a thumbnail of Renée jumped out at him, and he touched the screen.

A large profile picture of the young girl filled his screen, fresh-faced and beaming, surrounded by girlfriends, their arms around each other at the beach. Renée looked so alive that it was almost impossible to understand that she was dead, much less murdered. Eric glanced down on the page, and the only thing that showed about Renée were her past profile pictures and the most recent one, from about a month ago, had a caption that read CAN'T WAIT FOR SUMMER, BITCHES!!!!!! It showed her with a giggling group of girls wearing 3-D glasses, in front of the IMAX theater at the King of Prussia Mall. It was the same mall that Max tried to get himself killed in, despairing over her death.

Eric swallowed hard, imagining that Renée's last Facebook post would be on her page, with memorial R.I.P. posts from all of her friends at school and work. He suppressed his emotion and scanned thumbnails of Renée's Facebook friends, grinning, making faces at parties, wearing funny hats, or girls just trying to look their prettiest or their most provocative.

Their names were beside each face, and Eric scrolled down to the left and saw her friends' photos. He went back to Renée's page and saw the music that she liked: Iron and Wine, Bruno Mars, Katy Perry, Taylor Swift, and Faith Hill. Books like *The Fault in Our Stars,* the *Divergent* series, *Mockingjay,* and *Eleanor & Park.* All of it touched Eric's heart, making her more real to him, bringing the tragedy of her murder into poignant focus.

The phone on the desk rang again, and Eric still couldn't ignore it, so he picked up. "This is Dr. Parrish."

"I'm calling from the *New York Times* and—"

"I have no comment."

"But Dr. Parrish—"

"Thank you, but no." Eric hung up and returned to the task at hand. He was going to go through Renée's photos, trying to determine who was closest to her and see if any of them seemed remotely off or suspicious. She could've had a jealous boyfriend, a frenemy, a mean girl, or a bully. He knew it was a longshot, but it was a start and it was all he had. He clicked on the first picture on the left, which was of a young girl named Katie Shoop. Her privacy settings were in place, so he couldn't see much about her. However, Katie changed her profile picture often, and in almost every picture, she was hugging the same group of girls, including Renée. They appeared to be in the choir, because they were wearing blue robes, grinning with their arms around each other.

Eric grabbed a piece of paper and a pencil, and took notes as he went through the photos of Renée's Facebook friends. Almost all of the girls, but none of the boys, had protected their pages from the public, but Eric could still get information about the girls from their profile pictures, finding connections between them from their photo albums, Facebook friends, the groups they joined, and even where they lived. It was helpful, as well as scary, to see how much information he could glean.

An hour turned into two, and Eric ended up with a list of Sacred Heart sophomores, juniors, and seniors—nineteen girls and thirteen boys—who looked to be in Renée's inner circle. Oddly, Eric didn't see any mention of Renée's boyfriend, though he knew she had one from Max. He couldn't figure out which of the boys was her boyfriend, nor did any of the boys list her as a girlfriend on his page. One of the boys, senior Jason Tandore, listed Pickering Park as one of his favorite places, which set the hair on the back of Eric's neck on end, since Pickering Park was where Renée had been found dead.

Eric also learned that Renée was close to her Uncle Pat, a slick-looking single lawyer in Philadelphia who practiced products liability law. He'd also seen that Renée seemed close to her parents, Margaret and Anthony Bevilacqua, particularly her father. Anthony Bevilacqua was reasonably active on Facebook, and his settings were public, concerning his fruit-importing business, the amateur running club he belonged to, and his activity in the Masons. He posted lots of photos of him and Renée, riding bicycles and running together, and Eric couldn't help identifying with the dad, as a suburban father who adored his daughter. Anthony was about Eric's height and had thick black hair, but he was more muscular, in bicycle shorts. Renée resembled her father in the nose and smile, as best as Eric could tell; many of the pictures of Anthony Bevilacqua were taken outside and he was wearing either sunglasses, a ball cap, or a bike helmet.

Eric went to Renée's mother Margaret's Facebook page, which was also privacy-protected, with far fewer friends than her father. The only group the mother belonged to was Knurses Who Knit, on the labor and delivery service at Lankenau Hospital, so Eric noted she was a nurse, though out of his system. He could only imagine that Renée's mother would probably die a little inside every time she helped deliver a new life. He thought of Leah Barry, his patient who had lost her child to stillbirth, agonizing every time HGH played their lullaby.

His landline rang again on his desk, bringing him out of his reverie, and he reached for the receiver. "Dr. Parrish here."

"Dr. Parrish? This is Peg—"

"I have no comment."

"I'm not a reporter and I need to speak with you."

"I'm sorry, no, I can't—"

"Dr. Parrish, I'm Peg Bevilacqua. Renée Bevilacqua's mother."

Chapter Fifty

Eric kept checking the window in his living room, to see when Stan from Enterprise Rent-A-Car came to pick him up and deliver his rental car. Renée's mother had wanted to meet him in person, but wouldn't say more. The press was camped out in front of the Bevilacqua house too, and they were going to meet at an out-of-the-way restaurant. He dreaded the prospect of facing her, but at the same time, hoped that he could get some information.

Eric spotted the beige Buick from Enterprise slowing in front of his house, so he hustled back through the house, headed for the office, and let himself out the back door. He locked it quickly and hurried down the driveway just as the Buick came to a stop at the curb. He sprinted for the car, but reporters realized what was going on and surged forward, cameras focused on him and shouting questions.

"Dr. Parrish, where are you going?" "Dr. Parrish, please give us a comment." "Dr. Parrish, what happened inside the mall?" "Are you going to tell the police what you know about Max Jakubowski?" "What do you know about the Renée Bevilacqua murder?" "Do you want to give us a comment?" "Why did you take time off from HGH? How long are you taking off?" "Where are you going?"

"No comment!" Eric called to them, hustling down the driveway. Stan from Enterprise was already shifting into the passenger seat, as they had discussed, leaving the engine running. Some of the reporters turned around and ran to their cars, to give chase, but Eric made a beeline for the driver's seat, jumped in, slammed the door behind him, and sped off.

"Sweet!" Stan said, with a loopy grin. He was young, with spiky hair and diamond shaped earrings.

"Hold on." Eric knew all the back roads, so he took a sharp left turn, then the first right turn, glancing into the rearview mirror. The reporters' cars hadn't caught up to him yet, so he took another sharp right turn into a random driveway and pulled all the way up to the house, hoping the hedges along the driveway would give cover for him.

"Nice!"

"Duck." Eric slipped quickly out of view, and so did Stan, waiting. After a few moments, the reporters' cars sped down the street, passing the driveway.

"Bam! That was sick!"

"Thank you, I think." Eric ascertained that no more reporters were following him, then pulled out of the driveway, and headed back to Enterprise. He dropped Stan off, thanked him, and made his way west, toward the suburbs farther from the city, passing into Downingtown, where he navigated the strip malls until he found the one he wanted, pulled into the parking lot, heading toward Tudy's, a small restaurant that served only breakfast and lunch.

He hurried to the restaurant, opened the glass door, and looked around. The walls were painted brown with white paneling, and the floors were of the same dark hardwood. It was tiny, maybe only fifteen tables, and few were occupied. He caught sight of Peg's curly red hair, a more strawberry-blonde shade than Renée's, skimming her shirt collar in back. She sat along the wall in a booth, facing away from the door, wearing a crisp white shirt and a pair of jeans.

Eric signaled to the approaching hostess that he was heading for a specific table, then walked over, stopping tableside before he sat down. "Hello, I'm Eric. You must be Peg."

"Yes." Peg glanced up, then gestured to the other side of the booth. "Please, sit down."

"Thank you." Eric slid into the booth and folded his hands in front of him. "I'm very, very sorry about the loss of your daughter. Please accept my deepest condolences."

"Thank you." Peg met his eye directly, though hers were puffy, bloodshot, and shot through with pain so deep that it seemed to dilute the otherwise pretty blue color of her irises to a paler hue, as if they'd been washed out by too many tears. Her nose was pert, turned up at the end, with just the faintest smattering of freckles, like Renée. Her skin was pale.

"Not at all, I'm glad you reached out to me."

"I can't begin to tell you what a loss this is, for my husband and me." Peg swallowed hard, and deep wrinkles bracketed her mouth, which formed a flat, tense line, like a rubber band stretched to the limit.

"I really am so sorry," Eric said, speaking from the heart. He knew his voice carried the honest emotion he felt, so he just let it come.

"Are you a parent, Dr. Parrish?"

"Yes, I have a daughter, she's seven. And please, call me Eric."

"Renée, is, was our only child. She was everything to us. My husband was especially close to her, she was a true daddy's girl." Peg smiled just the slightest, bittersweet. "The two of them, they were two of a kind. They look so much alike, they acted so much alike. It's just too much for him, right now. I don't even know why I'm telling you this, maybe because I know you're a psychiatrist, you're used to listening to people. I know you work at HGH, I'm a nurse at Lankenau, so . . . we have that in common."

"Yes, we do." Eric didn't know exactly what to say, but just let her talk, knowing that she would find her way to the point.

"My husband is so upset, he's just beside himself. He won't get out of bed but he can't sleep. He cries so hard, its awful, awful. I had to call our doctor, we got him a sedative." Peg shook her head slowly. "Anyway, he doesn't know I'm here. I told him I was going to spend some time with my sister. The reporters are out in front of our house, it's like they're camped there. The whole thing, it's a waking nightmare, it truly is. It's just beyond what anyone should ever bear."

"I'm sure." Eric didn't mention the press on his front lawn. His troubles were nothing compared to hers.

"We picked out Renée's casket, can you imagine. My daughter's casket. I will bury my beautiful daughter, and knowing what they do to her body in the autopsy, that makes it so much worse."

"I'm sure." Eric could feel her agony.

"Well." Peg straightened in her chair, seeming to summon her strength. "I know you're wondering, I mean, I called you because I wanted to talk to you like a person, without lawyers or police, or anything like that. I'm not the kind of person to fall apart, or just do nothing, it's not my way. I feel as if it's a mother thing, maybe. Mothers, they take care. They act. They keep going, for Renée. You understand, as a dad."

Eric nodded. "Yes."

"So, I hoped that I could talk to you, parent to parent, and also with us both in the medical profession, I mean, I think we understand each other. We both want to help people, we take care of people, that's what we do, right?"

"Yes, right, exactly." Eric managed a smile that he knew looked pained, because that was the way he felt.

"Anyway, I know I'm not that coherent, I'm just so tired out." Peg rubbed her face with her index finger and thumb, leaving pinkish welts on her fair skin.

"I saw you on TV, and they showed you in front of the police station, and we saw everything that happened at the mall last night."

Eric didn't say anything, waiting for her to finish.

"And of course we followed everything else that the Upper Merion Police said, and Captain Newmire." Peg hesitated. "Anyway, the more I think about it, it doesn't make sense to me that you would kill Renée."

"No, of course not." Eric felt a wave of relief. "I didn't, I promise you. I did not harm your daughter. I would never do such a thing. It's absolutely out of the question."

"You didn't know her, did you?"

"No, I did not know her." Eric looked over as a young waitress approached, at the least opportune moment. "I'll just have a Diet Coke, that's all."

Peg looked over, unsmiling. "Me too, that's it."

The waitress nodded, getting the message. "Thanks, folks. Sorry to interrupt. Be right back."

Peg waited until the waitress was out of earshot, then picked up where she had left off. "Right, sure, that's what I thought. I mean, that would be the *least* likely conclusion to draw, that you killed her. I asked around about you, I talked to people at work. They've heard of you, they say you're very respected, a nice man, a good psychiatrist. You have no reason to kill Renée. Obviously, I think it's much more likely that it was Max, and you're Max's psychiatrist, and that you know information, he told you something about her."

Eric listened to her talk, her voice deep and calm, and though he sensed where she was going, he didn't interrupt her. In any event, he knew that he wasn't going to be able to give her the answer she wanted, if she asked him directly. So he was in absolutely no hurry to get there. It was as if he had to break her heart, in person.

"I'm going to be totally honest with you. Renée told me, rather she told my husband while they were running, that she thought Max had a crush on her. She liked him, too. Not in that way, but she told her father that Max definitely had a crush on her, she knew it from the first time he tutored her."

Eric said nothing, just told himself to listen, not react.

"She was never really worried about Max, she *never* thought he would do her any harm, but she was young, naïve. My husband and I, we're guessing he hid it pretty well. That all the time, he was planning to kill her."

Eric forced himself not to respond.

The waitress approached with two Diet Cokes, which she set down on the table. "Here we go. Feel free to let me know if you want anything to eat. Thanks."

Eric nodded at her. "Thank you, we will."

After the waitress had left, Peg continued, "We heard Captain Newmire say that you have information about who killed Renée and that you are not giving them the information because you have to keep your patient-doctor privilege." Peg paused, keeping her washed-out eyes on Eric and folding her hands in front of her. "I understand that that's the kind of concern you have in the hospital. I mean, I know, I'm employed by a system, too, but this is an exception. This isn't corporate or legal or anything like that. This is between us parents, and that's why I called you. I wanted to meet with you, and ask you, and really *beg* you, *beg* you, do you *understand what I'm saying?* I'm *begging* you, from one parent to another, to tell me what you know. You need to tell me what Max told you about Renée, and why he killed her. She didn't reject him, he never asked her out. She was nice to him, she was nice to everybody. She never did anything wrong. She didn't deserve to die like that, she was too young, too good." Peg's eyes filmed. "I want to know all of it because I'm going to get justice for my child. Anthony says justice can't bring her back, and I know that. But justice can be an end in itself. I want Max to *pay* for what he did to my daughter, and my family."

Eric sighed inwardly, not knowing where to begin. "Peg, I wish I could tell you what you want to know, but I can't. You know I can't. There's no way in the world I can tell you. But I will tell you something important, I will tell you that I'm not sure that Max killed Renée. You and the police could very well have the wrong suspect."

"What are you talking about?" Peg's tone darkened, but she kept her anger in check. "I know that he had a crush on my daughter, and so do you. I believe that he was planning to kill Renée, and so do you. I know that the police found her phone in his bedroom. Respect me enough to be honest with me. I'm an adult, I see life and death every day. I can take it. Tell me what you know."

"I can't tell you what I know, but I spent this morning—"

"Stop. You *will* answer me." Peg spat out the words, her blue eyes hardening like ice. "I know that Max killed her. You know how I know that? Because I read what they said about your whereabouts. That you went to Swirled Peace, that you talked to Renée, that you *followed* her home, that my neighbor saw you sitting on the street, right out front of our house. Why were you doing that?"

"I can't tell you, I can't answer."

"You don't need to, because I'm not stupid. I say to myself, there are two possible reasons that you would be doing that." Peg counted off on her index finger. "The first reason assumes that you have some relationship to Renée, that you're stalking her, and that you're trying to kill her. As I told you, I don't believe that. Not from what I know about you, and I see doctors like you every day in my hospital. They're healers. Even if they're arrogant, and so many of them are, they chose the profession to heal, not to do harm."

Eric swallowed hard, hearing a new note of certainty in her tone.

"The second possible reason is that you were *protecting* Renée. I think that after Max went missing, you were worried about Renée's safety. So you went where she worked, which you knew from Max, and then you followed her home, to make sure Max didn't hurt her."

Eric listened, knowing that she had enunciated a theory that made perfect sense, a lot more sense than the police-Svengali theory, but it still wasn't the truth. He hadn't gone to protect Renée, he had really gone to find Max, but he couldn't tell her that.

"Then, when my neighbor saw you on the street and told you to leave, you went home that night and went to bed. You let your guard down. You couldn't find Max, but Max knew *just* what he was doing. He found Renée. He got to her the next morning. He must've known she walked the dog in Pickering Park in the morning before school. She always did it. She loved the dog, she talked all the time about the dog, and she probably told Max that in one of their tutoring sessions. He *murdered* her there, in the park. He choked the life from her." Peg leaned over, her palms flat on the table, but pressing down so hard that her knuckles turned whitish. "You were worried about that, Eric. You tried to prevent it, but you failed. Tell me I'm right. Tell me the truth."

"The truth is that I think Max may be innocent."

"Really." Peg blew air through her lips, a little puff of disgust, then leaned back in the booth and folded her arms. "You think he's truly innocent?"

"Yes."

"Then tell me why, or better yet, go tell the *police* why you believe that. Because the police think he did it, and if he really didn't do it, then all they're doing is *wasting* their time trying to make a case against him, when they could be going after the real killer. Either way, you have to go tell them. You *have* to tell them what you know. You have to tell them why you think Max is innocent, then. You *cannot* just sit back and do *nothing*. My daughter is *dead*. Your daughter is *alive*. You have no idea how *lucky* you are."

"I am so very sorry for your loss, believe me, I am *so* sorry, but you have to know I haven't been sitting on my hands." Eric decided to be open with her, as tactfully as possible. "This morning, I was on my computer, did some research, and came up with a list of people who were close to Renée."

"How do you know who's close to my daughter or not?"

"From Facebook." Eric slipped a hand into his shirt pocket and pulled out his handwritten list. "Todd Schuler, Hudson McAllister, or one of her girlfriends, and Julia Clackney, Mindy Choretz, Gabi Mateille, and Cate—"

"Are you *serious*?" Peg recoiled. "You looked on my daughter's *Facebook* page? That's private. I set her privacy settings myself when we set up the account."

"Her page is private, but not all of her friends' pages are private. Most of the girls' are, but not the boys', but I couldn't tell which of the boys was her boyfriend—"

"You looked at her *friends'* Facebook pages?" Peg's lips parted in disbelief. "And what boyfriend? She doesn't have a boyfriend."

"She doesn't?" Eric remembered that Max had told him in therapy that Renée had a boyfriend, that she had cried once after a fight with him. Eric realized that Peg didn't know Renée had a boyfriend, so he couldn't disclose it.

"No, she used to see Todd Schuler, but they broke up a long time ago. We didn't like him and—" Peg scowled, catching herself. "This is none of your business! What are you talking about? What are you doing, looking up her Facebook friends?"

"Peg, I'm just trying to exhaust the possibilities. The police have the wrong person and they aren't looking for the real killer. If her murder wasn't an act of random violence, which is always possible, then it had to be someone she knows—"

"How *dare* you!" Peg frowned, her eyes flashing like polished steel. "Are you trying to tell me that you think her *friends* killed her? They've been best friends since *elementary* school, some of them. They can't stop crying since she died."

"I'm just saying that the real killer is still out there—"

"You think that her friends strangled her with their *bare hands*? You think that's likelier than your crazy patient Max doing it? Your troubled, damaged, *whack job* patient, who was dangerous enough to hold children hostage at *gunpoint* and threaten the lives of everyone at the mall?" Peg pursed her lips tightly, leaning forward. "Now you listen to me. I asked you nicely, I even *begged* you, and now I'm going to tell you what I'm going to do, if you don't tell me or the police what you know. I did some research myself and I asked a few psychiatrists I know, and they told me about a case called *Tarasoff,* and under that case, if a psychiatrist thinks that a psychiatric patient is going to kill somebody, he is legally *obligated* to tell that person or the police."

Eric felt the blood drain from his face.

"You knew that Max was going to kill Renée, and the proof is that you followed her to protect her that night. So if you don't come forward and tell the police everything you know, my husband and I are going to sue you. We have the money and will spend every last cent of it to sue you *blind.* You are going to lose *everything you have.* You will never work at a major hospital, or *any hospital* again." Peg spoke so vehemently that her words picked up speed, fueled by anger, pain, and grief. "I am not going to stop until I get justice for my daughter. I am not going to stop until I see that Max is punished to the fullest extent of the law. So if you value your own hide, you best get your butt to the *police*."

"I'm sorry, I can't—"

"Then *so be it.*" Peg got up abruptly from the table, jostling the sodas, then she grabbed her purse, turned away, and stormed off.

"Peg, wait!" Eric rose to go after her, but he stopped himself and sat back down. He had upset her enough already, and Peg was entitled to every emotion she was feeling. In her position, he would've felt the same way. But in view of what she had said, he wanted to follow up to see if Renée's boyfriend was Todd Schuler.

Eric took a sip of his Diet Coke, slid his phone from his pocket, and searched Facebook until he reached Todd Schuler's page. It was public, with none of the privacy settings engaged, and Eric scanned it with a critical eye. Under In A Relationship it read, It's Complicated. Eric realized if Todd was her boyfriend and Renée's parents didn't know about it, then Todd couldn't very well say it on Facebook. Eric would guess that Renée's relationship status was single, because she couldn't blow their cover, either. Todd didn't show as Renée's Facebook friend, which was why Eric hadn't found him before. She must have unfriended him, like Caitlin did, maybe to fool her parents.

Eric scrolled down and read the posts on Todd's page. There weren't many of them, and it looked as if Todd posted only every three or four days. He scrolled down to Wednesday, the day Renée's murder had come to light. His post read simply: **hrtbrkn 4eva.** There was no mention of Renée or explanation of the reference, which jibed with Eric's theory that they were keeping it under wraps.

He scrolled down to the previous posts and looked at them. There were pictures taken at a party, dimly lit, with lots of young people, red Solo cups, and backwards baseball caps, but in one of the photos, Todd was in a selfie, standing alone with Renée, grinning against some verdant backdrop. The caption said: **my bae.**

Eric wasn't completely unhip and he knew that "bae" meant girlfriend. Todd might have been careless in posting it, but he must have known that Renée's parents would have no reason to go on Todd's Facebook page. And they hadn't thought the relationship was current, at least not until now, when Eric had let it slip to Peg.

He checked the date of the picture, which was a month ago. Peg had said they broke up a long time ago, but the picture contradicted that; whether they were boyfriend and girlfriend or not, they were certainly in each other's lives. He eyed the picture again, which was easier to see in the restaurant than in his office with its panel of windows. He couldn't tell what was in the background of the lawn, but there were some hedges, then the corner showed some sort of pink object.

He swiped the screen and enlarged that section of the photo, but still couldn't tell what the object was; it looked like a neon-pink spike of some sort, a color and shape incongruous in nature. Then it struck him, he had seen that incongrous shape somewhere before, in one of the photos. He navigated from Facebook to read the Township website, then looked under Parks and Recreation, and skimmed through the listings to Pickering Park.

He clicked the link, and the phone screen filled with photos from the park: a mulched running trail, a parkour course, and the third photo, which made him gasp. It was of a life-size plastic cow, painted in neon-pink and chartreuse, one of those charity art projects that dotted public places in the area. He enlarged the photo with his fingers, squinted to see the pink tip of the horn, then navigated back to Todd's Facebook page and compared it with the pink sliver in the upper right-hand corner of the selfie. It was the same cow, from Pickering Park.

Eric's mouth went dry and he took another sip of his Diet Coke, his thoughts churning. The selfie proved that Todd had been in Pickering Park with Renée, so clearly he knew about the park. Eric remembered that Peg had said Renée walked the dog in the park every morning, as part of her routine. Eric wondered if Renée had been using the dog as an excuse to meet Todd in the park on those mornings, secretly. Maybe Todd had met her there Wednesday morning and killed her.

Eric thought about it, and it made sense. What if Renée had tried to break up with him and he had killed her? Or if he was jealous about something? The boyfriend was the conventional place to start a murder investigation, but the police didn't know Renée had a boyfriend and neither did Peg, until now. If Todd had taken her phone when he killed her, nobody would know about him. The police might find out when they got the records, but that was days away. In the meantime, Todd could destroy evidence or vanish.

Eric prayed that Peg was driving home thinking about what he had said, and after she'd calmed down, she went to Todd's Facebook page and saw the photo he had just seen. He hoped she would see the neon-pink bull's horn and that she would put two-and-two together. Eric scrolled upward to the most recent pictures, scanning them idly and planning his next move. There were pictures of textbooks with the caption **Only thing worse than school is summer school** and under that **you believe I paid 100 bucks for this effin chem book?** Eric checked the sidebar, under Education, and Todd had listed that he was a freshman at Delaware County Community College, Exton campus.

Eric thought a minute. Exton was only fifteen minutes away, and he had no other leads to follow. He wondered what kind of car Todd drove, because then he could find out if the car had been spotted around Pickering Park the morning that Renée was found dead. The neighborhood had an active town watch, so maybe someone would've noticed Todd's car.

Eric slid out his wallet and put a twenty-dollar bill on the table.

And got going.

Chapter Fifty-one

Eric navigated Lancaster Avenue in light traffic, the cell phone to his ear. "Hello, is this the registration office?"

"Yes, how can I help you?"

"My son is taking a chemistry class this summer, and I must have picked up his backpack instead of my own because I have his books. Do you know what time the class meets and in what building?"

"Let me check the time of the class. Yes, here, the class is from noon to three o'clock, so he's missed most of it. Too bad."

"What building is the class held in? I'm in the neighborhood, so maybe I'll drop it off anyway and say hi."

"Aren't you nice? There's only the one building, so you'll see when you pull into the parking lot."

"Okay, thanks." Eric hung up, checking the dashboard clock, which read 2:15. He wondered if he would ever again check the time and not wonder if Max was doing the same thing somewhere, counting down to the moment when he could perform his rituals.

Eric reached Exton, passed the Church Farm School, looking for signs for Springdale Road, and took a left into the parking lot, scanning the area. He didn't know when colleges started looking like corporate parks, much less being situated in them. He took a left into the parking lot, which was medium-sized, and reversed into a space farthest away from the entrance, cutting the ignition.

The space gave him the best view of what appeared to be the only entrance to the school, next to the signs that read Delaware County Community College Is a Smoke-Free Campus and Bucks for Books!

The entrance was of smoked glass underneath a brown-painted façade, and the building that housed the college was part of the corporate center and shared its architecture: new, modern, and orangey brick, with a few windows. There was no bucolic grass common on which to hang out, talk, or throw a Frisbee, and only a handful of students stood talking outside the entrance, their backpacks slung over one shoulder and their plastic headphones slung around their necks.

A few students headed toward their cars, and Eric watched as the doors opened and more young people trickled out in dribs and drabs, talking and laughing before they went their separate ways. He waited ten minutes, which turned into fifteen, then twenty, keeping an eye on the students leaving the building. Just when he thought that he'd missed Todd, he spotted a student who he thought might be him. The student was tall and about six foot two, with blond hair like Todd's, and he left the building talking with two pretty female students, all of them smiling.

Eric checked Todd's Facebook picture to be sure, and as the blond boy walked closer, Eric realized it was Todd. He had the same broad shoulders in a vintage gray T-shirt and droopy green cargo pants, and his smile was the same: easy and vaguely cocky. Eric edged up in his seat, waiting to see which car Todd would go to because the lot was still fairly full.

One of the girls laughed loudly, the sound coming through Eric's open window, then she waved good-bye and walked to a row of cars parked along the right. Todd walked to the left with the other girl, and in the next moment, he threw his arm around her shoulder and kissed her on the cheek, then she stopped and smiled up at him, whereupon Todd kissed her fully on the mouth.

Eric blinked, surprised. He didn't know what to make of it. Either Todd was Renée's boyfriend and had moved on heartlessly soon after her death, or he wasn't her boyfriend in the first place and Eric's theory was wrong. Eric didn't understand, but he didn't have time to parse it now. He scrolled to the camera function on his phone and started snapping pictures of Todd and the girl as they broke up the clinch, walked together to an olive gray Jeep Wrangler, and both of them got in, with Todd in the driver's seat. Todd reversed out of the space and exited the parking lot, and Eric took a picture of his license plate.

Eric eyed the photo of the license plate, in thought. What he had learned about Todd made him think that the boy should be investigated further, but for a moment, Eric wasn't sure where to go with the information. It would be foolhardy to go to the police himself, given that he was out on bail, nor could he call Marie, who would probably be eager to hear anything that could help to exonerate Max.

It struck Eric that the tables had turned, as an ethical and legal matter. Previously, his confidentiality had prevented him from giving to the police evidence that would put Max on the hook; now, it was preventing him from giving evidence that would take Max *off* the hook. The sword cuts both ways, and Eric was going to be principled about his confidentiality. But he could divulge what he'd learned today, outside of what Max had told him.

He turned to the phone function and pressed Call.

Chapter Fifty-two

"Paul, how are you? Got a minute?" Eric sat behind the wheel, idly watching students leave the college.

"Sure I was just about to call you."

"Let me go first." Eric didn't feel like his news could wait. "I discovered a viable suspect in Renée Bevilacqua's murder and I want to know what we do next. I'm thinking you could tell the police, because I know I can't communicate with them directly."

"You're kidding, right? Who are you, Nancy Drew? You find the hidden staircase?"

"Paul, listen. If you go on Facebook, you can find the page of a nineteen-year-old named Todd Schuler, who goes to Delaware County Community College, and there's a picture of him with Renée at Pickering Park, taken a month ago." Eric still had to be careful about keeping confidential what Max had told him in therapy, but he didn't have to keep confidential what he had learned otherwise.

"Okaaaay," Paul said, slowly. "So you're Facebook-stalking people, I can live with that. I do the same thing to a girl who dumped me. Looks like she's with a real loser now, which makes me very happy."

"I believe that Todd Schuler was Renée's boyfriend, and I think the police should investigate that. Isn't it fairly typical, that when a wife is murdered, they look at the husband? I think I even read that somewhere, that they look at the nearest and dearest. Well, Todd Schuler was the nearest and dearest, so we need to find a way to tell them. Can you tell them?"

"Eric, you're trying to do police investigative work by trolling Facebook, and I don't think that's how it works." Paul chuckled. "Even though the local constabulary isn't exactly the top of the law-enforcement food chain, I think even they can figure out to go look at her boyfriend. Let them do their job, and you need to chill. What's going on with the reporters? Are they still on the lawn?"

Eric didn't answer, since he was still in the parking lot at Delaware County Community College. "But the thing is, the police might not know she had a boyfriend."

"I'm sure the police can find out she has a boyfriend. I mean, that's not forensic expert stuff."

Eric hesitated. "I think the relationship was secret. Her parents didn't know."

"Then how do *you* know?"

"I just met with Renée's mother and—"

"You did *what*? You met with the mother of the murder victim? When? How?"

"She called me. She begged me to meet with her. I didn't tell her anything, and I didn't do anything untoward."

"Eric, meeting with her is *untoward,* whatever that means. Who uses words like that anymore? What is your deal? What happened at this meeting? Where are you?"

"It was a brief meeting at a restaurant. She asked me, she *begged* me, to tell her what I knew about Max, and I didn't. Then, at the end, she threatened to sue me, but I'm getting used to that."

"Are you kidding? This is so dangerous for you. Why didn't you tell me?"

"I knew you'd say no."

Paul snorted. "Who else was there?"

"No one."

"She didn't bring counsel or anyone?"

"No."

"Was she wearing a wire?"

"Of course not."

"How do you know?"

"I just do."

Paul groaned. "Did you record the conversation?"

"Of course not."

"She could call the police. She could tell them anything. She could make up something you said, a confession even."

"She's not going to do that."

"You don't know that."

"Yes I do. She's a heartbroken mother trying to get some justice for her child. What's important is that she did not know that Renée had a boyfriend, in Todd. And that means the police probably don't know."

"Renée's girfriends will know. My wife tells her girlfriends everything."

"They might not tell, knowing Renée wanted to keep it a secret. They'd have no incentive to reveal her secrets after she died, if the police already have the killer."

"Eric, if you could figure it out, the cops can figure it out. They have the Internet. I think."

"But they're not looking. Plus, Renée's mother told me that it was Renée's routine to walk the dog in the park every morning before school, and I think she was meeting Todd there. Todd could've killed her, and I have to tell you, I think he's really a player." Eric didn't need to add the part that he'd learned from Max, that Renée had been crying after she had a fight with her boyfriend.

"Eric, how do you know he's a player? High-school gossip? Is he in your homeroom?"

"Trust me, you don't want to know. I have his license plate, too, I'll text it to you. And the fact that Renée had a routine is significant. Anybody who was watching her would have known that she would be there walking the dog, all by herself."

"Eric, please, stop—"

"Would you just call the police and tell them about Todd Schuler? And ask them to ask if anybody on the town watch saw his car around Pickering Park on the morning of the murder, or on other mornings?"

"If I do that, they'll know it comes from you."

"So what? I'm not going to answer any more questions from them. I thought about calling the tip line anonymously, but I don't know if they follow through on that stuff."

"They do, I think."

"I don't want to rely on that. I want to know it got communicated. I'd love to give the information to Marie, but I know you're going to say we can't call her."

"Thank God, at least you listen to some of the things I say. No, we can't call her. I'll tell you why, I was about to call you. I just spoke with Max's new lawyer, Lionel Bolton. He's one of the best criminal defense lawyers in the city."

"Terrific."

"No, not terrific. I'm sure he's taking the case because it's so high-profile, and Lionel loves to take the little and make it big."

"I think the case deserves to be big. Max needs a psychological evaluation, so they can get him the treatment he needs, and in the meantime, his lawyer can hold Newmire's feet to the fire—"

"Eric, your naïveté, it touches me. You're like an extremely brainy newborn."

"What do you mean?"

"The only person whose feet are going to get held to the fire are *yours.* Lionel is not telling me his strategy, of course, but I've represented codefendants in conspiracy cases with him before. He doesn't play well with others. His MO is divide and conquer."

"How so?"

"He's going after you, Eric. He's gonna ride the theory that you manipulated Max, this weak-minded young boy."

Eric scoffed. "Like the cops were saying? Why would I manipulate Max to kill Renée?"

"He doesn't have to answer that question, not in front of a jury. All he has to do is create reasonable doubt. He'll serve up somebody more culpable than Max and flip the facts of the case on their head. He takes your going to the mall and getting Max out as proof that you have unusual power over the kid—who looks as innocent as an altar boy. You, on the other hand, are a powerful psychiatrist, who today looks like a big bully, because by the way, somebody named Linda Perino is talking to the press and saying that you attacked her husband on your psychiatric unit."

Eric couldn't believe his ears. "I didn't, that's not true."

"It doesn't matter what's true, it only matters what gets reported. I wouldn't be surprised if Lionel finds a way to get Mrs. Perino before every microphone in the tri-state area."

Eric sighed inwardly.

"Max is going to get the best psychiatric care on the planet because his new lawyer is going to want to prove him mentally unstable, whether to get him off on the murder charge on an insanity defense, or to derail a criminal trial, in hopes that he's not mentally competent to participate in his own defense."

Eric felt a small measure of reassurance.

"But the way it works for the defense lawyer is that he has to get the jury somebody to hang. That's going to be you. So here's new rules. From now on, Max, Marie, and her boyfriend Sasquatch are the enemy. We have nothing to do with them. Total and complete separation. Church and state. Love and marriage."

Eric couldn't smile.

"Do I have your agreement on that?" Paul's voice turned stern. "I'm not asking you, I'm telling you. If you don't follow my directions, I'm going to drop you faster then Julie Stein."

"Who?"

"The girl I Facebook-stalk. She dropped me in the middle of our first date. I took her to dinner and didn't even make it past the bruschetta. She went to the bathroom and never came back." Paul chuckled. "That's what's going to happen to you, Eric. I'm going to the bathroom and I'm not coming back. You're going to be left holding your bruschetta."

Eric could hear in the tone of his voice that he wasn't kidding.

"Now what are you going to do?"

"First, will you tell the police about Todd Schuler?" Eric scrolled to the text function and texted Paul the photo. "I just sent his license plate to you."

"Yes, I will do that. I'll look like a smacked ass for you. I'll tell them all the lunch-table gossip, who likes who, who's wearing what, did you see Jenny's eye makeup, whatever the hell you want me to do. But you need to go home and behave yourself. By the way, my sister says hi."

"Say hi back." Eric thought a minute. "Or I might go to the hospital, say hi to her, and sneak in a check on my patients."

"Yes, that you can do. But stay off of Facebook or you're grounded. Feel me?"

"Yes," Eric answered, reaching over and starting the car.

Chapter Fifty-three

Eric reached the hospital by the end of the business day, and rush-hour traffic was in full swing. He steered to the parking lot, stopped at the entrance, and slid his parking pass into the turnstile, but the parking attendant stepped out of his booth and waved him away.

"Sir, sir! That turnstile is for doctors only!"

"It's me, Bob!" Eric called back, sticking his head from the driver's side window.

"Sorry, Dr. Parrish. Didn't recognize the car. You get a new one?"

"Not exactly." Eric wasn't about to explain, but Bob was grinning.

"Hey, way to go last night at the mall! You did us proud!"

"Thanks," Eric said with a smile. The turnstile went up and he cruised through, drove to his parking spot, and turned off the ignition. He got out of the car, locked it up, and made his way to the breezeway that led to the main building. Hospital staff, doctors, and nurses flowed from the exit, and Eric approached, swimming upstream. As he got closer to the breezeway door, he realized that people were looking at him, doing double-takes, and his very appearance caused a frisson of reaction. He caught one or two of the staff smiling at him, and somebody flashed him a thumbs-up, but one of the nurses frowned, looking away.

Eric could read her expression at a glance, and he had anticipated as much. He'd hoped that most HGH employees would know
him well enough, at least by reputation, to know he wouldn't kill
anybody, but there had to be people who would disapprove of his
protecting the killer of a young girl or suspect him of murder
himself. Eric kept his head down, suddenly self-conscious, then
spotted Ken Shu, one of his colleagues in oncology, flagging him
down.

"Eric, my God, I saw what happened at the mall. What you did
was positively heroic. Was that young man one of your patients?
He could've killed you!"

"No, I'm fine, I wasn't in danger, thanks," Eric said, grateful,
though he wanted to keep going.

"I want you to know I'm behind you, and we know this thing
will get straightened out. I can't stand some of the negative things
they're saying, it's ridiculous. It's very difficult for laypeople to understand a physician's privilege. The police and the press, it's
obvious they don't get it."

"Right, but I have to go, take care. Good-bye now. Thanks again."
Eric barreled ahead, hearing the murmuring and feeling the stares
as he went by.

"Dr. Parrish!" A group of nurses looked over at him, and one
cupped a hand to her mouth to call out, "Looking good last night!
Way to go!"

"Thanks," Eric called back as he entered the breezeway, a long
corridor under a glass-walled canopy that led to the hospital, plastered on both sides with large multicolored posters of hospital PR.
He braced himself when he saw that Morris Brexler was coming
toward him from the opposite direction, his eyes hardening.

"Eric, you're certainly in the news. What a hullabaloo. Of course,
we're behind you a hundred percent. My wife was delighted that
you saved Neiman Marcus."

Eric forced a smile. "Yes, thanks."

"I was surprised to hear that you were taking the time off, though
I trust it's a good idea. Too many distractions. I imagine you have
meetings with counsel and the authorities, things of that nature."

"Yes, I do." Eric couldn't tell if Morris was suspicious of the reason for the suspension.

"How long do you expect to be off? A week, two weeks?"

"I'm not sure. Why?"

"We have a meeting of the Pharmacy Review Board next Wednesday. If you recall, we vote on Rostatin."

"Oh, right." Eric realized that Morris was asking because he had a vote to deliver to his cronies at the drug company. A golf boondoggle probably hung in the balance. "I'm sure I can vote by email. I'll email Mike and copy everyone on the committee."

"No, email won't do. I checked with Mike and you have to appoint someone to vote in your stead."

"Then I'll have someone vote in my stead. I'll tell Mike."

Morris frowned. "Eric, I emailed you some further information on the drug. I put in a request for those other studies you wanted. I never heard back from you. Did you get the information?"

"It probably came in but I'm behind on my email."

"I can also put you in touch with one of the reps, Clark Yoshida. He's very knowledgeable and he can answer any questions you may have. I know you're busy right now, but he'll work around your schedule. You can even discuss it over dinner."

"Thanks, but no." Eric tried not to laugh. Most doctors did everything they could to avoid drug reps, and Morris was sending him on a blind date with one.

"Eric, I wish you would keep an open mind."

"If you're asking me if I'm changing my vote, I'm not. We can agree to disagree." Eric wanted to go. "It isn't the first time, and it won't be the last. I'm the loyal opposition."

Morris frowned. "I hope you reconsider after you've read the email."

"Thank you, but I have to go. See you soon." Eric took off, going the wrong way through the crowds, acknowledging the shouted approval and expressions of support, and trying to ignore the narrowed eyes and tight lips of those who didn't. He found it difficult to believe that people would actually think him a murderer, but it wasn't out of the question. The newspapers were full of similar stories, every day, and he knew that the face someone showed the world could be at odds with the psyche.

He got on the elevator as everyone got off, and hit the up button, heading for his unit. He realized he did it reflexively, as he had every day for the past fifteen years, and he knew he probably couldn't be here in an official capacity, with the indefinite suspension. Still, he thought he'd check on his patients informally, see if there was anything he needed from his office, then stop down and see Laurie.

Eric got off the elevator on Wright as staff piled on, reacting to his appearance, and he smiled and acknowledged their comments, then went down the short hallway to the unit. He realized he didn't have his employee lanyard to swipe himself in, so he knocked at the door, waited, then knocked again. He couldn't see anybody through the glass in the airlock, so he picked up the intercom phone on the wall.

"Anybody home? It's Eric, and I don't have my swipe card. Can you let me in?"

"Dr. Parrish, it's Tina. I'll let you in. Hold on a second, I'm in the dining room."

"Thanks. I'll wait." Eric hung up, feeling a comfort being back on the unit, its schedule fixed and familiar. Tina would be supervising the patients at dinner, the shift was over, and most of the day nurses had gone home except for Amaka, who always stayed late. Sam, David, and Jack would be getting ready to go home. Eric wondered how the patients were doing, and, in particular, if Perino was improving. It was too bad that his wife had decided to go public with her complaint, but if this experience was teaching Eric anything, it was to let go of what he couldn't control. He probably should've learned that lesson already, but better late than never.

"Dr. Parrish?" said a voice behind him, and Eric turned to see two smiling security guards in blue uniforms approaching him from the elevator.

"Yes?"

"You were awesome last night at the mall, Doc. My daughter works in the Lady Footlocker, and the cops evacuated her. She was scared out of her mind."

"I'm sorry to hear that."

"It's good that it ended peacefully, thanks to you. Anyway, we got a call to check on you."

"Check on me? I'm fine, thanks."

"No, it's not that way." The security guard hesitated, shifting his feet. "You're not permitted on the premises while you're on suspension."

"Oh, please."

"Sorry, sir."

"But I want to check on my patients and get some things out of my office."

"They told us you can clean out your desk, but we have to escort you and wait with you while you do that. No suspended employee can be on the premises unescorted while they're on suspension. That's a procedure for all employees, including physicians."

"I can't bring you into the unit. It upsets the patients and they've had enough of that already this week. Can't you wait here while I go in and talk to my people?"

"No, sorry, no can do."

"Hold on a second." Eric picked up the wall phone and punched in Mike's extension.

"Legal Department," Dee Dee answered.

"Dee, this is Eric Parrish. Is he in?"

"Sure, Eric, hang on." Dee Dee put him on hold, and in the next moment, there was a click on the line.

"Eric, this is Mike. Jeez, I can't believe what you did last night in King of Prussia! I hope that kid knows he owes you his life. Now I understand what was going on yesterday, when the cops—"

"Thanks, but I'm outside my unit now, trying to get into my own office."

"I know, I heard. I would've come up to see you myself, but I'm in the middle of something."

"Mike, I need to check on my patients and talk to my staff."

"Sorry, it's not procedure. I know this seems formal, but it's out of my hands. Employees on suspension aren't permitted on the campus. I could cite you chapter and verse in the employee manual, if you wait a minute."

"It's a matter of patient care, Mike. I just want to know how they're doing."

"You're not supposed to be performing any of your duties as Chief. If you want to take belongings from your office, the guards will wait for you to finish and escort you out."

"Mike, I can't have guards all over my unit again."

"I'm sorry, but there's nothing I—"

Eric hung up in disgust, turning to see Amaka, Sam, David, and Jack, piling into the airlock and unlocking the outside door.

"Eric!" Amaka came over, gave him a big hug, then let him go, beaming at him. "Thank God you're okay. What a nightmare that must've been. We saw tanks and guns. It looked like a war zone."

Sam emerged, shaking Eric's hand. "Chief, great to see you. You were unreal at the mall. We were at a baseball game and one of the moms had a video live-streaming on her phone. What a scene!"

David grinned at Eric, his eyes shining. "Chief, I'm proud to know you. I was gaming and I stopped when I saw it online. I gave up the win because of you."

Jack leaned over and shook Eric's hand. "Chief, I'm telling everybody we're best friends. There's a really hot nurse in Endocrinology, and I think you just tipped the balance in my favor, if you follow."

Amaka gave Jack a playful hit on the arm. "Stop, you."

Everybody laughed except for Kristine, who showed up on the unit's side of the airlock, her only expression an interested smile. Eric ignored her. "Hi, everybody, thanks. I wanted to check on the patients and get some things out of my office, but I can't come in without security, so I'm not coming in."

Amaka frowned at the security guards. "This is insulting! Dr. Parrish is the Chief of the unit. This is *his* unit."

The security guard shook his head. "Sorry, but we have to follow procedure. The only way to admit Dr. Parrish into the unit is if he's escorted."

Eric let it go, because Amaka, Sam, and David looked uniformly upset. Only Jack seemed typically detached. "Troops, let's not sweat this. There's nothing in my office that I need, and I'm not going to disrupt the unit."

Amaka muttered, "This is ridiculous."

"Don't worry about it." Eric faced Sam. "Can I call you tonight and talk about Perino and the others?"

"Happy to do it. What time?"

"I'll call you at eight, okay?"

"Sure."

"All right everybody, take care." Eric managed a smile, though he hated to go. "Feel free to call me if anything comes up or if you have a question. I have a new phone number, and I'll email it to you."

"Bye, Chief," Amaka said, still frowning, and Sam gave his little hippie wave.

"We'll talk, Chief."

David nodded, somber. "See you later, Chief."

Jack flashed him his trademark too-cool-for-school smile. "Take care, Chief."

"Will do." Eric managed a smile back, though something about Jack bugged him, the attending's superior act wearing thin. Eric motioned the security guards to walk ahead of him down the hallway. "Let's go, gentlemen. I don't need you to walk me out of the building but we can share an elevator."

"Okay, Dr. Parrish," said one of the security guards, leading the way to the elevator lobby and pressing the down button

Eric waited for the elevator.

But he'd be damned if he'd be kept out of his own hospital.

He made a call as soon as he got outside.

Chapter Fifty-four

Eric left the hospital by the front entrance, only to walk around the building to the emergency department and enter through its automatic doors. He waved at the nurse in the glass-walled triage station by reception, then slipped past the double doors of the ED entrance when one of the physician's assistants left, doing a double-take as Eric went past.

"Dr. Parrish, great job!" the PA called to him.

"Thanks," Eric called back, over his shoulder. He entered the ED, and the two nurses looked up from the octagonal station.

The blond nurse smiled warmly. "Dr. Parrish, you were amazing last night! That was really something, the way you went to that mall."

"Thanks." Eric smiled. "Is Dr. Fortunato in?"

"She's in room D, but she's not finished. She said she'd meet you in her office. I'll let her know you're here."

"Thanks." Eric went past the examining rooms and ducked into Laurie's office, at the end of the hall. He closed the door behind him, glancing around, and the office looked like no place else in the hospital. Lining the walls were framed posters of abstract art from Matisse, Delaunay, Kandinsky, and Marz; the names of the artists were at the bottom of each poster, and though each painting was different, they all shared vibrant and vivid colors, like the Marz, which depicted a bright cobalt-blue horse. Laurie's framed diplomas had yet to be hung, stuck on a shelf between medical books and hospital manuals, and the top of the shelf was covered with the funky windup toys she collected: mechanical robots, walking cats, elephants with a Babar crown, ducks, and chattering teeth, next to a Magic Eight Ball.

Eric picked up the Magic Eight Ball and turned it over, and the triangle appeared through the black water, reading, *Cannot predict now.* Unfortunately, he didn't know the question.

"Eric, hey!" Laurie entered the office, closing the door behind her, then came over and gave him a hug. "It's so good to see you."

"Hi." Eric hugged her back, remembering that before he'd run into the mall, he'd kissed her on the cheek. He couldn't explain how that happened, so he hoped she didn't remember and his impulse would be consigned to let's-pretend-this-didn't-happen territory.

"Wait." Laurie looked Eric up and down, then made a funny face. "Why are you dressed like my brother?"

Eric smiled. "Because he dressed me."

"Creepy, yet it works."

"Thanks for hiding me."

"Do you believe such idiocy? Please sit down. You've been through hell." Laurie leaned against the side of the desk in her white coat. Her stethoscope was looped around her neck, her dark eyes looked bright and lively, and her curly dark hair was twisted into a topknot with a pencil. She smiled at him. "So you survived jail, *and* Paul. Which is worse?"

"I like Paul." Eric sat back down, smiling. "I bet he had no idea what he was getting into."

"Ha!" Laurie chuckled. "That's what he says about you. It's quite the bromance. So fill me in."

"You don't have time."

"You're right, and I have marching orders from him anyway. He wants me to talk to you. He thinks you're going too far out on a limb for Max, and I have to tell you, for once in my life, I actually agree with him. Do you know what a brat he was when he was little? I never, ever, *ever* thought that would happen."

"Why do you agree with him?"

"Why?" Laurie's eyes flared. "I saw you run past an armed barricade into that mall. That was insanity! Just because it ended up okay doesn't mean it was a smart thing to do, or even the right thing to do."

"The nurses approve," Eric said slyly, suddenly in a good mood. Maybe it was the colorful artwork, making him happy.

"Very funny." Laurie folded her arms, getting serious. "Eric, let me ask you a question, sincerely. Do you really believe that Max didn't kill that girl? Think about it. I mean, really think about it."

"Well, I just learned about this secret boyfriend that Renée had, named Todd Schuler, and I'm sure the police haven't even questioned him yet." Eric had been thinking about it on the way over, and the more he considered it, the more it seems like Todd had been overlooked as a suspect. "I found out that Renée used to walk her dog every morning in the park, at that same time. It was a well-established routine, because she was so crazy about the dog. But I don't think she was just there walking the dog. I think she used to meet Todd in the mornings, secretly, because her mother didn't like him. He could've killed her one morning and nobody would've known. He's a big guy, too. He could have overpowered her easily."

"That's not the answer to my question. Before you go off on a tangent, I want to bring you back to Max and ask you if you really think he's innocent."

Eric challenged his thinking. He flashed on Max last night at the mall, saying he didn't remember killing Renée, but seeming resigned to the fact that he had probably done it. "Okay, I'm ambivalent. Maybe he did it, but I can't imagine him doing it. It's just not like him."

"So that's how you feel, your intuition?"

"Yes."

"I know that you're intuitive, and you rely on your emotional intelligence as a clinician. But let's look at this objectively. Sometimes you have to look at the data."

"Do you think he killed her?"

"Yes."

Eric blinked, surprised. "I thought we were on the same page. I had the impression you thought Max was innocent, too."

"I did, before last night. But last night changed things for me." Laurie frowned slightly. "I have to be honest with you, when I saw the trouble he caused, when I saw the fear and even the terror he caused, those kids crying, police mobilizing from everywhere, the EMTs, first responders, guys I *know,* whose help is needed elsewhere. He caused all that to happen."

"So you're angry at him."

"Damn right, I'm angry at him. I deal with emergencies every day and I've seen how first responders work all night, picking up the pieces after accidents, rushing children in here, arms off, legs off, even *babies* in here after car accidents, shootings, stabbings, muggings, accidental poisonings, household accidents, every kind of horrible thing that can happen to human beings ends up in my ED." Laurie gestured at the door. "Right out there. The lives of innocent people could have been *lost* last night, it could've been a disaster. We drill for bomb threats, and when I heard that Max had a fake bomb, I could've killed him myself."

"I understand that you're angry, but that doesn't make him guilty of murder. I tell you, he was trying to kill himself last night."

"Eric, I'm not the shrink, but I think you're in denial about Max. You're projecting onto him, seeing yourself in him—or maybe even Hannah. It's like you're being protective without knowing the facts."

"What facts?"

"Exactly. You saw Max a total of three times, including the time you met him on Friday night here, for which I will be forever regretful. Do you really have enough facts on which to base this *ambivalence* you're sticking to?" Laurie threw up her expressive hands. "How well do you *really* know Max? You think you understand him, but would you have predicted that he would do what he did at the mall? Did you see that coming? According to you, that was wildly out of character, but he did it. It's a fact that he did it."

"I admit, I didn't see that coming. I worried he was suicidal, but this kind of scheme, with the bomb and everything, it doesn't seem like him."

"Hello, wake up, he did it. I saw it."

"But still, it's not like him. It's almost like he had another influence, as if someone was influencing him."

"You sound like a mother who says that her kids fell in with the wrong crowd. Doesn't that sound like denial to you?"

"Maybe, but I doubt it." Eric felt stubborn, but he couldn't bring himself to believe that Max was completely responsible for the hostage-taking at the mall. He was buying into the police's theory, that Max was weak and there had to be a Svengali. Eric thought back to Marie, telling him that Eric talked to someone on the phone at night, sometimes they fought. Whoever that person was, maybe *he* was the Svengali. But Eric couldn't talk to Marie, not after what Paul had said about the lawyer they'd hired.

"Eric." Laurie sighed. "You need to get your head out of your own ass. Take a look at the facts. Begin at the beginning."

"I did that. I read through my notes of my sessions with him."

"I took notes about Max the night you met him and his grandmother. They're in her file. Max was Chatty Cathy before you came down and he gave me an earful."

"He did?" Eric felt his ears prick up. "Why didn't you mention this before?"

"I didn't think it mattered, and it's not as if we've had a lot of free time to chat." Laurie snorted. "I don't know what he told you in his sessions, but I think you need to start over. Begin at the beginning. Look at this kid with new eyes. Objectively."

"Okay."

"Hang on a sec." Laurie walked around to the front of her desk, bent over her computer keyboard, and hit a few keys. In the next moment, her cell phone signaled an alert, as part of the two-step security system that HGH maintained for access to its electronic medical records system. She slid the phone from her pocket and typed in the security code that appeared on the text. Only then would she be permitted access to the record, then she'd also have to type in her own personal identity code, was which was also confidential. "Okay, here's his grandmother's file, with my notes from him that night, which came from my conversation with Max."

"Great." Eric started to rise to come around the desk, but Laurie held him off with a stagey wink.

"I'm sure you're not allowed to look at this since you're on suspended status. So, don't you dare look at this file. Oops, I think I hear someone paging me, so I'm going to leave." Laurie straightened up and walked out of the office without another word, closing the door behind her.

Eric rose, intrigued, and went around the desk.

Chapter Fifty-five

Eric scrolled through the first page of Virginia Teichner's electronic medical records, or EMR, skimming the logged entries of her vital signs on the night of her treatment in the emergency room and scanning the ghostly gray images of her chest X-ray, which showed the amorphous whitish tumor that interfered with her breathing and swallowing. He could see the telltale crosshairs where the X-ray technician had dutifully measured the mass, but you didn't have to be an oncologist to know that it would kill Mrs. Teichner sooner rather than later.

Eric felt a stab of pain, remembering how lively Virginia had been that night, and how funny, but he had to put that memory behind him for now. He scrolled to the back of the file, where Laurie had typed in her notes, and began reading, picking up the parts about Max: ". . . grandson vocal on subject of his mother . . . expresses anger at mother and her neglect of grandmother . . . grandson resents that mother has 'milked grandmother for all she is worth and then some' . . . grandson seems v. depressed and angry about grandmother's imminent death . . . says he 'can't stand idea of living with his mother' and he 'would be better off if the mother were dead' . . . grandson says that mother is 'useless whore' . . . and 'deserves to die' . . . . . . he 'hopes that one of her loser boyfriends kills her in her sleep.' . . . call Eric for psychiatric consult . . ."

Eric considered it, though he wasn't really surprised. Max had expressed anger at his mother in their sessions, and Eric could see with his own eyes that Marie was an irresponsible mother. The hostility was more than Eric might have expected, considering it was expressed to a stranger like Laurie, but that could be explained by the fact that Max was so upset that night, with his grandmother choking at the house, then having to bring her to the emergency room. It wasn't really a fair picture of Max, Eric thought, then he paused, wondering if he really was making excuses for the boy.

Eric scrolled to the next page to see if there were any more notes, but there weren't, though he hadn't reached the end of the Virginia Teichner file. The next page of the EMR was the first page of a previous admission of hers, and he checked the date of the admission. Evidently, two months prior to her admission to the emergency department, Virginia had been admitted to the third floor, which was cardiology, and had stayed there for three days, for observation and treatment of breathing difficulties and chest pain.

Eric remembered that Laurie had mentioned the previous admission that night in the ED, but he must have forgotten. He hadn't really focused on it before, because it didn't matter, and it made sense that Virginia, who had such an advanced cancer by the time he met her, would have been admitted to HGH before. Eric checked the top of the page to see which physician had been assigned to her case: Dr. Morris Brexler, Cardiology Chief.

Eric frowned. It was odd that Morris hadn't mentioned that he'd treated Max's grandmother. He had just run into Morris downstairs, and they'd discussed the scene at the mall last night, so it would've been a natural thing to mention. It didn't make sense that Morris was omitting it, for some reason. It seemed remotely possible that Morris hadn't made the connection between Max and his grandmother, but that was unlikely, given that Max had probably been the one to bring Virginia to the hospital in the first place and had undoubtedly visited her, if he even left her side at all.

Eric looked at the upper right side of the page, where the treatment team for each patient was always listed. The treating physician was Morris Brexler, the resident Sara Stone, the assigned nurse

Caleb Martieki, and the social worker Martha Girandole. Next to each of the names was the general phone number for the cardiology department. Under HGH procedure, the personal cell numbers of hospital staff were kept confidential, to avoid patients' calling them at all hours.

Eric scanned the report of Virginia's vitals and her bloodwork, idly noting the levels, then looked at her MRIs and X-rays of her chest and throat, in which the mass was barely visible, so it must have been a fast-growing tumor. He kept going through the file to see if Morris or anyone else had made any notes regarding Max, but he reached the last page, under Physician's Notes. There was one relevant note on the first day of Virginia's admission, on which Morris had noted: "patient accompanied by grandson, no other visitors . . . grandson is primary caretaker and familiar with medication and eating habits of patient." On day two of Virginia's hospital stay, after notes about her breathing issues, Morris noted that, "Patient very worried about mental state of grandson, given her diagnosis." On day three, Morris made a similar note, "Patient wants referral psychiatrist for grandson w depression, grief counseling."

Eric flashed on Virginia in the emergency department, how she had collared him and made him pay attention to Max's problem. Evidently, Virginia had been as insistent with Morris, but Morris hadn't tried to help her or Max. Eric was beginning to get a bad feeling. He knew Morris was busy, but no busier than any other chief, and Morris should have called him in on a consult, the way Laurie had that night in the ED. Eric wondered if Morris didn't refer the matter to psychiatry because of their bad blood on the Pharmacy Review Board. Eric wouldn't have ordinarily entertained that conclusion, but it did seem strange that Morris hadn't mentioned any of it to him in the breezeway.

"Hey," Laurie said, entering the office, then closing the door behind her. "Well?"

Eric changed mental gears. "I read it, and I admit it sounds hostile, but it really doesn't change anything for me."

"He called his mother a *whore*." Laurie frowned and folded her arms, standing on the other side of the desk. "Doesn't that seem beyond the pale?"

"It's inappropriate, but I wouldn't extrapolate too much from it."

"Why not? Like I said, I know I'm no psychiatrist, but do you know what my mother always told me?"

"What?"

"Men who hate their mothers hate women."

"That's not bad," Eric had to admit.

"Tell me about it. My mom is always right. Just ask her."

Eric didn't interrupt her, because he could see she was on a roll, her dark eyes growing animated.

"So it would make a lot of sense to me that Max hated women. His mother is so obviously irresponsible. Marie's a drunk. Zack is actually too good for her. A kid like Max, who has such anger toward his mother, could easily lose his temper on Renée and kill her, even impulsively."

"It's possible, but not likely—"

"Really? Plus I was thinking about what you said, that Renée had a boyfriend and this dog-walking routine. If she was meeting the boyfriend in the morning, then Max could've easily known about that routine, too. He could've known she had a boyfriend. What if she mentioned that to Max during one of her tutoring sessions?"

Eric didn't confirm that it was true, and that was how he himself knew about Renée's having a boyfriend in the first place.

"And if that's so, then maybe Max got jealous that she was rejecting him. Maybe Max knew she was meeting her boyfriend in the park, and so he went to the park that morning and killed her. It's completely possible, and it even fits with his profile. I know you don't see him that way, but I don't think you're seeing him objectively anymore."

"I hear you, but I think I am."

"So you're unconvinced?"

"I think so."

"Whatever, then close down the file." Laurie came around the desk, leaned over, and reached for the mouse, but her swipe called to the screen the log-in sheet, which showed a record of the times the EMR file had been accessed online, by anyone in the hospital. "Oops, sorry."

"Wait, don't close it yet." Eric glanced at the list, then did a double-take. The EMR had been accessed a slew of times during Virginia's three-day hospital stay, which was to be expected, but it had also been accessed in the two months since then—twice. "That's funny."

"What?" Laurie looked at the screen, the white light of the monitor showing the contours of her fleshy cheeks.

"Why was somebody accessing the file after the patient's been discharged?"

"I don't know." Laurie frowned at the screen. "Any test results or bloodwork that comes after discharge are imported into the file automatically. They don't show as accessing the file under the EMR system, do they?"

"No. The only people who would have any reason to access the file after discharge are the treating physician and his team."

"That's what I was thinking."

"Maybe if somebody has a question or wants to jog his memory for some reason. I've done that once, my entire career."

Laurie snorted. "I've never done it. Who has time? In the ED, if I start looking at files, somebody bleeds out. My practice is strictly plug-and-play."

"There's another reason I can think of for accessing the file—to alter it in some way."

"Whoa, why?"

"And who? I don't know if they added something or deleted something, but I'm going to find out." Eric scanned the access entries, and next to each one was a line of twelve asterisks, the encoded identities of whoever had accessed the file. Every physician, nurse, intern, and even orderlies at HGH were assigned an identity code, and the codes appeared as asterisks for security reasons, so that nobody could learn the code of another employee and use it to fraudulently access the EMR system under his name. Eric looked up at Laurie. "Would you be surprised if I told you that Morris Brexler was the treating physician?"

"Morris of Myrtle Beach?"

"Yes." Eric had confided in her his suspicion about Morris's taking kickbacks on the Pharmacy Review Board. "Morris treated Virginia Teichner on her previous visit. He even met Max. *And* he never mentioned it to me, even though I just saw him on the way up."

"What?" Laurie's eyebrows lifted in surprise, and Eric returned his attention to the list of access codes, a block set of asterisks, like the stars on the American flag.

"This is fishy."

"Maybe it's a mistake?" Laurie shook her head, nonplussed.

"I'm going to find out." Eric rose.

"What are you going to do? You're not allowed to be on the premises, officially."

Eric crossed to the door. "Then I'll be on the premises, unofficially."

Chapter Fifty-six

Eric took the stairs two steps at a time. He'd have to hurry if he wanted to catch the guys in the IT department before they went home. He raced downstairs, blew through the exit doors, then jogged down the hall. Luckily, the IT department was in the basement, consigned to an out-of-the-way location near the morgue, and only a janitor was coming toward him in the other direction, pushing an industrial-size floor polisher.

"Hello," the janitor said, nodding as Eric hustled past.

"Hi." Eric spotted the sign for the IT department and opened the plain gray door, but it was locked. "Anybody home? Can you give me a hand?"

"Hold on," said a voice from inside, and in the next moment, the door was opened by a young girl with supershort purple hair, black-framed glasses, and a slouchy summer dress. She appeared to be on her way out, a red knapsack over one arm and white earphones plugged into both ears, from a wire that went into her dress pocket. "We're closed for the day," she said, wearily.

"I work in accounting," Eric said, since she appeared not to recognize him. He had never seen her before, but her employee ID lanyard was around her neck, with the name Julia Meehan. "I'm wondering if you could help me with something, Julia."

"Not now, I gotta make my train."

"Please, it's really important and I have to get it done by to-night, but I forgot about it. It won't take that long." Eric pressed his way into the office, and Julia stepped backwards with a heavy sigh, setting her backpack on the floor and unplugging one of her earbuds.

"Okay, whatever."

"Thanks, I really appreciate it. We had a patient, Virginia Teichner, who was admitted a few months ago for heart issues. She was discharged after a few days, but recently passed away."

"That's sad."

"Yes, it is. Her file was accessed twice after her discharge. It's kind of unusual, and we're worried it might be a mistake. As you know, the log-in sheet in the file shows the codes for the IDs but not the names of the employees. We need to know their names so we can follow up, then make sure their time and treatment gets properly billed."

Julia nodded. "Okay, no problem. Obviously, I can't tell you which employee has which encoded identity, but I can give you the names of the employees who accessed the file after discharge."

"That would be great."

"I'll take a minute to get that, but it's easy. What's the patient's name again?" Julia went to the middle cubicle against the wall, which was decorated with My Little Pony posters, presumably iron-ically.

"Virginia Teichner," Eric answered, spelling the last name.

"This will just be a minute." Julia woke up her computer, and the monitor came to life with a My Little Pony screensaver, a speck-led white pony with a flowing purple mane. She typed in her pass-word, which showed as a line of ten asterisks, then started typing so quickly that it sounded like raindrops on a rooftop. "Please, don't look at my screen."

"Sorry, I'm just in a hurry." Eric turned away.

Suddenly the typing stopped. The room went completely quiet.

"Did you find it?" Eric asked, turning around.

"Who are you?" Julia's eyes had gone round with fear.

"What's the matter?"

"There's an alert with your photo in my email. I'm calling security."

"No, please," Eric said, but Julia was already reaching in her pocket for her cell phone.

He turned around, tore open the door, and bolted out.

Chapter Fifty-seven

Eric hurried down the hallway, his thoughts racing. If he couldn't find out from IT who had accessed the file, then the second best thing was to go to Cardiology and try to find out what had happened during Virginia's admission. The last admission wasn't that long ago, so somebody had to remember Virginia and Max, especially given what Max had done at the mall last night. He jogged past the framed landscapes.

He was about to take the stairwell but kept going, bypassing it. Fewer people worked on the basement level and he could run into the new wing of the hospital, which housed the Cardiology Department, and take the stairs from there. The security office was in the older wing, only one floor up, and the security guards would already be on their way down to IT, so he was running away from them. He ran down one hallway, then the next, passing rooms that contained the storage and the hospital's computer servers. He'd never been on this floor before.

The carpeting ended in glistening tile, and he knew he was headed toward the morgue. He kept going, spotting its stainless-steel double doors on his right. One was opening, and a morgue employee in blue scrubs emerged. Eric caught a whiff of the distinctive formaldehyde odor, then took a left turn down the hall and passed the pathology lab. A young lab technician came walking in the opposite direction, reading on his smartphone, but Eric kept his head down, jogged lightly by him, and reached the stairwell, where he went through the door.

He raced up the stairs, passing the first floor, then the second, nervous as he approached the doorway for the third. He anticipated being recognized in Cardiology because he'd been there for consults many times, since depression and anxiety were prevalent in heart patients. He didn't know how he'd deal with it, he'd have to play it by ear.

He reached the third-floor landing, opened the door, and took a left. He strode down the glistening hallway, trying to act as normal as possible as he passed into Cardiology. The hallway was empty except for a tall rolling food cart; the dinner service had begun. The nurses' station was on the left, with two nurses on computers behind the counter, and he recognized one of them, a slim, young African-American woman, Patty Allen. Patty had a lovely face, with a slight up-tilt to her eyes, and she wore her hair smoothed into a thick braid.

"Hi, Patty," Eric said, arranging his face into a professional mask as he walked to the counter.

"Dr. Parrish?" Patty looked up from her computer, and her broad smile showed that she hadn't seen the security alert yet. "Oh my goodness, that was incredible, what you did last night at the mall. I was so worried about you! How did that happen? Was that boy a patient of yours?"

"Actually, that's what I came to see you about." Eric slid his phone from his pocket, mindful that the other nurse, whom he hadn't met, was eyeing him warily. "His name is Max Jakubowski, and his grandmother, Virginia Teichner, was admitted here for three days, about two months ago. She had congestive heart failure, and he came with her. That's according to Dr. Brexler's notes in the file, and it makes sense to me. Max was her caretaker until she passed away last week."

"Okay." Patty blinked. "How can I help you?"

"Do you remember him at all, Max and his grandmother? She was in her nineties, very nice, and he's a seventeen-year-old boy. He's the one you saw on the news last night."

"No way. He was *here*?" Patty's eyes widened. "Do you know which room she was in? My patients are usually on this hallway. We've been shorthanded since Sheila went on maternity leave, so I keep close to the station because I cover the phones."

"Dr. Brexler was the grandmother's treating physician, but I know he's gone for the day." Eric remembered the other names of the people on the treatment team. "The resident was Sara Stone. Is she around?"

"She left for the day, too."

"The nurse assigned was Caleb Martieki."

"Caleb's out sick today."

"The social worker was Martha Girandole."

"She's on vacation. She's due back on Monday."

"Hmm," Eric said, temporarily stumped. He felt the disapproving eyes of the other nurse on him. "I guess I can get their cell phones from you, but here's my problem. When I look at the file, Dr. Brexler made notes that Max was depressed and needed a consult from psychiatry, but I never got a call for a consult. Do you know what happened?"

"No, I don't. A consult on a visitor, not a patient? That would be kind of unusual."

"Yes, it would. That's why I think somebody would remember it or there would be a note in the file. Do you think anybody else on the floor would know?"

"I know," the other nurse interjected, her tone chilly. She looked middle-aged, with her dark hair cut in a no-nonsense short style and a slim build, like a runner. Her employee ID lanyard read Nancy, and she folded her arms as she spoke. "They were in 308, on the other side. I don't remember the boy, but I remember the grandmother."

"Oh good."

"I think there was a psych consult. I heard that someone came down from Wright. I thought it was for the grandmother, but it could've been for the grandson."

"There *was* a psych consult?" Eric repeated, surprised. "Who came down?"

"I don't know. I wasn't here. I remember the boy visited at night. I only saw him once, when I was on my way out."

"But all my people know that they have to make a note in the file, regarding any consultation. Even if Max wasn't technically the patient, it should've been in Virginia's file."

Nancy frowned. "Dr. Parrish, why are you asking us these questions? You're not supposed to be in the hospital. We got an alert about you. We're supposed to call security if we see you on campus."

Patty recoiled. "Really?"

"Please, don't, but this is important." Eric turned to Patty. "Patty, do you have Dr. Brexler's cell phone handy?"

"Well, uh, sure, it's 610—"

"Patty, don't tell him," Nancy interrupted. "Dr. Parrish, you're putting us in a terrible position. We shouldn't even be talking to you, much less giving you patient information. I don't feel comfortable with this. I'm going to call security."

"No, please, don't." Eric edged away, as Nancy picked up the phone.

"Hello, Operator? Can you connect me to security?"

But Eric was already on the run, heading for Wright.

Chapter Fifty-eight

Eric ran down the hallway, burst into the stairwell, and climbed the stairs as fast as he could. He was running out of time. Security could predict where he was heading, especially if Julia from IT had called them, followed by Nancy. He had to get to the psych unit ahead of them. He didn't know if he'd get another chance, and an urgency he couldn't parse drove him. He didn't understand what was going on, but he had a bad feeling.

He put two-and-two together, hurrying up the stairs. If a psych consult for Max had taken place but wasn't in the file, then somebody could have accessed the file to delete the reference. Eric didn't know why one of his people would hide the fact that they'd been consulted for Max, but he was going to find out. He reached the fourth-floor landing, and suddenly a fire alarm went off. The ear-splitting siren reverberated in the concrete stairwell.

Eric's brain defaulted into Chief mode, ticking off the procedures during a fire alarm, which affected the psych unit differently from other services. When a fire alarm went off, they were to listen to its location on the loudspeaker. If the alarm area was away from the psych unit, they did nothing except wait for an all-clear. Patients weren't evacuated from the psych unit, even for a drill, because of their tenuous mental states or their dangerousness, unless the fire took place on the unit itself. An HGH fire team responded to every pulled fire alarm with extinguishers and called the fire department if there was an actual fire.

The loudspeaker blared, "Code Red, Wright Wing. Code Red, Wright Wing."

Eric felt his heart seize at the words. They meant there was a fire on the psych unit. He raced up the stairs, mentally rehearsing the procedure, which he'd been through only one time. In the event of a fire on his unit, it would be all hands on deck, every staff member utilized to evacuate patients and minimize upset to them. The staff would release any restrained patients from their beds and put them in soft restraints that held their arms around their waists. A staff member would be assigned to accompany any patient in soft restraints and make sure he didn't harm himself or anybody else during the evacuation. Eric prayed the only patient under restraint was Perino.

The loudspeaker kept blaring, "Code Red, Wright Wing. Code Red, Wright Wing."

Eric reached the fifth floor, flew through the door, and tried to see what was going on at the unit, but employees from other services congested the hallway, talking excitedly. The air smelled like something burning. A silty blackness was beginning to filter through the air. The ceiling sprinklers would probably turn on any minute. The HGH fire team would arrive with extinguishers.

"Everybody!" Eric forced his way through the crowd. "Please get back to your work area! You need to make room for the fire team!"

"Hey, it's Dr. Parrish!" somebody called back, and the crowd burst into chatter. "We saw you at the mall last night!" "Dr. Parrish!" "We're here to help!" "Tell us what to do!" "Can we help, Dr. Parrish?"

"I know you're trying to help, but please get back! This is too dangerous, get back!"

Eric felt relieved to see nurses and patients from his unit, looking dazed and wet, already evacuated into the hallway, off to the side. He acknowledged them with a quick nod, then threaded his way to the door. Inside the psych unit, smoke clouded the air with blackish haze. Ceiling sprinklers in the entrance hall had switched on, spraying water.

"Amaka!" Eric called, as she was coming out of the airlock, escorting an anxious Mrs. Jelik through the exterior door. Tina was on their heels with Mr. Jacobs, an aging depressive who looked dazed and frightened.

"Eric, thank God!" Amaka cried, her nerves under shaky control. "We didn't wait for the alarm. Sam ordered everybody to evacuate. I don't know where Jack is. David's trying to put out the fire, it's in the kitchen. God knows how it started."

"Okay, just keep going, get everybody out of the unit." Eric helped Amaka and Mrs. Jelik into the hallway, then Tina and Mr. Jacobs. "Brief me. You're evacuating patients from the north side?"

"Yes, we're almost finished."

"Great job." Eric knew that most of the unit's patients were on the north hallway, while the south contained conference rooms, the offices, the kitchen, and the smoking patio, with one patient room reserved for belligerent or dangerous patients like Perino. "What about Perino? Is Sam getting him into soft restraints?"

"Yes, I think so, but I was on the north side, so I don't know for sure."

"Nobody else is in restraints, right? Nobody new came in while I was away, did they?"

"No."

"Okay, go. See you later!" Eric hurried into the unit. Cold water poured from the ceiling like rain. The staff hustled remaining patients to the exit, their hair and clothes drenched, some rolling IV bags. "Great job, everybody! Who's left inside?"

"This is the last of 'em!" one of the nurses called back, smiling gamely despite her dripping hair. "Everybody's out but Perino!"

Eric hurried into the south hallway, asking another nurse, "Where's Sam and Perino?"

"Perino's room!" she answered, coughing.

"What about David and Jack?"

"David's in the kitchen, putting out the fire!" shouted another nurse behind her, escorting Leah Barry, The Ghost. "I don't know where Jack is!"

Eric darted down the south hallway. Smoke billowed from the kitchen on the left side of the hall, filling the corridor in front of his office. Orange flames raged from the microwave and trash, but Jack and David were nowhere in sight. Eric's office door was open, which was odd, and he looked inside. He could barely see anything for the water raining on the thickening smoke. He thought he heard a strange gurgling noise near his desk.

He ducked inside to see what it was, but the sight was so shocking and horrific it took a moment to register. Kristine was lying on the rug, her throat cut open, grotesquely. She was still alive, her gaze moving sightlessly around the room. Blood geysered from the gash on her neck, soaking her chest and shoulders. Blood bubbled from her mouth. Water poured onto her face and body. Her hands lay at her sides.

Eric rushed to Kristine and knelt at her side. Instinctively he covered her wound with his left hand, trying to stop the flow of blood, while he got his phone with his right hand, and pressed Redial to call Laurie directly. "Laurie!" he said, as soon he heard a click. "Get up to my unit! I got a kid with her throat cut."

"Oh my God! Cover the wound with your hand! We're on our way!"

"Hurry!" Eric hung up the phone, tossed it aside, and used both hands to cover Kristine's neck wound, leaning over her. Her warm lifeblood filled his palms. He could feel her pulse, only faintly. Eric didn't know how this had happened or who had done it. He was reeling, stunned. It had to be Perino.

"Eric . . . ?" Kristine whispered faintly.

"Yes, it's Eric. Hang in there. Help is on the way." Eric could feel air rushing through her windpipe and her blood bubbling against his palm.

"I'm sorry . . . what I did to you . . ."

"It's okay, Kristine, it's okay." Eric knew she meant the harassment claim, but that didn't matter anymore. Her lifeblood leaked through his very fingers. He could feel her breath wetly against his palm, with every syllable she spoke.

"He's . . . evil . . ."

"Who's evil? Who did this? Perino?" Eric leaned close to her mouth to hear her answer.

But in the next moment, he felt a stunning blow to the back of his head. Pain arced through his skull.

And the world went black.

Chapter Fifty-nine

Eric woke up on his back, being dragged quickly by his feet, sliding along the wet floor of the hallway. He struggled to think, foggy from the head blow. Smoke billowed everywhere. Water poured on his face. He coughed and sputtered. He couldn't stay conscious long enough to see who was dragging him. It had to be Perino. Oddly, his head didn't hurt.

Eric didn't know where Sam, David, or Jack were. Kristine would bleed to death. He didn't know what was going on. Somebody was dragging him away, fast. He couldn't remain conscious. He felt snowed under, as if he'd been drugged. If it was a drug, he'd been injected with it. Perino couldn't do that.

Eric felt a bolt of terror. It had to be one of his own people. He tried to fight back, save himself. Tried to struggle, get up, or run away, but he couldn't. He was too weak. He heard the HGH fire team shouting at the other end of the hall. The floor vibrated with their footsteps. They wouldn't see him this far, past the smoke. They'd stop at the kitchen and put out the fire.

Eric was dragged past Perino's room and heard him sobbing, "Please, untie me. Untie me, I can't breathe."

Suddenly, Perino's door closed. The man dragging Eric called out, "All clear back here! Everybody's evacuated back here!"

Eric felt shocked, despite the drug haze. The voice was Sam's.

Eric struggled to put the pieces together. Sam was the one who had hit him. Sam was the one who had killed Kristine. Sam was dragging him out to the patio. Sam was going to kill him.

Eric felt a whoosh of warm fresh air. The patio door opened as he was pulled outside. He felt sun on his face. Warm wind whirled around him. The patio was a concrete balcony, surrounded by a wall, four feet high.

Eric tried to twist away but couldn't. He opened his eyes but couldn't stay conscious. His back scraped against the rough concrete as he was dragged to the wall. His brain struggled to function.

Sam had killed Kristine in his office. Sam was framing him for her murder, the motive would have been revenge for the harassment claim. Sam was taking him to the wall. Sam was going to throw him off the building. Sam was going to make it look like he'd committed suicide. The HGH fire team wouldn't see them until it was too late.

"Sam . . . why?" Eric could barely speak. Terror crept over him. He tried to save himself but couldn't control his limbs. His head bumped against the wall.

"I'm sick of being your bitch. I want to be Chief and I don't want to wait. I want the Pharmacy Review Board. *I* want a house on *Myrtle Beach.*"

"No . . ." Eric felt himself hoisted bodily upward under his arms. He tried to defend himself but could only flail.

"That's the morphine. They'll find it on your tox scan. The Physician Impairment Committee won't be surprised." Eric heard Sam grunt with effort as he tried to lift him up. "I set you up from the beginning. I've known Max since the grandmother's hospitalization, when Brexler called me. I worked Max to bring his grandmother into the ED. I knew you'd get called on the consult and take the bait. You always were a soft touch, especially for kids."

"No . . . please." Eric grasped at the wall's edge but his fingers wouldn't close. Still, he couldn't give up. He thought of Hannah. She needed him. He loved her, above all else. He couldn't die.

"I've been working Max all along. I knew he'd tell you about

Renée. I knew he'd break when the grandmother died." Sam shoved Eric onto the ledge, so the top of his body flopped over the wall. "He drunk dialed me after he called you that night. I met him and slipped him Rohypnol. He played right into my hands. He would never kill Renée. He doesn't have the balls. I killed Renée, to ruin you."

Eric faced down, in horror. The sidewalk was five stories from here. People were walking back and forth to the hospital. Eric felt Sam's hands grip his shoulders. Sam was about to throw him off the wall. Eric tried to grab on to him but missed. He would fall to his death.

"Good-bye, Eric."

Chapter Sixty

Suddenly, Eric felt Sam release his shoulders and heard Perino raging on the patio.

"Dr. Ward, stop!" Perino bellowed. "You have to stop! No, stop!"

Eric turned to see what was going on, but almost fell off the wall. He tried to hug it with useless arms as he watched Perino come running onto the patio, trailing his broken restraints.

"Dr. Ward!" Perino charged at Sam, grimacing in fury, his beefy arms outstretched. "You have to be stopped! This is over, here and now!"

"No, don't! Don't!" Sam raised his hands.

"You're evil, Dr. Ward!" Perino lunged at Sam, grabbed him by the shoulders, wrenched him off his feet, and sent him crashing into the small metal table and chairs where he landed on his back like a broken doll.

Eric watched the explosive violence in horror, his emotions in turmoil. He still couldn't believe that Sam had been trying to kill him. Still he didn't want Perino to murder Sam before his very eyes, but he was powerless to interfere, stop Perino, or even move his limbs.

"You're a bad doctor! You gave me those pills! I feel worse after them, not better!" Perino went after Sam, who scrambled, terrified, to his feet, his head bloodied and his blue eyes wide with fright.

"Don, no!" Sam picked up the metal chair and brandished it at Perino, keeping the raging man at a distance. "Don, don't blame me, blame Dr. Parrish! Dr. Parrish made me give you those pills! He told me to do it! Go get him! That's why I was trying to kill him! For you!"

"I don't believe you! You're a liar!" Perino grabbed the leg of the chair that Sam was holding and whipped it hard, wrenching it from Sam's grasp and throwing it aside. "You lie all the time!"

"No, don't . . ." Eric watched, terrified, as Sam leaned backwards over the wall. He summoned all of his energy to fight the druggy cloud in his brain and hang onto the wall.

"Don, I'm sorry!" Sam put up his hands, panicking. He kept backing up, edging toward the wall, desperate to save his own life. "I won't do it anymore, I promise! No more pills! I swear!"

"I don't believe you!" Perino cocked his fist and was about to punch Sam, when there was a shout at the door.

"Everybody, freeze!" shouted a security guard, drawing his weapon. "Freeze right there!" Two other security guards rushed onto the patio behind him. Smoke wafted through the open door.

"Don't shoot!" Perino raised his hands, but Sam wobbled backwards, caught dangerously off-balance.

"No! No!" Sam cried out in abject fear, but in the next awful moment, he began to topple over the wall and over the side of the building, his hands grasping and clawing at thin air.

"Dr. Ward!" Perino lunged to grab Sam before he fell, but it was too late.

"No!" Eric felt agonized tears spring to his eyes as Sam tumbled over the side of the building, screaming all the way down.

Then Eric squeezed his eyes shut.

He couldn't bear to see any more.

Chapter Sixty-one

Eric lay in a hospital bed in the ED examining room, coming back to his senses thanks to Narcan, an inhalant that directly blocked the effect of morphine, usually given to patients who were overdosing. He had a plastic clip on his finger to monitor his vitals and an IV port on his hand for a saline drip. He was still dressed in his clothes, damp from the sprinklers, and his shirt and hands were covered with Kristine's blood, which hadn't been completely washed away. Kristine was in surgery, and Eric didn't know how she was doing. He sent up a silent prayer for her recovery.

He closed his eyes against the harsh fluorescent lighting, trying to chase from his mind the image of Kristine bleeding on the office floor, her throat a crimson gash. He could hear the police, hospital administrators, and Laurie talking in low tones outside the examining room. Paul was on his way to HGH, having instructed Eric not to speak to the police without him. The chances of that were slim to none, anyway. Eric couldn't tell the police what had happened before he'd had time to process it himself.

Eric let it sink in that Sam had tried to kill Kristine, as well as the fact that Sam had actually been the one who had killed Renée. On the way down to the ED, Eric had told the police that Sam had admitted that he, and not Max, had murdered Renée, and they had promised him they'd tell the Radnor Police and Max's attorney. Eric remembered that first night, when he had met Max and his grandmother, and it struck him that he was now in the very same examining room, so matters had come to a full, horrifying circle.

He kept his eyes closed, feeling the loss of Max's grandmother, as well as Renée and Kristine. It broke his heart to lose Sam, so horribly. So much violence, so much death. He flashed on Perino, trying to save Sam's life at the last minute, which would take a toll on the man's already fragile emotional state. Eric would have to study his file and follow up on Perino's beliefs that Sam had been giving him pills that made him worse, not better. It was completely possible that Sam had manipulated and used Perino the same way that he'd manipulated and used Max.

Eric shuddered, inwardly, to his very marrow. He would be replaying in his mind for a long time how he had put so much trust in Sam, which had been so profoundly misplaced. Eric knew as a psychiatrist that so many of us wore masks, showing one face to the world when our psyche was much different, so he should have known better. He realized he had a mask of his own, perhaps one that he had been wearing too long. The mask of the perfect Chief, who was number two and perennially trying harder. The mask of the perfect father, who protected his daughter too much. The mask of the perfect husband, who simply hadn't been the man his wife wanted, in the end. Maybe it was time to let all the masks drop and to see what was really beneath them. When this was all over, maybe he'd call Arthur and get a refresher course.

Eric felt his eyes film, and although he didn't understand exactly why, he didn't try to analyze his emotions. The only thing he knew for sure was the purity of the love he had for Hannah, and his heart felt light that he had cleared his name, not only for his sake, but for hers. His daughter, her friends, and the other kids at school wouldn't think he had murdered anyone. He could go back to being a psychiatrist and a father, however imperfect. He would still think too highly of people he cared for, like Sam, and maybe even Caitlin. For him, love would always be blind, at least in the beginning. That couldn't be helped, nor should it be. He was a human being, after all.

"Hey." Laurie peeked around the patterned curtain. "May I come in?"

"Sure." Eric smiled, happy to see her, and Laurie smiled back, walking over to the bed.

"How are you feeling?"

"Better."

"The police are waiting until you feel well enough to make a statement, but I told them to cool their jets."

"Thanks."

"In the good-news department, it looks like Kristine is going to make it, two transfusions later. We got to her just in time."

"Great." Eric felt relief and gratitude wash over him.

"In a final irony, her blood is AB negative, which is rare, and we ran out. Guess who had to give her a bag?" Laurie made a face, screwing up her nose adorably.

"*You?*"

"Yes. Don't think it was easy."

Eric laughed. It felt good. "How's my unit? A wreck?"

"Getting cleaned up, but everybody's calming down. Amaka's in charge."

"Thank God. And Perino, how's he?"

"Down the hall, doing fine. His wife isn't happy."

"I'm sure not." Eric couldn't think about it now. "Where were my other attendings, during the fire? David and Jack?"

"David passed out trying to put out the fire. Turns out he has asthma. Jack was in Endocrinology, chatting up some nurse." Laurie picked up his hand lightly, her fingers around his wrist. "Meanwhile, I'm here in a professional capacity, as your ED doc."

"Are you taking my pulse?"

"Not exactly." Laurie smiled.

"Then you're holding my hand."

Laurie smiled, wider. "You kissed me that night at the mall, in the car."

"That was your imagination. The whole thing, it was a fantasy of yours. It didn't really happen. I didn't run into the mall, either. Who would do something that stupid? Not me, I'm the Chief."

"You're talkative, you know that?" Laurie leaned over and kissed him on the lips, once, then again, softly.

"Wow," Eric said, feeling a stirring in his heart that he hadn't felt in a long time.

Laurie straightened up, smiling sweetly. A dark curl fell over her eye, freeing itself from her pencil topknot. "You like my bedside manner?"

"Don't get ahead of yourself."

"Ha!" Laurie's expression changed, growing serious. "Well, I suppose I should say you were right, and I'm glad of it. You believed in Max a lot more than I did, but he didn't kill that girl. So happy ending, right? Kind of?"

"Kind of." Eric felt a pain in his chest. "It's just awful that Renée was murdered, so young, and for such a stupid reason. As if any reason could justify murder."

"Why did Sam do it, again?"

"He wanted to be me. More accurately, he wanted what he perceived I had. He wanted the applause, and really, he wanted the money." Eric thought back to what Sam had said on the patio. "I'm going to talk to the powers that be and tell them to investigate Brexler on the Pharmacy Review Board. If that jerk is getting kickbacks from the drug companies and that's how he built that damn Myrtle Beach house, I want him in *jail*. Enough with the gossip. It's criminally actionable and I'm not going to tolerate it anymore."

"You're a changed man." Laurie smiled, proudly.

"You're damn right I am."

"Then I'm with you." Laurie bent over and kissed him again. "How about dinner tomorrow night, after work? I owe you a gin and tonic."

"Your place?"

"Perfect." Laurie smiled at him again, just as the patterned curtain was moved to the side and they both turned to see Paul sticking his head into the examining room, looking from Laurie to Eric with a slowly spreading grin.

"When's the wedding, kids?" Paul asked, in delight.

Chapter Sixty-two

Eric spent the next two hours in the conference room on the executive floor, meeting with Captain Newmire, Detective Rhoades, and the assistant district attorney. He'd changed into another set of generic sweats from Paul and had told them everything that had happened, from when he found the omissions in Virginia's medical file to the horrifying fight on the patio. They asked detailed questions, which he answered as completely as possible, subject to objections from Paul, who never let the authorities get anywhere near the issue of confidentiality. Sitting to his left during the questioning was Mike from Legal, and beside him Tom and Brad, all of whom listened quietly and took notes, but asked no questions.

When that was finally over, Eric still had a question. He turned to Detective Rhoades. "Now that you know Max is innocent of Renée's murder, what happens?"

"It's not quite that easy. We'll follow up on your statement, investigate, and touch base with his lawyer, to see if they will cooperate and give us an interview. Obviously, it isn't enough to rely on what you said, though that's no reflection on your credibility, but rather on the credibility of Sam Ward."

Eric winced at the mention of Sam's name. It was still so hard to believe that Sam was gone, having died such an awful death, and Eric was still wrapping his mind around the fact that Sam had tried to murder Kristine and sabotaged Perino's health, much less betrayed their friendship. Eric knew it would take some time to sort out his conflicted feelings, but at bottom, he felt raw and aching, the pain of loss and grief.

"Max still has to deal with criminal charges stemming from the hostage-taking at the mall. That will be a matter not for us, but for the Upper Merion Police and Captain Newmire." Detective Rhoades nodded in Captain Newmire's direction. "Would you like to address that?"

Captain Newmire cleared his throat. "Dr. Parrish, I'll have to discuss it with the assistant district attorney, who will discuss it with the district attorney."

Eric thought it sounded like law-enforcement buck-passing, but every institution had its own bureaucracy, whether they wore badges or white coats. "Where is Max now?"

"Max is being moved to one of the local mental health facilities for evaluation and treatment."

"Which facility?" Eric felt Paul kick him under the table, but he was beyond worrying about that anymore.

"I'm unsure, at this juncture." Detective Rhoades glanced at Captain Newmire, who was already getting up, getting his notes in order, and slipping his ballpoint pen into his pocket. "I think we're finished here, though we'll have to ask you to remain within jurisdiction."

"What, why?" Eric asked, surprised.

Detective Rhoades frowned. "Just until we've investigated your statement, Dr. Parrish."

"Fine." Eric read between the lines, that was just a matter of time.

Paul shook his head. "Don't make me sorry we played ball with you, Detective. I'm not out of ammunition yet and I can still do you damage in the press, especially after today."

Detective Rhoades stood up heavily, picking up his pad and slipping it inside his sport jacket. "Gentlemen, thank you very much. We'll be in touch."

Mike sprang to his wingtips. "Officers, let me show you out."

"Thank you." Detective Rhoades crossed to the door with Captain Newmire and the assistant district attorney. They said their good-byes, then left, and Eric could hear Dee Dee outside, offering to take them to the elevator.

Mike came back into the room and closed the door behind him. "Eric, we need to talk."

"I'll say."

"Allow me, please." Mike glanced at Brad and Tom as he returned to the conference table, pulled out his chair, and sat back down opposite Eric and Paul. "I know I speak for Brad, Tom, and the entire PhilaHealth Partnership and HGH family when I say that we appreciate your efforts—"

"Enough." Eric held up a hand. He couldn't hear another word that sounded like an employee manual. "First, I want to be reinstated as Chief immediately. It should be obvious by now that Kristine's sexual harassment claim was bogus. She did it at Sam's behest, probably for a recommendation, and you can verify that with her when she's well enough. I want you to issue a press release immediately, and I'll start back to work tomorrow, to keep some semblance of continuity for the patients and clean up the unit."

Mike blinked, flustered. "Uh . . ."

Tom nodded. "Done," he answered simply.

"Second, I'm concerned about any drugs Sam may or may not have been giving Donald Perino while he was treating him and—"

Mike interjected nervously, "I'm sure Mrs. Perino will file suit."

Eric let it go. "Lawsuit or no, it's important for the integrity of my unit, and the hospital, that we apppoint an independent investigator to look into this matter. I would do it myself, but I think that will raise the question of a conflict of interest."

Paul added, "You want to avoid even the appearance of impropriety."

"Right." Eric nodded at Paul, then turned to Mike, Tom, and Brad. "I don't want to pull any punches on this investigation. We have to have somebody look at it with a hard eye and let the chips fall. If Sam did anything to harm Perino's care, I want to know about it, even if I'm held responsible as his boss and even if the hospital is held responsible as his employer."

Mike's eyes flared. "As a legal matter, any such acts or wrongdoing by Sam would be criminally negligent acts and outside the scope of employment, and therefore the hospital would not be liable. You have the most to lose, Eric, in the event of a lawsuit by Mrs. Perino. I'm sure her attorneys would argue that you were negligent in your supervision of Sam and—"

"Stop." Eric held up a hand again, shifting his attention to Tom. "Do I have your word on that? We start an independent investigation?"

"Yes." Tom nodded. "We would order such an investigation, given the potential liability of the system as a whole. The last thing the PhilaHealth Partnership desires is to allow any such wrongdoing to taint our reputation for patient care. As you know, I'm a surgeon. If we need to cut, I'm not afraid to cut."

"Good." Eric read between the lines, hearing that he might have to take the fall for Sam, but be that as it may. He knew now that if he got fired, he would survive. He'd certainly been through worse.

Tom cleared his throat. "Then we agree. It's my hope that we will weather the storm, no matter if Mrs. Perino files suit, and that you wouldn't be liable for any negligence, especially given your number-two ranking, which we are about to roll out and—"

"No rolling," Eric cut him off. "Stop the rolling."

Paul chuckled. "You mean slow your roll."

Eric smiled. "I do. How did you know that?"

"I might be in love with you."

Eric faced Tom, his smile fading fast. "Third, you need to send a letter to *U.S. Medical Report* telling them that we withdraw the HGH psychiatry service from the ranking. Given this debacle, with patient care so grievously compromised, we cannot go forward and accept that ranking. I will not go in front of any camera, smile, or make any speech."

Mike gasped. "Eric, really?"

Tom frowned. "Eric, think about what you're saying."

Brad looked at Eric like he was crazy. "You can't mean this. You've been through hell today, this past week. You're under enormous stress. We apologize for the role we may have played in that, however inadvertent, because we were completely misled by that young girl—"

"Stop." Eric shook his head. "Kristine was a victim. She was Sam's victim as much as Renée Bevilacqua. I'm not going to play ball with the ranking. I suggest you withdraw us before it becomes public, then nobody will be the wiser." Eric paused, thinking clearly. "And I promise you this—next year, we'll *earn* that ranking. And it won't be number two. It'll be number *one*."

Tom and Brad exchanged glances, and Mike clammed up.

Paul interjected, "Eric, I do, I love you."

Eric ignored him. "Last point." He turned away from Mike, to Tom and Brad. "I want an independent investigation, by outside counsel, of Morris Brexler and any financial misconduct he may have been engaged in on the Pharmacy Review Board. We've heard the rumors about him taking kickbacks to promote certain drugs, most recently, Rostatin. You don't need me to tell you that there's corruption in our profession, from which drugs get approved by the FDA down to what gets carried in the hospitals, and what's given as 'free samples.' I'm not content to turn a blind eye to my suspicions any longer. I want to do something about it. At the same time, nobody knows better than I do that it's unjust to be wrongly accused. If Morris is taking some kind of kickbacks, we need to stop him and punish him. If he's not, we need to clear him."

Brad, Tom, and Mike fell momentarily speechless.

"Well?" Eric said, coolly.

Tom answered, "You're asking a lot, Eric."

"It's about damn time, isn't it?"

"We'll take it under consideration."

"You'll see the wisdom of my suggestion, or the press will." Eric glanced at Paul, slyly, then back to Brad, Tom, and Mike. "Did you know that Harry Truman never said, 'Give 'em hell'? He said, 'I never said give 'em hell, I told the truth and they thought it was hell.' Now, boys, take care. I'm going home."

Eric rose, and so did Paul, almost in unison. They walked to the door, and it struck Eric that the last time he was in this room, he'd been asked to pee in a cup.

He left without another word.

Chapter Sixty-three

It was dark by the time Eric left the hospital parking lot, holding up his hand against the camera flashes and klieglights of the media, which were being held back by HGH security guards. The local TV was already running the story of Sam's grisly death on a continuous loop; Eric had shut off the examining-room TV when the breaking news banner had come on, HORROR AT HGH.

He accelerated until he left the hospital campus and noticed a few news vans in his rearview mirror, so he turned right, then left, trying to lose them. It didn't work, and he stopped trying. They had his home address already, and he had something more important he wanted to do.

He stopped at a traffic light, slid his phone from his pocket, and dialed Caitlin's cell number, so he could speak to Hannah. The dashboard clock read 10:23, but he still wanted to give it a shot. The phone rang a few times, then went to voicemail, so he hung up. He tried the house number, and it rang and rang, then went to voicemail, too. He hung up, and the traffic light turned green, so he drove forward, vaguely defeated. He'd wanted to talk to Hannah to let her know that he was okay, but at a deeper level, he knew that he wanted to hear her voice.

Eric set his phone aside, drove home on autopilot, and turned onto his street without even realizing how he'd gotten there. A line of parked cars, news vans, and reporters thronged in front of his house, but he cruised past, turned into the driveway, cut the ignition and got out of the car, tuning out their shouted questions as he jogged down the driveway to his office entrance.

He shut the door, finally exhaling and looking around at the books and papers scattered all over the rug and the empty space on his desk, where his computer used to be.

He walked through the office, entered the house, and went almost reflexively to the kitchen, where he opened the refrigerator door and got out a beer. He reached into the silverware drawer, left open by the police, rummaged around for the church key, popped the top off the bottle, and took a cold slug. The beer was chilly and delicious, and his gaze traveled over the open drawers, pots and pans on the butcher-block countertops, and the weird black smudges of fingerprint dust.

Eric wanted to put it all behind him, and there was no time like the present. He took another tug of beer, set the bottle down, and started putting things away, returning the colander, pots, and frying pans to the base cabinets, closing the silverware and utensils drawers. He shut the freezer door and took another sip of beer, then crossed to the sink, wet a sponge under the faucet, and tried to scrub off the fingerprint dust. He found himself getting a second wind, somehow feeling that if he could clean up his house, he could put the pieces of his life back together.

The reporters out front kept up a constant noise level, but he screened them out, fetching the dishwashing liquid and squirting a green squiggle onto the fingerprint dust, then scrubbing and rinsing until he got the first patch of clean. He was about to start on the second, when he heard some knocking coming from the door to his home office. He threw down the sponge, cranky that the reporters were getting aggressive, and he stalked back down the hallway and into his home office to confront them.

"You guys have a lot of nerve," Eric said, opening the door, and there on the step stood Caitlin, with Hannah.

"Daddy!" Hannah cried, raising her arms.

"Honey!" Eric shouted with happiness, scooping her up and burying his head in her warm neck.

And suddenly, his world felt complete.

Chapter Sixty-four

"I'd offer you something to drink, but you see how it is. Want some water?" Eric gestured self-consciously at the kitchen, unable to hide his surprise at Caitlin's being here with Hannah.

"That's okay, no worries." Caitlin forced a smile, eyeing the debris. "Love what you've done with the place."

"How did you know I'd be home?"

"I heard they were finished questioning you."

"Oh. Well, good to see you." Eric felt so awkward, standing near Caitlin in a kitchen that wasn't theirs, turned upside down. It didn't help that she looked great, in a white T-shirt, cutoffs, and pink sneakers, with her hair in a ponytail. She even had her glasses on, a look he particularly liked, an older version of Hannah. They were even dressed the same.

Hannah bopped into the living room. "Daddy, your house is so messy! You need to clean up!"

"I know, you're right," Eric said lightly, without elaborating. "That's what I was doing when you guys came here. What a nice surprise, and on a school night."

Caitlin motioned vaguely, at nothing. "We saw the news, and I thought it would be a good thing for Hannah to see you face-to-face, not just talk on the phone. She was worried about you."

"Wow, thank you," Eric said, touched. "Sorry about the reporters."

"Par for the course. So you're okay, that's all that matters. It must be some story, but I'll have to hear it another time."

"Right, yeah."

"Weird about Sam. I'm sorry, though. I know you liked him."

"Thanks." Eric felt at a sudden loss for words, glancing over at Hannah, who was gathering books that had been tossed onto the floor and shelving them. "Hannah, you're cleaning up for me over there? Thank you very much!"

"Daddy, it's like you had an earthquake!"

"I know!" Eric called back, managing a smile as he turned to Caitlin. "It's late, you guys must be so tired."

"I figured she could go in late tomorrow, if she wants. Maybe sleep in."

"Right, great idea." Eric hid his surprise, since it was so unlike Caitlin to bend any rules.

"Anyway, I knew that, uh, your place might be a mess, so I figured that if you wanted to, you could come stay at the house tonight." Caitlin shot him a look. "Don't get the wrong idea. I'm going to stay at Brian's."

"The wrong idea? Perish the thought." Eric forced a smile. He had gotten the wrong idea, but a part of him wasn't so sure it was the right idea anymore, and in any event, it wasn't her idea.

"You and Hannah can have breakfast together, then you can take her to school." Caitlin reached in her back pocket and took out her key ring, a silver disk with the scales of justice, which he'd given her a few years ago. She unclipped the ring, slid out the key, and handed it to him. "Here."

"Thanks." Eric accepted the key. "When I'm finished with it, I'll put it under the coffee can in the garage."

"Keep the key. You don't have to return it." Caitlin glanced in the living room, where Hannah was busy shelving books like a future librarian.

"No, that's okay," Eric said, touched. "It's your house. I'm clear on that now."

"No, not anymore." Caitlin lowered her voice and met his eye, directly, if a little sadly. "I blew off the deal with the German buyer."

"What?" Eric didn't understand.

"Let's make a new deal. I'll sell the house to you for the appraised value, if that's what you want. I don't want to live there, but you can. Then maybe, going forward, we can share Hannah's time, fifty-fifty. A week with you, then one with me. The transitions won't be too hard for her if one of the houses is hers. What do you say?"

Eric's throat caught. His heart felt full at the prospect of living with Hannah again, under the same roof, especially in his own home. He could mow his own lawn and weed-whack his butt off. It was the perfect solution. He asked, "Are you *serious*?"

"Yes." Caitlin nodded, her eyes filming, but she held off tears.

"Why are you doing this?" Eric couldn't help but ask.

"You going to make me say nice things about you?" Caitlin shrugged, swallowing hard. "I thought about what happened at the hospital, after the mall. You're dedicated and committed. You're a good guy. I changed my mind. *You* changed my mind."

"Thanks." Eric smiled. He felt a bittersweet knot in his chest that he knew would be there forever.

Caitlin smiled back. "And you're a great father."

"Thank you. You're a great mother." Eric saw Caitlin's eyes brimming again, because he knew she didn't believe that about herself. "You *are* a great mother."

"Well, anyway." Caitlin cleared her throat, moving past the emotional moment. "As I was saying, I decided that the best thing we can do for Hannah, as her mom and dad, is to work together. We have to be able to talk to each other, too. We can do better than this, I know we can."

"I know we can, too." Eric felt his spirits soar. "So, no more lawyers?"

"No more lawyers. Present company excluded." Caitlin smiled crookedly. "Do we have a deal?"

"Did you ask *her*?" Eric whispered, nodding toward Hannah, still shelving books.

"I SAID YES!" Hannah called back.

Caitlin laughed, and so did Eric, throwing his head back, happy and finally free.

"Then we have a deal, Caitlin."

Chapter Sixty-five

The next morning dawned sunny, and Eric got to work at the regular time since Hannah hadn't wanted to miss any school. He crossed the parking lot with a slew of other employees, aware that heads were turning in his direction. Hospital employees were nodding to him, smiling at him, or trying to catch his eye, and Eric smiled back, though he was looking forward to the day when his every fart wasn't cause for celebration.

He hit the breezeway at the same time as Sharon McGregor from the Pharmacy Review Board, elegant in some kind of gold tweed suit. She waved him down, fell into step beside him, and patted him on the back. "Eric, my goodness! I can't believe what I'm hearing about you! What a nightmare that must have been. Is it finally over?"

"Hell, no." Eric looked over, with a smile. "It'll continue at the next Pharmacy Review Board meeting."

"Ha!" Sharon laughed, and so did Eric, but only he knew he wasn't kidding. They parted ways in the lobby, when he went to the elevator bank that led to Wright and hit the up button in front of an adoring audience. He climbed into the crowded elevator, accepting congratulations, answering questions, and generally feeling the love, though he suddenly realized that he didn't have his red employee lanyard, with the red W for Wacko. He made a mental note to get a new ID, though he didn't know how the rest of the hospital would view the psych unit, from here on out. The horror of what Sam had done would never be forgotten, and Eric could only hope that his deeds had redeemed the unit. Either way, he was proud of his team and he couldn't wait to get upstairs, pick up the pieces, and get back to taking care of his patients.

He got off the elevator on his floor and didn't have to look far to see the damage from yesterday's fire. The air still smelled burned, and there was the slightest haze. Water had damaged the floor tiles, causing some buckling at the edges, and rolling water buckets with mops were lined up against the wall, next to two folded yellow signs that read, Caution—Slipping Hazard.

Eric crossed to the unit, mentally gearing up. He'd gotten emails from three different hospital departments about cleaning up the water and fire damage, which would require a major effort. Fortunately, the HGH sprinkler system was zoned and the sprinklers on the north side of the unit hadn't been turned on, so most of the patient rooms had gone undamaged. It was the south side—the TV lounge, dining hall, and the nurses' station at the front—that were water-damaged.

He unlocked the first door to the unit, entered the airlock, then unlocked the interior door and entered the unit to find his staff milling around in confusion, amid the water puddling on the tile floor, smelly and slightly hazy air, and the waterlogged nurses' station with defunct computers, monitors, and telephones.

"Hey, everybody!" Eric called to them, and they turned their heads, Amaka, Jack, David, Tina, the other nurses, nurse's aides, psych techs, caseworkers, and a crew of janitors in blue jumpsuits.

"Eric!" "You made it!" "You're back!" everybody called out at once, surging toward him like a crowd of reporters, but in a good way. "Are you staying?" "Are you okay?"

"Yes, I'm back." Eric threw open his arms, gave Amaka a big hug when she came forward, then waved for order. "Thank you for holding the fort in my absence. You've done an amazing job."

"We're number two, we're number two!" Jack called out, but Eric didn't burst his bubble, just yet.

"Okay, everybody, please settle down. I have something I want to say." Eric centered himself for a moment. "Consider where we find ourselves. We have been through hell this past week. We've seen the suffering of our patients. We've been betrayed by someone we held dear, yet we grieve his loss in many ways. The loss of who we thought he was. The loss of his presence and his contribution to our patient care, before he took his terrible turn." Eric could see faces falling around him, his staff struggling with conflicted feelings over Sam, their anger, bewilderment, and grief. "We've seen gruesome violence and death. There has been fire, and a deluge. It has simply been an impossibly difficult and traumatic time, for all of us."

Amaka clucked in agreement, heads nodded, and eyes filmed all around, including Eric's.

"Normally, we focus on the care of our patients, but we can't overlook or neglect our own care, not after what we've been through. It will take us awhile to process the events of this week, and we will discuss it, and overthink it, and analyze it every which way from Sunday. Our specialty is talk therapy, and we will talk until we're blue in the face."

Amaka broke into a smile, and the nurses laughed.

"Going forward, we will *heal* this unit. We're trained to deal with trauma. In fact, we're the only service in this entire hospital trained to heal emotional trauma. So, as a matter of fact, it couldn't have happened to a better group of people. We didn't choose this test, it chose us. And we will get through it together, with flying colors. Are you with me?"

"Yes!" everybody cried.

"Thank you!" Eric said, feeling himself smile from the very depth of his soul. "Okay. The first thing we're going to do is have a quick morning meeting in the conference room, as usual. I want the same bad coffee and the even worse décor. I want Amaka to tell us how every patient spent last night, because they are our first priority. And then, we're going to roll up our sleeves, clean up this unit, and get it back in business. Ready, set, go!"

Chapter Sixty-six

After a long day of putting the unit back together, Eric parked in the visitor space in front of Laurie's garden apartment, walked up the front walk, and knocked on her door. He'd bought a bouquet of daises from the grocery store. He'd showered and changed. He'd put on aftershave he'd found in the bottom of his Dopp kit. He was about to have his first real date in over a decade, which was harder than breaching an armed police barricade at the King of Prussia Mall.

"Hey, hi." Laurie opened the door and smiled. "Flowers, how nice!"

"I'm here." Eric realized it sounded idiotic the moment he said it, though he saw that she had showered and changed too, into a soft blue work shirt and denim shorts, with her dark hair finally worn down, making thick rich curls around her chin. She was barefoot, which he thought was cute.

"Come in, thanks!" Laurie accepted the flowers, then kissed him on the cheek lightly, and Eric tried to relax as he stepped into the apartment, which smelled like something delicious was cooking, with cheese and tomatoes. The table was already set with another loaf of artisanal bread, a block of butter, and a wooden bowl full of arugula, avocados, cherry tomatoes, and onions. He remembered that Caitlin would never even kiss him if he'd had onions. At the end of their marriage, he found himself choosing the onions.

"What's for dinner? It smells great."

"My specialty, eggplant parm. It's hearty and comforting, which is just what the doctor ordered." Laurie went into the kitchen with the bouquet, opened the cabinet, and retrieved a glass vase.

"Can I help?" Eric followed her into the kitchen and leaned against the counter. He stopped short of kissing her on the cheek. He was trying to slow his roll, now that he'd learned the expression. He watched Laurie put the bouquet in the sink, get a scissors from the drawer, and cut the twine around the wrapping.

"The eggplant's already in the oven, but you can make us both a drink." Laurie nodded toward a bottle of Tanqueray, one of tonic, and two tumblers, next to a juicy lime on a small plate, which had been cut into perfect eighths. On the chopping board was a sliced mound of parsley and fresh green basil.

"Will do. How do you like your drink, light or heavy?"

"Light. So how was work?"

"Tough, you can imagine." Eric crossed to the refrigerator with the tumblers, used them to scoop some ice out of the bin, and returned to the counter. "Lots of hugs and tears from the staff. Lots of nerves and worry from the patients. The logistics were a mess, trying to use humidifiers to get rid of the water, then we had to go begging for computers, phones, and new chairs. We tried to salvage what we could. My phone rang constantly, everybody had a million questions."

"I bet. How was Perino?"

"I spent some time with him, talking to him and his wife. It will take him some time to come to terms with this." Eric untwisted the cap off the gin and poured them both a light drink.

"The poor guy. It's traumatic."

"I also looked through his file. Perino was on risperidone and fluoxetine, and I suspect Sam was dosing him with Ritalin, too. Sam had an expertise in ADHD and Ritalin, Vyvance, and that family of drugs. They would've wound Perino up and made him aggressive, and it would explain why he wasn't responding to treatment."

Laurie groaned. "Why would he do that?"

"I think he used people, as pawns. My sense is that he would use Perino as another kind of weapon against me, or maybe even to set Perino up to attack me. I learned today that Perino has a lot of delusional beliefs about me and I'm betting that Sam filled his head with them." Eric cracked the cap off the tonic bottle with a satisfying hiss and filled the glasses.

"That's horrible."

"I know." Eric squeezed in some lime juice, relaxing as he realized that it was completely possible to go from being friends to maybe being lovers. The two of them always talked shop when they ran, and this was like that, only stationary. He felt natural around Laurie, and he liked the whole scene: the aromas of the food, her easy way with him, how nurturing she was. Eric had always heard the expression that you didn't know what you had until it was gone, but he suddenly had a different insight—that you didn't know what you were missing until you had it. It looked like he was going to have it, and he felt good inside.

"Everybody's saying the wife is going to sue. That's all anybody ever worries about in administration."

"I know, right?" Eric handed Laurie her drink. "Here we go. Cheers."

"Cheers." Laurie raised her glass, then took a sip. "Perfect."

"Really?" Eric sipped his drink, which tasted tart and great. "Not bad."

"No, it's perfect." Laurie smiled, more warmly. "Everything's perfect, really."

"That's just what I think," Eric said, touched and happy. He leaned over and was about to kiss her when his phone started ringing. "Damn it."

"Saved by the bell."

"Very funny." Eric slid the phone from his pocket, and the screen showed the hospital's number. "I should take this."

"Go ahead. Dinner's in ten minutes, but I can lower the heat if I have to."

"Thanks." Eric touched the screen to answer the call. "This is

Eric Parrish," he said, but all he could hear was static, and the voice on the other end was breaking up. "Hello? Hello?"

"Eric, go to the hallway," Laurie called to him. "Remember, the reception's bad lately."

Eric hustled from the room and into the hallway. The phone call was still breaking up. "Hello? Can you hear me?"

"Dr. Parrish . . ." a woman started to say, but static swallowed her sentence.

"Hello? Hello?" Eric kept moving to get a signal, passing the bathroom and walking toward the two rooms off the hallway, Laurie's home office and her bedroom. "This is Eric Parrish. Hello, hello?"

"Dr. Parrish? Are you there?"

"Hold on, can you hear me now?" Eric ducked through the open door to Laurie's office, which he'd never seen. It was small, cozy, and characteristically cheery. White shelves full of books ringed the room, ending in a white metal file cabinet. A white desk and a black ergonomic chair sat next to the door, against a wall covered with colorful art posters by Chagall, Miro, and Rothko.

"Yes, hi, this is Julia Meehan. I got your number from the directory."

"Julia who?" Eric heard her clearly but didn't recognize her name. He sat down at Laurie's desk.

"From IT, at the hospital. Anyway, remember you asked me to look up who accessed Ms. Teichner's file after her discharge?"

"Oh, yes. Hi." Eric remembered.

"Sorry I freaked out when you came in yesterday. It's so spooky working near the morgue. I hate when I'm the last one to leave work, that's why I lock the door."

"That's okay. Sorry I didn't give you my real name." Eric eyed the things on Laurie's desk, a silver laptop, and a row of windup toys—a bright yellow chick, a blue robot, and a tiger that did back-flips.

"No worries. My boss told me it's okay to give you the info."

"Go ahead." Eric knew the name would be Sam's, but it would be good to have it verified.

"That file was accessed by Dr. Sam Ward and Dr. Laurie Fortu-nato."

Eric didn't think he'd heard her right. "Who did you say? The last one?"

"Dr. Laurie Fortunato."

Eric realized the explanation. "Oh, of course. She accessed it yes-terday for me. She showed me the file."

"Yes, Dr. Fortunato accessed it yesterday."

"Okay, thanks."

"Wait, hold on. She also accessed it two months ago. Post-discharge."

Eric didn't understand. "That can't be."

"It is. She logged in twice, once yesterday and once two months ago."

"Are you sure about that?"

"Positive. If you want the exact dates and times, I can give them to you. I can even tell you how long the file was kept open, each time. Do you have a pen and paper?"

"Hold on." Eric looked around for a piece of paper, but there wasn't any on the clean desk. He glanced at the black mesh waste-basket next to the desk, which was almost empty except for a few crumpled bills and envelopes. He grabbed an envelope and slid a pen from his shirt pocket. "Go ahead."

"Dr. Fortunato accessed it yesterday, and on April 18. The pa-tient was discharged April 15."

Eric felt too numb to even make a note. "When did Dr. Ward access it?"

"The same day as Dr. Fortunato, April 18. Dr. Fortunato accessed it at 9:05 A.M., and Dr. Ward accessed it at 9:30 A.M. She had the file open for five minutes, and he had it open for ten minutes."

Eric felt stunned. He couldn't speak. He didn't understand. Laurie had told him she'd never accessed a patient's file after dis-charge, but she'd accessed Virginia's, right before Sam. His gaze fell on the windup toys, without really seeing them. Then some-thing shiny caught his eye, glinting at him from the bottom of the wastebasket.

"Dr. Parrish? Are you there?"

"Yes. Fine, thanks. Good-bye." Eric hung up, shaken. He didn't know why Laurie had lied to him or why she had accessed Virginia's file, especially the same day as Sam. He didn't think Laurie had even heard of Virginia until last Friday night, when Max had brought her into the ED.

Eric found himself staring at the shiny spot in the wastebasket. He set his phone and pen down, reached inside the wastebasket, moved aside a tissue, then did a double-take.

Blood rushed to his head, striking him dumb. It was almost beyond belief, but at the same time, it was absolute confirmation.

Eric felt his heart break.

But he knew what he had to do.

Chapter Sixty-seven

Eric came back into the kitchen, trying to compose himself. The room still smelled delicious, but now it turned his stomach. "The phone's been crazy like that all day. Sorry about that."

"No worries. Have a drink." Laurie turned, draining the last of her drink. "I might be getting tipsy. Don't try to take advantage of me until after dinner. I have everything planned, you'll see."

Eric faked a smile, but his blood ran cold. It terrified him to think what she had planned. Unless he missed his guess, he'd walked into the lion's den. But he had a plan of his own.

"What's the matter? You don't look so good."

Eric thought fast. "Oh, it was just the phone call."

"Who was it?" Laurie uncapped the Tanqueray and poured herself another splash.

"Amaka, checking on some things for tomorrow, but she's so sad. It's been tough on them about Sam. They're taking it hard."

"I'm sure." Laurie emptied the leftover tonic into the glass. She didn't bother to get new ice, and Eric wondered if her drinking was part of her plan.

"They need time to process it. We all do. We all loved him, so it's hard to believe what he did and what he was. It doesn't jibe with the person we knew."

"Of course not. It's such a betrayal."

"That's part of it, but not all." Eric started speaking from the heart. In a way, he couldn't not. "I wish I'd seen it coming, I wish I'd known. I liked him. I . . . trusted him. I can't believe it."

"I know, it's tough." Laurie puckered her lip, in sympathy.

"He was a friend." Eric paused, taking a chance. "I wish you had known him better."

"Yeah, me too. He seemed like a nice guy." Laurie nodded, her expression sympathetic.

"He was. We all felt that way. I wonder if his wife knew. She probably didn't. I wish I'd known, I could've helped him."

"Helped him do what?" Laurie cocked her head, pausing in mid-drink.

"Helped him get better. Alleviated his suffering. I could have treated him. He didn't want to be the way he was, or to do the harm he did. He was sick."

"You're wrong. He wasn't sick, he was evil. He chose to be the way he was. He must've liked the choices he made." Laurie frowned as she set down her glass, her mood darkening, and Eric wasn't sure where it was going, but he was going along.

"I disagree. Evil isn't a choice, it's a label. A short answer. Evil doesn't go far enough. Evil doesn't stand up to analysis, from a psychiatric point of view. Sam had an illness."

"What was his illness then, from a psychiatric point of view?" Laurie folded her arms, and Eric met her eye.

"He manipulated others for his own gain. He used people as puppets so he could ruin me and become Chief. He felt nothing for others. All of his emotions were for show. His act fooled everyone on the unit, for years. He even fooled me. But none of that was a talent, a skill, or a choice on his part. It was a *symptom*."

"Of what?"

"He was a sociopath. Whatever his motivation, it wasn't the root cause of what he did. His illness is the root cause. His planning only proves how very, *very* sick he was." Eric watched her face darken, eyes harden, and smile flatten, and Laurie began to change before his eyes, becoming who she really was, about to shed the mask

completely. He kept talking, provoking her. "We're unsure whether sociopaths are born or bred, but I think it's a bit of both, and the weight of the literature agrees. Sociopaths are sick people and they lead horrible lives."

"How do you know that?" Laurie lifted an eyebrow, betraying her contempt. "Have you ever treated a sociopath?"

"Yes, two. I did med checks in the clinic at Albion Penitentiary in western Pennsylvania during my training. Both of the sociopaths I treated were in prison for life, for murder. I remember when I was with one patient, his eyes were stone cold. He had the 'shark-stare,' all of the stereotypical symptoms."

"Like on TV." Laurie snorted.

"Yes. The prisons are full of sociopaths, where you would expect to find them. In point of fact, there are more of them in everyday life than on death row. Most of them look normal, whatever that is." Eric paused, thinking of Hannah. "But normalcy is a fallacy. Normalcy is an appearance. Normalcy is just for show."

"I never heard you talk like this." Laurie frowned again, standing by the sink.

"I'm a changed man, like you said, and frankly, I never got it before. I said it, but I never really *got* it." Eric was telling the truth. He'd just had an insight, but he just wished it didn't take a life-threatening situation to bring him there. "A sociopath has a very well-defined theory of mind. He thinks he's superior, but it's a false belief. He's arrogant, but like any arrogance, it's only a façade. A sociopath thinks he has a strong ego, but he has a very weak ego. Basically, a sociopath is delusional."

"I don't agree with any of this." Laurie recoiled, her lip curling in distaste. "I don't know why we're even talking about it."

"Because I was thinking about Sam. I feel sympathy for him. I pity him."

Laurie's eyes hardened, but Eric couldn't stop talking now. He knew he was poking a tiger in a cage, but he wanted to know if it was really true. She would never confess, but he wanted her to show herself, even to attack.

"Laurie, think about it this way. A sociopath is hollow inside, empty of feeling. They're sick, but they can't face that fact. Because they can't face that fact, they never get the help they need."

"What if they know what they are, but they don't want help?"

"That's exactly how a sociopath feels—but it's merely a symptom of the illness. That's what the illness does."

"What if they *like* being the way they are?" Laurie's eyes narrowed.

"Also a symptom of the illness. But in reality, they're missing out on the feelings that everyone else has. Love, joy, sorrow, grief, true happiness. The full array, the stuff of a real life. You call me Captain Emotion, but what else is there to life? What are the things we remember but the feelings we have? Any family photograph we own, it's not about the picture, it's about the emotion the picture provokes." Eric felt his throat catch but stayed the course. "Sociopaths never know that joy. They hide behind their mask. They keep life at arm's length. I pity them. They're not living, and if they didn't hide their mental illness so well, they could get the treatment they need. If we couldn't cure them, then at least we could alleviate their suffering."

"You don't know what you're talking about, Eric." Laurie raised her voice, and her dark eyes flashed with new anger. "You don't know anything. All this mumbo-jumbo, there's no science in it. You talk about a 'theory of the mind,' but it's only theory, all of it. You're the one who acts superior, but isn't. You don't know anything. Look at the choices you've made in your life."

"What do you mean?" Eric asked, modulating his tone.

"Look at how long you stayed with Caitlin. You made a fool of yourself over that woman." Laurie scowled. "You couldn't see that she wasn't worth the trouble, all this time. I've known you since medical school. Years and years, I've been your friend. You had to know I wanted you. You had to know I was waiting for you, but you didn't choose me over her." Laurie waved her hand angrily at the flowers. "You choose me *now, after* she dumps you. But that's too little, too late. You never dumped her *for* me. You never saw

that I was better. Prettier, smarter, more successful—I'm *sure* I'm better in bed. But you were too *stupid* to see it. And you're too stupid to see anything with Sam. You're too stupid to see anything right in front of your face."

"Am I?" Eric went into his pocket, pulled out the tissue, and watched Laurie's eyes follow his motion.

"What's that?"

"Never mind." Eric swung the tissue low and away from her, like a tease. "Why did you access Virginia's file after her discharge? Why did you lie to me about it?"

"What are you talking about?" Laurie shot back. "I didn't do that. I didn't lie."

"Yes, you did. You accessed the file right before Sam did. You went into the file, saw his notations about the consult, and told him to delete them. You knew Sam better than I did. You used him like a puppet. He wasn't the planner, you were. He wasn't the mastermind, you are."

"What's in that Kleenex?" Laurie glowered, and Eric took a step backwards, still holding the tissue away from her, taunting her.

"You set me up from the beginning. It wasn't happenstance that you called me to the ED for that consult Friday night. You had a plan. You wanted to ruin me because I didn't choose you over Caitlin."

"What's in that Kleenex?" Laurie grimaced, as fixated on the tissue as a wolf on fresh meat.

"Were you sleeping with him? Was he in love with you? Is that how you got him to kill Renée? That's my bet, and here's the trophy that he brought you, proof that he did what you told him. Proof of his love."

Laurie looked down at the tissue, as Eric opened it without touching its contents—a delicate gold necklace with a little plate on it that read FEARLESS. Eric remembered seeing it at the frozen yogurt shop. He remembered Max's talking about it in session. It was Renée's Bevilacqua's necklace, and it would have Sam's and Laurie's fingerprints.

426 | Lisa Scottoline

"No!" Laurie shouted. Suddenly, in one horrific motion, Laurie grabbed the scissors from the sink and slashed her lower arm, sending blood spraying in the air like a gruesome red fan.

"No, don't. Stop." Eric edged backwards passing the entertainment center. He spotted a video game player from the shelf, yanked it free, and threw it at her, but she ducked and it landed on the hardwood floor.

"We were on a date, I drank too much." Laurie started talking, as if to herself. "You tried to date-rape me, you grabbed a scissors. You held it to my throat. We struggled for it."

"No, Laurie, don't!" Eric kept moving backwards toward the door. He heard noise out front. He had to stall for only a few moments longer. He'd called Detective Rhoades from Laurie's home office after he'd found the necklace.

"I got the scissors away from you, I tried to run out the front door." Laurie advanced on him, the scissors poised. "I was almost outside but you tackled me. You ripped my shirt open. I had to kill you. It was self-defense."

"Laurie, stop." Eric flung open the front door just as Laurie tore her own shirt open, clawing at the buttons and trying to rip them off, only to see Detective Rhoades running up the front walk with uniformed police, drawing their weapons and aiming them at her.

"Dr. Fortunato, freeze!" Detective Rhoades shouted. "Freeze right there!"

"No!" Laurie screamed, in a rage that came from her tortured psyche. She raised the scissors high, but Eric lunged for them on the downward stroke and wrested them from her hand.

Just before they reached his chest.

Chapter Sixty-eight

It was December, and Eric was pleased to see that the visiting room had been decorated for the holidays, though it wasn't easy to make a juvenile detention center look cheery. Artwork by the residents lined the walls, painted Christmas trees, crayoned Santa Clauses, plus Hanukkah dreidels and Kwanzaa Unity cups drawn with varying degrees of skill; juveniles from ages ten to eighteen lived in the center's secured detention wing, which contained thirty-six rooms, one of which was Max's.

The visiting room was modern, clean, and medium-sized, with thin blue carpeting and large glass windows that let in indirect light even on an overcast morning, with snow in the forecast. Ten small tables with heavy-duty plastic chairs filled the room, and Eric took his customary table and waited for Max. He kept his coat on because there was nowhere to hang it. In the corner of the visiting room stood a decorated Christmas tree, festooned with colored lights and inexpensive ornaments, and beneath it sat wrapped presents on a cottony carpet of pretend snow. This wouldn't be the happiest Christmas for Max, but the boy was lucky to be here, not in a state prison for adults.

Max had been sentenced as a juvenile as a result of a plea agreement orchestrated by his lawyer, his motion supported by three psychological assessments: the pre-trial evaluation from the psychiatric staff at the detention center, a risk-assessment and evaluation by a psychiatrist hired by Marie, and a substantial report by Eric himself. All three mental health professionals had agreed that Max suffered from OCD and depression with suicidal ideation, which had impaired his decision-making at the time of the offenses.

The federal government had dropped its charges under the terrorism statutes, and the district attorney of Montgomery County had dropped the kidnapping charge in view of the fact that Max had no intent to inflict bodily injury on the hostages, as he'd been unarmed. In return for being sentenced as a juvenile, Max had pleaded guilty to counts of unlawful restraint, reckless endangerment, and terroristic threats, and received a sentence of a year in the detention center and three years' probation thereafter, the maximum possible so-called "long tail" sentence. The judge had accepted the deal and ordered the sentence despite opposition from King of Prussia business groups, who wanted Max tried as an adult, if not burned at the stake.

Eric looked over to see the door to the visiting room opening, and Max was brought in by a uniformed detention officer. The boy had no handcuffs on or anything of that sort, and the detention officer remained by the door as Max crossed the room toward him, with a smile. Eric rose, thinking the boy looked better than he had last visit, two weeks ago. His aspect seemed brighter, his brown hair cut away from his eyes, and he'd put on some weight, which made him look stronger in his gray sweat suit, the winter uniform here. He seemed taller, too, but that could have been Eric's imagination.

Eric extended his hand. "Max, are you *growing*?"

"Little bit." Max grinned, shaking his hand firmly. "The doc said I'm in a growth spurt. Can you believe that?"

"Ha!" Eric sat down. "Good to see you. How're you doing?"

"Good, thanks." Max sat opposite him, meeting his eye with a new animation. "Guess what, my mother's getting married."

"That's great," Eric said, meaning it. He had visited Marie and Zack recently, at their invitation. Marie had gotten out of rehab two months ago, landed a job, and Zack had moved in with her.

"I'm getting a dad for Christmas." Max rolled his eyes.

Eric chuckled. "When's the date?"

"December, next year. They're waiting 'til I'm out."

"Great. So, how do you feel about it?"

"I'm happy about it." Max nodded. "It's a good thing. I like him. He's a nice guy and he's a good influence on my mom. I don't think she would've gone to rehab without him pushing her."

"You're probably right." Eric remembered Laurie's saying that she thought Zack was too good for Marie, but he pushed that from his mind. "How's school?"

"Boring and easy, but that's okay." Max shrugged. "I'm tutoring fifth-graders in math. They need the help."

"That's nice of you."

"You know what I like? The Language Arts class. I never liked it at Pioneer, but I like it here. How weird is that?"

"Not weird, good. Good for you."

"They make you do what they call 'reflective writing,' which is like writing in a journal, but you can write whatever you want, like, free-form. It sounds stupid, but I like it. I'm trying poetry." Max shrugged, sheepishly. "Only because there's nothing else to do, since they don't allow video games."

"Poetry is better than video games."

"I knew you would say that. It's such a dad-thing to say."

"There's a reason I say dad-things." Eric smiled, though since the summer, he'd clarified his relationship to Max in his own mind. Eric no longer felt so paternal toward Max and was clear now that the only person he parented was Hannah. He had his hands full with her, since she was currently lobbying to repaint the entire house pink. Outside.

"Therapy's going good, too." Max smiled, happily. "I really like Dr. Gold."

"She's terrific." Eric had been happy to refer Max to one of his old friends, Jill Gold, an OCD expert affiliated with the Beck Institute in Philly, which was on the cutting edge of cognitive behavior therapies. The juvenile detention center had cooperated in coordinating its treatment of Max with Dr. Gold's private treatment, which would aid in Max's progress not only now, but after he left their care.

"She's been talking to me a lot about Gummy, and that's sad."

"I'm sure." Eric could see Max's face darken when he thought about his grandmother, his grief evident.

"It's like, I see these good things happening now, like my mom quitting drinking, and I think, why didn't she do that before? Like, when my grandmother was alive? It would've made her really happy."

"Right, of course. But you know, sometimes people grow up only after their parent passes. I'm not saying that's the case with your mother, but it might be."

Max pursed his lips, sighing. "Anyway, I'm doing better with my OCD. Dr. Gold's been working with me, doing the flooding techniques. I'm down to tapping once an hour, on the hour."

"Good for you."

"It takes forever, though. It took all this time to get it down just that much."

"I know, but it works if you stay with it."

"I'm good 'til ten o'clock." Max's gaze shifted to the wall clock, which read 9:10.

"It will get easier, you'll see."

"That's what she says." Max met Eric's eye, with new animation. "You know, she's single."

"Dr. Gold? No she's not, she's married."

"No, she got divorced. It was final last month. I heard her talking to one of her friends on the phone." Max cocked his head. "Are you ready to, like, date?"

"No, I'm not, Max." Eric was still processing the fact that Laurie had turned out to be a sociopath, and she was currently in prison, awaiting trial. He prayed that she was getting the help she needed, but he was in no position to help her. Paul had never spoken to him again, which he understood.

"Dr. Gold reminds me of you, and you guys have a lot in common. She has a daughter, too, about Hannah's age. Maybe you should give her a call, like, for a date."

"I'll think about it." Eric still felt so sorry that all of this had happened because someone was trying to ruin him, leaving so many lives in pieces and so many people in grief, including Max. He had said as much to Max, Marie, and Zack, as well as to Anthony and Peg Bevilacqua, who had accepted his apology with grace and courage. Linda Perino had filed suit against the hospital, but she had pointedly not named Eric as an individual defendant, and HGH had already offered her a substantial settlement.

"Dr. Parrish, you should do more than think about it. I think Dr. Gold's *hot,* for someone, like, her age."

Eric smiled. "Her age is my age."

"I know. See, that's another thing you have in common. You can be olds together." Max laughed.

"Enough. I have a surprise for you."

"What?"

"Merry Christmas." Eric reached in his coat pocket, pulled out a present, and placed it on the table in front of Max. It had been wrapped by Hannah in giftwrap from *Frozen.* He didn't have time to get any proper holiday paper, between his job as Chief, his private practice at home, and being a hands-on dad, which he loved. He was even getting along better with Caitlin. His life felt as if it were finally falling into place, even though he was, well, crazy busy.

"What's this?" Max smiled, picking up the gift. "You didn't have to do anything."

"It's something little. Open it."

"Aw." Max tore the wrapping paper off to reveal a black Eveready flashlight. "Ha!"

"Remember what I said about the flashlight?"

"That it's a phallic symbol?"

"No!" Eric laughed.

Max laughed, too, then it subsided. "I'm joking. I remember."

"So, this is your flashlight. You're just at the beginning of exploring the cave. Keep it with you at all times."

"But you're supposed to be with me." Max grew serious, his face falling.

"You don't need me, not anymore. You can do it yourself and

you're doing a wonderful job. If you need a hand to hold on to, you have Dr. Gold's. She's right there with you."

Max swallowed hard. "So what are you saying?"

"I've been visiting you every week, but I'm thinking that from now on, you should call me when you want me to visit. Whenever you want me to come, just call. I'll be in your life as long as you want. How's that?"

"Okay." Max blinked, nodding. "Just so you're not ditching me."

Eric's throat caught. "No, I'm not ditching you."

"Good. Because Dr. Gold will be here any second."

"Here? Why?"

"I told her you wanted to take her to brunch."

"You did *what*?" Eric looked over to the door of the visiting room, and it was swinging wide open.

Acknowledgments

I'm a big fan of thanks-yous. Here's where I thank the experts and kind souls who helped me with *Every Fifteen Minutes*. It should go without saying, but doesn't, that any and all mistakes in the novel are mine.

First, I'm indebted to my best friend, Sandy Steingard, whom I knew well before she grew up to be one of the most well-respected psychiatrists in the country. She's brilliant, compassionate, funny, and generally wonderful, and she helped me understand how psychiatrists think, and in particular, how the fictional psychiatrist in this book might think. I am forever in her debt, for this and many other reasons. That's why this book is dedicated to her, with gratitude and much, much love.

Thanks to Dr. Marc Burock, Medical Director of the Inpatient Psychiatric Unit at Bryn Mawr Hospital, part of the Main Line Health System. Dr. Burock took time out of his busy day to answer all of my questions, not only about psychiatry but about practice and procedures in a typical suburban hospital. Though the hospital in this novel is completely fictional, it was during my interview with Dr. Burock that I heard the hospital's delivery lullaby, which plays in the novel, so even though that custom may be hard to believe, it's true.

Thanks so much to Tom Mendicino, Esq., senior counsel of Main Line Health System, who took time to meet with me and helped me understand the legalties of life in a large hospital system. Tom was invaluable in getting the facts and law right, and I thank him very much. Thanks, too, to his colleagues Jane Herling, Esq.; Della Payne, Esq.; and Sharon Sorokin James, Esq., who met with me as well, so I was brainstorming with a crack legal team. Last but not least, thanks to Terry Dougherty, Director of Human Resources at Bryn Mawr Hospital, and here's a big hug of thanks to the hardworking and adorable Mary Kate Coghlan, who helped facilitate the interviews!

Thanks to psychiatrist Dr. Lisa Goldstein, who spent hours with me, answering all my questions about adolescent psychiatry, and in particular the treatment of OCD. Dr. Goldstein is a sweetheart, and she helped me construct the treatment and understand other facts that underline the fiction of this book.

Finally, I read a lot about the life of a psychiatrist, a patient, sociopathy, and other mental illnesses. Here are a few of the sources I used, and I heartily recommend them: Simon Baron-Cohen, *The Science of Evil*; Judith Beck, *Cognitive Behavior Therapy*; Louis Cozolino, *The Making of a Therapist*; Kevin Dutton, *The Wisdom of Psychopaths*; James Fallon, *The Psychopath Inside*; Peter and Ginger Ross Breggin, *Talking Back to Prozac*; Robert D. Hare, *Without Conscience*; Kent Kiehl, *The Psychopath Whisperer*; Jane McGregor and Tim McGregor, *The Sociopath at the Breakfast Table*; J. Reid Meloy, *The Psychopathic Mind*; Dinah Miller, Annette Hanson, and Steven Roy Daviss, *Shrink Rap*; Daniel Smith, *Monkey Mind*; Scott Stossel, *My Age of Anxiety*; Martha Stout, *The Sociopath Next Door*; M. E. Thomas, *Confessions of a Sociopath*; and Robert Whitaker, *Mad in America*.

Thank you to the Radnor Police Department, which is real, but again, the personnel and characters in the novel are fictional. Still, I needed help to get the procedure right and for that I want to thank Lieutenant Christopher Flanagan, who patiently answered all of my questions. Thanks, too, to Chief/Superintendent William Colarulo, Detective Christopher Four, and Corporal Walt Sherman.

And a hug to Mary Ann Donnelley, who helped so much! Thanks to the Upper Merion Police, too.

And thank God for the King of Prussia Mall.

I'm a lawyer, but criminal law wasn't my field, and this novel raises cutting-edge criminal law questions. I needed help, even rescuing, and I turned to my dear friend, as well as brilliant and dedicated public servant, Nicholas Casenta, Esq., of the Chester County District Attorney's Office. Nick answered all of my middle-of-the-night email questions, and he cited chapter, verse, and statutory provision, as always. Nick has helped me with every single book so far, and I wouldn't dream of writing without his advice and expertise.

Thanks to Stephanie Kalogredis, Esq., for in-the-clutch trust-and-estates advice.

Now to my publishing family!

Thank you to my editor, Jennifer Enderlin, who improved this manuscript so much with her expertise and great good heart. And big love and thanks to the brilliant, fun gang at St. Martin's Press, starting with the terrific John Sargent, Sally Richardson, Jeff Dodes, Jeanne-Marie Hudson, Brian Heller, Jeff Capshew, Jen Gonzalez, Paul Hochman, Kim Ludlam, John Karle, Tracey Guest, Stephanie Davis, Anne-Marie Tallberg, Nancy Trypuc, Caitlin Dareff, and all the wonderful sales reps. Big thanks to Michael Storrings, for astounding cover design. Also hugs and kisses to Mary Beth Roche, Laura Wilson, Brant Janeway, and the great people in audiobooks. I love and appreciate all of you.

Thanks to my agent, Molly Friedrich, who has guided me for so long now, and to the amazing Lucy Carson and Nicole Lefebvre.

Thanks and another big hug to my dedicated assistant and best friend, Laura Leonard. She's invaluable in every way, and has been for more than twenty years. Thanks, too, to my pal and assistant Nan Daley, and to George Davidson, for doing everything else, so that I can be free to write, write, write!

Thank you very much to my amazing and brilliant daughter, Francesca, a wonderful writer in her own right, for her love, support, and great humor.